# SKINS AND BONE

John Baird Rogers

Gotuit Publishing LLC

Cover design by Books Covered
978-1-7322262-5-8 (trade paperback)
978-1-7322262-6-5 (e-book)

Library of Congress control number: 2021908793

“Joe’s intriguing struggles prove just how violent, controlling, and downright dangerous even an advanced world can be. … The high-tech atmosphere never overshadows the timeless quality that fuels the action: human greed. And the main motivation of avarice and those willing to do anything for their own benefit produce some engaging friction.” —Kirkus Reviews of Skins and Bone

… Reviews of Fatal Score (Mayfield - Napolitani #1)

“With memorable characters, precise writing, and a very human story all of us can relate to, Fatal Score is a brilliant debut thriller” – STEVE ULFELDER, Edgar finalist author of Purgatory Chasm.

“Rogers has grasped both the marvelous advances and future of technology, big medicine and big government, as well as the insidious dark and dangerous aspects of human greed.” – CARL BROOKINS, author of the Sean Sean and Tanner/Whitney mysteries.

“Carried to the finish line by a strong plot and a cast of intriguing characters, Fatal Score’s take on problems that are just over the horizon is both chilling and thought-provoking.” –TIM MAHONEY, novelist and author of Secret Partners, a Minnesota gangster history.

"An accomplished and appealing debut thriller, Fatal Score features vivid, appealing characters, an evil, labyrinthine cyber-scheme, and relentless suspense. It delivers on all counts." – BRIAN LUTTERMAN, author of the Pen Wilkerson mystery/suspense series.

“A rousing launch to a thriller series that has potential regardless of which character takes the spotlight.” – Kirkus Reviews.

Join me, Joe Mayfield, and Louise Napolitani at *johnbairdrogers.com* or on facebook at *@johnbairdrogers* to sign on to my newsletter. for free books to advance copy readers, discussions about the next book in the series. Perhaps help me navigate the interesting world of a few years from now.

Also by John Baird Rogers

*Fatal Score* (Mayfield - Napolitani #1)

For Beverly, and for Geoffrey, Edward, and James—who have grown into admirable men.

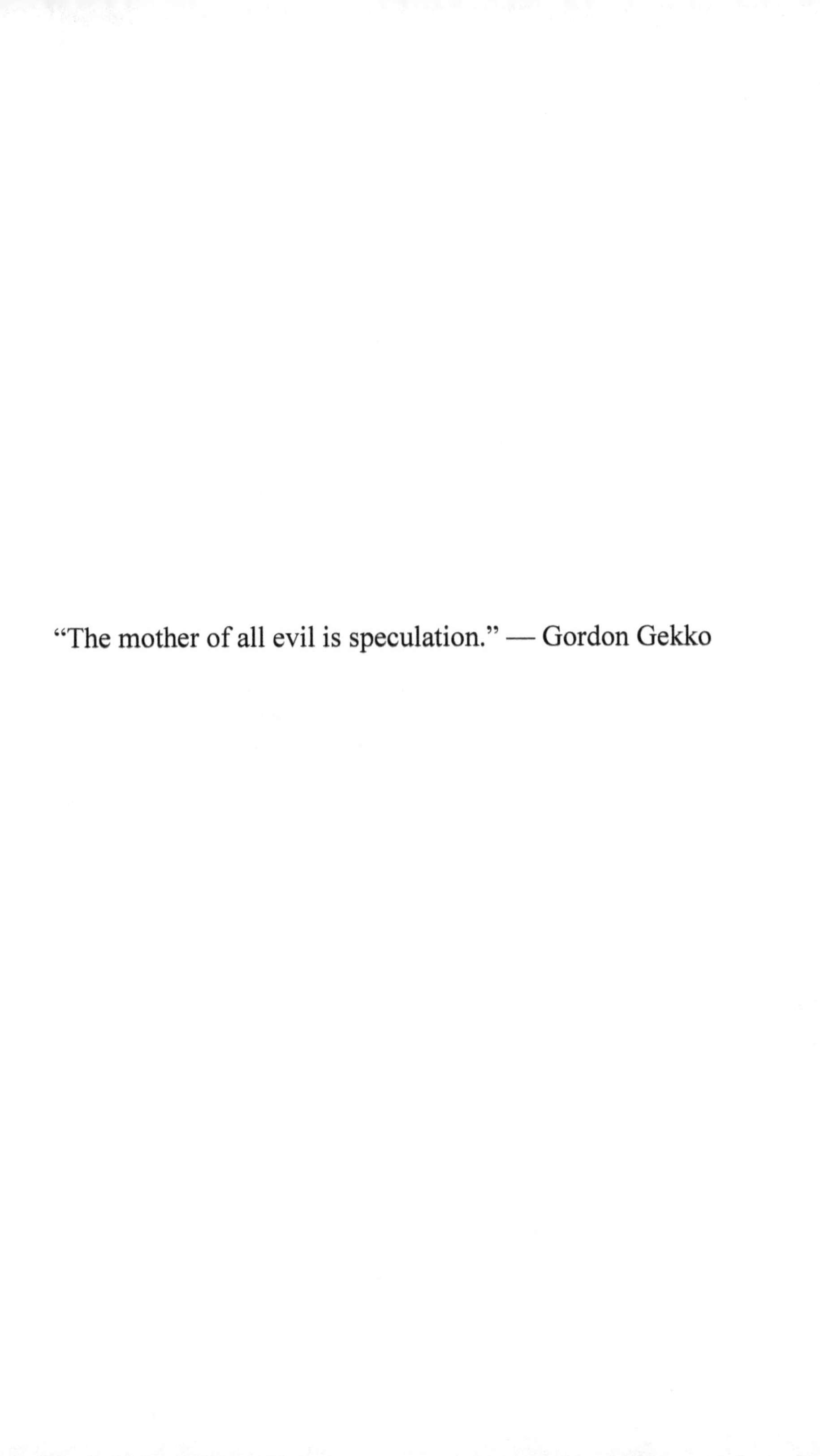

"The mother of all evil is speculation." — Gordon Gekko

# ONE

JOE MAYFIELD STOOD to stretch. The floor-to-ceiling windows in the quiet conference room looked toward Trinity Church and New Jersey. Thirty-four stories below him, the frenetic activity of the world's largest financial district played out as silent ballet.

A pretty woman half opened the door. "Would you like a water?"

"Yes, thanks."

"Evian?"

He started to say that tap water was fine but sensed that would be a mistake.

"Uhh. Sure. Thanks."

Earlier, the original artwork, the butter-soft leather chairs, the long maple table framed in burl oak, the cloth towels in the men's room had been intimidating. But now, waiting for the final two interviews of the day, the luxury seemed understandable, the natural result of hard work by smart people. He had never dreamed of having a job at a prestigious investment bank. When the headhunter called a couple of weeks ago, he had expected another interview for a mid-level corporate job in Central Florida. Now he was in Manhattan, and he wanted this job—the money, the challenge, being part of something big. Maybe most of all, living close to Weezy. But below the wanting ran an undercurrent: I don't belong here. Why are they interviewing me?

He knew, of course. Phoenix, RazorBlue. Sports stars sold athletic shoes to teenagers—maybe the bankers at Zhou, Cadwallon and Gordon thought the guy who helped bring down the largest financial scam of the decade would help sell their services to chief financial officers.

The woman returned with a tray holding three bottles of Evian and three crystal glasses. "We have to change the schedule a bit," she said with an apologetic smile as she set water at Joe's place. "Mr. Ackerman is running late." She shrugged. "He said it's a crazy trading day." She crossed to the other side of the table and placed the two bottles and glasses. "Mr. O'Malley said he will come in a little early."

She turned to the door, then stepped back as it flew open. A bear of a man barreled in. Tall and on the far side of well-fed. Curly red hair wrapped around a large dome and thick, unruly eyebrows gave him a gnomish look despite his size. Features a polite observer might call craggy.

"Eric O'Malley," the man said and gave Joe a handshake which would pass for a mauling if delivered in anger.

"Pleased to meet you, Mr. O'Malley."

"Eric, it's Eric." He waved toward Joe's chair. "Sit."

O'Malley reached across the table and snagged one of the bottles of Evian, sat down next to Joe, unrolled an e-pad, and took a slug of the water.

"I usually look at a candidate's file before the meeting, but they pulled me in early. Ackerman's going to be late. Crazy trading day, apparently …"

Joe tried not to fidget while Eric scrolled the file, nodding occasionally, chuckling once, raising his eyebrows and saying "great test scores" under his breath.

Finished, he focused on Joe. "Phoenix, huh?"

Joe was caught in a bright but friendly spotlight. "Must be interesting going from a comfortable job in a Florida utility to being famous," O'Malley said with a grin. "So, tell me about Phoenix and Panacea, Florida."

Joe told him the story of hacking the US firewall to discover the Phoenix software that had co-opted the medical reimbursements system, his off the grid meander to hide from Phoenix thugs, and the final exposé.

"Everyone saw how that turned out," O'Malley said. "FBI grabbing the bad guy right in the Senate hearing."

He paused, peeling the label on the Evian bottle.

"Of course, you're not the model of our normal hire," he said. "And, yes, there is a model."

Joe took a sip of water, using the opportunity to look away from O'Malley. The polite brush-off was coming. Good test scores worked for the already well-connected, but not for a guy with an accounting degree from a technical college ranked 239th in the country.

"That's why we're interested in you."

*Huh?*

O'Malley kept talking.

"I'll be candid. Of course we like the Phoenix story. It's no secret that financial firms have a reputation for being unethical. Do whatever we want to, then explain why what we did was perfectly legal. In ten-dollar words, of course." He cracked a grin that made him look even more like a gnome. "But you showed the world a rock-solid moral compass."

The door opened part way. A hand on the handle, followed by an arm. "Move those other interviews earlier and cut them to ten minutes each." The rest of the person entered. He was a couple of inches shorter than Joe but carried himself as if he was taller than anyone in the room. Not bad looking, though his facial features were small, and his mouth was fixed in a petulant bow. He wore his dark blond hair longer than most of the people Joe had met at ZCG. There was some gray, which gave him a distinguished look. Not a fighter, not a lover, but surely a winner.

He strode to a seat across the table from Joe, looked him up and down, then extended his hand. "Ross Ackerman. Sorry for the schedule mess up," he said, looking not a bit sorry. "Crazy trading day."

***

Ackerman took a seat across from Eric O'Malley and Joe. He drummed his fingers, affecting boredom. Why hadn't Braithwaite called? He glanced at his watch. Must be night in Africa.

O'Malley was explaining the firm to Mayfield. He had Mayfield hanging on every word. Maybe it was the big man's enthusiasm. Maybe it was that he reeked of honesty, goodwill, and concern for the customer's interest. Of course, with O'Malley, those feelings were genuine.

Ackerman sighed and tapped his e-pad. The file on Mayfield came up. Oh, yeah, the famous one. So, here he is in the flesh. Not bad looking. Dark hair receding a little, strong features, solid. Intensity that might come off as phony. Off-the-rack suit. He scanned the résumé, then the psych profile. He hesitated at the 99.6th percentile in reasoning capacity. He stopped dead at the note, "High moral conviction rating and a strain of egalitarianism." Gotta be careful of true believers.

O'Malley was saying, "If you can foresee the worst-case scenario, you can protect against it." He paused for effect, as if talking with an important client, not an accountant-turned-hacker from East Bumfuck, Florida. "That's what we do at Zhou, Cadwallon and Gordon, and we do it better than anyone else."

Ackerman glanced at his watch. Why hadn't Braithwaite called?

O'Malley continued, "We have the best experts on call, the best quants putting together the derivatives that deliver the protection and" he extended an open hand toward Ross like an impresario introducing the next act "— the best derivatives trading desk."

Ackerman took his cue. Enough of this love fest. Time to send this country boy home.

But …

He paused for a moment. O'Malley was waiting, eyebrows raised. Mayfield had turned to him.

… or maybe this Mayfield was just what he needed.

"So, Florida Northeastern University, huh?"

Mayfield nodded.

"They actually teach math there?"

The guy went red, shifted in his chair.

"Uh, sure."

Ackerman nodded several times, letting Mayfield know this was surprising information.

"You know, we only take the best of the best," Ross said with a challenging smile. "Gotta be absolutely top of the pile to do the work at Zhou Cadwallon. Think you're up to that?"

Mayfield stammered, "Yes. I hope so."

"Hopes and dreams, huh?" Ross raised an eyebrow. "You know, we don't make mistakes here. Maybe somewhere else they pat you on the back and call it a learning experience, but we do it right the first time. No excuses."

Now he had this really smart, famous guy on the defensive. And he had laid down the marker he needed.

He gave Mayfield, then O'Malley, a little grin, snapped the e-pad shut, and stood. "Gotta get back to Jersey," he said. "Crazy trading day." He gave Joe a nod, no handshake, and strode toward the door. He paused with his hand on the handle.

"Enjoy your trip back to Panacea, Florida." He was sure Mayfield caught the way he said Panacea. 99.6th percentile, after all.

Outside the conference room, he scanned the outer office. Satisfied that he was alone, he opened his e-pad.

"Call Braithwaite, secure."

***

Nick Braithwaite was in Johannesburg. With the copper project nearly in the bag, he was in a delicate conversation on one of his encrypted lines about his next assignment, the Chromium Skin. The general of a self-styled liberation army on the border of South Africa had just upped his price.

Nick sighed. "I can get you ten Denel Y3s and four hundred grenades. Same as South African Defence uses." The operation was getting expensive. There would be more demands as the time for execution drew near. He would meet them. Peanuts compared with the financial upside.

The general cleared his throat, preparing to negotiate some more.

Nick's implant tapped him, and a pleasant computer voice announced: Incoming. Ross Ackerman, Secure.

"I've got to sign off, General. I can do these grenade launchers, but then I'm tapped out."

He disconnected without waiting for a counteroffer and answered Ackerman.

"Where are we on the copper situation?" Ackerman said.

Nick glanced at a window on his monitor. An internet chess game with Father Time was paused, waiting for a next move.

"I'm awaiting confirmation."

"Awaiting confirmation? Oh, my, veddy British are we today? Well, when do you expect to finish a-fucking-waiting, Rennie?"

Nick swallowed a tart response. No one dared call Nick by his given name except the man who represented sixty percent of his firm's revenue. "I expect confirmation about midnight here, four o'clock your time."

"Good." Then, "Remember the backstop you wanted me to set up? To protect myself in case one of these projects blows up?"

"I do."

"I think I met my backstop. See me when you're back in the States."

Ackerman disconnected before Nick could answer.

Nick shook his head. Bugger never says goodbye. A chime from his monitor announced a move by Father Time, Nxf2#. He let out a small sigh of relief. Copper was done.

# TWO

JOE LEFT THE Zhou, Cadwallon office with mixed feelings. Eric O'Malley and Joe had finished the interview on a cordial note. Eric made Joe want the job. Ross Ackerman made him think the chance was slim to none.

As he walked to the subway, he put all that out of his mind. Weezy had agreed to come up from Bethesda for the weekend. It had been nearly a month since they had seen each other.

Penn Station was busy, the rush to catch outbound trains beginning, but Joe saw Weezy right away. Tall and slender, looking ten years younger than she was. She could pass for a runway model, or maybe a grad student based on the cargo shorts and T-shirt. No one would identify her as the last, best defense against intrusion into the national firewall protecting the IAC—the most secure, sophisticated database in the world.

She gave him a half wave—when they met, a warm hug.

"How'd it go?"

"Interesting."

"What kind of interesting?"

Joe chuckled and put his arm around Weezy's shoulders, pulled her to him. "Let's just say that an offer is unlikely. But"—he leaned to plant a kiss above her ear—"the trip gave us a chance to enjoy New York. Let's make the most of it."

They took the subway to the New York Athletic Club where ZCG had put Joe up. Weezy's clothes earned a disapproving look from the doorman, who informed them that business attire was required to cross the lobby. He directed them around the back of the building to the freight elevator. They dropped Weezy's bag, escaped the NYAC, and bought coffee from a street vendor. They crossed Central Park South and squeezed around a dog walker being dragged along by her pack of pedigreed and exquisitely groomed canines.

"So, tell me," Weezy said, "why aren't these guys falling over themselves to get the smarty-pants, real-world-sophisticated guy called RazorBlue by his four hundred forty thousand adoring Internet friends to consider a generous six-figure offer?"

Joe chuckled. "You mean Florida Northeastern University Joe?"

"Aha! Panacea Florida Joe, right?"

"Yup. They probably interviewed me out of curiosity. RazorBlue and Phoenix. I think they realized I don't fit their profile."

Weezy snorted. "Profile? You mean guaranteed mediocrity?"

Joe shrugged. "No, I don't think so. Most of the people I met were ferociously bright. Plus, they had all the advantages of fine upbringing and the best education money can buy. No, they're not mediocre." He stepped aside for a jogger intent on owning the path. "I had been daydreaming about living in Panacea, working at a job to keep body and soul together, buying a little boat, taking time off whenever I wanted. Now … well, Zhou, Cadwallon is the big time."

They found a bench and sat.

"You'd be bored in a month working that Panacea dream, anyway."

"Yeah, I know. And the work the firm does is interesting … challenging."

Weezy cocked her head. "So, tell me."

"They call their main product 'Skins.' Some kind of acronym. Basically a basket of financial derivatives designed to offset risk at the geographical source of a commodity." He took a sip of coffee. "The one they're working on now is covering copper for a big client with operations in the Copper Belt … mostly Zambia. They slice the derivatives up so the customers can buy whatever level of protection they want. They sell pieces to investors and hedge funds, too."

"Like they did with home mortgages back in 2008, which brought the financial system to its knees, right?" Weezy said.

"Always the skeptic, eh?"

Weezy arched one eyebrow.

"Just trying to figure out what they do." She stopped, then continued, "Tell me about the interviews."

"In the morning, I got a thorough workout from their personnel department and a psychologist. All sorts of written tests. Then an analyst who let me know right away that he went to Harvard, was extremely bright, and didn't really have time to talk to me. Now I can picture 'looking down your nose at.' "

Weezy chuckled and Joe continued, "This afternoon, I talked with Eric O'Malley and Ross Ackerman." He unrolled his e-pad, tapped it, and passed it to Weezy.

"Here's Eric."

She smiled at the picture, nodded as she read the bio. "Hmm…Princeton, cum laude, all Ivy as a defensive tackle. Wharton MBA, consulting firm for a couple of years, then with small startups for ten, ZCG five years ago. Pretty impressive."

"Impressive in person, too," Joe said. "Eric manages the investment bankers who sell the firm's services and the crew of analysts who support them. I would start as an analyst, and Eric would be my boss."

"And Ackerman?" Weezy asked, fiddling with the pad. "Oh, here he is." She squinted, then nodded. "Uh-huh. Yale undergrad, straight on to Goldman Sachs in trading. Can't be too stupid," she said under her breath as she scrolled. "Then the London Desk and on to Zhou, Cadwallon as head of trading.

Not bad for a guy who got gentleman's C's at Yale. But, of course, he is the scion of *the* Ackermans."

"*The* Ackermans? Wait a minute! You know Ackerman's *grades*?"

Weezy gave Joe one of her can't-believe-you're-that-slow shrugs. "I *live* in cyberspace. Remember?"

"Sure. Of course," he said, looking away.

Weezy handed the e-pad back.

"You really want the job, don't you?"

"I … yeah, I do."

He leaned forward, elbows on thighs. "I was at my Florida job for fifteen years. Got hired straight out of college. I liked most of the people, and I did good work. It wasn't difficult."

He turned to Weezy. "You know how people sometimes talk about their day job? And you know what they're telling you is they have a different passion than their work?"

Weezy nodded.

"Well, my job was a day job. I was proud of what I did, but my life was my wife, her art, our friends. Once a year, though, the investment bankers from New York came in. They did exciting, challenging work. Interesting, difficult stuff. I did routine things. I always wondered what it would be like to do really hard stuff."

"And make big bucks," Weezy said.

"Sure. That too. And"—Joe leaned close to put an arm around Weezy's shoulder—"be only a couple of hours away from you."

***

Ross Ackerman had returned to the New Jersey trading floor after his interviews in Manhattan. It really had turned into a crazy trading day. He was deeply involved in trying to decipher the markets when his implant tapped him. Braithwaite. Ross tapped his e-pad, connecting.

"Yeah, what now?"

"Not a nice way to treat a chess partner," Braithwaite said.

*This guy's getting too familiar,* Ross thought.

"Checkmate," Braithwaite finished.

Ross's irritation vanished. He punched disconnect and pinged Arty Pov.

Artyom Povreshenko turned from the four monitors on his desk and looked across the trading floor to Ross's slightly elevated window. He looked surprised, but he always did. Ross wondered idly how much of that was the coke. Hell of a trader, though.

Arty pulled his headset mic into place.

"Yeah, boss?"

"Arty, execute those buy orders for RedSock on the Copper Skins, will you? You kept your log up on the negotiations, right?" Ross couldn't read the look he got back. But Arty nodded. "Uh-huh."

***

The men's seemed to be empty. Arty checked down the row of stalls for occupants. *Good.* The RedSock buy orders couldn't be originated in the Zhou, Cadwallon system. Arty and Ross had been careful to record the pseudo-negotiations leading to the trades Arty was now about to execute to prevent the regulators' software from reversing the transactions in what traders called a "stuff up."

In the last stall, Arty dropped his pants for verisimilitude. Enthroned, he turned his pad to silent, signed on to Quantitec Financial and placed orders from fifteen accounts at the hedge fund RedSock, LLC for the Copper Skin. Arty ordered the highest risk portion of the Skin, the stuff the bankers called "industrial waste." Watching the trades go, he smirked. Brian Garrity would be shocked to find out what he had done.

Ackerman had taken Arty along when they went to Quantitec to open the account. Garrity must have thought he had scored big. They got the one fancy conference room in the place. Quantitec catered to smaller accounts and struggling retirees. Garrity had led with a rambling description of market conditions. Ackerman handed him a memory cube and said with an amused smile, "Drop your ideas on this." Somehow, that cube got Arty access to Garrity's trading account.

Drawing a breath, Arty reached to get at the small pocket carefully sewn into the inseam of his pants for a small envelope of gloriously white, soul-inspiring powder and a thin ceramic tube. He opened the envelope, hands shaking. He had to take the coke directly out of the packet and spilled most on the floor. *Shit!* The men's room door opened. He waited while someone took a leisurely piss. The guy spent an interminable amount of time washing his hands. Finally, he left.

Arty pulled off a piece of toilet paper. Licked it a little. Pressed on the white grains on the floor. Didn't even consider thinking about what else he was getting. He folded the paper, put it between cheek and gum. Waited for the blissful infusion. Heaven.

Fortified and calm in the antic sort of way he got after a hit, Arty opened a new channel. He purchased sixteen copper call options, four each from four online brokers where he had accounts. A one-penny increase in the price of copper got two hundred fifty dollars for the person holding the contract, but the option holder gained or lost much more. Arty expected there to be lots of pennies, and the options gave him lots of leverage. Hundred k, maybe one-twenty. Just a taste.

# THREE

JUST AFTER SUNUP, Joe woke to the clank and crash of trash being collected on the street behind the New York Athletic Club. He extricated himself from the twisted sheets, Weezy's arm and ankle.

The bed was uncomfortable and too small for two adults, particularly if one of them rarely settled in one position. Joe twisted to stretch his sore back, wishing for the chain hotels he was used to with their premium mattresses, choice of firm or soft pillows, and adjustable shower heads. He rotated his head, hearing the pop and snap of vertebrae.

The television set belonged to the twentieth century. Joe switched it on at low volume as he made coffee in the tiny electric pot. Weezy was making waking up noises, kicking off covers.

She sat up, stretched, and said, "Do we have to stand in line with a tin tray for breakfast, or is this a minimum-security facility?" Joe drank in her nakedness.

"Uhh …"

"Breakfast. We were talking about—"

Joe turned to the TV.

"Hold that thought," he said.

The ticker scrolling across the bottom of the screen read *Assassination in Zambia?* The picture switched to a correspondent standing in front of an impressive building surrounded by uniformed troops.

"We have breaking news from Lusaka, Zambia," he said in a clipped British accent. "It appears that a regional governor, Jameson Chitimukulu, has been found dead in his headquarters north of here, near the Copper Belt." He motioned toward the building. "The government statement says that he died of complications of a heart condition. It expressed shock that the strongman, much loved by his people, had been 'taken in the prime of life.' " The video switched to a still of large man beaming as he took flowers from a child. "Chitimukulu was a shadowy figure in the politics of the region. He ruled the northern area of Zambia and parts of Congo through a militia that has been accused of barbarous crimes, but he also built schools and medical facilities." The report continued, mentioning political unrest building since the government had jailed a handful of "terrorists" thought to be members of Chitimukulu's militia. "Rumor has it," the reporter said, "he may have been assassinated, and the head of the national police force has declared an emergency."

The anchor took over, noting that Chitimukulu had enforced relative calm in the Copper Belt, and several multinational mining firms had been rebuilding a moribund copper industry.

Joe turned to Weezy, who was fastening her bra, her back to him.

"That's the product—"

"The Copper Skin," Weezy said, stepping into her shorts. "So, someone made a lot of money, someone lost a lot, and your friends at ZCG are going to look very smart and raise their rates."

She turned toward him and must have seen that she had, yet again, interrupted with a conclusion.

"That's what you were going to say, wasn't it?"

Joe chuckled. *You like having a girlfriend with a 160+ IQ, right? So, roll with it.* "Yes, that's right."

"I wonder," she said, "why they put together that Skin now, rather than a year ago or a year from now. Were they lucky? Or smart?"

***

On Friday, copper moved up two cents on the news Chitimukulu's death was possibly an assassination. This was confirmed over the weekend, and copper shot up ten cents when markets opened on Monday. As the country's factions fought for control, a rebel group thought to be associated with Chitimukulu blasted the new rail line from Chimbolo to Angola, effectively cutting off the third-largest world supply, and copper climbed thirty cents a pound. This destabilized the recently established African Currency Unit, turning a bad cold into contagion.

The next Wednesday, Ross Ackerman sat in his kitchen fully dressed for his semi-regular 4:00 a.m. call to his firm's president, Zhou Qiáng, in Hong Kong. While he waited for the call to go through, he scrolled his e-pad, watching the value of the puts and calls that made up the Copper Skin gyrate. A window opened revealing Mr. Zhou.

"I see there was a disturbance in Africa."

"Yes, sir." Ackerman said. "A tragedy. But the Copper Skin protected our clients, and someone made a hell of a lot of money on the high-risk tranches."

The elder Zhou nodded almost imperceptibly. "Good for business."

"Yes, sir. It should help us sell the Chromium Skin," he said, thinking, *and if you make the worst case happen ….*

***

Later that day, Ross Ackerman and Nick Braithwaite met in Ross's Manhattan office.

"Chromium plan in place?" Ackerman asked as Braithwaite sat down in the visitor chair in front of Ackerman's desk. He knew it was. The question was a way of finding out whether Braithwaite was recording the conversation. He had no illusions about Braithwaite working for anyone but Braithwaite. And the money, of course.

Braithwaite gave him his anodyne stare. "It is. I finished the arrangements before I came back. This one's not as precise as Zambia. Mine owners are playing singing out of their normal hymnals, refusing to negotiate with the union on wages and safety conditions. We can control when the cave-in will happen, but we don't know how long it will take for all hell to break loose afterwards. Depends on how hard they work on the rescue and how many workers die. Should be a couple of days, a week at most. They don't spend much effort on saving kaffirs."

"Kaffirs?"

Braithwaite looked a little embarrassed. "Blacks." He unwrapped a stick of gum, folded it, and popped it into his mouth. "Then the Liberation Army, or whatever they call themselves, is going to see an opportunity, cross the border. The Defence Force will have to step in. A couple of officers killed by snipers should set off a bigger conflict and shut the mines. Then the infrastructure will blow, which will eliminate the people we put in place to start the riot. Of course, they don't know that." He cracked his gum.

"Sounds like we're hoping and praying stuff will happen."

Braithwaite didn't bother to hide his irritation. "Look, if you want to create a massive clusterfuck halfway around the world, you have to plan for the contingencies and then improvise as the situation develops. No way to make it precise and surgical." He shifted in the chair. "But I improvise better than anyone. It'll work."

He stood, turned toward the door, then back to Ackerman and said, "Speaking of contingencies, you mentioned you identified a back stop?"

Ross scowled. "You're the one who said I needed something more. I'm not sure why. I mean, the trading's all done through Garrity, right?"

Nick gazed out the window, working the gum. "Usually, the feds are lazy. If there's a problem and they look only at the electronic record they won't catch on. Garrity's licensed to trade derivatives. Of course, if they send out an investigator with any common sense, they'll realize that pissant retail brokerage he works at wouldn't be trading derivatives at this level. If they squeeze his head a little, he'll probably pop. It'll roll back to Arty, and you'll have to wail and moan and sacrifice him. But it'd be nice to have something more … a diversion."

"What do you mean?"

"Confuse 'em. You know how fighter planes send out chaff to confuse missiles when they're under attack? That kind of diversion."

"So, someone that's part of the company, maybe," Ross said. "Someone who's not high enough in the power structure to attract notice until the shit hits the fan, right?"

Braithwaite nodded.

Ross tapped the screen of his e-pad and began scrolling. He stopped at Mayfield, Joseph E.

"Like I said the other day, I think I found my backstop."

# FOUR

ERIC O'MALLEY HAD said Joe would hear from ZCG soon. "Soon" turned out to be a couple of weeks, and the offer came through the headhunter his former employer had hired as part of the Phoenix settlement. "Damn, Joe. The Personnel Director at Zhou, Cadwallon called." She leaned close to her e-pad's camera, her excitement more than the gloss of enthusiasm she normally put on for her clients. "What would you say to $250k? I mean real, serious two-hundred-fifty-by-god-k? And a bonus?" The wide-angle lens made her nose huge, and her eyebrows rose high enough to risk cracking her carefully applied makeup.

As she detailed the offer, Joe looked around the small interior of the trailer with its worn, comfortable furniture, Cynthia's art and her guitar. He hadn't planned to stay in the trailer—just hide out when Phoenix was after him. But after all that happened … losing Cynthia, RazorBlue, meeting Weezy … it had become home. The offer was everything he had dreamed of. But could he leave all this? "Uh, yeah, I'll take a look at it. That's great, really great."

"Whaddya mean you'll look at it? It's better than 'great.' I mean, it's a no-brainer, right? A chance to move into the big leagues." She didn't hide her disbelief in Joe's hesitation.

"Look, Joe. Be realistic. Yes, you're famous because of the MedRecords scam you exposed, and you're a very smart guy. But you got yourself a nice size five résumé. Here's an opportunity for a size ten job."

She pulled away from the camera and held up the offer letter.

"My advice, honey—jump on it."

***

Joe took the offer. The following day a perky young woman from ZCG's Personnel Office called. The firm expected to make his transition to New York seamless. He was introduced to a personal shopper at Brooks Brothers, given advice as to barbering, and received an invitation to become a member the New York Athletic Club. He was introduced by video to a bubbly woman anxious to find him the perfect apartment.

He picked a place on Sullivan Street in the center of Greenwich Village because it had the feel of a smaller town, like Panacea with an Italian accent. For the first few nights, he didn't sleep well. Panacea nights were silent but for the occasional chortle of a barred owl or the cackle of a heron perturbed by the alligators in Spencer's pond. In the Big Apple, the sirens were nearly nonstop, interrupted by enough silence to let him drift back toward the threshold of sleep. Then conversation wafting up the narrow divide between the buildings threw his brain into analysis mode, startling him awake.

He called Weezy, complained about the noise and sent her a video of the apartment.

"Nice," she said. "Very stylish. You'll get used to the noise in a couple of days."

"And," he said hopefully, "it's only about an hour from Bethesda on the Acela. Lots of good things to do in Manhattan."

Weezy gave him a pixie grin with a hint of promise. "I bet there are."

***

On his first day at ZCG, Joe found the Sixth Avenue subway near his apartment. The placid mornings in Panacea flashed through his mind as he was muscled forward into the dark maw of the entrance. Once in, he stopped at the system map. A mistake. People shoved by, seemingly on autopilot. A guy absorbed in his e-pad bumped him, spilled coffee and said *Shit,* glaring at Joe as if not moving was a sin. After a few rides, he'd be like them, he thought.

The ride to Wall Street was short, and the transfer to the New Jersey PATH at the Trade Center was easy. It took a couple of minutes to pass under the Hudson, and he was in Jersey City.

Joe found the ZCG offices in a tall, sterile building in the Exchange Place complex. He got out of the elevator on fourteen and held out his new security badge to the severe-looking receptionist. She nodded toward a smart pad. He swiped the badge; she consulted her monitor.

"Fourteen-E." Then, with an irritated sigh, "Down the hall."

Following the receptionist's pointing finger, Joe was halfway across the open area when Eric O'Malley bounded out of his office, grabbed Joe by the shoulder with one hand and offered a handshake with the other.

"C'mon, I'll show you where you're going to live."

O'Malley took off at flank speed, with Joe almost race walking to keep up.

Fourteen-E turned out to be a big room filled with mahogany-trimmed cubicles surrounded by partitions enclosing L-shaped workstations. Names were already up, and Joe saw his.

"We team a new analyst with both a new banker and an experienced analyst," Eric said. "Charlie Gray's your banker, also your classmate. Your mentor is Felicity Banasiak. She's been with us for five years and knows the ropes."

Eric cocked his head slightly to the right and said, "Tap." He held up his finger to Joe and spoke to the invisible other party, "Yeah. I'm in Jersey. I'll be at the meeting on time."

Finished, he grabbed Joe's hand again and pumped. "Glad you're with us. You're going to have a good time."

***

"I'm Felicity. You're Mayfield, right?" The scent of flowery perfume had preceded the woman now leaning over the wall of his workstation. "Felicity Banasiak," she said, offering a handshake. "I haven't got much time today. I hope you actually know how to do this shit, because I have a full plate all the time. I mean, I can answer sensible questions …"

She looked around his workspace. He had gotten as far as putting several math books on the bookshelf and a picture of Weezy mugging for the camera on his desk. Felicity's look said she was assessing him. She was perhaps a couple of years older than he, short and broad with blue eyes and blondish hair starting to gray. "But go to the first training, and don't be intimidated. The quants … the guys who run the course … are gonna drive you crazy. Just remember, you don't have to do the math, it's all in the templates we use. You only have to understand how to apply them."

Left on his own for the hour before the class started, Joe finished moving into his desk. He found his computer console required a thumbprint to enter. A Ramos Security page popped up, asked a series of questions, seemed satisfied with his answers and let him into the ZCG portal. His personal page included a calendar with his schedule on it and quite a bit of background on the current Copper Skin, as well as the math refresher he was given along with his acceptance letter.

The refresher intimidated him at first but got easier as Joe remembered the courses he took fifteen years earlier. When he hit the discussion of stochastic calculus, he was tempted to call Weezy for help. But he didn't want to get the pitying look as she explained what she considered to be intuitively obvious.

Joe dug into the Skins background. He got immersed in the commentary, charts and graphs and was halfway through his review when he realized there was a person standing next to his workstation.

"Charlie Gray." The man put out a hand. Joe stood and shook. Charlie was a nice-looking guy with longish dark blond hair and an aquiline face. He was slightly overweight and had a genteel southern accent.

"Hear you and I are going to be working together." He chuckled. "Or, more likely, you're going to be working and I'm going to be hangin' on for dear life."

Joe grinned, unsure of how to answer.

"And you're RazorBlue, right?"

"I am."

"Hot damn. Well, I hope you're as good at math as you are at hacking."

Joe noticed people were moving purposefully by his workstation toward the hall.

"You goin' to training, Joe? Don't want to be late the first day."

"Thanks for reminding me," Joe said with a grin as he stood and joined Charlie. "I was lost in the exciting material we're going to be studying."

The training was in a large conference room down the hall. Twenty people were milling, most near the back, where a table held coffee and snacks. Charlie made for the coffee. Joe stood aside picking out the few classmates he had met. Almost all were younger, almost all from fine universities. All smart, most willing to tell you so within a minute or so of meeting you.

The front wall was a whiteboard. To the side, a lectern and a stand supporting a brushed-metal cylinder. Windows on the outside wall gave a view of lower Manhattan. A tall, lanky guy with thinning red hair pulled into a ponytail stood at the lectern. He pushed his glasses up the bridge of his nose and stared intently at a small pad. He tapped it a couple of times, and a hologram of ZCG's logo rose from the cylinder, followed by a title, *The Mechanics of Political Exposure Assurance Units*. This faded and under it *How We Give You the Skins* appeared.

Joe crossed to the window side and picked a seat in the second row. Charlie appeared with a coffee cup and took the one on his left.

"Let's do this, RazorBlue."

"RazorBlue, huh?" The woman in front of him turned to inspect him. She put out her hand. Joe shook it, searching for her name tag. "Khadijah Mahyadi Sengupta. Don't bother. It's unpronounceable to you Anglos. Just call me Ida." Prickly, but she smiled.

An Asian woman, tall and willowy, entered and walked toward the lectern. She laughed at something Ponytail said, and he blushed. She surveyed the room and said loudly enough to stop conversation, "Good morning. I hope you have all had a chance to meet at least some of your classmates."

Coffee drinkers moved toward chairs. The woman waited while conversation tapered off, then said, "My name is Stacey Cheung. I'm the internal coordinator for several of the groups you'll be assigned to. I also help with customer relations." Charlie gave an appreciative murmur. "As is usual for Zhou, Cadwallon, you are an impressive group. As you'll note in the résumés for the class, we have nine bankers, seven analysts and a couple of us overhead folks." She smiled at a portly woman in the back row.

An index of résumés came up on Joe's e-pad. Those around him paged through them. Up to now, he'd been a celebrity. Now they'd discover how ordinary he was.

Stacey continued, "Your classmates' résumés are on your e-pads. You're in fast company. Five Harvard MBAs, four from Wharton, a Yale Ph.D., several CPAs, two CFAs, and a genuine hero." She directed a radiant smile at Joe.

Good, and now they'd know he was ordinary and hate him.

"Anyway, we need to keep to schedule, so let's get started. In the next week, I'll be taking you through a lot of procedural material, but it is the processes we use to develop ZCG's proprietary financial products will be the focus. The best known of these are the Political Exposure Assurance Units, which everyone calls 'Skins.' I suppose those of you with a liberal arts background … she delivered the 'liberal arts' with an archness that drew a chuckle from Charlie …will recognize that the acronym is PEAU … not too zippy … but also French for 'Skin.' Thus, Skins. Now, I will turn the meeting over to our best-known quantitative analyst, Martin Docherty. I wish you all the best of luck in following Martin's presentation."

Ponytail's résumé appeared on Joe's e-pad. *Martin Docherty, MSc, Language Evolution and Computation Research Unit, University of Edinburgh; Ph.D., Caltech.*

Docherty smiled nervously. "The subject today, as Stacey said, is Skins." A bit of a Scots burr. "But really, it's risk. We're in the business of offsetting risk." Docherty steepled his fingers as if to pray. "But first, let me ask you, with respect to risk, what are we missing?" He looked expectantly over the audience. Beside Joe, Charlie shifted uncomfortably. Ida's hand went up. "Language," she said, with an almost inaudible question mark.

"Language, absolutely right." Docherty beamed. "And as you all know, mathematics is a language. Perhaps the simplest and most powerful product of the human mind to date, but a language, nonetheless." A cartoon character popped up on Joe's e-pad, rolling its eyes before performing an act of self-gratification, then disappearing. A muted chuckle ran through the room … someone hacked the training network.

Docherty looked up from his notes, furrowed his brow, but continued, "Our algorithms use mathematics to give risk a language." He glowed as if speaking of a love interest. "And the nice thing is that allows us to turn risk into a visual representation that even a CEO can understand." Another chuckle.

"Let's look at our new South African Chromium Skin." A three-dimensional graph appeared out of the holoprojector, the axes marked "currency," "politics," and "environment." Docherty continued, "Now, here's the price of chromium. Trending at three dollars per kilogram over ten years, except seven years ago, when there's a peak for about six months at nine dollars." He peered over his glasses to be sure everyone saw the anomaly. "And the new African Currency Unit is anything but stable." Another graph, showing wide but seemingly random fluctuations in the new currency. "So, here we have the problem: South Africa has the richest sources of chromium in the world, but"—he pointed to the 'politics' pane of the holo—"during the last few years, it has a political risk profile that would send shivers down the spine of even the dullest politician." He smiled broadly. "And in that risk and uncertainty, there is enormous value to be mined. Value we mine with our Skins."

***

The second week of training began with a senior analyst explaining financial derivatives. He interlarded his presentation with obscure technical terms, seeming to dare the class to ask what he meant. When he came to a point he deemed particularly weighty, he puffed out his cheeks, reminding Joe of the blowfish he often saw in the waters off Panacea. Fully expanded with spikes protruding, the dull little creature probably looked impressive to a predator sizing him up for lunch.

Joe chuckled.

"Do you find long straddles humorous, Mister … uhh … Mayfield?"

He puffed out his cheeks again. Joe nearly lost it.

"Not a bit, sir," he said, trying to contain a laugh.

Martin Docherty took over the next day, driving the group deeper into mathematics.

Back in his apartment, Joe called Weezy.

His e-pad showed her sitting in her overstuffed chair balancing a cup of tea precariously on a knee, her lap occupied by Sappho the cat.

"I think I need some tutoring."

"Behavioral? Life skills? Sartorial?" She grinned, looking down at her faded T-shirt and much-worn pants.

"Nope. Mathematical."

"Phew!" Weezy said. "I was afraid you were going to ask me about your wardrobe."

"I get plenty of unsolicited advice on that from ZCG." He chuckled. "But about the math … I think I'm doing okay. I mean, it's clear they don't want me to actually do it, but the accountant in me doesn't like winging it about something I don't understand. My college math carried me through the first week, and my masculine pride kept me from calling until now. But we're getting into some pretty heavy lifting."

Weezy leaned forward. "Yeah, go on."

Joe exhaled and said, "Okay. This will be a good test." He pursed his lips. "Of course, it will also be a violation of ZCG's confidentiality agreement. You and Sappho need to cross your hearts and swear …"

"Sappho makes no promises to humans."

"... The secrets of ZCG will remain in your possession and your possession only."

"Mmm. Okay. I can hear the corporate-speak seeping into your vocabulary. Is that a function of your big salary or the New York air?"

Joe settled back onto the daybed that also served as his couch. He laid out what he had learned over the past few days about the combination of puts and calls and the end product.

Weezy said, "Pretty simple. What's the deal with the math?"

"I can trace the outcomes of putting several puts and calls together, but yesterday and today, Docherty has been waxing eloquent on the subject of stochastic calculus. Which makes the whole thing more complicated."

"Well, 'stochastic' is Greek for 'guess at,' " Weezy said. "So it's just calculus with some estimated component, probably some projection from one of your high priced outside experts."

Joe's brain coughed and threatened to die at "just calculus," then restarted.

Weezy went on, "Your guys are doing the research to estimate better than your clients could, at least that's what they must think."

She cocked her head. "What kind of fees do you have wrapped into Skins?" One corner of her mouth turned up in an almost-sarcastic smile.

"I don't know for certain. Maybe five percent. They keep the profit models close to the chest."

"Five percent seems pretty reasonable and pretty unlikely. I bet it's more." She sipped her tea. "After all, you have to pay for the office towers and original art you talk about and all those salaries. And if you have to charge a lot, you have to make it mysterious. Right?"

Joe grinned. "We call it the 'value proposition.' Sure, a mining company could do its own simple derivatives. But ZCG gets the best minds in the world to look forward at the likely political development of, say, South Africa and then wraps it into our Skin."

Weezy smiled at Joe's use of "we" and stroked Sappho, who waved the tip her tail.

"So, you go out with these Skins," she said. "You talk vaguely but impressively about all the things you do, including stochastic calculus. You convince those folks they could never achieve the level of protection you offer on their own. Right?"

"We do, Weezy, and I do think Skins *are* better than they could do by themselves." Joe realized he sounded defensive. He changed the subject to a story of his neighbors' operatic arguments in a mix of English, Neapolitan dialect and didactic hand-gestures, trying to get beyond the doubt in her eyes.

# FIVE

AFTER THREE WEEKS of pressure-cooker study, all but four members of Joe's class were passed, if grudgingly, by Martin Docherty.

Friday evening, Joe arrived home to a basket of exquisite trinkets—a note congratulating him on finishing the class, a Hermes tie, a bottle of fine bourbon, an embossed business card holder, chocolates monogrammed with his initials—and an engraved invitation to a reception at Ross Ackerman's West Village townhouse.

Joe looked ahead at the weekend, wishing he hadn't put off asking Weezy up to New York. He'd heard the doubt in her questions while he explained Skins. He had been torn between wanting to see her and feeling as if he might have to defend the work he was coming to love. The basket and the invitation forced the issue.

He called her N-Ops number. The computer said she was unavailable but would respond as soon as possible. An hour later, she called from home, in the overstuffed chair, anchored by Sappho.

"So, what's up?"

"I'm a graduate. And, with your help, I understand as much, maybe more, about Skins as my impressive classmates. Anyway, they sent each grad this over-the-top basket of goodies and an invitation to a reception next Friday evening. I'd like to show you off." Nervous as a seventeen-year-old asking for a prom date.

"And my wardrobe? Right?"

"Mainly you. I can almost promise you the chief quant, Martin Docherty, will try to bird-dog you."

"Bird-dog?"

"Yes, a fine old tradition. Docherty will fall for your mathematical capability and good looks."

"In what order?"

"I decline to answer on the grounds—"

"Damn, they've put some polish on you, haven't they?" She gave him the grin he loved. "But, sure. Of course I'll come."

***

The new graduates and several of the instructors had been invited to join the company directors in the Manhattan reception area. It was simply laid out, elegant without being showy. Several pieces of original art graced the interior wall, and a tall, slender bronze of a woman, beautifully top-lit, commanded the center. There was a table of fruit and pastries, largely untouched. As Joe walked across from the entrance, Charlie Gray raised a hand in greeting. Ida Sengupta nodded. Even Martin Docherty gave him a half smile of recognition. Being accepted was a nice feeling, like slipping into comfortable clothes, long misplaced.

Ross Ackerman was talking with a couple of Joe's classmates. He was impeccably dressed in a flowing shirt, slacks and expensive-looking loafers. Eric O'Malley was talking with Ida Sengupta. A short, pudgy young Asian man was making his way through the room, stopping to greet each person. His dark hair combed back, he was dressed in an old-style pinstripe suit, perfectly pressed shirt and a fine silk tie. Joe knew from his class book this was John Zhou Min, son of ZCG's founder Zhou Qiáng and head of US Operations. Everything about Zhou Min was precise, down to the same number of words exchanged with each person, followed by a double-pump handshake.

Across the room, Eric excused himself from Ida, gave Charlie Gray a peremptory nod and kept on coming toward the refreshments and Joe.

"I hear you beat the pants off all those Ivy-Leaguers." Eric beamed and extended a big hand.

"I don't know about that. It was more like keeping my nose above water."

Eric inspected a platter of dainty fruit tarts, picked one up with surprising delicacy and popped it whole into his mouth. He chewed a couple of times. "Well, that aw-shucks self deprecation has made you a lot of friends around here." He swallowed and brushed a flake of crust off his shirt and smiled more broadly, "You're going to have to lose it when you get in front of our clients. But, congratulations. Hope you can teach Charlie a thing or two." He palmed another tart and moved off toward a group surrounding Martin Docherty.

John Zhou Min finished his brief conversation with Charlie, double-pumped, and turned toward Joe. "Good Morning. John Zhou Min. And you are Joseph Mayfield, are you not?" His smile was pleasant, a formal mask.

"Yes, sir." Joe stifled the urge to bow or salute.

"We are happy to have you on our team." Careful with words as well as actions.

"And I'm honored to be here."

Zhou Min asked how the training went and whether Joe was settled in the city. Joe felt the double-pump coming. Then John's expression softened, and he drew closer to Joe, surprising him. "We value your courage and honesty."

Joe fought the temptation to step backwards.

"Thank you."

John put his formal face back. He grasped Joe's hand and shook it twice.

As Zhou Min moved on, Ross Ackerman sauntered toward Joe.

Felicity had hinted that Ackerman, not John Zhou Min, ran ZCG. Joe saw it playing out as the leading men circulated. Eric was outgoing and upbeat, a salesman at heart, not a plotter. John carried the burden of being young and son of the owner. His polite, formal manners diminished him in the competitive world of finance. Ackerman clearly had his hands on the wheel.

"Joe Mayfield, right?" Ackerman looked him up and down, taking his measure. "They say you did well in class." A hint of surprise in his voice.

Joe shook Ackerman's offered hand. "It was a great training session. Hard, but very interesting."

"Man, I've never heard Docherty called interesting before." Ackerman smirked. "And, hell, you had to get through it without having gone to Haahvard." Ackerman didn't quite sniff.

Joe, remembering Eric's admonition about the aw-shucks drawl, said, "Yes, good old Florida Northeastern for the basic stuff, and my tutor."

"Tutor?"

"Yessir."

"Who?" Ackerman looked … perturbed?

"You will meet her Friday evening."

# SIX

WEEZY WAS AT work in Bethesda at the National Operations Center of the Interagency Channel. She was seated at her workstation—six monitors arrayed in a semi-circle around her and her high-back, five-wheeled chair. Thirty identical cubicles occupied an area half the size of a football field, open but for an office tucked in one corner. The cubicles housed trackers: the last, best defense against intrusion into the most secure, sophisticated database in the world. The office housed Keith Sanders, the recently-appointed, wet-behind-the-ears Assistant Director, Operational Security. Weezy's boss.

She had worked most of the morning tracking down a hack attempt from Montenegro, trying to ignore the mosquito whining in her ear: What to wear to Joe's party. The thought was lurking, bringing back memories. Her Aunt Tonia saying "you could be byootiful" and urging her to concentrate on unimportant, time-wasting activities like grooming and clothes selection that occupied the lives of the popular girls. Those girls sneering at her, exuding the inward certainty that pretty clothes were considerably more important than being able to do base two arithmetic effortlessly. Junior high boys calling her Boney Maroney.

She had put off the inevitable. It was less than a week until she was to leave for New York. Properly attired, of course.

She heard a ping on monitor 4. She glanced at it, not wanting to be interrupted.

```
Sanders: Bone, how do you want to
handle the power management
implementation team meeting?
```

Weezy grimaced at "Bone." Keith was fond of nicknames, which he supposed projected a devil-may-care informality that would endear him to the tracker staff. Weezy became Bone based on her slenderness and perhaps the penetrating gaze that often froze critics into silence.

She sighed, tapped at her keyboard to suspend her report on sequential DNS-spoofing algorithms. The meeting was going to be another two-hour session with several other department representatives. She knew she was one of the Freaks & Geeks to them. The teleconference would be all guys, the same ones she had called dumbasses at the last meeting. After that came the "little talk" when Keith held forth on good communication and smoothing ruffled feathers. Weezy wrote:

`How about Maddie?`

A window opened and Keith's face appeared, lines of concern across his forehead. "Can she handle this? Is she up to speed?" Keith asked.

Weezy stifled her response that "up to speed" meant arthritic oldster with a walker. Stifled it because she saw that Keith was trying his best to live up to his predecessor, P.E. Smith. Everyone admired P.E's common sense and her knack for protecting the Freaks & Geeks from the irritating quotidian bullshit of governmental bureaucracy. Keith aspired to fill P.E's size nines by having his finger on the pulse of the larger organization at all times. He often concluded discussions about form and protocol with a cheery "Got you covered" to remind them all that he, too, produced important "work product." (Watching Keith pass through the bullpen loaded down with a e-pad and several briefing packets, someone said, "Work product? Really? Sounds like he's constipated.") Someone in the OddBalls, Weezy's lead team, dubbed Keith "the dweeb." It had stuck.

"Keith, Maddie's far more impressive in a group presentation, if you know what I mean."

You *do* know what I mean, she thought, as Keith blushed. But it would be sexist to admit that Madeline Hollingsworth's soft Atlanta drawl, cotillion-trained eyelash flutter and voluptuous figure was guaranteed to captivate the largely male audience.

"If you say so …" She knew he was afraid because he had seen what happened when some poor doofus decided he could tell the book by its cover, made an insinuating remark, and got sliced up too thin to fry.

"I do, Keith. I'll bring her up to speed."

Weezy signed off and restarted what she had been working on. In the dead time between the program's need for instructions, the mosquito whine returned, this time too loud to ignore.

Of course, she knew how to dress, but her carelessness about clothes had become part of her persona, particularly at work. P.E. Smith tolerated it. Keith Sanders actually thought it was cool.

She looked down at her clothes, embarrassed for the first time in a long time. She wore an ancient sweatshirt with a force formula and underneath it, 'MIT Football', an in-joke few outside of Boston would understand. A pair of wrinkled work pants and bright green socks that smelled pretty good that morning completed her outfit.

She saw Maddie at her pod, had an inspiration, and tapped out a message:

`Got a minute?`

Two workstations away, Maddie made a coffee-drinking gesture. Weezy nodded *Sure.*

In the employee lounge, Weezy dialed up a coffee. Maddie made a cup of the Oolong tea she liked.

Weezy started from a comfortingly practical angle. "I need you to represent Trackers at the power management team meeting tomorrow."

Maddie chuckled, "So you're sending me in to heal their tiny little egos after you fried them in the last meeting. Thanks." But she smiled.

They spent five minutes outlining Maddie's talk.

"That all?" Maddie asked when they finished.

Weezy looked down at her coffee, formulating her question.

"Uhh, I think I need some wardrobe consultation."

Maddie didn't entirely succeed in suppressing a grin.

"I mean, well, you know how I dress isn't exactly, you know, the most important …"

Maddie's grin turned to a chuckle.

"Yes, I've noticed."

Weezy inspected the tabletop, then blurted out, "I'm going to New York to see Joe Mayfield. I have to go to some sort of party with the people he works for. He tells me outward appearances are important to them. He said it apologetically, but I know he's scared I'll turn up in hiking boots or something. I don't know what to wear."

Maddie drew herself up and slipped into her best deep south accent, "Well, y'all came to the right gal. I been bein' primped an' propered for this kind of challenge since I was a young thing."

She pursed her lips. "First off, it's going to be pretty easy. You're a pretty woman, and being as thin as you are gives you lots of options."

She glanced down at her own more substantial figure. "See, the best compliment I've gotten recently from a gentleman was that I have a lush body. 'Course, he was sayin' lush but lookin' lust. I have to be careful about which of my attributes to accentuate. If I go too low-cut, I can't get most guys to squeeze out a conversation. You, on the other hand, have a lot of positives to pick from."

She cocked her head at Weezy and grimaced, "Well, you'll have to worry more than you do now—I mean, bright green socks and a worn-out sweatshirt? You are really trying to fly under the fashion radar, aren't you?"

Weezy's defenses rose. Clothes shouldn't matter. Intellect should.

"Aw, c'mon Weezy." Back to the deep south voice, but with a grin, "I was just funnin' you."

She paused, shifted out of the accent. "Okay. Let's treat this like any other problem."

"There's an algorithm for clothes style?"

Maddie started laughing.

"I saw you! You actually thought there might be, didn't you?"

Weezy colored, but said stiffly, "Of course not. I was joking."

"The good news is the fashion world has one or two good ideas, and it cycles through variations on them. Right now, we're moving toward conservative again, and the Little Black Dress is back in style, if it ever went out. I think the thing to do is find an LBD for you that emphasizes your slenderness, pretty legs and the very nicely formed derriere. If you're going to a conservative party, it's probably best to leave the breasts to their imagination."

Weezy relaxed. Maybe this wouldn't be so bad.

"Now, about makeup."

"I really don't wear—"

"Hold on, tiger. You'll be able to get away with a little lipstick and—" Maddie looked closely at Weezy's eyes, "Maybe a little mascara. Not much needs doing on you. Oh, and we're going to get your hair cut by a professional."

"I do get my hair cut by a professional!"

"I mean, something other than the five minute special from Redi-Kutz."

The weight of the fashion world descended on Weezy. Maddie must have noticed the stubborn look that often preceded an ejaculation of 'dumbass' and held up her hands in mock defense.

"Weezy, it'll be easy, and if you give this girl thing a chance, you'll like it. Guaranteed!"

***

Friday. Joe met Weezy at Penn Station. She was carrying her usual back pack. No suitcase.

"I have to introduce you to my neighbor," Joe said as they strolled through Washington Square. "Mrs. Gagliardi pretty much runs the neighborhood. If she likes you, everyone will think they know you within a week."

After the meeting ("I don't think she approved," Weezy said. "You're Italian. She was charmed," Joe said), they made slippery love in the shower, she on tiptoes, one leg coming up to wrap his thigh. In the aftermath, sensual washing of each other and giggling until the water began to run cold.

Weezy hummed to herself as she dried her hair, caught in the warm afternoon light filtering in from the courtyard in back of Joe's apartment. Joe watched her from the kitchenette. She had a natural grace, lifting her arm as a ballerina might to wipe her flank. She looked up and saw him watching, began to cover herself but smiled, turned toward him and continued.

Joe was mesmerized, drawn into the motion and the light, the beauty of her movement, but the momentary reverie brought a discordant thought: What the hell was she going to wear?

Finished drying, Weezy picked up her backpack and the hiking pants she had worn on the train. "Maybe I should dress for the party now."

"Not a bad idea" Joe said a little stiffly. "We should get there about eight. It's a nice evening. I was thinking we could walk over. It's about a mile."

Weezy looked at the boots she wore with the hiking pants. "Oh, fine. I have comfortable shoes."

Joe looked as if he might get ill.

Weezy smiled. "Now, give me some privacy."

***

Finished dressing for the party in his Brooks blazer and slacks, Joe paced the small kitchenette, straightening utensils that needed no attention, flipping through a cookbook that held no interest. Temporizing.

Weezy had been in the bathroom for about fifteen minutes. Dressing in the small place had to be hard. One muffled 'Shit!' a couple of minutes ago. Joe had never seen what she might mean by "dressed up." Maybe she would choose something weird, maybe too ornate. Or try to do something too fancy with her hair. Whatever it might be …

Weezy stepped out of the bathroom.

Good Lord.

She was wearing a black dress that took advantage of all her curves and angles. Her hair looked natural, as always, but artfully shaped to accent her strong facial features. Her eyes were beautiful, maybe more so than usual, and … was she wearing a little lipstick?

Good Lord.

Joe drew a slow breath.

Weezy cocked her head. "Well?"

"You are … gorgeous. I mean beautiful. I mean … Wow!"

# SEVEN

ON THE WALK to Ackerman's, a brisk March breeze cut through Weezy's thin jacket, but she was warm, buoyed up by the shower, Joe's high spirits and, she had to admit, by her new look. Pretty hadn't mattered much to her before seeing the effect on Joe. They chatted about ZCG, Joe's classmates and the people Weezy was about to meet. The wind brought the hopeful, green scent of new leaves sprouting, overlaying the undercurrent of day-old restaurant trash and dog castings thawed after the last snow of the season.

They followed Fourth Street west, crossing Sixth Avenue and Seventh. Weezy began to wonder at the gritty shops and bodegas. This is a rich guy's neighborhood? But after another block, discreet galleries offering art and high-end accessories took over. Joe consulted his invitation and turned onto Bank Street. The Ackerman townhouse was tucked between a patisserie and a former packing house transformed into aggressively elegant condos. The townhouse was more discreet, its century-old facade conservatively dressed in beautifully restored red brick.

They climbed the steps, and Joe held the door. Weezy remembered scolding him for doing it when they first met and him apologizing for being a southern boy. But she had come to like it. The nice, old-fashioned touch reminded her to act like a grown-up.

Warmth, distant conversation, and muted jazz reached out to enfold them. The first floor was a cauldron of activity. Several women in starched uniforms queued up canapés in the compact, chef-designed kitchen. “Mmmm. Smells good,” Weezy said, getting a smile in return.

A greeter took their coats and directed them up the stairs. Weezy felt her prickly defense shield rising. This was about as far away from her childhood in Boston’s North End and her comfortable wraparound chair in the epicenter of N-Ops geekdom she had ever been. She caught herself in an ornate mirror at the top of the stairs and was both startled and steadied.

Hot damn! She was attractive in fancy clothes. She looked like these people. She squared her shoulders. Time to act like she looked.

The stairs led to a high-ceilinged open-plan room that occupied the whole floor. The furniture was modern and spare; the art, nouveau and valuable; the jazz, classic and tasteful. A live trio, well-known in discriminating circles as heirs to the beat generation, stood aloof, wrapped in a protective coating of cool against contact with these square cats. They were finishing *Take the A Train* as Joe and Weezy stopped at the top of circular staircase. Weezy was uncomfortable again. Wealth, tastefully displayed. But wealth, nonetheless.

Joe checked out the groups scattered around the room. He leaned toward Weezy. “The good-looking guy with the longish hair in the big group at the far end of the room is Ross Ackerman. The big man with them is Eric O’Malley. Right next to him, John Zhou Min, the managing director. They’re the top three at ZCG. To our right, some of my classmates listening to Martin Docherty.”

He nodded toward the window. “The woman over there is Ida Sengupta, a classmate, and the big guy she’s talking to is Nick Braithwaite.”

Weezy watched as Braithwaite scanned the room. Clearly in data acquisition mode. "What does he do?" He seemed out of place, like a predator watching the flock and waiting for an opportunity to strike.

Joe said, "Not sure. Data security, I think. I haven't met him, but he sat in the back of the class for a couple of hours, and one of my classmates who works in the data center said he does security work, whatever that means in an investment bank."

A pretty, slightly plump woman made her way toward them, smiling a greeting.

"Good evening," she said. "You must be Joe Mayfield. I am Emily Ackerman." Joe took her offered hand.

"Pleased to meet you. This is my friend Louise Napolitani."

Emily smiled at Weezy. Warm. Friendly. A heart-shaped face, light brown hair carefully arranged. A touch of green eye shadow. All in all, a gracious hostess, easing the entry of guests. She turned to Joe, "Ross speaks highly of you, and I'm sure you will want to introduce Louise." She touched Weezy's arm, a friendly pat, and led them across the room toward Ross Ackerman, who was talking with a short, sixtyish guy Weezy knew she had seen somewhere before. Closer up, the prominent nose and pockmarked face finally registered. A Harvard prof much loved by his students. He was on several blogs she followed. Ingoff, wasn't it? Rolf Ingoff. He was surprisingly short, but she realized she had only seen him on television as a witness at the Senate hearing on IAC funding after the last cyberwar. Ingoff, the news show's expert, had savaged the IAC director's wooden presentation, his precision and slight German accent driving his points home mercilessly.

The circle opened to include Weezy, Joe and Emily. Ross Ackerman was nodding sagely to Ingoff. He glanced at Joe, then at Weezy and did a double take. She was both flattered and uncomfortable.

*He can't see through my clothes, but he'd like to.* She turned to Joe and saw him frown.

Emily started to introduce Joe and Weezy, but Ingoff was not going to be diverted. He gave them a cursory nod and turned back to his audience.

"There are two and only two determinants of wealth." He paused, making sure everyone hung on his words. "Information and natural resources. However," he raised a hand as if to stave off disagreement, "information allows control of natural resources, so there is really only one determinant of wealth: information."

Ingoff allowed a moment for his conclusion to sink in, then continued. "Until Cyberwar I, most information was controlled by private entities. Then the government stepped in, creating the IAC and sequestering military, infrastructure, financial and a range of personal information behind its firewall." He sniffed. "Our business depends on deploying our superior information systems to control natural resources wherever they exist. We must fight the tendency of government to control our use of data under the rubric of 'security.' "

Weezy looked sidewise at Joe, letting a little smile tug the corners of her mouth. She saw his nervous glance and tried to hold back, but not very hard. "So you'd like to see free and open use of all data?"

Ingoff, two inches shorter than Weezy, managed to look down on her. He swelled up, preparing to answer.

Emily interrupted, "Dr. Ingoff, Ross, Eric, this is Joe Mayfield and his friend, Louise Napolitani."

Polite but somewhat chilly greetings followed, but Ingoff would not be sidetracked. He half turned to Weezy, but mainly addressed Ross, "Yes, free and open access. People who are worried about security should supply their own. The most powerful tool of control and wealth creation in modern society should not be handed over to the government. It is too much power. Too tempting. Particularly for a group of faceless bureaucrats."

Eric turned to Ingoff. "Dr. Ingoff, Joe has joined us as an analyst. He has quite a bit of experience with the IAC." Ingoff turned to Joe, expectantly. Eric continued, "Joe is the man who exposed the Phoenix Project. You probably remember the intrusion into the IAC MedRecord data last year."

"Of course."

Eric continued, "And I believe Ms. Napolitani is the somewhat mysterious tracker he worked with in so doing."

Ingoff glanced at Weezy, then back at Joe. "So, you must agree with me. A person with limited technical expertise, this Phoenix, was able to penetrate the 'most sophisticated security system yet developed,' I believe the government calls it, and it took an ordinary citizen with no technical expertise to catch him."

Weezy watched Joe try to formulate a polite answer and told herself to shut up. But how did a blowhard like this get to be an expert?

"But we did catch him," slipped out. "After all those systems you think should operate on their own sat idly by while Phoenix moved large sums of money and data. It took the IAC and an unusually smart and persistent 'ordinary citizen' to shut it down."

Color rose in Ingoff's thick neck, and Weezy belatedly realized she had challenged his standing as an expert in front of the very people who paid him. Stupid!

Stupid or not, she couldn't stifle the *coup de grace*. "So, after we go to personalized security systems, I'd like to know where you bank so I can clean you out."

There was a moment of leaden silence. Various shades of amusement hid under the surface of the faces in the circle. She shrugged, tried a grin, and said, "Just kidding."

Ingoff fixed Weezy in an icy glare, and she saw he was preparing to demolish her with the weight of his erudition. Eric O'Malley put a big hand on Ingoff's shoulder. "Better not tell her your bank name, Rolf," he said, followed by a guffaw. O'Malley's goodwill bulldozed its way through the impending argument. The group laughed politely but, uncomfortable, broke up.

As they walked away, Weezy shrugged an apology to Joe. "Sorry."

Joe said, "Well, he needed his shirt unstuffed … you can claim community service, I guess. Now, for the big challenge. You have to meet Martin Docherty."

They joined the group of Joe's classmates and found Docherty addressing the art of making Scots whiskey.

"Now this one, this one, it has a bit o' the peat in it, nestled as it has been down near Dunkeld, cradled in the oaks of Birnam Wood these last eighteen years. They're still there, you know, the trees. Great enormous oaks remembering their promise to Macbeth."

He took a sip of the scotch, hiccuped discreetly, and declaimed, "Macbeth shall never vanquish'd be until Great Birnam wood to high Dunsinane hill shall come against him."

"Martin."

Docherty sipped again, smacked his lips, and turned to Joe and Weezy.

"Ah yes, the well-known Mr. Mayfield. The man who actually tried to do the math. The one with the tutor."

He paused and peered at Weezy.

"This cannot be the tutor."

Joe smiled. "Yes, it is. Martin Docherty, this is my tutor, Louise Napolitani."

Docherty bowed somewhat unsteadily and took Weezy's hand. "Ah, the tutor. Well met. I shall be extraordinarily pleased to discuss a few points these sparkling Ivy League graduates could not possibly comprehend, even though I may be somewhat affected by several samples of barley-bree, the ardent spirits from the land of my birth."

He weaved slightly, then seemed to focus.

"I don't know whether he's really smart or you're a good teacher, but he did a good job."

Weezy felt a hand on her back. A congratulatory pat?

"Your well-known work on the Indus Valley codices is exciting," Weezy said to Docherty.

"You've read the papers?"

"Sure," she said. "Stats class. The intersection of the Sumerian and Akkadian languages. It was non-obvious, but you showed the relationship through statistical analysis."

Docherty's eyes lit up, and he began to explain the methodology he had used.

The hand on Weezy's back moved down and rested on the curve of what Joe called her delicious derriere.

Strange that Joe would do that in this formal setting. Trying to concentrate on Docherty's explication, she wiggled a little in appreciation of the hand, then glanced around the room. With most everyone relaxed and lubricated, would anyone notice? The big guy across the room, Nick Braithwaite, had them fixed in a cold stare.

Joe was several feet away.

Weezy hesitated. Could it be a mistake, an unintended brush of the hand? A tipsy husband maybe, about to be mortally embarrassed?

The hand squeezed her suggestively.

"What the f…?" The hand lingered, then slipped away. Docherty looked at Weezy quizzically, perhaps thinking she had discovered a flaw in his reasoning. She wheeled to find herself staring at Ross Ackerman, who wore a lubricious smile, eyes tinged with arrogance.

"Nice," he said.

Her fist started to come up. But the new self reflected in the mirror a few minutes ago took over. This was Joe's new life.

"Brains and a nice ass. A winning combination. Mayfield seems to know what he's about."

Weezy was speechless, nostrils flaring, jaw locked to bite off the torrent of expletives she ached to spew.

Ackerman gave her a lopsided grin she supposed was meant to say 'no big deal' and strolled toward the bar.

***

Ackerman sauntered up to the bar and ordered a drink. He glanced back over his shoulder at the Napolitani woman. She looked shocked, but she might be titillated, too. Maybe a little. But she might be dangerous. Docherty had worked up an enormous mathematical hard-on explaining some esoteric crap about a dead language to her. Probably was that IAC tracker, like Eric thought. Nice ass, though.

He caught Braithwaite's eye, tilted his head toward the stairs. Braithwaite was talking with the Indian broad, Ida something-or-other. He waited for her to draw breath, gave her a tight smile, said something, and walked to the spiral staircase.

Ross watched Braithwaite disappear down the stairs. He got a little rush of pleasure from being able to control a clearly superior physical specimen like Braithwaite.

He leaned toward Emily, put a hand on her waist, then slipped it down, caressing. "Nice party." The bartender poured his scotch. He sipped it, put the glass on the bar and followed Braithwaite.

***

Emily watched Ross disappear down the stairs. She studied her half-full wine glass, feeling sad and a little angry. Another opportunity for intimacy lost.

She turned to the friendly Russian, Artyom Povreshenko, who was next to her at the bar. Arty Pov, they called him. She remembered Ross mentioning his love of jazz and watched him bask in the music.

"You seem to be enjoying the Amos Trio," Emily said.

"Yes, I am," he said absently, watching the bass player solo. "You don't usually get to see them this close up."

When the number finished, Arty turned to her and said, "You must be really happy about the Skins in your accounts."

"Pardon?"

"You know, all those Scholze accounts Ross is managing. They've made a fortune over the last several months."

Fortune? Ross said they're "doing okay, conservative." When she asked more pointedly, he sighed and a few days later tossed a report on the coffee table. "See, making a decent return, nothing amazing." Fortune? She knew her face must give away her surprise, but Arty had turned to watch the trio.

She composed herself and leaned over to touch her shoulder to Arty's. "How do you do it? Make a fortune on those Skins?"

"Dumb luck," he said. "Dumb luck and maybe a little inside information." The trio lay down the last few bars of *Stormy Weather* and prepared to take a break.

Arty turned to Emily. "The thing is, Ross is putting the highest-risk tranches of Skins in RedSock," he said. "Most of the time, you'd expect them to be worthless, because they only pay if the worst-case scenarios happen. But the bad stuff seems to keep happening, and Ross gets the bad news before anyone else. RedSock's tranches have cashed out millions."

Millions?

***

Arty had taken in Ross's hand on Emily's hip and her surprise when he said millions. He was pleasantly high. Cocaine amplified by vodka. The music was great, and Ross's wife was, well, captivating. *Zaftig*, his dad would have said. Friendly, too.

Possibilities and questions began spinning in his mind, and the coke inspired brilliant answers. She leaned closer, bringing a hint of her perfume and under it … possibilities.

***

On the first floor, Ross jockeyed around the activity in the kitchen and went toward the back of the house. "I want you to check out the woman who came with Mayfield," he said as he stepped onto the patio.

"Yeah?"

"She's some sort of mathematical whiz-kid. She helped Mayfield thrive in Docherty's training, and she cut Ingoff's nuts off and handed them to him on a platter."

"Anything specific?"

"Nope. A suspicion, but I tend to trust my instincts. Get me some in-depth background on her."

Braithwaite's look said he was thinking ahead of the problem and didn't give Ackerman's instincts much weight. "Are you tracking Mayfield? Is he implanted?"

"Not yet. There's been no reason."

"I'd get it done. Any problem with the woman is most likely going to show up through Mayfield. With the implant, we'll see it."

# EIGHT

THE MORNING AFTER the party, Joe and Weezy sat at a table in the coffee house down the block from his apartment. They had taken a cab home after the party and had some desultory conversation about Joe's classmates. Weezy had not mentioned Ackerman's weird, embarrassing grope.

The smells of coffee and pastry, the morning light shafting through the window, the quiet conversations around them signaled a relaxing weekend coming. Weezy, not looking forward to what she had to say, crossed her legs, foot bobbing.

They chuckled over Rolf Ingoff. "I really should have buttoned my lip," Weezy said. "But the guy is such a pain in the ass."

"And now you have the undying affection of Eric O'Malley, who truly dislikes Ingoff."

Remembering Braithwaite's cold stare, Weezy said, "That big military guy … Nick Braithwaite? … is one scary-looking dude. I felt like we were sheep, and he was a wolf contemplating his next meal. Every time I looked at him, he had his eyes on me, and I bet everyone else, if they noticed him at all, had that same impression."

"He probably puts it on for effect," Joe said. "I think you're right that he's former military. Or maybe he's just interested in pretty women."

"He was there to observe. The only question is, observe what?"

"I wouldn't make too much of it," Joe said. "I bet he was invited for the same reason Ingoff was … to be part of the team. Maybe he was uncomfortable."

Weezy brightened. "Anyway, Martin Docherty is a sweetheart." Which brought back Ackerman's hand and his sense of entitlement. She looked at Joe for a long moment, unused to the kind of computation she felt forced into.

Joe looked puzzled. "What?"

"I'm thinking."

"I can see that."

"Joe, if someone you're close to gets insulted, but it's by another person you're close to …"

She restarted, "Um, say there was a situation in which a very uncomfortable …"

Joe nodded encouragement.

She stopped again, took a sip of coffee.

"C'mon Weezy," Joe said. "Spit it out. You don't do oblique. Just say it."

In a rush, "Ross Ackerman grabbed my ass last night. On purpose. I don't want you to do anything about it, and I wish I didn't have to be telling you." She took in the shock on Joe's face, exhaled and continued, "I don't want it to come between you and a person you have to work with. But it pissed me off. It was so arrogant. It was … he was almost daring me to be a little girly-girl and go crying to big strong Joe. I think he was hoping you'd make a fool of yourself."

Joe's jaw worked. His hands clinched, and Weezy saw raw fury in his eyes. Out of place on a bright morning in a Village coffee shop, but she felt a rush of pleasure anyway.

"Maybe I shouldn't have said anything. But I can't be pleasant to him again without having you know what went on."

"Where was I?"

"At first, I thought it was you doing it. But then I saw you were talking with Charlie Gray"

Joe exhaled sharply. "I'll talk to him about this."

"No, no. I'm sure it's exactly what he wants. The only reason I told you is so it won't get between us."

"It's totally unacceptable!"

Weezy smiled sweetly at Joe. "Please, don't do anything. It's enough for me to know you care. I'm a grown woman. And I can wreck that lizard's life if he really pisses me off. I mean there's a lot of stuff about him in the IAC, I'm sure, and it's all subject to… um …edit."

"You wouldn't."

"No, of course not, dumbass. But I can dream …"

They were silent for a moment. It hit Weezy how important it was that Joe cared so much.

"Anyway, Martin recovered nicely from those scotches and told me about the Skins. Pretty simple, actually. Neither he nor I can see how ZCG makes any real money on them, but we had a good talk."

"The example in class showed we are charging something like a half percent for the not-too-risky tranches," Joe said.

Weezy shook her head. "Gotta be more, Joe. ZCG is not assuming any real risk. You're putting fancy insurance in a pretty package, taking a reasonable fee from the people who are buying Skins mainly for the protection. Then you sell some of the pieces off to investors. Somewhere in there must be what, maybe a three hundred million net payoff to run an operation like ZCG's, wouldn't you say?" Weezy waited for Joe's accountant mind to tally the rent, salaries, lavish travel, and the artwork.

"Something like that," he said.

Weezy continued, "So you'd have to sell sixty billion-worth of Skins if you were charging half a percent. Forget about the fancy math. Do the arithmetic. Do you sell sixty billion-worth of Skins every year?"

Joe looked at her quizzically, no doubt re-running the numbers in his head.

Weezy gave him a hint of the dumbass look. "No, I didn't slip a decimal point."

***

Joe listened to Weezy work her way through the logic of skins. He heard her skepticism. Probably because of her job, plus that 160 IQ. If he tried to keep it humorous and tweaked her, she would tell him the unexamined life isn't worth living. Then she'd tell him it was Socrates who said it and repeat it in Greek.

But she didn't know Eric and Charlie and Felicity and the others the way he did. She couldn't see how exciting it was to get up in the morning, get on the subway, go to work. Yeah, the money was great, but the belonging, the being admired by admirable people, that was like nothing he had experienced in his work before.

Ever since Cynthia died, he'd been in limbo, holding on to beautiful memories, awash in pain. In the months after meeting Weezy and the MedRecords discovery, he'd lived in Panacea, surrounded by Cynthia's art and his memories. And feelings about Weezy—infatuation mixed with guilt. Now, finally, he was moving forward, not living in the past so much. He saw Cynthia in his mind's eye. She was smiling, encouraging him. Weezy was part of that past, and he realized how much he wanted her to be part of the future, too.

She was waiting for a response for the decimal point comment.

"Weezy, there's got to be something I'm missing. I think it's probably what someone called the 'lottery effect' the other day. People buy tickets with a virtually zero chance of making an enormous amount of money. Investors fall for that, too. I bet we sell those sell high-risk parts of the Skins to them at huge premiums."

"Could be," she said, not looking convinced.

"Well, now I'm doing real work, not just exercises. I'll find out soon enough."

He rearranged the sugar bowl and tiny vase with someone's idea of an artistic arrangement of fern shoots, feeling like a teenager asking for a date.

"How about next week? Bethesda?"

"Are you asking for a date, Mayfield?"

"I am."

"Next week might be tough, but how about Boston the weekend after?"

When they said goodbye at Penn Station, she gave him a long, soft kiss that was a perfect memory of their lovemaking.

Boston, he thought as the subway rocked and rolled him back to the village. She's asking me to meet her family.

# NINE

ROSS AND EMILY Ackerman sat at the cherry-wood breakfast table in the corner of their kitchen. Ross scanned the Wall Street Journal feed on his e-pad. Their maid Constanza was at the stove, humming as she prepared a soft-boiled egg. Ross raised his eyes from the pad to watch Constanza deliver the egg to Emily, stoop to pick up the napkin Emily had dropped, and deliver it with a radiant smile. The few thousand Emily talked Ross into throwing at the dump of a Harlem school Constanza's son went to really mattered to her. Maybe enough for … no, she had made it clear she was a righteous woman. Besides, good help was tough to find.

Emily buttered a piece of toast, scraping the surface and irritating Ross. Always so methodical, so focused on little things. He stared at the toast until Emily realized he was watching, waiting for her to finish. She gave a tiny shrug and moved on to spreading marmalade. Smucker's for chrissake. Bought her three or four fancy ones from Gristede's. But no, she had to use the ordinary crap from the dingy grocery store down the block.

A lot of things about Emily irritated Ross. So practical, so down-to-earth. Sex? Not inventive, not enthusiastic … it was a duty, not a craving. But she was pretty. Substantial in the right places, with a trace of wholesome farm girl. Now she was beginning to spread. A good hostess, though. And there was her family, of course.

After their wedding, Ross and Emily had made the obligatory trip back to Iowa to meet her extended family, the Scholzes. They were polite but most seemed uncomfortable. Ross assumed it must be his East Coast manners or the money.

One evening, after they escaped the stuffy parlor to the privacy of the guest room, Ross admitted he was afraid he might be intimidating her Uncle Silas.

Emily chuckled. "No, Ross. To him, you're odd. He's a practical man. Ask him about corn choppers, tractors, grain moisture loss and he sounds like a Ph.D. But you do something which, in his mind, doesn't produce anything. He can't figure out what you're good for, and he's too polite to say so."

At the time, Ross was offended. ZCG could buy fifty farms like Silas's. Now it was more like a hundred. He didn't care any more, because Emily's extended family was going to be an unwitting part of the mechanism of RedSock, LLC. Plenty of cousins, aunts, and uncles. A lot of them getting senile now. Uncle Silas wouldn't find out he had an account at RedSock, held in trust in Emily's name in the Netherlands Antilles.

Let them keep thinking he didn't produce anything.

Emily finished spreading marmalade to the absolute edge of the slice of the toast and, as usual, cut it into two triangles and took a bite out of the exact center of the first.

"Emily, I'm putting some more investments into the Scholze RedSock accounts."

"Oh?"

"I just thought you'd like to know. We're doing quite well for those folks."

"Why the secrecy? Why can't I tell them what you're doing?"

"Well, baby, the only instruments RedSock trades are high-risk. I don't want one of your aunts or uncles crapping out from a heart attack because they're watching the value of their account jump around."

She picked up a piece of toast as if to take a bite, stopped, and said, "You're worried that these farmers, who are more at home with real risk … hail, crop failure, drought, flood and freezing … these farmers will become faint of heart at the thought of a stock account going bad? Seriously?"

"Look, baby, I—"

"You know I don't like being called baby."

Their delicate marital balance wobbled. "Baby" was for those "clients" he entertained in clubs and upscale bistros. The ones who wore perfume that clung to his clothes along with their scent.

"Okay. Sweetheart, sorry. But, dammit, we're doing these people a favor, even if they don't know about it."

"All right, Ross. I understand the part you've explained to me, and I hope it works out well for all concerned."

"This should be a nice surprise for them when the time comes." Ross smiled and restarted the WSJ feed.

***

Emily took another bite of toast. The man across the table from her was still the handsome, urbane person she'd met nearly twenty years ago. Her prince charming, she had told her parents. Having graduated from the family farms in Iowa to the big city, Ross was their dream come true, too. He was charming, wealthy, and a Yale man. It fit their plan for her so comfortably.

Tears came upon her, surprised her, and she coughed.

"You all right?" Ross didn't look up.

"Just crumbs," she said, wiping her eyes.

Where did it all go? Ross had been so sweet, and she thought she could overcome his parents' never quite openly expressed opinion that Ross had married down. Babies would have helped, but after the shock of Ross's routine infidelity, Emily didn't let it happen and Ross didn't care. Their marriage had become one of convenience. The thought brought her near tears again. She suppressed them, as she did so many of her feelings.

The year before, Ross had come home late from one of his client meetings. He had undressed quietly, brushed his teeth and slipped into bed. Emily rolled over, groggy, as he put a hand on her hip.

"You're late."

"Yeah. Customers to entertain." The standard excuse. "You know. Tired, but …" he slipped his hand under her chemise to cradle her breast.

Emily rolled away from the invitation.

"I'm mostly asleep, Ross. I have to be at PS123 at nine."

A small, resigned silence. "Okay, but I have some papers I need you to sign before you go."

In the morning, Emily found a sheaf of documents on the breakfast table, trust agreements naming fifteen of her elderly relatives as beneficiaries. Emily was halfway through the Definitions section of the first document when Ross appeared in his pajamas, yawning and stretching.

She flipped pages, not looking up. "What are these?"

"I told you. Remember? The trusts for your family. We're doing some really creative financing, and I'd like to help them out a little."

"Why am I trustee?"

"You know they'll be much happier to be getting it from you than from me."

"Then why are you the secondary if anything happens to me? Why not my cousin William? He's younger and a lawyer in Cedar Rapids."

"I'd rather have this be a nice surprise if anything comes of it."

Emily went back to reading, registering Ross's supposition that her cousin William wouldn't maintain confidentiality. Ross shifted from foot to foot.

"You don't have to read it all. It's legal jargon. S'all in order."

Emily turned a page, flipped back to the front of the document to review a definition. Then to the body again, tapping her pen absently as she read.

Ross's irritation finally came to the surface. "Just sign the documents. These are complex financial transactions that may possibly benefit your family. That's all you or I really need to know."

Ross's irritation piqued Emily's curiosity because he usually liked to brag. Why was he doing this, anyway? Why not give her the respect of explaining why, all of a sudden, he wanted to help out her relatives. She pictured Uncle Silas saying, "I hear the BS-o-meter running."

Emily tilted her head, mouth set. "Ross, would you sign a legal document without reading it?" She answered her own question. "Of course you wouldn't. So at least grant me the respect of assuming I wouldn't either!"

"Goddam it, Emily! Of course I don't read that crap, but I hire lawyers who do. I'm sure those documents are all in order. Just sign them."

In the end, Emily signed each of the documents. Ross, satisfied, went off to shower. When he returned, Emily had dressed for her volunteer teaching in Harlem and was moving essentials from the hand-finished leather *sac à travailler* Ross gave her for a recent birthday to a simple canvas bag.

"Don't like my present?" Ross said.

"It's lovely, but too fancy for PS123," she said, sliding her e-pad in. On it was a copy of one of the trust documents she had scanned while Ross was showering.

***

Emily Ackerman was alone at the kitchen table with a fresh cup of coffee and her e-pad. Arty Pov said millions?

She had read the trust document carefully in the days after she copied it. On page fourteen, it mentioned financial reports would be sent to a RedSock electronic address. A couple of weeks later, she had asked Ross, off hand, to bring home the reports.

"Nothing to bring. They're electronic. Anyway, it's pro forma financials. You probably couldn't understand 'em."

Swallowing a tart remark, she had asked him to forward the reports.

A week later, she asked again.

"Oh crap. Yeah. I forgot."

Two days later, the reports appeared on her pad. Uncle Silas had a tidy sum, $43,000 and change. The other fourteen trusts were identical. About $650,000 total. A lot of money, but Arty said "millions" as if there were at least several of them.

There was probably a good reason. I'm missing something, she thought, but the thought didn't satisfy her. After all, Ross had no compunction about lying about other things.

Arty Pov's warmth, his willingness to talk about his work and the millions comment came to mind again.

"ZCG … Artyom Povreshenko," she said to her e-pad.

A pleasant automated voice asked, "Trading or personal?"

"Personal."

The voice asked her to leave a message.

"Arty, this is Emily Ackerman. I was intrigued by our conversation at the party, and I have a couple of questions. Uhh, confidential questions." And I'd like to talk to you more. "Please give me a call."

# TEN

WELL INTO JOE'S first week in the saddle, Eric O'Malley walked past his workstation. He turned as if struck by a thought and said, "We have a major prospect coming in, Morgan RioTinto. I make first contact, then assign a banker and an analyst. At the first meeting, it's usually just me, sometimes with Ackerman or John. This time, we're going to have you, Charlie, and Ida sit in to get the flavor of how we present Skins."

"Thank you. That will be exciting … uhh, interesting."

Eric glanced around the open area, then leaned closer.

"I'm going to send you the financials, and I want you to scrub 'em and let me know what you think. And … let's keep this between the two of us."

Joe attacked the project with gusto. It was home territory, given his accounting background. He used the standard analysis template Felicity gave him to spin the numbers, but also dug deep into the RioTinto's history and world metals mining background.

Finished, he started a quick review before he sent the package to Eric. As he flipped through the critical spreadsheets, he noticed a tab called Profitability that he had not needed for his work. Curious, he selected it. The original template had been set up for a client, apparently a big one, purchasing the Copper Skin. At the bottom of a column pricing the various risk levels, Joe noted that the profit should have been four percent. The actual profit was negative, a loss. He sent the work to Eric but kept a copy—he'd look at it again.

On the morning of the meeting, he got a note, "Meet in Conference 1 in Manhattan at 12:45. Meeting's at 1:00. Very impressive analysis, Joe."

When he walked by Felicity's office, she raised an eyebrow. "What are you so jaunty about, Mayfield? Love life improving?"

***

Joe entered the Manhattan conference room, the same one he'd been interviewed in.

Eric was at the center of the table, concentrating on his e-pad. Charlie and Ida sat in chairs at the end of the room. Eric's assistant Ghoshi was setting out papers, ZCG coffee mugs and water. Eric looked up, smiled briefly at Joe, nodded toward an empty seat next to Charlie and turned back to his e-pad.

Charlie gave a half wave and Ida smirked; Joe took the seat. Ghoshi turned a projector to standby and checked a connection. Must be a teleconference.

"The connection to Kalispell is set up. Mr. Petrescu has not yet joined," Ghoshi said. "Mr. Washburn is in the lobby."

As Ghoshi left, Eric turned to the three newbies.

"You are here to observe, not participate in—"

Ross Ackerman entered the room.

Red anger took Joe by surprise. He thought he'd buried the party and Ackerman's violation of Weezy. Charlie turned to him, eyebrow raised.

"You okay?"

Joe nodded, trying to push it down, push it down.

"Why are they here?" It seemed to Joe as if Ross was staring only at him.

"I want them to see a presentation," Eric said. "Washburn is fine with it." He turned to the three and said, "Try to disappear into the wall." But he smiled.

Ross frowned and plopped into a chair facing Eric.

"Over here, Ross." O'Malley indicated a seat next to him.

Ross's fair complexion showed his irritation. He got up with a scowl that reminded everyone how much bullshit he had to put up with and moved.

Fred Washburn arrived, an amiable banker in his pinstripe suit. Ghoshi came in and activated the connection with Montana. Don Petrescu appeared, sitting in front of a window with a view of mountains. A trout mounted on the wall behind him snapped at a fly.

Fred chuckled. "Don Petrescu, our Chief Operating Officer. Looks like a cowboy, but he's the best minerals guy in the U S of A, maybe the world."

Don was indeed the picture of a western rancher, face weathered by the sun, bushy white eyebrows, lanky as a longhorn bull. He shifted in his chair and looked a little embarrassed. "Fred can put a high shine on pretty much anything. That's why he's talking to the market makers and I'm keeping the home fires burning."

Joe saw genuine friendship between the two men, unusual in his experience with large public companies.

Eric introduced Ross, then turned to Charlie, Ida and Joe, introducing them as new additions to the ZCG team.

Eric started his presentation, "You have no doubt read about the recent crisis in Zambia."

Both men nodded.

He spun out the story of the copper crisis, the cost to the companies in the Copper Belt shut off from the outside world and the financial lifeline the Copper Skin gave those who had purchased it. Eric made the presentation a conversation rather than a pitch. The hundred or so hours of research behind the numbers he wove through the story were never obvious. He finished and introduced Ross to talk about the new Chromium Skin.

Ross gave an up-tempo description of the trading process studded with terminology, referring several times to ZCG's proprietary algorithms and implying the protection the Skin provided could not be achieved by ordinary folks.

Fred Washburn watched Ross reel off his speech, his look polite but guarded.

Ross concluded, "You need to protect at least three hundred million of current revenues. We have capacity available in the Chromium Skin, at least for the next few days."

Joe knew the capacity was almost infinitely adjustable.

"Can I ask a question?" Don peered out of the monitor.

Ross turned away from Fred and nodded.

"What's the present value of the revenue stream you assumed when you estimated the coverage we need?"

Ross hesitated. He should be able to reel the answer off from the summary sheet Eric gave all of them, which included Joe's answer to that question.

Eric turned to Joe. "Mayfield?"

Joe answered, "Our analysis suggested five hundred million." Fred Washburn shifted in his chair to look at him.

"We could do this ourselves couldn't we? I mean, it's puts and calls, right?"

Everyone turned toward Joe.

Joe took a moment to gather his thoughts, knowing he was moving into dangerous territory.

"Yes, you could."

The intake of breath almost created a vacuum, or at least it seemed so to Joe. Ross didn't mask his fury. Eric raised an eyebrow.

"But it doesn't make sense for you to do it."

Washburn's look hardened. "Why not? Your one percent fee is five million dollars. I bet we could get the job done pretty well for that kind of money."

"Sure," Joe said, "But ZCG has spent far more than you will pay to put together the models we use. Best spend your five million on what you do better than anyone else."

Washburn dipped his head.

Joe caught a small 'well done' nod from Eric, and Ross's color was changing back to normal.

The focus moved to Morgan RioTinto's operations in South Africa and its expansion plans. Ross excused himself halfway through, using the market's-open-twenty-four-seven excuse.

By the end of the meeting, Fred Washburn had asked Eric to come to Montana to see the Morgan RioTinto operation and meet Don Petrescu in person. They filed out of the conference room, Joe peeling off to the elevator with the other newbies while Eric and Fred headed toward Eric's office. The elevator door opened. As Joe turned to face the front, he saw Fred put a hand on Eric's shoulder, look back toward the elevator, and say something. Eric inclined his head toward Joe and smiled.

***

Joe rode from the Manhattan office over to Jersey in high spirits, but with the issue of Skins profitability picking at him. It didn't make sense that ZCG would plan to lose money on a Skin. Maybe there was something obvious, or maybe the Morgan RioTinto spreadsheet was wrong.

*Felicity. I bet she can clear this up.* He hesitated—she was becoming relaxed and a bit too intimate with Joe. But he needed an answer.

She was, as usual, focused on one of her monitors, graying hair falling over one side of her face. Stacks of journals, notebooks and file folders weighed down her desk. She had said defensively the first time he went into her office, "I know where everything is."

"Felicity, I have a question on the template."

"Pretty busy, Joe."

"Okay. I'll come back."

"What's your question?"

Joe handed over his e-pad with the copy of the RioTinto analysis open to the profitability page.

Felicity scanned it, then exhaled.

"What the hell were you doing on that page? I told you to stay the hell away from pricing. That's the senior banker's job."

"I was reviewing the analysis before I sent it off, and this page looked odd."

Felicity stood. "Walk with me."

When they were out of earshot of the others in the analyst area, Felicity said, "First thing you do is wipe that sheet off your e-pad. Carrying a copy like that is a violation of company policy."

"Uhh, okay. Is it really that big a deal?"

"Yes, it is. I got curious a year ago, started digging and found that we should have gone out of business about four years ago. Next morning, I got a visit from Nick Braithwaite."

"The security guy?"

"That's the man. Now how, you ask, would he have known I was checking profitability? I hadn't sent anything out. Nobody should have seen it but me."

She tapped her temple with her forefinger.

"Because, I answer, he's monitoring the work we do in the system."

She started to turn back toward her office, and stopped.

"So be careful, Joe. And, no, I don't know how we make money."

***

Joe went back to his desk, his thoughts in turmoil. But his monitor had a message from Fred Washburn himself asking a couple of questions, a signal honor for an analyst. Right up his alley. He pushed the question of profitability to the back of his mind and ran numbers for Washburn, imagining his presentation and finding ways to make it tighter and more impressive.

A ping announced an incoming message. My office. Ackerman. appeared on his monitor. Not a call. No video. Not "can you meet?"

Joe climbed two flights of stairs, emerging at the glassed-in trading floor—forty monitors arrayed around the five traders. Ackerman's office was a raised area between the trading floor and the ceiling-to-floor windows overlooking the Hudson River and lower Manhattan. The man himself was lounging, feet on an open desk drawer. He stayed in the relaxed position as Joe entered, a tight, almost challenging, expression on his face. "So who's this, uh, pelvic affiliate of yours? Louise, wasn't it? Almost made Ingoff have a stroke, and Docherty must have had to go home and jerk off after the exciting conversation about whatever the hell they were talking about."

Joe retreated behind a wry smile. "Louise doesn't hide her light under a basket."

"She's some sort of math whiz, right? Where'd you meet her?"

There was something behind Ackerman's offhand manner.

"She caught me hacking into the IAC. She works for them, and I was trying to find information on my wife's—"

"You mean the whole Phoenix thing with the medical records scam, right?"

"Yes. I stumbled on the problem. She caught me and figured out what really was going on."

Ackerman nodded, broke eye contact, and gazed out over the Manhattan skyline.

"You know, this Skins product is very lucrative." He turned back to Joe. "I'm sure a math whiz could figure out how lucrative pretty quickly with your help."

Ackerman kicked the drawer closed, sat up and picked up a folder on his desk. He paused, sizing Joe up.

"O'Malley and the bankers you support sell the legs that the Skins stool rests on. We need those big companies that buy the low-risk stuff. The high-risk tranches go to retail brokers and hedge funds. That's where the profits are, and that's my part of the business."

Ackerman fished a document out of the folder and slid it across to Joe.

"We put fifteen basis points from trading into a bonus pool. Usually only bankers get included, but you did a good job in the meeting with Washburn. If you and O'Malley sell the chromium Skin to Morgan RioTinto, you stand to make half a million at the end of the year."

The compliment took Joe by surprise. It took a moment for the amount to hit. Six years of salary at his old accounting job.

*Is he buying me off?*

Joe stammered, "Th-thank you."

Ackerman's hard look returned. "You're part of the team now. I expect loyalty. The people I sell to aren't your squeaky clean, always above-board Morgan RioTinto types. Any one of them would pay a lot to find out what my pricing strategy is."

*He knows I've asked questions about pricing?*

"No discussion with the pelvic affiliate. Understand?"

"Yes. Of course."

How am I going to explain this to her?

Ackerman pushed a pen across the desk.

Joe scanned the first page and turned to the second.

"It'll be in your personal file. You can read it later. Just sign it." He cracked a sardonic grin. "Or the gift horse might trot his ass out of here."

Warnings blared at Joe, but he took the pen and signed the last page.

***

Ida Sengupta was concluding a carefully thought-out but dry presentation in the Friday status meeting when Ross Ackerman slipped into the back of the room. He was in the middle of a phone conversation, which he continued without lowering his voice. With him was a dark-haired, professionally dressed woman carrying an armful of folders. Joe's attention shifted from Ida to Ross, who signed off, oblivious to the interruption.

"How many of you are implanted?"

About half the class raised hands.

"Transit specs?"

Several hands went up.

"Okay. Here's the deal: The specs need to be off. You don't really need to be streaming every goddam moment of your day, exciting as it may be to you. Video recording violates every confidentiality agreement we have with clients, so turn 'em off and take 'em off." He looked around the room. "Now." Ida looked pained and said, "I need to have glasses to—"

Ross sighed. "Fine, but get some regular glasses. Second point: Everyone needs to have an implant, at least G-two level. I don't want to be sending smoke signals if I need to get in touch. See Kirsten to get it done." He nodded toward the woman with the brochures.

Joe exchanged a glance with Charlie, who gave him a no-big-deal shrug and tapped his ear. Implanted already, apparently.

Why did they need to have constant communication with him? And why was the head of trading demanding it? Why not Eric?

Ross finished giving instructions and left. Ida restarted her presentation.

Maybe he was too used to staying off the grid.

At the break, Joe joined several classmates clustered around Kirsten.

She showed the group her own implant, which had received fourteen taps in the last couple of hours. It was on Silent/Private for the meeting, and the fourteen messages were filed on her e-pad. Her e-pad had Personal Recognition, so the messages disappeared from the display when she walked a few feet away from it. "See?" she said. "Completely private."

Kirsten held up a tiny device. "This small Bluetooth transponder goes just under the skin behind the ear. The procedure to implant is minor. We do it in our office with a local anesthetic. It goes into your mastoid bone, right behind your ear and is totally invisible." She pulled her hair aside to expose the area behind her ear, a surprisingly intimate gesture. The tiny lump was not totally invisible, but close.

Joe willed the warning bells in his head to stop. Ross gave everyone in the room a direct order, but Eric was his boss. Probably no big deal. The implant was not much more than an extension of an e-pad. Why was he so goddam touchy about this?

The answer tapped him like the implant would do: Once they're in your head, what can't they do?

***

"Got a minute?"

Eric looked up from his screen. "Sure, Joe. In fact, I wanted to talk with you. Sit."

Joe took the chair in front of Eric's desk.

"Joe, you'll come along with us on the western trip. Fred Washburn wants you to see the Montana operation and have you meet Don." He cleared his throat. "I probably don't have to tell you we usually don't take first-year analysts on a trip like this."

"It's a … great … uhh, thank you for the opportunity."

Eric smiled through Joe's clumsy response and said, "The clients we're going to see, they're salt-of-the-earth people. You're one of those people, too. Fred and Don will be a hell of a lot more comfortable with you than with a squeaky-clean Ivy League graduate they can't relate to. So, don't retreat into that self-effacing thing you do. Speak up."

"I … I'll do my best."

"And nice job in the meeting the other day," Eric said, and turned back to the document he had been working on, then, "Oh, you wanted to talk, right?"

"I did." Joe hesitated. "Eric, is it necessary for me to be implanted?"

Eric raised his eyebrows, as if this particular question had never occurred to him.

"Well, Joe, pretty much everyone in our business is these days."

"Analysts, too?"

"I think so." Eric said. "But ask Felicity. She'd know."

Apparently, nobody else thought an implant was unreasonable. Joe had a momentary vision of trying to explain the rationale for having one to Weezy, but she would probably think it was just another piece of technology and shrug.

Eric went back to his document a second time. His body language said the meeting was over.

Joe stood, deciding whether to ask the more serious question.

Eric looked up from his work.

"Anything else, Joe?"

"Eric, the standard template I used for the Morgan Rio Tinto analysis seems to be saying ZCG is losing money. I'm afraid I'm missing something."

Eric closed the document he was working on and leaned forward.

"We should be," he said. Then, with a sigh, "I'll tell you what I know, because a smart guy like you is going to figure it out over time anyway."

He gazed out the window, then turned back to Joe.

"A couple of years ago, our whole business was creating custom-designed Skins for big companies trying to protect their operations in risky parts of the world. Then there was a revolution in Mali. We had a Skin that covered that part of the world." Eric paused. Picking words carefully, he continued. "The high-risk tranches, the ones we'd sold off to brokers because no sensible investor'd touch 'em, paid off big time. A couple of small investors ... day traders, really ... made millions. The *Journal* ran an article and interviewed Ross." He smiled. "Ross was the picture of a rapacious Wall Street shark, which made those high-risk tranches suddenly sexy. Hedge funds got interested. We can sell the high-risk stuff at huge margins, and those margins have been driving our profitability."

Eric shifted in his seat.

"Keep this conversation to yourself. There's nothing wrong with selling to people who are essentially gambling, but I can sense you're uncomfortable with it. I am, too. People buy and sell futures all the time, though. Some, particularly the little guys romanced by fly-by-night hucksters, are making horrible decisions. But it is, like it or not, part of what we do." He finished with a shrug.

"Thank you for the explanation. It helps me understand the business. And I'll do my best to justify your confidence in me."

Joe returned to his cubicle, dazed and elated over being included in the trip west. At the same time, Eric's explanation of profitability disturbed him. He hadn't signed up to provide the raw material for unscrupulous securities dealers to fleece widows and orphans. He tried to put his reservations to rest but kept seeing Weezy's skeptical look.

How do I justify this to her? To myself?

Later, he made an appointment to get the implant done. After all, no harm being connected to the grid, as long as you could control it.

***

Business Communication Technologies had a small office in the Exchange Place complex. Joe emerged, newly implanted, a sore spot behind his right ear. Kirsten explained how incoming messages are "taps," and ZCG expected Joe to set its Main Office, Ackerman, Zhou and O'Malley, as "privileged," meaning they could send a "hard tap" that would appear as a message marked Urgent on his e-pad.

"Can they monitor me?" Joe asked.

Kirsten's smile let Joe know she's been asked the question many times. "No. It just means they can high-priority tap you whenever they want, but they can't force you to answer."

"I mean—I mean, there are times when a tap would be… intrusive."

Kirsten pursed her lips. Her friendly demeanor cooled.

"I mean, you know, personal," he said, embarrassed. How many guys had used the question to segue into an intrusion of their own?

"Yes, I understand." She drew back and continued, "The Do Not Contact option in Settings won't prevent a tap from your high priority contacts, but it will show them a warning before they tap you. Most people understand and leave you a tap that pops up when the DNC goes off. And here..." She pointed at the screen. "You can set it to turn on DNC when you're sleeping. The device monitors your movement, heart rate and respiration. It figures you out after a few days."

After Kirsten's introduction, Joe sat on a park bench across the tramway from the storefront, reading the instruction manual on his pad and trying the controls. He added Weezy's private and IAC contact information to the privileged list and shook his head a few times to verify the device was getting the tiny charge it needed from his motion. Finally, he set the default to Complete Privacy. No outgoing broadcast without him making a call, no position monitoring, no helpful advertisements. Only calls he controlled and taps from his privileged contacts when not on DNC. He still felt uncomfortable, but he told himself having the implant was no different than any other communication device.

A flicker on Joe's display made him wonder if he had mistakenly changed something. He checked Personal Settings again. It still said Complete Privacy.

# ELEVEN

Ross Ackerman, Rolf Ingoff, John Zhou Min, and Eric O'Malley were arrayed around the burnished aluminum-and-burl-wood table in the Main office. Ackerman was bored, and the room was stuffy. Ghoshi, Eric's assistant, had cleared the remnants of lunch and was opening the door to push the cart out. Nick Braithwaite appeared, his size and purposefulness intimidating the young man to pull the cart back and stand aside.

"What?" Ross said.

Nick leaned down and whispered, "Mayfield's woman may be a problem."

"Okay. Later." Then louder, so the group heard, "Why don't you sit with us? Maybe you can bring some real-world experience to this rarefied atmosphere."

"What's the subject?" Nick took a chair along the wall.

Ross put on a bland look. "We're planning where to target the next Skin." Only Braithwaite understood the little twitch of Ross's smile at the word "target."

Ingoff cleared his throat and began. "I am sending my white paper on minerals to each of you, encoded through the ZCG system." He waited a minute for the file to appear on each person's e-pad.

"Although the technical detail may be daunting, the conclusions are straightforward. I'm suggesting—"

"I don't have the paper," Nick said.

Ingoff looked to John Zhou Min, then Ross. "I sent it only to the planning committee. Should I—"

"Forward it to Nick," Ross said.

Ingoff tapped his e-pad. "Done." Then, as if suddenly realizing, "Of course, it's encoded. Unfortunately, you won't be able to read it. Ross or John will need to give me permission to decode it, which may take some time." Watching Ingoff's face, Ross imagined he was fantasizing about ways to restrain and torture the big South African.

Nick leveled a look bordering on disgust at Ingoff. "I have the paper."

"I'll be sure to decode it for you when I have clearance—"

"I have the paper, and I can read it."

"It's encoded. I doubt—"

"I wrote the code." The implied "you idiot" hung in the air.

Ingoff ducked and fumbled his e-pad, tapping on it harder than necessary, his lips pressed tight. A map of Sweden emerged from the holo projector.

"Up until the late twentieth century, we were discovering new sources of minerals on a regular basis. We were breaking rocks and extracting in increasingly remote places, but there was plenty of opportunity. In the last forty years, new discoveries have fallen off. Today, we are bumping up against serious constraints. Particularly in indium, gallium, tungsten and the rare earth minerals. They exist everywhere, but in small quantities." Ingoff tapped his e-pad again, and a red highlight appeared on an island northeast of Stockholm.

"Ytterby, Sweden is currently the only commercial source of Gadolinite, which yields four of the rare earth metals, Ytterbium, Yttrium, Terbium and Erbium. Gadolinite is also present in Central Africa and the Russian Commonwealth, particularly the -stan countries, but unexploited. I believe there is opportunity to—"

"Kazakhstan."

Ingoff tensed, angry at the interruption and not hiding it well.

Nick stared him down and continued, "Sweden's stable, with a strong democratic government controlling the Ytterby mine. No big risk, so no big reward for putting together a Skin."

"A good point, but, as I was saying—"

"There's a lot of rare earth in the CIS countries," Nick said. "Could be some Gadolinite. But Uzbekistan and Afghanistan are political nightmares, hopeless for foreign investment. Kazakhstan is a better target. Got its own currency. Pretty unstable. Here …" He tapped his e-pad. Ingoff's map of Sweden blinked out, replaced by a chart, *Теңге/USD*, showing wide fluctuations in the Kazakh currency. "And …" Nick tapped again. A pie chart appeared, showing Kazakh total output by type. "Something like sixty percent of its GDP comes from extractive industries. Got a lot of oil, but oil demand is way down, so the government is desperate for foreign investment in the mining sector."

"And, as I was saying …" Ingoff fought to wrest control of the room's attention from Braithwaite.

Nick rolled over him again, "Big mining companies are probably tempted by Kazakhstan, but nervous of the politics … They have one of those 'president for life' systems going with the granddaughter of the original strong man—"

"Dinara Nazarbayeva, named for her mother." Ingoff was determined to stay in the conversation. Ross chuckled as Nick continued.

"—and it's not going so good for her. Lots of charisma, but she doesn't like to do the nasties her granddaddy did to keep a lid on the country."

By the end of the meeting, a plan for the next Skin covering the broad spectrum of minerals in Kazakhstan had been sketched out.

As they rose to go, Ross gave Nick an almost imperceptible nod.

# TWELVE

JOE PACKED HIS newly-purchased Mobibag, concentrating on doing it efficiently. The packing was orderly; his mind was not. The conversation with Weezy about Skins, Felicity's suspicions about being monitored, and Eric's explanation of profits kept repeating on him like the Italian sausage he'd had for lunch.

His group would be on the road for two weeks. He had asked for a few days off after the trip, days he hoped to spend in Panacea with Weezy. The day after Ackerman's party, when they had gone to Penn Station for Weezy to get the train back to Bethesda, she had been cool, kissed him on the cheek, not the mouth. No hint of wanting him to come down to Bethesda or a repeat of the almost-invitation to Boston. Maybe more upset about Ackerman than she let on.

He had called her yesterday night. She seemed a bit distant, answering questions, but not asking. Sticking to describing daily activities and forcing out humor in what seemed like an attempt to steer around anything personal. After a few too-long silences, he said, "I've been looking at ZCG profitability to the extent I can, and I thin k you're right."

"Yeah?"

"I don't have a complete picture, but—short story—the high-risk tranches got sexy a couple of years ago, and they're very profitable. Otherwise, everyone's close-mouthed around the junior staff."

He got a genuine smile. "You knew you didn't sell sixty billion of Skins."

Finally, the real Weezy.

"Will you take a couple of days—maybe a long weekend—with me in Panacea when my trip is finished?"

Hesitation ... hoping ... "Sure."

Joe was so relieved he almost told her about the implant, but decided it was not the right time.

***

The ZCG group was due to depart from Grand Central on the new Acela, increasingly popular for high-end business travel since air travel had moved from exciting to banal to disgusting. Joe walked across Washington Square toward the Astor Place Green Line, carrying his e-pad and letting his Mobibag roll along on its electronic tether a couple of feet behind him. It was mid-morning, and the subway was not crowded. A few people checked out his formal clothes and probably speculated about the likely contents of his bag, contemplating grab and run. But nobody made the move, even though the transit cop at Grand Central looked like he could make a fast waddle at best.

A heavy glass door off the dingy corridor leading from the Green Line was marked "Acela." As Joe approached, the door sensed his ticket and opened.

The group of bankers was assembling. The ZCG cars included one compartment car with compact living quarters for each person and one car fitted out with a large meeting room and dining area. O'Malley shooed them into the meeting room car, where an Acela greeter assigned compartments and explained the wonders of the communication systems, the latest model personal Holographis machines, and the amenities in the shared bathrooms.

As Acela accelerated out of Grand Central, Joe unpacked his shaving kit and a couple of shirts. Finished, he sent a message to Weezy: On the train. Fancy, but a nice way to travel. Chicago later today, a day in meetings there, then off to the West. Give me a call when you get a minute.

He checked his e-pad to be sure his implant had gone live as scheduled. He'd almost forgotten it was there. As if to verify its activity, a pip followed by O'Malley's voice, "Meet in conference car, ten minutes. Let's cover assignments and agendas."

Joe was reviewing company backgrounders when a tap announced an incoming call from Weezy. He opened video on his e-pad. Weezy was at her N-Ops console. "Well, well. Looks like you're on the road. Is the Lizard with you?"

"You mean Ackerman?"

Weezy gave a tight smile. Joe chuckled.

"No. We're with O'Malley. Eleven of us are on a separate Acela car. Much nicer than a plane and almost as fast. We'll get to Chicago in four hours. Just thought I'd call … I miss you."

The 'I miss you' slipped out, unintended but true.

Weezy's look softened, but she said, "Now, don't get sappy."

She paused, looked away to someone asking a question, then turned back to Joe. "Gotta go." A little smile. "I miss you, too."

***

Weezy was happy Joe missed her. She expected to end the call on a sassy note but what came out was, "I miss you, too."

Maddie nodded approval as she passed Weezy's station. "Joe?"

"Yup. He's off on the Acela to Chicago and points west."

Weezy dove back into her work, but on another level she was thinking about Joe, Skins and ZCG. What the hell were they doing? All this hand waving about complex risk, higher-level analysis. Like a magician using misdirection to pull a coin from behind your ear. Smoke and mirrors.

On the other hand, Joe loved the job. He was getting recognition he deserved. ZCG made a lot of money doing something that didn't make sense. So what? Haute couture didn't make sense, either. Even so, the designers made a lot of money. So, what was the problem? Enjoy the relationship, don't ask too many questions. Chalk up Ackerman's party behavior to bad manners. Option One: stifle the thought there's something askew in the logic of Skins. *Caveat emptor*, right?

Really, she told herself, that was the only sensible approach. But the questions kept coming back, and Weezy kept landing back on Go.

Finally, she reminded herself unlawful manipulation of IAC data, which included all financial transactions, was a trackable condition. Slim pretext for Option Two, but enough.

***

Weezy's weekly review was usually brief. Keith Sanders liked the appearance of control it gave him. Weezy had made it clear that the window for conversation was open for about ten minutes. At eighteen minutes, clouds of Dumbass began to form, and the review could take a bad turn.

Keith ticked off the project names as he read them. "Hmmm. Cal Occult still productive." Weezy nodded. "Rumania bad guys on hold. OddBalls have them under control." And so on, through a dozen more. "Zhou, Cadwallon Gordon. New entry. This didn't come through me. What's it about?"

"A suspicion, more than anything else. They may be misusing IAC data to sell their products called Skins."

"Why open a case on it?" Keith asked. "Why not query the Securities Exchange Commission?"

"It might be data manipulation, not a financial trading issue," she said.

"I know it's a bad idea to ignore your intuition, but this one does seem to be a stretch," he said. "Let's put it on hold."

Clouds began to form.

"Not really within our charter, is it?"

Weezy's mouth set. "Our charter is to protect the database, right?"

"Well yes," he said.

"And the database includes all financial transactions, right?"

Keith nodded.

"And how much damage can manipulating markets through apparently normal channels do?"

"Probably a lot," he said. "That's what the Securities Exchange Commission is for."

"And they do *such* a good job …"

"Well, they're understaffed, but the fact remains …" Keith brightened. "I know one of their investigators. Let me run this by her."

Weezy saw she had lost the battle for Option Two and said, "Sure." Time for Option Three.

***

Energized by the bike ride home from work, Weezy opened a can of Feline Treat for Sappho and made a quick dinner for herself.

While she ate, she said to her e-pad, "Open Net, Olegarten Fabricating." The screen came to life, showing a flat 2D business website with not much animation. One of those millions of superannuated sites ignored by its creators. In keeping with Olegarten's apparent Norwegian heritage, there was a small white, spiky flower called a Bakkekløver in the lower corner. Weezy tapped the flower, and a long string of HTML code appeared, concealing the entrance to a chat room. She signed in as Hotcakes.

`HoHum, you out there?`

HoHum was one of twenty or so cream-of-the-crop hackers and computer visionaries Weezy stayed in touch with through Olegarten. They were like-minded people … friends … but also potential sources of scuttlebutt for her day job. Getting no response, she left a ping for him to call.

She put on some classic jazz and was about to settle down with a book Maddie had read and loved when Joe called.

"How are you?" He sounded loose, as if he'd had a couple of drinks.

"I'm good. How's the trip? Where are you?"

"We're rolling out of Chicago."

They chatted, he seeming tentative. She was a little closed, wondering if there had been a turn in the relationship.

After a few minutes, they said a pleasant, impersonal good-bye.

An hour later, Weezy's computer chimed.

`'Zup, Hotcakes? Wanna boogie lo and slo?`

HoHum's normal greeting for Weezy, reminding her of his infatuation.

Weezy said, "Video."

HoHum was in the basement Weezy had seen before, surrounded by electronic gear, wearing a threadbare 'Telluride Blues and Brews' T-shirt and his usual Einsteinian tangle of hair.

"Nihow. How's it going?"

"Nihow. I need advice."

"For you, always."

"I'm curious about some financial transactions."

"Part of your hacker-bashing job?" HoHum and Weezy went way back. On the other hand, she was, in some sense, the enemy.

"Yes and no. Not part of playing straight defense, like I usually do."

Weezy explained Skins and her concerns. HoHum listened and finally said, "So who's dumb enough to buy these Skins?"

"Dumb enough?"

"Hell, anyone can buy and sell futures. How do you think American agriculture survives? My dad ran an elevator for years. Used to call it 'a large concrete structure full of puts and calls.' If you're a business going into a foreign country, you'd better by God understand the risks involved. If you understand the risks, you buy your own damn derivatives."

"Not everyone is as clever as you, HoHum."

"Then they shouldn't be risking other people's money, should they?"

"No, of course not, but the picture ZCG creates of its so-called 'comprehensive knowledge of risk' is pretty impressive. Something doesn't smell right, though. The big companies buying Skins for risk protection probably pay rational fees. Maybe, like you said, they're overpaying a fraction of a percent for something they could do themselves. The way ZCG makes a lot of money is by slicing and dicing the riskier parts of the Skins and selling them as investments. Can you see who is buying?"

HoHum thought for a moment. "Those transactions all go through the Securities Exchange Commission system, which is buried behind the IAC firewall since CyberWar I. I can't get into the IAC. That'd get you on my case, which I wouldn't mind, but maybe some federales, which I definitely would mind. Can you get me a list of ZCG's clients?"

"I think so," Weezy said.

"Good. Maybe I can learn something from them."

They signed off, HoHum with his signature "boogie lo & slo."

Weezy stroked Sappho, who had taken up residence on her lap. She let her plan percolate, trying to ignore potential penalties associated with the flatly illegal parts.

***

"Structurepuppy." It was evening the next day, and Weezy was at her console at N-Ops, calling on the reference work for IAC systems and files.

Keith wouldn't open a project on ZCG, but it should be easy to identify who ZCG's trading with.

A color-coded tree appeared, and a sad-looking Bassett hound cartoon asked, *Where to?*

"Financial transactions," Weezy said.

A new map came up.

"Damn."

The system fed all hits back to an algorithm that would identify Weezy if she went in and searched the transaction files. Two hours later, several levels deeper in Structurepuppy, she discovered daily transactions washing back against history after market close to determine whether they were long or short term. She hung a trace on the backwash but realized it would take a week or more to get a good sample.

At home, she texted HoHum:

`Will get you data in 7-10 days.`

# THIRTEEN

WEEZY STEPPED ONTO the platform in Tallahassee. Humidity wrapped itself around her and the sweet smell of flowers with a hint of rot intruded on the metallic scent of the train. Joe was at the end of the platform but hadn't seen her yet. Same sharp features, good-looking but not quite handsome. Try as she might, she couldn't keep her breathing from quickening.

He saw her, waved and jogged down the platform, a smile tentative. A quick kiss. Weezy felt his desire to make it last longer. "Good to see you," he said.

"You, too," she said.

They walked back to the Element. Weezy carried a small backpack and a shoulder bag, no suitcase. One advantage of not being fashion-conscious.

"How's the old gal doing?" Weezy said as she stowed her pack.

"Still holding up." Joe chuckled. "Everything seems to work."

Joe bought the Honda Element in New Orleans at the beginning of his off-the-grid meander a little over a year ago. It was old and quirky, but both Joe and Weezy were fond of it. Joe engaged the autopilot and the Cajun voice of its prior owner, BeeBee, said "Where to?"

"Home. Autodrive," Joe said.

"Awright. You got it. Home. Auto."

The Element backed out of the slant space in front of the station on its own, jerking to a stop to allow a bicycle to pass. Then they were on their way.

"What have you been up to?" Joe said.

Weezy realized she was uncomfortable. They had talked a few times while Joe was on his western trip, but she hadn't let him get under her funny, sassy shell. She told a funny story about Sappho the cat, but realized Joe was anxious to talk.

Joe told a story, laughing at the memory, about Charlie Gray's slow-motion slide off the path around Anaconda's open pit copper mine "going' Eeep, Eeep' kind of like one of those back-up warning signals."

Then there was Don Petrescu, Chief Operating Officer of the world's second largest minerals conglomerate, excited as a twelve-year-old boy when Joe showed him a map of the fishing holes on the Ochlockonee. "Can you believe it," Joe said. "Only problem he's going to have is figuring out where to land the corporate jet when he comes down to camp out in the trailer."

Weezy stared out the window, as much to shield her face as take in the scenery.

These people were his friends now. How would she keep her opinions to herself for the whole weekend?

As if prompted by Weezy's thought, Joe said, "When I started out in the training program, I was just odd. The black stone in jar of white ones. I didn't come from a fine family, and I didn't have an Ivy League education. My home address was Panacea, Florida. The notoriety I got—we got—from the Phoenix project made people assume I was hired because of that, and they didn't expect much of me. I heard 'country bumpkin' more than once."

He turned to Weezy. "Now, Panacea has graduated from odd to very cool. I did well in training, thanks to you. All of a sudden, my differences are being celebrated rather than mocked. These are good people, smart people, and I'm lucky to be where I am."

"That's great for you, Joe." Weezy realized she sounded polite, a little formal, maybe a little nervous.

***

They finished dinner at Pelican's Roost and sat on the edge of a dock in the park down a side street from the restaurant. They had exhausted the safe conversational territory of work and shared experience and sat quietly for a time.

"What's wrong, Weezy?"

"Nothing."

"We're distant from each other. I can't figure it out."

"Takes two to be distant," she said, picking apart a piece of dry seaweed.

"I don't like it," Joe said.

Weezy tossed the seaweed in the water, brushed off her shorts. "It's no big deal, Joe. But we don't see each other too often, and you're different each time I see you. It takes me a while to adjust."

"Adjust?"

"Yeah, adjust. I mean, when I first met you, you were angry and scared and on the run. You were turning yourself inside out trying to be a regular guy. Willing to risk your life for a bunch of people you didn't know. After Phoenix, you were hoping to get a plain-vanilla accounting job somewhere in Central Florida and go back to your former life. You were such a nice home boy it was almost painful. But underneath it all, your moral compass never wavered."

She snapped her fingers. "Now you're living in New York City, realizing you're a really smart guy, flying with the finance eagles. Except nobody seems anxious to explain your main product in simple words. That's dangerous, Joe."

She looked out over the Gulf, then said almost to herself, "I can't always tell where your compass is pointing. Nothing's wrong with me, Joe, except I get whiplash every time I see you."

Joe stared into the water, jaw muscles working.

Why was she being so goddamn picky about ZCG?

"So, you're worried about my moral compass all of a sudden."

"Yours and mine both. Always."

"It hasn't changed."

"Good."

They were silent for a while, back at square one.

As they walked away from the dock, Joe reached for Weezy's hand. She gave it, tentative.

At the trailer steps, Weezy stopped and turned toward Joe. She put her hands on his chest, holding him at arm's length and searched his eyes for a long moment. Then she leaned forward and gave him a light kiss.

Sometime in the dark of the early morning hours, Joe woke. Weezy had slipped into his bed. Outside, an owl asked "who?" and a fox barked. Joe turned to Weezy and started to say something. She put a finger to his lips. The other hand stroked his belly and he thought he saw a smile. She straddled him, and their cries blended with the night sounds.

An algorithm sorting through the feed from his implant did not pass judgment, noting simply 'exercise component' then 'sleep.'

***

Weezy woke to light shafting through the window and the smell of coffee and bacon. Slipping out of bed, she stretched, yawned and picked up the shirt she had dropped on the floor last night.

Joe was in the kitchen, humming and cooking bacon in a square pan, strips aligned like soldiers at review.

"Coffee?" he asked.

"Sure. Mmmm. Smells good."

Joe concentrated on flipping bacon.

She leaned to give him a sisterly kiss on the cheek. Then another, this time less casual.

Joe turned.

Weezy ran a finger down the front of his shirt, then came into his arms.

"The bacon..." Joe said.

"I like it crisp."

A long kiss.

"Hmmm. Well, now I know where your compass is pointing."

Another kiss.

She pulled at his shirt, and he pushed hers up, caressing her breasts.

She kissed along the line of his jaw, then his ear.

"Joe?"

"Umm."

"You ... have ... an implant?"

"Z'off."

Weezy pushed him away. "When were you going to tell me?"

"What?"

"You got an implant."

"It's on 'private' for the weekend. We all have to have them. It's a tool. Like a new e-pad or something."

Weezy jerked down her shirt, stomped down the hall into her room.

"Weezy, it's no big deal, really."

No big deal. Right. Ackerman grabbing her ass was no big deal, maybe. But this? Why hadn't he told her? She realized she was near tears. She looked around the bedroom, found a scrap of paper, scrawled out a message and stormed back out. Joe stood in the kitchen, mouth open, between astonished and angry. The bacon, forgotten, had begun to burn.

Weezy shoved the note at Joe: *Follow my lead. Point to your e-pad.*

Joe seemed to wake up, sniffed the bacon, reached to turn the burner off. He pointed with his fork at his e-pad on the little fold-out table in the living area.

"I thought those implants always transmit …" She made her tone a little fearful.

Joe shrugged. "No, like I said, I can set it to private. If someone wants to get in touch with me, they can leave a message, and I get a 'tap' in my ear. I haven't had any taps since you arrived."

Weezy carefully, quietly, picked up a cast iron skillet from the kitchen. Joe flinched. She wondered if he really thought she'd hit him. She said, in a voice she hoped acted out false uncertainty, "Really? I don't want anyone listening in to …." Coyly, "You know …."

She inverted the skillet and lowered it over the e-pad, covering it.

She put a finger to her lips, went to her room and retrieved her own e-pad, tapped on it and watched the screen for several seconds, finally relieved.

"Okay. The skillet kills the signal. I tried to send you a tap and got 'out of range' back."

"Weezy, isn't this overkill? I mean, I told you it's on Private." He said it lightly, maybe hoping for a restart of where they were a couple of minutes ago.

Weezy tossed her e-pad onto the recliner. "I don't like our personal life being monitored by some bot back at ZCG security."

"Goddam it, Weezy. I've got it set to Private. It's a piece of technology, an extension of my phone."

"Joe, I hate to break it to you, but when your employer screws a device into your mastoid bone, number one, you've just taken a step toward being a clever robot and number two, your employer can do anything he wants with the device."

"Why do you always see a conspiracy around every corner?"

"Joe, how'd you get to be so naive? You do remember you and I were nearly incinerated in this tin can you call home, don't you? Because the bad guys traced our signal."

"That was different. ZCG is a respected organization. These people are my friends. Why would they care about tracking me? I'm just a wet-behind-the-ears analyst."

Weezy remembered Joe's enthusiasm, his animation when he told the stories of his trip. He was being drawn into a circle of people he liked and admired, a circle she didn't belong in. And didn't want to belong.

Was she making too big a deal of this? But all she said was, "If I were you, I'd want to know for sure."

"How would I know for sure?"

She could tell from his look that he was unconvinced.

"You'd have to have a scan up close. I think the official line of the implant company is there's always a signal coming out of the device at some level. But a good scan would tell whether you're actually being monitored."

"How can I get a good scan?"

"I can arrange it," she said.

"Not yet," he said. "Let me do some checking first."

Joe inspected the damage to the bacon.

"Well, you said you like it crisp," with a wry grin.

"I do," she said, and saw Joe's relief as she smiled. But tension hung over them for the rest of the day. Weezy told Joe she needed to catch the Sunday morning train.

"Didn't you say you were leaving this afternoon?" Joe asked.

"Work."

Joe sighed. "Okay. Seems a shame to waste a lazy Florida afternoon over work, though. I'll go with you and see if I can get an earlier one, too."

They packed and closed up the trailer. When Joe removed the skillet, there are two taps, both from "ZCG switchboard." One announced a meeting on Monday, and one was from Felicity wondering where in the hell Joe had got to. He sent "Panacea Florida" to Felicity.

Weezy and Joe chatted on the trip up to Tallahassee. Friendly, inconsequential banter about whether the Sox had any chance at all, some gossip about IAC people. No more of Joe's stories.

They embraced like old friends before Weezy stepped on the train. She found her seat, looked out the window and waved at Joe. When he was out of sight, she opened her e-pad. Maybe a novel. Then the tears came.

# FOURTEEN

WHEN JOE ENTERED his cubicle on Monday morning, there was a sticky note on his monitor screen, "See me re: Rio Tinto analysis — F."

Felicity met Joe at the door to her office.

"I need some coffee."

In the hall leading to the coffee room, she stopped him. "Mayfield, I owe you big time. Not sure whether it's a kick in the balls or a big, sloppy kiss, though." The look on her face suggested that she would prefer the kiss, or more.

"What?"

"You do remember I warned you about the pricing spreadsheet, don't you? Like, *two times*?"

Joe gave her his "busted" grimace.

"Well, that scary security dude Braithwaite came to me Friday to do a 'security review.' It didn't take long for him to get around to asking if I'd noticed whether 'the new guys' were especially interested in pricing."

She put her hand on his arm and gave him a long, warm kiss on the cheek.

"Been here five years and always suspected that dude was monitoring us. Now I know."

***

The eleven o'clock Monday meeting was a regular status for Eric's investment bankers and analysts. It was held in the larger conference room in the New York office. Most of the time was spent planning for an upcoming conference in Austria. Joe wouldn't attend, but it was an interesting session. The Skin being developed was based on a place, Kazakhstan, rather than any one commodity.

Joe was collecting his papers and preparing to go over to the Jersey office when Ackerman's assistant stopped him in the hall. "Mr. Braithwaite wants to talk with you before you leave." Braithwaite? What would he want?

Joe followed her to a small interior office. Braithwaite was concentrating on an e-pad. He motioned for Joe to take a seat and went back to working on the e-pad. Joe waited for a couple of minutes, then cleared his throat. Braithwaite finished, looked up and smiled. "Sorry. Had to get that done." He didn't look sorry. "Can I ask where you were over the weekend?"

"At home in Florida."

"A couple of taps were refused by the system. Apparently poor signal strength." Braithwaite produced a small black box. "Mind if I test your implant?"

"No. Go ahead."

Braithwaite passed the device around Joe's head.

"Well, the implant's working fine. So it must be phone reception."

"Yes, I'm sure it is. I'm in a trailer. Metal skin, you know, carefully grounded. We live in the lightning capital of the States. I have a hard time making calls from inside. Besides, Panacea coverage is iffy at best."

"Okay. Well, I was concerned when the taps failed." The friendly smile was like a thin coat of paint, exposing more than it covered. "O'Malley is probably going to want you to do something about the reception problem when you're in Panacea."

***

"I think Mayfield suspects he's being monitored." Nick Braithwaite said as he entered Ackerman's office. "I checked his implant, which is working fine, and upgraded the positional tracking. He gave me some bullshit excuse about living in a trailer down in some remote burg in Florida. Might be bad phone reception like he said, or he could be masking the implant."

Ackerman frowned. "I really don't care about his personal life, except—"

"Oh, and the Napolitani woman was with him. Seems from some of the broken-up stuff she discovered his implant and was pissed. Of course, she might just be sensitive to us listening in while she has it off with Mayfield."

"Could you tell if he told her anything?"

"No. There was one Friday night conversation came through clearly, some happy horse shit about 'moral compass,' but otherwise nothing."

***

Joe was somewhere under the Hudson. The roll and jerk of the subway was hypnotic. He rotated his neck, relaxing muscles that had gone without exercise for too long. Drifting into … Felicity's discovery. Braithwaite's smile—was he really 'testing' the implant? Weezy's "clever robot" comment that cut him to the quick. Felicity's kiss. The beautiful carefree Weezy before the discovery.

The train jerked to a stop at Exchange Place. Joe was up and out, the reverie evaporating in noise and people surging.

He emerged from the station into a beautiful day. People on park benches, talking, eating lunch. His reverie was still with him, particularly Braithwaite's insincere smile. He walked the two blocks toward his office but stopped at the entrance.

When had Weezy's intuition ever been wrong? She was skeptical of people he liked and admired. She hurt his feelings. But that was okay—just Weezy being … Weezy.

He turned away from the office entrance and found a park bench with no one nearby.

He tapped out a text to Weezy's personal number:

```
Hw R U? Thought about ur suggestion for
the skillet recipe and want to try it.
```

***

A brown paper-wrapped metal box arrived in Joe's Sullivan Street mailbox Tuesday with a return address in St. Libory, Nebraska. The small black device in the box was featureless but for an 'on' switch and a small LCD screen. The handwritten instructions told Joe to turn the device on, wait until the screen displayed "1" then walk "completely and slowly" around his apartment. Then he was to tap "on" again, wait for "2" to appear, make sure his implant was on "active," hold it "not closer than 10 cm from the implant, but not farther than 20 cm," and make a call. The note said scan 2 was the "null scan."

Joe ran the null scan while he ordered Chinese.

The final instruction was to press "on" at bedtime. After "3" appeared, he was to set his implant to Private and repeat the scan process, making some "bedtime noises or talk to self."

Joe followed the instructions. He sang a couple of bars of *Sweet Home Chicago*, feeling a little foolish.

Wednesday morning on the way to work, he sent the package back to Nebraska.

# FIFTEEN

FIVE DAYS AFTER sending the scanner, Joe was in his cubicle in New Jersey, going through an analysis with a skeptical manager at Morgan RioTinto. A tap alerted him to an incoming message, which turned out to be a text from Weezy.

> Hw R U? HoHum day for me. Check out Stevie Ray.

There was an attached song, "Love Struck Baby," from the great bluesman Stevie Ray Vaughn. Joe named one of his avatars Stevie Ray when he was trying to hack into the IAC a year ago. He saw the country road in North Dakota, the day Weezy found him in the diner in Underhill, the day he drove away, furious. Why was she telling him to check out Stevie Ray?

The phone, of course. He had used several disposable phones registered to his avatars back then, when he was running from Phoenix.

He texted back: Thanks. Stevie Ray takes me back. I have a meeting this aft'noon, then call tonight?

She answered immediately, Cool.

***

Joe passed the rest of the day talking with potential clients, joking with Charlie Gray, doing an analysis of what was being called the Zambian Copper Crash. But Stevie Ray was never far from his mind.

He was more relaxed emerging from the subway at Sixth Avenue. This was his new home life. Even Sixth Avenue was pretty in the soft twilight of a long day. Noise was pleasant after the quiet purposefulness of the expanse of cubicles at ZCG.

Kids played on Third Street. He said good evening to Ms. Gagliardi in the foyer of his building.

In his apartment, he dug to the back of a kitchen drawer to find the disposable phones he used a year ago. He remembered dropping Stevie Ray, putting a nick in the case. He found a charger, plugged it in and waited a few seconds for the display to spring to life.

Five texts showed on the screen.

```
<Monday 13:44>Call me on this phone.
<Monday 16:03>Call me on this phone,
dumbass
<Monday 22:31>Aw C'mon Joe
<Tuesday 09:03>I'll text you on your
oh-so-public address
<Tuesday 09:12>You're being monitored.
```

Oh, shit!

```
See attached. Safe to read it on your
e-pad. Afterwards, give me a call.
```

Joe dropped into a kitchen chair. *Monitored?*

He realized he was almost hyperventilating. Sweating, clammy. Braithwaite. The forced friendliness.

Monitored?

He remembered Panacea and accusing Weezy of seeing a conspiracy around every corner. Thinking she was justifying her antisocial nature and still prejudiced by one small, probably cocktail-induced brush of her ass by Ackerman. Thinking less of her.

Maybe they did this with all newbies? But what about the risk of getting caught and slimed for such an egregious violation of privacy? Not likely. Not these people, not after the repeated righteous warnings about confidentiality, probity and honor.

He picked up Stevie Ray, clicked on the attachment, and said, "Forward," then winced. He heard Weezy saying, "What part of 'monitored' don't you understand, dumbass?"

Hand shaking, he tapped out 'forward' on the phone, directing the document to his e-pad, and opened it.

Joe,

HoHum tested your apartment and your implant. Seems like the apartment is not being monitored, unless someone's co-opted your neighbor A. Gagliardi's wi-fi. Your implant is another story … it's mainstreaming all the time, regardless of what you think the setting is.

So the question is what to do about it. I'll skip the part about the illegality of what somebody's doing and who it is. Of course, maybe the setting was a mistake. But not likely.

One option is to have the implant removed and provide the scan we made to the police. Another option is to fix the transmission problem.

We can't talk, but we can text through Olegarten.

First, give me an innocuous call.

Joe entered the Olegarten chat room, using text only.

Hotcakes?

::I'm here.

Nice to see you. I already hate not being able to talk with you freely.

::Me too.

I read your note. Thought about it. I want to eliminate the possibility it's a mistake.

::Okay. Then you have to discover the problem yourself. Best way: break your phone, take it in for repair and hope the tech who fixes it sees the problem. HoHum said they might have used the setting the police use to monitor

```
criminals. If the tech notices that
configuration, it will be illegal for
him to reset it. You might pretend
ignorance, get him to raise the issue.
Then go back to the implant place and
raise hell.
```

***

Joe's e-pad bounced off two stairs and came to rest, case cracked, on the tunnel entrance at the PATH station. He tried to look horrified, picked it up and continued to the train.

On the Jersey side, he went to his wireless provider's storefront.

"Can this be fixed?" He asked the young woman at the counter.

She took the e-pad, turned it over, pushed the 'on' button a couple of times, snapped her gum.

"Nope." She gave him a half-sympathetic smile with the ennui of a twenty-year-old who's answered this question several hundred times. "At least, doesn't make any sense to fix it. Cheaper to buy a new one."

She showed Joe several models, and he settled on one similar to the broken one.

"Okay. Can you set it up for me?"

"Takes a few minutes." The gum, bright green, moved to the other side of her mouth. *Snap.* "You want it set up the same as the old one?" *Snap.*

'Make it plain vanilla. Just transfer the contact information. I'll handle the rest of it."

"Okay. You can wait or come back." *Snap.*

"I'll wait."

She took the broken e-pad and the new one through a door marked "Tech Service," then returned. After a half-hour during which Joe realized how wedded he was to his e-pad, a guy appeared from the back room. "Linda?"

Linda turned from a woman checking out pastel-colored e-pads with her excited ten-year-old. "Yeah?" *Snap.*

"Uhh. Setup question."

Linda gave a little shrug and walked back to Tech Service.

There was a whispered conversation.

Linda returned, angry.

"We gotta set you up the way it was." The carefully trained commercial non-accent slipped back toward her original Canarsie.

"The way it was?" Joe tried to look sheepish. Not hard.

Disgust, a little head shake, and another snap of the gum. "Electronic monitoring? Ring a bell?"

She didn't say douchebag, quite.

"Oh, yeah. I forgot about that. Minor issue. About to drop off anyway. I doubt the police care …"

A half smile. "Well, we got a choice here, Mister … uhh … Mayfield. If we set it up the way it was, I keep my job and you stay out of jail. Or you can take your broken pad and the new one to somebody else. Your choice."

"Okay. Okay. Set it up like it was."

She said over her shoulder, loud enough so the woman and her daughter could hear, "Benny, set it like it was, with the electronic handcuffs active."

Ten minutes later, nine minutes after the woman left the store dragging her disappointed daughter, Joe had a new e-pad.

***

Joe went the few doors down the pedestrian mall to Business Communication Technologies, asked for Kirsten and found she was with a client.

He waited.

When she appeared, smiling expectantly, Joe said, "I broke my e-pad."

"Ohhhh … Too bad. We don't do e-pads here, but there's a store …"

"I've been there. My pad, the broken one, was set up as an electronic monitoring device, like the police use for criminals."

Kirsten's smile changed.

"That could be a mistake by the provider. It's an electronic switch … they might have set it by mistake."

"But when the police use electronic monitoring, don't they do it through an implant?" Joe asked. "So my implant must be set up as a monitor, too, right? And they must need a court order, don't they?"

"Not necessarily. Let's check it out for you."

She went to a monitor, said Joe's name and hers, and the screen filled with several documents. Kirsten squinted, a small 'v' on her brow. "Nope. No court order, and the implant seems to be set up the usual way. Hold on a minute, I'll scan it."

She reached under the counter and produced a small device that looked like the one Joe got in the mail. She came around the counter.

"Hold still."

Kirsten circled Joe's head a couple of times with the scanner, touched Joe's implant gently, then plugged the scanner into a port on the side of her e-pad. Data marched across the screen. She glanced at Joe, assessing, maybe suspicious.

"Find … Mayfield, Joseph E."

"Something the matter?" Joe said.

"Just checking." More data marched. Finally, Kirsten looked relieved and the smile came back.

"Looks like it was a setup error. You're not in any of the monitoring databases." She pointed to a stool at the counter.

"Sit here." She sat down next to him and put her e-pad between them. "Let's set this up to be password protected."

She opened a channel to Joe's implant, searched for a minute. "Put in a password." She looked away, and Joe typed in "sappho."

"Now it shouldn't happen again," she said. "I told corporate about this problem last year, but did they change the software? Of course not."

She leaned toward Joe, familiar now. "If you ever want to see exactly what's going through the implant, run a diagnostic. You got your e-pad?"

Joe pulled it out of his folio.

"Here, this is the routine you run. Same thing we use to diagnose transmission problems." She tapped instructions and some code on an electronic sticky note on his e-pad. "You can see all activity for whatever time you specify up to ten days." She turned to him, smiling. On his side now against the random jerkfulness of the rest of the world. He left with her card, a personal number written on the back.

***

When the transmission from Joe's implant shut down, the 'bot at Ramos Security put a flag on Nick Braithwaite's computer.

Nick was packing for a trip to Johannesburg to make sure his operatives understood the plan for the Chromium Skin. Maybe catch a little R&R if everything was on schedule. He saw the flag, swore under his breath and tapped Ackerman. "No time to talk now, but Mayfield's implant just shut down. Maybe a routine problem … I'll put somebody on it." A spider web of suspicion was forming. The implant. The IAC tracker woman. The searches for Skins profitability. Someone nibbling at RedSock's firewall. No reason to believe there was a connection, but … He said as an afterthought, "You'd solve a lot of potential problems by dumping him."

Ackerman appeared on the screen, "Why? He's done well so far. Besides, he's my chaff."

"Chaff?"

"You told me to set up a diversion, remember? You said, 'like a fighter under attack, some chaff to confuse missiles.' "

"Okay, it's only a suspicion. Let me run this down. I'll get back to you."

"You in a hurry?"

"I am. Plane to catch." Nick glanced at his watch, picked up his bag. "South Africa. Last strokes on Chromium. This one will be the biggest payoff yet."

# SIXTEEN

At home after work, a can of Feline Treat for Sappho and a hurried bologna sandwich for her, Weezy signed into the Olegarten forum.

She tapped out `Private to HoHum: Whatcha got?`

HoHum answered almost immediately.

`Nihow, Hotcakes. Boogie lo and slo?`

`Nihow, HoHum. Save the boogie. Video?`

Video opened, and HoHum said, "Lovely, as usual, Hotcakes." His T-shirt advertised Cargill, a departure from the usual computer gear or obscure bands.

"I got some results on those trades you sent me," he said. "Skins customers fall into three groups: Nine large multinational corporations doing big transactions to protect their operations, a raft of brokers buying smaller pieces to resell as investments, and about twenty hedge funds. The brokers and hedge funds buy the higher risk stuff, and the hedge funds do quite a lot of secondary trading, presumably protecting investments in commodities."

"Man, you are some kind of financial whiz."

"Nope. Just a farmer. Put seeds in the dirt, hope for rain and sell puts and calls." He cracked a grin. "Anyway, there's a fund that buys and holds the risky stuff. Seems like a losing proposition long term, but this guy happened to buy in shortly before a couple of catastrophes. The fund must have made millions."

"Do you know anything about it?"

"Not much. It's called RedSock, LLC. It's registered to a corporation in Netherlands Antilles, a tax haven."

"How would you feel about taking a look at RedSock?" Weezy asked.

HoHum interlaced his fingers, stretched, taking time to think.

"Those folks are pretty touchy about having their affairs looked at ..."

His tone revealed he had experienced what "pretty touchy" meant.

"I don't doubt it. That's why I'm asking the best."

"Aha! A transparent appeal to my ego. I'll take it, Hotcakes ... from you, I'll take it. Let me knock around and see how security-conscious they are."

***

HoHum signed out of Olegarten, stretched, twisted the cap off a Mountain Dew and shifted in the big armchair. He had brought it to the basement from the front room where his father used to read the paper and listen to the crop report every morning at six.

HoHum knew and respected the IAC's protection scheme. After all, he designed part of it from his prison cell, then scrambled the code to negotiate early release. In the aftermath of Cyberwar I, after the electrical grid had been repaired and the homes destroyed by fire and water had been rebuilt, companies belatedly took computer security seriously. HoHum became a consultant to many of them. Most companies admired his advice and intended to follow it. But when their CEOs couldn't get messages from their retreat in Martha's Vineyard, the Hamptons or La Jolla, the IT departments dumbed things down. As a result, HoHum approached RedSock supposing it had security he could easily circumvent.

RedSock, LLC looked like it used a standard commercial security software. It took HoHum ten minutes to slip through a crack in its firewall.

*Hmmm. Transaction files. Pull those.*

*What else?*

*Legal documents … copy those. Messages … copy those.*

*Now, erase your tracks.*

After four minutes in the site, HoHum backed out, stepping only in his electronic tracks, sweeping them away as he retreated. Or so he thought.

***

Nick Braithwaite stretched, relaxed his shoulders. He was at his flat in Johannesburg, enjoying a morning coffee. The R&R was going well. Keza, a beautiful African woman of indeterminate age moved gracefully across the balcony to join him. Her height and regal bearing reflected her proud Zulu heritage. People who didn't know her assumed she was Braithwaite's concubine, but she was much more. Keeping order over a business with so many contractors and so many moving parts required a hub, a center of gravity. Keza was that hub and, despite Nick's feelings about blacks in general and Keza's disgust with most white men, they were lovers.

She put her hand on his shoulder as she leaned to pick up his empty coffee cup. He caught her scent. It would be so nice to relax for another day, but he couldn't ignore the intrusion into RedSock.

He opened his e-pad and found the data dump he had downloaded after the little piece of code he called Doornail warned him of an intrusion.

Nick knew the IAC scheme well and had designed the ZCG website to mirror it. Stupid of the government to run a seminar in which they laid the whole thing out. One of the weaknesses of democracy. Like the IAC, the Ramos Security firewall protecting RedSock and ZCG allowed minor intrusions, much the way a medieval castle might have several walls protecting the inner keep. Behind the walls, algorithms sorted outliers. At the IAC, these outliers went to a group called trackers. Mayfield's woman was one of those. Ramos outliers came to Nick.

It took him half an hour to see what happened. The hacker was capable, making the problem of catching him an interesting challenge. This guy had been very careful once past the firewall. No hint of what he took, except it must have been quite a lot. On the way out, he tripped Doornail. Like a little nail sticking out of a door frame that grabs your shirt as you pass through, keeping a few threads. Nick followed the threads to their source.

He pushed back from the table and grimaced. "Deader than a doornail," he muttered.

***

Ross Ackerman was in his Manhattan office, negotiating the sale of a tranche of the Chromium Skin with a hedge fund manager up in Greenwich.

"You're hosed if you don't take the higher level. That's what gives you potential for a big win. The guys at XLTM already bought. They're trying to blow you right out of the top five." Ross felt the guy hesitating, tempted. The fish, bumping the bait, sensing it, ready to bite.

Nick Braithwaite stuck his head into the office.

"We need to talk."

Ross glanced up from his monitor, breaking eye contact with the man on the other end.

"Dunno, Ross," the man said. "Gotta look at all the positions in the portfolio. Good idea though. I'll be back to you." He clicked off.

"Dammit. I had him." Ross shook his head. Braithwaite sauntered over to a chair in front of Ross's console.

"You can't walk in when I'm in the middle of —

Braithwaite fixed Ross in a flat stare. "We had an intrusion into RedSock."

"When?"

"Late last week."

What started as irritation at the lost sale boiled into full-fledged anger.

"When were you going to tell me?"

"I was in Johannesburg when I saw it. I had to validate it."

"Validate it? I thought RedSock was hack proof. 'As strong as the IAC,' you said."

"It is." Braithwaite's steady stare usually intimidated Ross, but this time he had a head of steam.

"You're supposed to catch this stuff. Who was it? A dozen funds would give their left nut to see RedSock up close and personal."

"We don't know yet. Not one of the big funds, and it's not any industrial spy I know of."

"Well, find out, dammit. You're supposed to be better than the hackers."

"We'll find him. It may take a few days."

"Meanwhile, I have to wait for the market to start capitalizing on whatever they learned about RedSock?"

"It might be worse." Nick's face showed no emotion.

"Worse?" Ross's anger drove his voice up half an octave. "Might be worse? How could it be worse?"

"Whoever infiltrated didn't stay long enough to look at much. One reason the firewall couldn't track him. He must have grabbed transaction history, but he took a lot more gigabytes than that."

"A lot more gigabytes … what the fuck does that mean?"

"It means he copied other stuff. Maybe trust agreements, maybe … communications."

"Communications?"

"Did you communicate … text, voice, anything … through the RedSock site?"

Ross gave Braithwaite his dumbshit look. On the street below, a siren punctuated the background of muffled conversation from the other offices. "Of course I did. Can't very well do RedSock business through the ZCG system, can I?"

Braithwaite leaned forward, speaking slowly, as if to a recalcitrant child. "Did you flush the communications?"

"You're supposed to handle the details, dickhead. Find out what's going on."

***

HoHum's detailed report arrived on Weezy's e-pad three days after their conversation. Weezy saw it but couldn't trust reading it at work after Keith had shut down the project. The last half of her workday slipped by much too slowly.

At home, she wanted real food, so she pawed through her freezer and picked out a package of manicotti her mother sent home with her last time she was in Boston. She set it in the oven to warm. Sappho looked askance at her. A new can of Feline Delight solved the immediate problem. She clicked through her music library and selected Bach's "Well-tempered Clavier." She liked the rigorous logic of counterpoint when she did serious work. She took her e-pad and a glass of red wine to her overstuffed chair to wait for the manicotti and opened HoHum's report.

Sappho jumped onto the arm of the chair, trailing tuna breath, and settled into Weezy's lap. "So," she said to Sappho, who had begun a complicated exercise in feline toilette, "most of these funds are buying and selling all the time. HoHum doesn't see a pattern, except for this one called RedSock, LLC."

Sappho appeared uninterested.

Was there some significance to the name RedSock? Combining the warning color with an airport wind-direction indicator? Or "Red sky in the morning, sailors take warning"? Or maybe the owner likes baseball?

The report detailed long strings of transactions, mostly purchases of Skins. Each Skin purchase got distributed to fifteen accounts, all of which must be members of an extended family called Scholze.

Okay, so this was a family fund. Not too unusual for a small hedge fund, HoHum noted. Most of what Weezy took to be communications were encrypted, but there was a group of trust agreements hanging out there in plain English.

The first one was in the name of Eldon Scholze. Managed by "Trustee" or "Co-trustee." Weezy flipped through definitions, read a vague statement of how funds would be invested, noted the Sint Maarten depository bank and its identifying numbers and came to the signature page.

The signature was more like a chop … A big E-line-corkscrew and what might be a y, Big A-ck-line. Typed below, Emily Ackerman.

As if on cue, the Bach minor adagio jumped to major presto.

Half an hour later, Weezy had a list of fifteen names of the beneficiaries of RedSock trusts and a map locating all of them in central and northeastern Iowa. Over the last several months, relatively small investments in the highest-risk Copper Skins tranches produced six hundred percent returns. Close to twenty million, all told. Recently, the trusts put most assets into the highest risk Chromium Skins.

Why so risky for a bunch of Iowa farmers? They should want conservative investments.

Weezy stood, stretched a leg that had gone to sleep and rotated her neck. *Guess I have to crack those encrypted messages.*

It took Weezy about an hour to crack the first message, wishing she had the Harley-Davidson power of the IAC supercomputer rather than the moped of her e-pad. But eventually the work paid off and her algorithm spat out an innocuous string of characters.

A chess move? An hour's work to get a friggin' chess move? It was going to an online forum. Why encrypt it?

The second message followed her algorithm's learning curve and took only fifteen minutes to decipher. A short note to Ramos Security, *Status of S. Africa Project?*

Weezy decrypted ten messages, several of them chess moves. Her rudimentary knowledge of chess didn't give her a clear picture of the progress of the game. But why would someone be receiving chess moves at a hedge fund? A hobby? Then why encrypt them?

Weezy switched to the Olegarten website and left a message:

```
DingDing, you there? Got a chess
question. Check out the moves I'm
attaching.
```

No immediate answer … it would be mid-morning in Shanghai. Probably at work.

She pinged HoHum. He was far savvier than she about the ugly underside of the Internet.

No response. The clock said one a.m. Even hackers have to sleep.

She put a stack of decrypts in HoHum's mailbox and signed out of Olegarten. She could still catch five or six hours of Zs. Sappho woke and startled, then fixed Weezy with one of those dumb human looks, and Weezy sniffed.

"Dammit!" She opened the oven. The manicotti was dry but salvageable.

Sappho's stare reminded Weezy of why people had thought of cats as supernatural in the Middle Ages.

"Sappho, I do believe you are omniscient."

Sappho waved the tip of her tail.

Weezy ate, leaving the crunchy ends. If it had been store-bought, she'd have thrown it out. But it was the warmth and smell of the Napolitani kitchen in Boston. Mom saying, "Mangia, Mangia." Brother Petey giggling. Love.

Even as she ate, questions roiled her mind. High-risk investments for farmers? Chess moves in financial conversations? Strange.

***

Braithwaite was sorry to lose his man in charge of the Dwarsrivier chromite mine project. Smart guy, and flexible, too. The "liberation army" of mostly ragtag teenagers were excited by the shiny grenade launchers Braithwaite had given them and jumped off too early. Braithwaite's man had to pull the cave-in forward. Two miners died, and the rest walked off the job.

The miners had been restive for over a year. A union organizing attempt had been quashed by truncheon-wielding government police. The cave-in was a painful example of what the miners had feared without modern work rules and safety standards.

There was an ugly video of miners pelting the mine manager's car with rocks. Word came that the liberation army had broken over the border with Namibia and was coming down the N7, threatening Cape Town. The National Defence Corps mustered and met the liberation army near the mine. A tense standoff broke into a firefight when Braithwaite's sniper picked off a National Defence captain, and the project rolled forward according to Braithwaite's careful plan. Over one hundred were killed and at least three hundred wounded; no one knew for sure. Video from the field hospitals showed pitifully thin child soldiers crying out as their wounds were tended.

There were numerous acts of sabotage of equipment and buildings, so the bombing of the main shaft would surprise no one. Braithwaite gave the go-ahead, assuring the man he had twenty minutes to get to safety.

Unfortunate to lose him.

# SEVENTEEN

ON THURSDAY MORNING, Eric O'Malley sat in the headquarters conference room overlooking the financial district and the East River waiting for John Zhou Min and Ross Ackerman to join him. It was review time, and Eric needed to cut six from the new class. Everyone had been on pins and needles for the last week. John Zhou Min entered, carrying a cup of tea. He sat down across from Eric, extracted the teabag from the cup and put it neatly on the saucer.

"What do you think of the class in general?" John's smile was the formal one he retreated behind when unpleasantness threatened.

"Certainly above average. The ones we cut loose will be better than some we've kept in the past. Hate to lose 'em." Eric, the indefatigable optimist, opened every year's discussion this way.

Ross Ackerman swept into the room ten minutes late and plopped into the chair at the head of the table.

"So, who's on the list?" Ross said. "I need to get over to Jersey."

Eric tapped his e-pad and a list of six names appeared on John's and Ross's pads.

"Where's Mayfield? He should be on the list." Ross said.

Eric startled, then tamped down his temper. As the head of investment banking, all these people ultimately reported to him.

"Mayfield? Why Mayfield?"

Ross looked down and exhaled. "I know the guy looks good now. But, like I've said to you, Eric, he's a loose cannon. Everybody thinks of him as the hero of the fiasco with the

MedRecords last year, but he went up against his employer, violated their trust." Ross's voice softened. "Got to be careful of true believers. He put his conviction before the needs of the people he worked for. We can't have that happen here."

Eric rubbed forehead in frustration. "He only went up against his employer because they were involved in a conspiracy that cost at least a dozen lives. We've got nothing to hide."

"He doesn't really fit the ZCG model. I want him gone," Ross said.

"And I want to keep him," Eric said without rancor. "He's too good to let go. Smart … they all are, but he has the best analytical chops of all the newbies. Maybe as important, he speaks the lingo of the people we sell to. Hell, the best story out of the western sales trip was Washburn, the CEO of Morgan Rio Tinto, talking with Joe about fishing holes in Florida. Besides—"

"Eric, he turned off his implant, and—"

"Off? You mean Private?

"No, he went offline entirely," Ross's eyelid twitched.

*How the hell did Ross know about the implant problem?* Eric opened his mouth to ask but thought better of it. Another question to file under What's Ross Up To?

"He told me. It was malfunctioning. Apparently it was mistakenly set up as electronic handcuffs. But it's fixed now."

"Okay." Ross shifted in his seat. Irritation? Or something else? "But I don't like having a smart guy who's doing the horizontal mambo with possibly the best hacker in the U S of A hanging around our trading system. Too big a risk."

Eric watched Ross. The conversation had been polite, but Ross's face and posture betrayed his anger. Why the hell did it matter so much to him? And where did he get this "best hacker" business?

Eric looked to John Zhou Min. It was up to John to make the call, at least in theory. But Ackerman was the goose that laid the golden eggs. At least Zhou Qiáng thought so. A vote against Ackerman was a vote against Zhou Qiáng, and John Zhou Min did not cross his father.

Eric sighed inwardly and thought about jumping ship. There were plenty of opportunities, given the success of the firm. He would hate to let John down, but this power structure was unhealthy, a bad cold fixing to be pneumonia.

"Joe's in," John said.

Eric couldn't contain a smile.

"Pardon?" Ross said, clearly shocked. John would pay later, big time, Eric thought. But, damn, he did the right thing.

"Joe's in. For now. Let's move on."

Eric took over, feeling bad about the next item of discussion.

"On the subject of Mayfield, I need to have him in Vienna at the IAEC conference. We're there to discuss Skins, and Washburn is sending Don Petrescu, the guy we met in that first teleconference. He expects Joe to be there, and I can't very well tell him we don't include first-year analysts in this meeting."

"Aw, fuck!" Ross stood, not quite slamming his hands on the table. "Gotta get to New Jersey to get some real business done. I don't like having Mayfield around, but I see you two have bought into his aw shucks, good ol' boy bullshit." He picked up his e-pad, half opened the door and turned back to Eric and John. "So be it. But it's going to be hard to explain to Zhou Qiáng why we kept and promoted a proven hacker who does not fit the profile of a ZCG banker. You surely know our success in trading depends on keeping our data safe. And you can guess how understanding Zhou Qiáng will be if critical information becomes public!"

Ross slammed the door. His references to Zhou Qiáng hung in the air. John's face had drained of color.

"Thank you. You did the right thing." Eric said. But he was sure the conversation would find its way to Hong Kong.

***

Ross kept the look of anger until he was alone in the elevator, where he let it fade to a half smile.

He got into the town car waiting outside the building to carry him to the Jersey offices and told the chauffeur to go. He raised the privacy glass and called Braithwaite.

"Remember that contingency plan we talked about, the one where we create a diversion?"

"Sure."

"I said I had an idea. Now I'm sure," Ross said. "Set Mayfield up to buy Skins. He's survived review, and I made a big stink everyone will remember. He has a reputation as a hacker, so we'll be able to divert SEC's attention to him for long enough to clean up our act if we have to."

"Perfect."

Braithwaite's approval shouldn't have mattered to Ackerman, but it did.

"Go through one of the do-it-yourself brokers and have him buy a little of the Chromium Skin. Say, thirty k," Ross said.

"Where do I get the thirty k?"

"How about the security budget?" Ross put a little edge on his voice but didn't get a rise out of Braithwaite.

"Make it look like a bonus," Braithwaite said. "That would be believable to regulators. They'll think he went right out and opened a personal trading account and bought the Chromium Skin. He took the class that covered conflict of interest and securities law. It will seem obvious that there was intent, as well as criminal action."

Ross thought the idea over. Braithwaite was right, of course. As usual. It also detached Braithwaite and Ramos from the transaction. Ross stowed that thought in the back of his mind.

"You set up the account," he said to Braithwaite. "I'll make the transfer."

***

All the newbies knew Cut Day was coming. Each of them waited for the call to "join me in my office" and feared the walk across the broad expanse of the thirty-fourth-floor reception area. Joe got the invitation on his implant on a Sunday night. At least he could go directly to Eric's office rather than going over to New Jersey and have everyone speculate about the outcome when he left for Manhattan.

Eric was good at letting down bankers about to be let go. The year before, one of those cut told her best friend, "After our talk, I walked out of his office so pleased with his kind words that I didn't figure out I'd been sacked until I was halfway back to New Jersey."

The next morning, Joe stepped out of the elevator on thirty-four, with its fourteen-foot ceiling, imposing oiled walnut entrance door, and the polished brass of the firm's name. He tried to look … nonchalant? Busy? Purposeful? Anything but nervous.

"Going to see Eric," he said to the receptionist. She smiled … knowingly? As he walked down office row, the senior bankers studiously avoided eye contact.

Eric's office was more like a living room than a corporate space, which fit both the purpose and the personality of the man whose title was Managing Director - Investment Banking and whose job was managing relationships.

Eric stood to greet Joe. They shook hands. A shake from Eric was like a hug, a big hand wrapping you in good will.

"Joe, sorry to make you do the perp walk." He chuckled. "Getting a call this week to come to the Manhattan offices has got to be nerve-wracking."

Joe mumbled agreement.

"Don't worry. You're a keeper."

Tension rushed out of Joe. "Great. I mean, thank you."

"Don't thank me. Thank hard work and the western trip." He waved at a chair. "Sit." Eric seated himself in a black straight-backed chair with the Princeton emblem, crossed his legs and looked out over Manhattan.

"Joe, I'd like to have this conversation stay in this room. Understood?"

"Sure."

Eric cleared his throat. "Trust is the currency ZCG or any other investment bank trades in. When we say 'open the kimono' to our clients, we expect them to trust us with strategic plans, financial strategies, embarrassing weaknesses, all of it. Before they're willing to do that, they have to trust us implicitly. A century ago, banks hired almost exclusively from the Social Register … everyone in the blue book knew everyone else, which built trust."

Joe nodded, wondering where this was going.

"These days, we look back on that as quaint at best, but the trust issue is still crucial. We look for people who are not only smart but personally conservative, as well. In the review, there were no questions about smart, but—"

"I'm not personally conservative?"

Eric shrugged. "I know you better than the other principals do. They're perhaps swayed by your reputation. They see RazorBlue and your lady friend, who is maybe the best hacker in the country."

"Best hacker in the country?" Joe's anger rose, the know-nothing, hand-on-Weezy's-ass establishment outlook closing in on him. "Best hacker in the country? Eric, goddammit, that's stupid. Weezy's the opposite of a hacker. She tracks hackers for a living. She caught me because I'm an inept hacker. If John and Ross want to find a way not to like me, they really need to pick another avenue."

"Whoa." Eric spread his arms. "As I said, you're in. But I want you to know there were concerns. Remember, after CyberWar I, anyone whose job and reputation depends on information has a bias toward worry and suspicion when it comes to data security. You never would have seen an investment bank retaining a Nick Braithwaite ten years ago. But now … file the concerns away. Don't stay angry, but be aware."

Joe swallowed. "Okay. Thanks for the heads-up. And thanks for your support."

Eric leaned back and laced his fingers behind his head.

"On to the next item. You're probably aware that we're going to the International Atomic Energy Commission conference in Vienna next month."

"Sure. Rollout of the Kazakh Skin, right?"

"Right. All the big exploration and mining companies will be there. We typically take only a few senior bankers … it's expensive, what with Vienna prices, entertainment, wives attending, and so on. I need to make an exception in your case because Fred Washburn is sending Don Petrescu, and he's expecting Don to talk with you."

Joe started to protest. The other people in Jersey would hate him for this. But he mumbled his thanks.

Eric stood. "Please don't discuss the Vienna conference with your colleagues. At least, not yet. It will cause hurt feelings." Joe stood, too. Eric reverted to his normal upbeat self, grabbed

Joe's hand and clapped him on the shoulder. "Welcome aboard!"

Joe left the office feeling elated. But something dragged at him, too. The dock in Panacea and Weezy saying, "I get whiplash every time I see you."

***

Weezy's pad beeped as she pedaled from work. Arriving home, she slipped her Bianchi into the garage below the apartment. She climbed the stairs and greeted Sappho, who bounded across the lawn toward the bushes. The message was from Joe. She took a long drink of water, then called him.

"Hey, babe." He was on a bench with the Washington Square arch as backdrop.

"Got your ping on the way home," she said. "But of course I'm not wired for sound."

Joe grinned. "Neither am I, anymore. Thanks to you and HoHum."

Weezy gave him a thumbs up.

"Today, I survived review … I'm in. I think it was my tutor …

"Congratulations," Weezy said, hoping it didn't come out too flat.

"Yeah, and they asked me to go to Vienna," he said. "Part of a conference where we'll be talking about the Kazakh Skin. My guess is there will be a lot of interest after the strike in South Africa and the riot that sent chromium over the edge."

"Chromium?" Weezy went cold.

"Yes. The Skin ZCG put together about six months ago, the one we used in training. It's going to cash out big time. A couple of days ago, miners in the biggest chromite mine struck, then the police shot into the crowd. There were more than a dozen casualties, then rioting and an explosion that killed more. The mine's shut down for months, and the price of chromite is up eighteen percent. A couple of our clients who'd bought the Chromium Skin offset some pretty big losses."

RedSock bought that Skin for all those Iowa farmers.

"Nice to see the work we're doing help our clients out."

He sounded serious, but proud and happy, too.

How was she going to tell him?

"Anyway," Joe still smiling, riding high. "I was thinking you could join me after the conference for a few days. Vienna, maybe Prague … or Tuscany. It'd be on me."

"I don't know, Joe …" *Don't go making wild accusations until you know what's going on, dumbass.*

"Well, anyway, think about it." Weezy saw his disappointment.

"Sure. Really, it sounds wonderful. I have to see if I can get away."

After they disconnected, Weezy fixed herself a simple dinner, dreaming against her will about Vienna and the Tuscan hills.

But the subtext was there, no matter how much she tried to push it away. This wasn't coincidence. She should have known something would happen to chromium as soon as she saw Ackerman tied to those RedSock investments. Why didn't she say something, at least warn someone? Ackerman was involved, but what about ZCG? She had to tell Joe what she had found out. Even if it meant losing him.

# EIGHTEEN

THE MORNING AFTER Joe's review, a message from Braithwaite popped up on Ross Ackerman's monitor. "Need to talk. My office."

Ross, offended, pinged back, "No, my office."

A monitor window opened showing Braithwaite, expression serious as usual.

"Ross, this is a security matter, and I know *my* office is clean."

"*Jesus.*" Ross muttered. "Going down to thirty-two," he growled at his long-suffering assistant and huffed out to the elevator.

Goddam Braithwaite was getting too big for his britches. Ordering him around. A fuckin' contractor, goddam African, parading around like some sort of Foreign Legionnaire. All the women in the office hyperventilating when he walked by, and he might as well be gay for all the attention he gave 'em.

"Braithwaite, you can't be interrupting me—"

"Close the door, will you?"

"—when I'm in the midst of a contract review."

Braithwaite looked as patient as his thousand-yard stare allowed.

"Sit, please. We have an important matter to deal with."

"Better be, because …" The righteous indignation drained out of Ross. He forgot what the "because" was about.

"It's about the intrusion into RedSock. I have identified the hacker. He is a well-known computer consultant. He's been working with another hacker called 'Hotcakes.' I now know

Hotcakes is the woman Mayfield brought to your party, Louise Napolitani."

"They're after the bank account, right? Nationale Handelsbank assured me it's fully protected—"

"They're not after money."

Ross paled.

"I tracked back Napolitani's conversations on the Internet portal they use," Nick said. "After they hacked RedSock, Hotcakes sent off questions to a Chinese chess player, asking about the moves used in our communications for the past six months. She probably suspects they're bogus."

"But she can't make anything of them, can she?"

Braithwaite shrugged. It was the first time Ross remembered him looking resigned.

"I'm pretty damn good at decrypting stuff … identifying Napolitani was harder than finding a flyspeck in a pound of pepper. I'm up against the combination of HoHum…that's what the guy who got into our site calls himself … Napolitani, and the software and hardware resources of the IAC." Braithwaite massaged his temples and winced. "I'm a firecracker and they're a hand grenade.

"Chances are they will figure out some of what's gone on. They may not be able to prove we sent the guns to Mali last year or the action on Chitimukulu for the Copper Skin. I mean, I can't be sure of what they know, but I think they will eventually figure out why Skins are so profitable."

Ross chewed a fingernail. "But if they can't prove anything, screw 'em."

"I can't track this HoHum guy in real time," Braithwaite said. "He's too clever and too paranoid. Maybe I can monitor the Napolitani woman. She's not working on this through the IAC, and she lives in an apartment that should be easy to break into.

Of course, she might find any device I put in and silence it." Braithwaite laced his fingers and cracked his knuckles. "Short story: Right now, I can't be sure of getting advance warning if they decide to expose RedSock."

Ross considered the ramifications of having RedSock or the Kazakh Skin compromised. It was the biggest one yet, and because it covered several different commodities, the sales potential was several times that of the earlier copper and chromium skins.

"So, what do we do?"

"The safest approach is to eliminate the entire communication chain before someone can't resist dishing the dirt on the Internet or calling the SEC."

"The communication chain?"

Ross ticked through the possibilities. Upside: Braithwaite was good at what he did. He could probably eliminate the three without raising suspicions. Downside: Anything went wrong, Braithwaite would disappear to Dubai or South Africa, this conversation would go to the FBI, Skins would implode, and Ross would be standing alone with his dick in his hand.

"Yeah," Braithwaite continued. "HoHum and Napolitani surely suspect something. Hard to tell how much Mayfield knows. He's been looking at stuff he shouldn't have in the system, but that may just mean he's trying to impress O'Malley."

Braithwaite opened a desk drawer and produced a container of breath mints, popped the cap took one, then offered it to Ross.

He wants a go-ahead, Ross thought. Be careful. He might be recording this conversation.

Ross shook off the offer. "Maybe the first option is to intimidate the hacker and get to Napolitani through her boss," Ross said.

Braithwaite sucked his mint, eyes on Ross. After a moment, he said, "If we try and fail, it will pull the trigger on exposure."

"True enough. So, best take 'em all out, right?"

Another pause. "The hacker is probably easy if we make it look natural. There'll be no obvious connection to us or RedSock." He took another mint. "Mayfield wouldn't be too hard, either. Botched mugging. Guy goes for his wallet, they struggle, guy sticks a shiv in him. It'd probably get caught on camera if we did it in the Village, which would make it believable."

Braithwaite drew in a breath. "But Napolitani … not a good idea at all."

"Not a good idea?" Ross said, eyebrows rising. "She's our main problem, isn't she?"

"Ross, she is the best tracker the IAC has. No matter how she died, the FBI and several other agencies would be all over it. We have to assume she'll have left telltales pointing to us. Cutting out the other two, like I said, could look natural. It would take away her source of information and her reason to stay on this."

"So, what do we do?"

Braithwaite exhaled.

"Best get rid of HoHum and Mayfield. But it has to look natural."

*Got him to propose it. Good. He must not be recording.*

"Two. Two for now," Ackerman said.

***

It was evening, and Herman Suttermeier walked the fence line, something he did when he needed to figure things out. He grew up on this farm, and he loved the stillness that gathered as the western sky grew pellucid in the setting sun and birds settled in for the evening.

Herman was never cut out to be a farmer. Most of the family land was leased to Dan Schmidt, next section over, after Herman's father died. Herman was infatuated with computers as a kid, began programming and discovered he was gifted. That led to legendary feats of derring-do as HoHum, a run-in with the FBI, a short stay in the federal penitentiary, and a career advising companies how to protect themselves against Internet pirates like himself. The advisory service meant a lot of travel, but he always came home to the farm his father loved and he loved, too.

He walked, kicking clumps of dirt, thinking.

Something was wrong. He couldn't put a finger on it, but it seemed like someone was out in cyberspace, watching him. Like a flicker in the corner of his eye. When he looked, nothing there. Was it Hotcakes? She could do it, but she had no reason to. Maybe a competitor?

The gate behind the barn was ajar. Unusual. Schmidt was very tidy, very careful about the gate to keep his cows in pasture, and he was hardly ever in the barn in the evening. Herman didn't think much about it, his attention captured by RedSock what-ifs. He closed the gate and turned to walk through the barn to be sure Schmidt was not bringing hay down from the loft. The forklift was where Schmidt always parked it. He must have forgotten to lock the gate, that's all. Halfway through the barn, Herman heard the swish of a bale moving, looked up to the haymow.

"Schmidt? You up there?"

He saw the three-hundred-pound superbale before it hit him, but too late to move.

# NINETEEN

JOE HAD BEEN working late like all the other new bankers and analysts. Some of it was fear, some was pride at having survived review, some was because the job was exciting. And of course, the competition. Charlie Gray looked owlish from lack of sleep and overindulgence in caffeine. Senior bankers reminded newbies that what they were going through was far less stringent than when *they* joined the firm.

Joe trudged up the cracked and dirty stairs of the Sixth Avenue subway feeling gritty, tired and sore from lack of exercise. He walked down to Third Street, then east toward Sullivan, relishing the opportunity to stretch his legs. Gotta get a run in soon.

Macdougal Street was in full party mode, even on Monday night. High school kids strolled, trying to look innocent and hoping to score some drugs. Out-of-towners partied on expense accounts, and street people tried to score anything they could.

A block over, Sullivan Street was quiet.

At the corner, he saw a few lighted windows in his building. Mrs. Gagliardi, his neighbor. Bellanti's repair shop on the ground floor. A bluish flicker of TV in several. Otherwise quiet.

He started to cross the street to his building. A man he hadn't noticed before walked toward him, tossing a cigarette into the gutter.

"Buddy, can you tell me how to get to the Sixth Av station?"

"Sure. You go down—" Joe lifted his arm to point when he felt more than heard something approaching. Then impact … a shoulder in the ribcage. Hard. His head hit the building. Rough brick scraped his cheek and nose.

"Hey!"

He twisted toward his attacker. Something hit him like a rabbit punch in the lower back. Then pain, and his right leg went numb.

"Fucker's wearing a backpack! Go high." An arm over his left shoulder, pulling him backwards. The street was fading. His leg buckled, and he began to fall, trying to twist toward the pressure. A woman shouted, "What the hell youse doin'?"

Then a sharp pain in his collar bone. He raised his right arm, but he was fading.

Black.

***

Ross Ackerman leaned on the bar in a dance club downtown, head throbbing from the cacophony that passed for music, as well as a couple or four drinks. His date, Kelsey—Kaitlyn? Kayla?—was somewhere on the dance floor. It looked like she was more interested in dancing the night away than the horizontal sport Ross had in mind. He sighed, tired and wondering what he'd feel like at fifty.

His implant tapped him. Braithwaite. He took out his e-pad.

```
Link One confirmed. Link Three
completed, probable.
```

Ross barked a laugh that startled the guy next to him and, energized, left the bar to look for K-something.

***

Joe came to slowly, his brain sorting through sounds that made no sense. Electronic pips, muffled voices, a sharp clang somewhere distant, the *whoosh* of something … a door opening? Then a voice.

"Mr. Mayfield?"

He opened his eyes, and a face came into focus. Black, many beaded braids, generous mouth, concerned eyes. Beautiful.

"Can you hear me?"

Joe grunted.

"Welcome back." Big smile. "We thought we might lose you."

"Where ... ?"

"You're at Belleview Hospital. I'm Amelia. You gonna be all right. You just rest up."

Sometime later, a new face presented itself. Long nose hung over rubbery lips, a world-weary expression. "Mr. Mayfield?"

The face drew away, revealing a man in an ill-fitting suit, a badge hanging from the coat's pocket.

"Hubik," he said. "NYPD."

Joe tried to push himself up in bed. Amelia hovered, then reached to support him, sending an evil eye toward Hubik.

"Looks like somebody wanted your wallet," he said, extracting a small notebook from an inside pocket. "Can you describe your attacker?"

"There were two."

"Uh-huh." Hubik nodded as if Joe had confirmed his suspicion. He made a short note.

"I only saw one of them. A maybe five-seven or five-eight guy. Broad-shouldered. White. He asked me where the subway station was." Hubik's tight grin said he had heard this before. He asked a few more questions. Identifying marks? Beard? Accent? Joe began to drift, and he heard Amelia scolding Hubik. Joe felt his covers being tucked and a pat on the shoulder as he drifted back into never-never land.

A harried doctor appeared later, waking Joe. She explained that he had been brought in last night. There was a deep stab wound that fortunately missed his right kidney. Substantial blood loss, a nasty slice across the clavicle as well, non-serious facial contusions. "We sewed you up," the doc said with a smile.

"You're a lucky one. An inch to the left on the stab wound, and you'd have died. Better aim on that clavicle slash, they'd have hit your carotid and you'd have bled out."

The next face that appeared was Eric O'Malley's, a huge grin appearing as Joe opened his eyes. Nighttime, by now.

"Joe, everyone sends their best. Man, we were worried about you. I guess your parents are away from home, and your sister gave permission for me to see you. You want me to contact your lady friend?"

Joe surfaced from his soft, warm drug-induced cocoon, said, "Lmme caw er."

Eric chuckled. "Better let me make first contact."

# TWENTY

ON THE SECOND day, or maybe it was the third, Joe woke to see Amelia bustling around the room, arranging vases of flowers. He watched her for a minute. Was this the same beautiful black woman he had first seen, now transformed into a rather ordinary looking, somewhat pudgy nurse? Same braids and beads, though, and when she turned to look at him, same smile.

"Wake up sleepyhead. A whole lot of people want to see you."

As if in response, the door opened. Weezy, followed by Eric. He raised his left hand, and Weezy took it, her face gaunt.

"Hey."

He gripped her hand tightly, not wanting to let go, wanting a hug he knew he couldn't have, but pulling her to him awkwardly, anyway. She sat on the edge of the bed.

"So good to see you …" He closed his eyes, suddenly overcome. "Both of you." He kept holding Weezy's hand.

"What happened?" Weezy leaned close, her lips trembling and eyes full.

"I was almost home. A mugging—"

The door opened, and Detective Hubik appeared.

"Glad to see you're awake," he said. "I'd like you to explain what happened. In detail this time." He turned to Eric and Weezy. "In private."

"They're my friends."

Hubik shrugged. "You can stay," he said. "Have a seat there," pointing to hard plastic chairs along the wall on the other side of the bed. "But no conversation, no body language, or you're out. Understood?"

Eric and Weezy nodded and moved to the chairs.

Hubik began asking the who-what-when questions, establishing that Joe was coming home from the office, it was 11:20, and he'd just turned onto Sullivan Street. Joe got a few words into describing the attack when Hubik began nodding.

"One guy asked a question, other guy hit you from your blind side, right? Drove you into the wall?"

Joe hesitated.

"Yes."

"Standard mugging procedure."

"Five point four percent," Weezy said.

Hubik's eyes narrowed. He turned toward Eric and Weezy. "I said, no conversation."

Weezy cocked her head. Joe saw the dumbass look forming.

"Right," She said. "No conversation. Just data. Out of the NYPD database."

Hubik's jaw set. "Whaddya mean, five point four percent?"

"Over the last decade, knives have been used in five point four percent of similar robbery attempts between Canal and Fourteenth." Weezy locked eyes with Hubik. "So the knife wounds are not 'standard procedure.' "

"I don't know where you got that, Miss."

"Out of your database."

Hubik's pained look said he'd heard this kind of BS plenty of times. People get all kinds of crap off the Internet. "You couldn't have—" Hubik stopped, reconsidered, then gave Weezy a tight smile. "Okay, Miss. Let's assume you *did* hack our database. That's a felony now that we got the IAC firewall. You wanna wait outside while I question Mr. Mayfield, here, or would you prefer a holding cell downtown?"

"Detective," Joe said. "She *is* the IAC."

***

Ross Ackerman's implant told him an important personal message was coming in.

He read it and spat out, "Call Braithwaite" into his computer.

The computer voice, cheery and oblivious, asked "Direct line? Interrupt?"

"Interrupt!"

A minute or so later, there was a tone in his implant, followed by Nick Braitwaite's voice. "You called?"

"My office, now."

"Can't do it, Ross. I'm across town. Working on the trading security project."

Nick disconnected.

Goddammit. The guy was always acting like a spook. Ross opened the bottom drawer of his credenza and rooted around in the accumulated junk he used to cover the simple disposable phone Nick had given him. "Trading security project" meant he was supposed to use it. Nick had programmed it with one number, so Ross had only to push send.

When Nick answered, Ross practically shouted, "What do you mean, 'Link Three was not successful'? I thought you said —"

"Meet you at, say, Battery Park at Greenwich Street in an hour. And bring that phone."

Nick disconnected, leaving Ross fuming.

When Nick appeared at Battery Park ten minutes late, it had begun to rain, a gray, cold mist. Nick had an umbrella big enough for the two of them only if they stood uncomfortably close. Nick ceded enough area to shelter Ross.

"Nick, goddamn it—"

"Give me your disposable."

Ross handed it over, and Nick gave him a similar one. One call per phone, then swap. Nick had explained the procedure as a security precaution when it first became obvious they were going to need to have some very private conversations.

"Damn it, Nick. What's going on with this link three problem? How can you fuck up offing an unsuspecting accountant? I though you said it'd be easy."

Nick turned and looked down at Ross. He was chewing peppermint gum, which he cracked. "It needed to look like a random attack, which made it harder. Given the budget, I had to use some semi-professional help."

The uncomfortable closeness of Nick made Ross hold his anger in check, at least outwardly.

"You said we need to adjust tactics. What's your plan?" A smirk. "Professionally speaking, of course."

The big man tensed, then returned to control.

"You may need to take out the two remaining links. What we did get from Mayfield's implant before he shut down the monitoring made it seem likely Napolitani shares more than bodily fluids with Mayfield. He must know about her suspicions by now."

"So, what do we do?"

Nick thought for a moment. "Discover that account with the Skins. Fire Mayfield. When he's out of the company, it'll be easier to deal with him."

"Yeah, great idea…except he has to go to Austria. Everybody thinks he's a cool, brave guy thanks to your semi-incompetent thugs. He's impressed the biggest potential customer for the bottom side of our Kazakh Skin, and we're down to the short strokes on that deal. If Mayfield's breathing, he's gotta go. When we get back here, we can pull the trigger. How about the woman?"

"She's a bigger problem. Like I said, anything happens to her, the FBI and Homeland Security will be all over it. Only way to take her out is a believable accident. A car, except she doesn't drive much. Drowning, except …" Nick paused. The corner of his mouth twitched.

"Except what?"

"Any way you can get her on the Vienna trip?" Nick said. "That would keep her from working the problem with all that governmental computer power while we're gone for a week and a half. Also, it'll be a lot easier to make an unfortunate accident happen on foreign soil."

"Most of our senior bankers bring spouses or whoever they're screwing. I'm sure we can make it happen for our star junior analyst. Eric will do back flips to get it done."

"Okay. Get her to Austria. But we'll have to pay for Le Pic."

"Le Pic?"

"Guy I know. Out of Corsica. His favorite tool is a stiletto. Not a thug. Very smooth, very continental. The kind of guy who follows you into a revolving door and ends up coming out in front. He'll blend in with our crowd. We'll figure a way to make it happen to Napolitani." He cracked his gum again. "This time, it'll be expensive. If the accident blows up somehow, it'll be obvious Le Pic did the job, so we need to have a cover story."

Nick smiled. "Maybe Napolitani's hacker friends have connections. She must have pissed some of them off."

Ross squinted, thinking.

"I've got a better one. The thirty-k bonus is set up in an account at Quantitec, right?"

Nick nodded.

"So, say Napolitani's nosing around ZCG. Maybe she finds out about the account. She confronts Mayfield. There's a big blowup—we still have the recording of her talking to him about 'moral compass' back when his implant was transmitting, don't we?—and Mayfield decides to protect his investment. Maybe our investigation then discloses what he's been doing. We, being good corporate citizens, fire Mayfield and express our utter embarrassment that one of our own did such a thing. Mayfield, in his agony, hangs himself or … I'm sure you can figure something out."

Nick took out his gum and rolled it into a ball, thinking.

"Good idea," he said and tossed the ball onto the grass.

***

Joe left the hospital after three days with strict orders to stay off his feet for another three. He had called his parents to say he was okay; they didn't have to make the trip from Illinois. He heard more relief than concern. They hadn't been close since he left for college and they moved back to Illinois to be near his sisters and their expanding crew of grandchildren.

Weezy stayed for three days, fending off offers of help, working from his kitchen table while he slept. Eric stopped by daily. Felicity and Charlie Gray came bearing gifts of food and wine. Mrs. Gagliardi checked on them often. She was polite, but disapproval of the living arrangement and likely violation of one if not several of the seven deadly sins was written on her face. But after a couple of days and Weezy's compliment about her five-hour sauce, Mrs. Gagliardi started calling her a "nice Italian girl."

"Joe," Weezy said after he had politely turned down yet another of Mrs. Gagliardi's offered dinners, "take the food. To an Italian family, food is love. She saved your life, and she wants you to love her for that."

"Saved my life?

"She was watching the street from her front window when you turned the corner." Sure, Joe thought, remembering the lighted window. "She yelled at the bad guys, called 911. She saved you. How did you think you got to the hospital?"

"I … I don't remember much."

"If Mrs. Gagliardi hadn't interrupted them, there would have been another slash, Joe. They'd have killed you." Seeing Joe's shocked look, she held up five fingers. "Dumbass cop thinks it was a robbery attempt. But they didn't get your wallet. Five percent, Joe. Five percent. The cops may not be able to draw the logical conclusion from their own data, but I can."

"I … I can't imagine why anybody …"

"Something's wrong, Joe."

Is she paranoid? Joe lay back into the daybed, feeling spaced out, hearing his dad's voice. Alligators. What did Dad say? When you're up to your ass in alligators, it's damn hard to remember your objective was to drain the swamp. Bits and pieces of what he'd learned over the last month circled. Like alligators. Weezy had to be right. Gotta drain the swamp.

***

On the last day of Weezy's visit, she took Joe on his first walk outside. He felt as if the whole street was watching. The story had gotten around. Mrs. Gagliardi's son, Tony Jr., sat in his usual spot on an upturned plastic pail in front of the parking lot across the street and smoked an electronic replica of a guinea stinker. He nodded at the pair as they made their slow progress up the street. Mr. Bellanti looked up from his work table as Joe passed in front of his shop, then went back to tinkering with a decades-old robot vacuum cleaner. A woman Joe didn't know smiled at him as she passed.

Joe had a sudden rush of feeling. This was *his* neighborhood now.

Weezy left for Penn Station mid-afternoon. Joe was settling in for a nap when a knock at the door roused him. He shuffled to the door, put his eye to the peephole. Tony Gagliardi, Jr. stood in the hall, the fisheye lens accenting his five-foot-nine, 240-pound frame. Imposing, but not scary. Probably bringing instructions or questions from his mom.

Joe opened the door, and Tony held up a small bag.

"Ma thought you'd like a cannoli."

A dark spot on the bag promised fresh-made goodness.

"Uhh, sure. Thanks."

"Too bad about those guys hurtin' you."

An opening line, not a conclusion. Joe stepped aside. "You want a coffee?"

Tony came in. "Nah. Thanks."

He gave a little shrug with his hands, a quick opening upward, neighborhood sign language translating to "It doesn't really matter to the world in general, but …" or "this is a little embarrassing, but …"

"These guys what hurt you. They weren't neighborhood guys."

"No?" Joe said. Where was this was going?

"But you got somebody pissed off at you. Somebody who doesn't know you don't do that kinda business in this neighborhood. Not ever."

The story Joe had heard…and discounted…that the neighborhood was quiet because so many of the families were "connected" came back to him. Or maybe the pain pills were shredding his logic.

"The police couldn't identify the guys from the security camera pictures, so how—"

"Yeah," Tony sniffed. "We know who they are."

"But if the police …"

"We got better eyes." Tony tapped a stubby finger on his temple. "Anyway," he shrugged. "Those guys won't be back. Ever."

"You didn't kill…"

"Nah. That don't make no sense." Tony looked the patient teacher. "Then they'd just disappear and there'd be no, whaddya call it?" He cracked a half smile. "Teachable moment. You know, to all the other guys that might wanna do bad things in the neighborhood. Curb job's better."

"Curb job?"

"Yeah. Y'now, put a guy's jaw on a curb, stomp on his head. Twenty grand of dental work, he drinks through a straw for a long time. Reminds people they shouldn't bring their dirty business to the neighborhood."

Tony paused, his eyes hardened, "You oughta fix whatever problems you got."

Joe was shaking his head No. "I just moved here. No problems, really."

"Oh, you got problems. You wanna stay here, you better fix 'em."

# TWENTY-ONE

WEEZY ARRIVED IN Bethesda anxious to dig further into the RedSock data. She had spent most of her time in New York caring for Joe; now, she had time and secure Wi-Fi.

She took a seat in her overstuffed chair with a cup of tea and rotated her head to loosen muscles cramped by tension and the train ride. When her headache began to wane, she signed into the Olegarten chat room and checked her message board. No message waiting from HoHum. No "Boogie lo and slo?" Surprising, because he checked in often, sometimes a little too often. Must be on a consulting trip.

The decrypts were almost complete, but the picture they painted was not clear. There were the legal documents and transactions she'd seen before. While she was in New York, DingDing had sent a note with the header "Chess Moves." But the note added nothing valuable. "All end-game moves. Seems like they're arbitrary, maybe from different games. Or a code of some sort."

She began sorting through cryptic messages to Ramos Security from RedSock originating from a Brian Garrity. The messages sounded like physical security rather than computer issues. Talk of guards and physical layouts, a discussion several months ago of Chitty liking little girls. Puzzling. Maybe HoHum could make sense of them.

Garrity turned out to be a lower-level trading guy at a small retail broker, not RedSock, but he was listed as Managing Director in RedSock documents. She googled Ramos Security. Its website site offered physical security and "cutting edge data protection." Offices in New York, Johannesburg, London and Dubai. Interesting.

A soft ping on Weezy's e-pad announced

`HoHum to Hotcakes`
`Nihow`

*No "Wanna boogie lo and slo?"*

She tapped out: `Nihow. What do you make of the RedSock decrypts I sent?`

She expected video to come up and wondered which of his five T-shirts HoHum was wearing. But all she got was text.

`Haven't had a chance to look at them in detail.`

Odd. He was usually obsessive about this stuff.

Weezy reported DingDing's comments on chess moves and the cryptic messages to Ramos Security. Another text response: Thanks for the input.

"Thanks for the input." From HoHum?

`You going corporate on me?`

He came back a little too quickly.

`Just finished a seminar. Anyway, nothing to report here. I'll look at RedSock and get back to you.`

Then he signed off. No banter. No joking offers of matrimony. He never had stepped out of character before. Maybe some personal problem?

Still in the Olegarten chat room, she tapped:

`Jake, you out there?`

Jake's video came up almost immediately. A sprightly older woman. Still the lovely white hair. The neatly kept kitchen and the "Gramma Rocks" coffee mug seared into social media memory as a result of Jake's part in the exposure of Phoenix a year earlier.

"Hotcakes … I guess I can call you Louise now … how are you? Are you in, what is it? Panacea?"

"No. Back home near Bethesda. I was wondering, have you talked with HoHum lately?"

Jake looked pained. "You haven't heard?"

"What?"

"Herman was … Herman was killed in a farm accident."

A leaden silence. Weezy's shoulders slumped. The headache came back full force.

"No."

"It was a farm accident, Louise. Happened about a week ago. There's a long article in the Grand Island, Nebraska paper." Jake reached to tap her e-pad. "Here, I'm sending it. I talked with his mother … I'm planning to go out and see her. He was a brilliant man." Jake paused to remove her glasses and pinch her nose.

Somebody else was pretending …

"Ohmygod, I got him killed."

Jake ran her hand down her cheek. "Nothing to do with Olegarten, Louise. A bale of hay fell on him."

"A farm accident?" Weezy pictured HoHum in his cave full of gear.

"Yes."

Rage surged. *Accident, my ass!*

"Have you had any contact with anyone trying to use HoHum?"

"No one would dare co-opt his handle."

"Well, someone has. I just got off the line with a HoHum lookalike."

Jake's mouth hung open. "In Olegarten?"

"Yes. I called you because the conversation was odd. He sounded … umm … corporate and didn't use video, which is unusual—"

"Because he's infatuated with you and always wants video. Yes, I know."

Weezy felt tears stinging her eyes and blinked.

Jake squared her shoulders. "We'll have to grab whoever it is whenever they come in again. I'll see to it."

"Sure. I—"

Jake interrupted. "There's going to be a public webcast about him. Here, I'll give you the address. If you joined and said something, it would mean a great deal to all of us and to his mother."

"Of course. Of course I will."

How would anyone know to track HoHum?

*I am going to find the sonofabitch who did this, and …*

***

Joe startled awake. How long had he slept? The stitches over his collarbone itched. His left hand tingled, caught at an odd angle to allow a semi-comfortable position on the daybed. He shifted his butt, causing a stab of pain to rise from his lower back.

Problems.

Ever since Tony Jr. said, "You got problems," the threat of that unknown had been on his mind. How the hell was he supposed to solve problems if he didn't know what they were? And what about Braithwaite's interest in his implant? Felicity's warning not to look too deeply into how ZCG makes its money? Weezy's suspicions?

He rolled to his side and sat up slowly.

Weezy had left him yesterday with detailed instructions about taking it easy, worry in her eyes. She had hugged Mrs. Gagliardi, now completely won over. Mrs. Gagliardi checked on him every couple of hours, each time reminding him of several of the items on Weezy's list. Today, finally, he was coming out of the fog caused by the painkillers. Beginning to worry. Eric had called earlier "to check in" but Joe heard hope that he'd return sooner rather than later. The Vienna trip was less than three weeks away. So much to do. But Tony's "you got problems" hung over him.

Joe stood. The pain was receding. For the first time, he didn't feel dizzy.

He made a cup of coffee and pulled out a biscotti that came from the bakery a couple of blocks away.

Tony was telling him the mugging wasn't random. Only the cop thought that, and he was blinded by experience.

Joe dunked the biscotti, bit off a piece and was back in Orlando and those months before Cynthia died. He had believed the MedRecords issue was some sort of mistake when he knew in his heart something was terribly wrong.

He was not going to do that again.

Joe picked up his e-pa d and called Weezy.

***

Weezy was assembling pieces. Like those antique wooden puzzles her grandmother had that drove you crazy because there was no picture on the box. At some point, though, you'd get enough pieces in place and the picture would click. Finishing the rest was a lot easier.

Someone figured out HoHum was hacking for her and had traced conversations back. In the course of a very hot, very long shower, she constructed how it must have been done.

She was drying her hair when her e-pad chimed. It was Joe, sitting on his daybed. "I've been thinking about the Skins issue and …"

He stopped and brought his face close.

"What's wrong, Weezy?"

Warmth spread over her. He had read her so well.

"HoHum …"

Her voice caught in her throat.

Joe's brow knit. "What about him?"

"HoHum's dead."

"My god! How?"

"They said it was a farm accident, but it wasn't. It was because of RedSock, Joe. I'm sure of it. You were supposed to be next." She was rushing her words, voice hitching, on the verge of sobbing. "It all makes sense now."

Joe shook his head, as if trying to dislodge something painful.

"Why HoHum?"

"I asked him to help me look at RedSock. Joe, it's owned by Ross Ackerman and his wife in trust for a family out in Iowa."

Joe rocked back from his screen but followed with a half-shrug.

"Which is not too unusual," he said slowly, "for a financially successful family to—"

"Sure. Let me finish. RedSock invests in the high-risk pieces of Skins, which may be odd, but—"

"Yeah, really odd," Joe said. "They'd most likely go for conservative—"

"Right. But the interesting part is RedSock has made multiple millions because—guess what—they invested right before an impossible to predict event happened. Like the strongman and copper or the chromium mine catastrophe."

"Jesus!"

Silence for a long moment. Realization and then fear washed across Joe's face.

"Yeah," Weezy said. "I started looking because I couldn't make the numbers work. I asked you about pricing and you found out exorbitant fees nobody wants to explain are built into the high-risk tranches, right?"

Joe nodded.

"Then you got your implant and someone started monitoring it."

"Or there was some glitch, some mistake." Joe said, but without conviction.

"Uh-huh. Right." Weezy kept rolling. "So then I go to HoHum and he discovers much more. Then the assassination attempt they wanted to look like a robbery."

*"They?"*

She shook off the question.

"When I tried to contact HoHum last night, he sounded odd."

"Odd? How so?" Joe looked like he was having trouble following. Maybe the painkillers, she thought, and slowed down.

"You remember 'boogie lo and slo' and all that? Anyway, last night HoHum came off like a stuffed shirt and didn't want to go on video … *very* unlike him. Then … then I found out about the accident, and I know—" her voice began to tremble, "the last time I supposedly talked with him, he was already dead."

There was a silence as Joe digested.

"Whoever's doing this knows," he said.

"Right."

"The only question is *who.*"

Weezy tilted her head. "Surely Ackerman. Not sure about anyone else. Might be the whole damn company."

Joe grimaced. "There's got to be someone doing the dirty work. Not Ackerman. Tony Gagliardi says the guys that did me were 'very bad guys' and that I 'got problems' I need to fix.

Remind me to tell you how Tony fixes *his* problems." Then a smile. "How about you do your famous, mysterious tracker riff on Ackerman? I seem to remember you were tempted to ruin his life data-wise, so you must be able—"

"I'm sort of hogtied," Weezy said. "Keith, my dumbass boss, shut down the project I wanted to start, so I can't use the system. Until I told you about this, Keith, HoHum, and an SEC contact of Keith's were the only people who knew about it." She paused, gave a quick shake of her head. "I can't imagine Keith is part of some sort of conspiracy, but his contact at the SEC might be. That's the only way I can see how anyone might have gotten suspicious of HoHum or me. Unless HoHum stumbled."

"Stumbled?"

"Got seen by someone or some software. Very unlikely."

"Maybe we shouldn't be talking so openly?"

Weezy considered. "Probably okay through your home feed because HoHum's scan showed no problem. Also, I check my home feed every day. But to be safe, maybe nothing electronic for now. And when we're anywhere that could be monitored, we should have some sort of shorthand."

"Shorthand? You mean code words?"

"Yeah. Like, say, 'heightened awareness' to say 'let's find a safe place to talk.' "

"Good idea," Joe said. But his face held a look she couldn't quite read.

"Weezy, don't ride to work tomorrow. Better yet, come stay with me."

"Joe, I can't do that. I'm busy. Besides, I'm gonna run these bad guys down."

"Weezy, can't you count?"

"What?"

"Three, Weezy, three. They got HoHum. They almost got me. You're number three."

***

Weezy thought about Joe's warning and took a U-callit cab to work the next day. When she arrived at N-Ops, she beelined to Keith Sanders' office. He was in a turf battle on video with an ex-military stuffed shirt at Homeland Security. He didn't immediately notice she had slipped in, taken a chair and now stared at him tight-lipped. He finished the conversation, signed off and turned to her.

She dove right in. "Did you tell anyone about the Political Exposure Unit project I wanted to start?"

Keith pushed back into his chair. "I did ask a contact at SEC if there were any open actions against the investment bank you mentioned. Z-something."

"Zhou, Cadwallon and Gordon."

"Yeah. She said it's a boutique bank specializing in risk management, no open actions." Then, "Louise, did you continue to work on that project?"

"On my own."

"You know it's SEC business, right?"

"I understand, Keith. Just a tip, though. This problem is not going to be solved by ever-so-polite Ivy League lawyers entering into Socratic debate on esoteric trading practices. The SEC won't fix this, Keith."

"Well, Louise, it's not within our purview."

"Got it." Her tongue curled as if she'd tasted something spoiled. "Not within our purview" she repeated.

"Louise, I don't want to leave this conversation up in the air. You're obviously upset. When you feel better, please come and talk to me."

Weezy pushed herself out of the chair. "When I feel better?" Her voice trembled. "Thanks, boss. Gotta go."

"Louise …" Keith's voice followed her as she left his office, shaking with rage.

Back at her console, she appeared to burrow into the backlog of work built up over her time in New York. Questions about the Romanian hackers and Cal Occult popped up on various monitors in the bullpen. The smokescreen worked with everyone but Maddie Hollingsworth.

A soft ping sounded on Weezy's console, accompanied by *Got a minute?*

In the break room, Weezy made a coffee, Maddie a tea.

"What's going on?" Maddie asked as they sat down.

Weezy stared into her cup, not knowing where to start or how much to say. Finally, "Joe's mugging probably wasn't an accident."

Maddie's hand went to her throat, her eyes wide.

"How do you know?"

"Because the attack was an outlier, Maddie. The vast majority of muggings in that neighborhood are young guys attacking a woman or older man. They don't use weapons, and they never go after a big guy like Joe. Cops may not be able to figure it out, but I can."

Maddie's nod encouraged her to continue.

"Remember HoHum?" Weezy said.

"Sure."

"He's dead."

Maddie gasped again.

"Supposedly a farm accident. I'd believe it, except someone's on the website where I meet my hacker friends posing as HoHum. Which means the website has been penetrated. It also means I've given away quite a bit about research I've been doing."

"Research?"

"How much do you know about derivatives?"

Maddie, it turned out, knew quite a bit. Her father lost a substantial portion of his "family money" in the real estate bubble in 2008.

Weezy told Maddie about her suspicions and the work HoHum had done on RedSock.

When she finished, Maddie asked, "What are you going to do?"

Weezy shook her head. "I don't know, Maddie. I can't use the IAC … I tried that and Keith nixed it."

Maddie's eyebrows drew together, indicating analysis in process.

"What were you trying to find out?"

"When I started," Weezy said, "I was just curious how this investment bank Joe works for makes all the money it does. The whole damn system hangs on someone buying the highest risk parts of the financial product they call Skins for prices no one should be willing to pay. Then I asked HoHum to help me out —" She paused to compose herself. "Two hedge funds buy most of the highest risk stuff. Looks as if they pay pretty high prices for them. Neither fund seems to be trying to protect a financial interest in some real project, and they're not hedging other financial exposures."

"So they're gambling, plain and simple," Maddie said. "And if they're paying very much for a scenario that's not too likely to happen, they're looking at a guaranteed loss over time, aren't they?"

"In a fair game."

"Right, in a fair game," Maddie said. Then she brightened. "Let me summarize, here. Your curiosity has been piqued because Joe's firm is selling these risk products to at least two fund managers who are incredibly stupid."

Finally, Weezy laughed, a welcome release after the last few days. Then, serious again, she said, "If the most recent purchases are any indication, they profit enormously. Do you remember reading about a revolution in Zambia? The strongman died unexpectedly, and the country came unglued."

"A couple of months ago?"

"Yup. Well, these two little hedge funds happened to hold Skins insuring against political unrest relating to copper production. Zambia is an important copper producer. So, when the strongman died, the price of copper went nuts and the African currency unit did some wobbles that wrecked a pretty big group of speculators."

"Maybe those two investors are extraordinarily clever outliers?" Maddie's raised eyebrows said skeptical.

Weezy nodded. "Ordinarily, I'd say you're probably right, but both funds are tied to ZCG. Without full access to the financial system, I could only look at patterns of purchases, not pricing. But the timing of their trades in the Copper Skin barely skirted the SEC's trading rules." She leaned toward Maddie.

"They knew about what was going to happen."

***

Weezy and Maddie had tossed around ideas for a few minutes more but in the end had come to no conclusion about what to do. No matter how logical the case, they had only suspicions. They had gone back to their workstations.

An hour later, Maddie appeared at Weezy's desk.

"There's what we know," she said, "there's what we need to know, and there's puttin' it together. Looked at that way, the solution's simple. What we know makes us suspicious. Between the two of us, we have plenty enough horsepower to do the puttin' together. But there are some things we still need to know, and we can't get at them because we're not authorized to look at financial transactions in detail."

Weezy nodded. Obvious.

"You remember the FBI guy down in Orlando?" Maddie said. "The one who really solved the murder the Phoenix guys did to cover up the MedRecords scam last year?"

"Sure. Henry Barber."

"Wasn't he some kind of numbers guy? Fancy accounting. That sort of thing?"

*Of course. Why didn't I think of that?*

"We've got two thirds of the problem on the run, and we need to solve the 'what we need to know' part. I bet the FBI—"

Weezy opened a window on her monitor and said, "Henry Barber. Video."

"—has access to the financial section of the IAC."

The picture came up. Same friendly face, tie not knotted, suit looked as if it had been slept in.

"Mr. Barber, you may remember me."

Barber seemed at a loss for a moment, then said, "Of course I do, Ms. Napolitani. Phoenix, right?"

"Good to find you," Weezy said. "I didn't know you'd moved to DC. A good thing, it sounds like from your title."

"Well, higher on the org chart. And, yes, a good thing. More interesting cases."

"I … we … need some advice on how to proceed with a … situation." Weezy panned the picture to include Maddie. "This is my associate, Madeline Hollingsworth. I think you met her last year."

"I did. Of course I remember."

"We have an issue with possible financial manipulation," Weezy said. "Not precisely hacking, and it needs someone who can make sense of financial transactions. We thought of you …"

Weezy went on to outline Skins, the transactions with RedSock and her suspicions. Finally, "I wouldn't have run into this except Joe Mayfield—"

"Panacea, Florida. Sure, you and he in that trailer they were going to torch."

"—went to work for ZCG—"

"And your intuition tells you something's fishy." A smile crinkled Henry's face. "That's enough for me, given your history. Why don't you send me the particulars, and I'll take a look."

# TWENTY-TWO

ERIC O'MALLEY DISCONNECTED from Ross Ackerman.

First, he wanted to fire Mayfield and had a temper tantrum when he learned Joe was going to Vienna. Now he put him in the trading bonus pool without asking and suggested... well, demanded ... that Joe bring his lady friend along.

The about-face made no sense, but Eric didn't spend a lot of time speculating about Ackerman's inner feelings. He knew a bunch of people like him at Princeton. The vestigial tail of the Old Boy network. Didn't want to talk to the big football player from Milwaukee. As far as Eric could tell, they didn't have inner feelings to speak of. But the abrupt change was, well, curious.

Eric was spending the day in his Jersey office, ostensibly to write a report but mainly because he liked the Jersey side better than Manhattan. There, he could roll up his sleeves, draw on the energy of the new bankers, and eat hot dogs (extra sauerkraut) rather than sushi.

He made a trip to the men's room in order to walk past Joe's cubicle and say, seemingly as an afterthought, "Joe, can you give me a few minutes?"

When Joe appeared, Eric said, "Glad I caught you. Say, when I mentioned the Vienna trip the other day, I should have been clear that most of us take spouses. I hope you can bring Ms. Napolitani. You cover the transportation, but we do everything else."

Joe looked surprised.

"Can I speak candidly?"

They both smiled at the formality. "Sure."

"Eric, I understand why I was chosen to go. I think most of my friends here know why, too. But there were some hurt feelings because others who are more senior and more successful aren't being taken."

"I appreciate your sensitivity, Joe, but everybody should know the drill. Business is business. If a guy from Montana likes fishing and wants to see you there, you're going to be there. Besides, Ross specifically mentioned Ms. Napolitani. Apparently she was a hit with Emily Ackerman, and we're all looking forward to seeing her … except maybe Rolf." A broad smile. "Anyway, it's a good time. She'll be an addition. See if you can get her to join us."

***

Later that day, Weezy's console chimed, announcing a call from Joe.

She redirected the call to her e-pad and walked out to the courtyard.

"You alone?" she said.

"I am." He panned his pad to show a small park surrounded by a black wrought iron fence. A woman and a man sat on the grass, incongruous in their business suits.

"Remember that I asked you about meeting after Vienna?"

"Sure."

"It turns out they want … I mean, it's usual …" then, in a rush, "I mean, I want you to come with me. To the meeting itself."

"Gee, a heartfelt invitation." A half smile.

"You know what I mean. It's a beautiful city, I'm told. There will be a trip down the Danube to Budapest. Then maybe Tuscany on the way home. Eric said Emily Ackerman asked after you specifically."

"I barely met her."

"You apparently made an impression."

Weezy grimaced. "Sounds bogus to me, Joe. More like, 'let's get 'em together and make another accident happen.' A twofer. Maybe there's a fancier term in assassination-speak."

"I had the same thought when O'Malley asked me, but I'm pretty sure he is not part of this. It *is* normal for the US folks to bring wives …" he smiled, "and I guess that means a personal guru in my case."

He stopped to mull over something.

"What?" Weezy, impatient.

"Honestly, Weezy, I was sorting through my motives. I don't want to leave you for almost two weeks. You're so damn tough and brave, you're going to blow these guys off—whoever they are—and keep on poking their hornet's nest. And get hurt. Completely irrational on my part, of course. How am I going to protect you?

He shrugged. "Then there's the ulterior motive: I want to draft on you."

"Draft on me?"

"You know, bask in reflected light of your brilliance." Joe said. "Have everybody thinking, 'That Mayfield is some kinda guy, having a woman like her.' "

Weezy chuckled and said to an imaginary audience, "Accountant-turned-investment banker tries out his new-found skills on girlfriend and gets …" her grin turned impish and she tapped her finger on her chin "… hmmm, what do you think he gets?"

Then she remembered the chop on the trust document. E-line-corkscrew. Ackerman's leer. HoHum. The mugging.

Bet your sweet ass I'm going.

"Joe, you're right, but for the wrong reasons. Both of us have to go. We're gonna smoke these bad guys out."

***

Emily Ackerman woke with a start. Where was she?

Morning light poured in, illuminating clutter and scattered clothes.

Arty's loft in SoHo.

Arty slept, snoring softly. Not handsome in repose. She tried to feel guilty, but only succeeded in feeling angry at Ross. He let this happen.

When she'd called Arty a couple of months ago, he had answered the same day. She could tell he was flattered, maybe because it was the boss's wife calling, maybe something more. Their first meeting was for coffee. She explained her confusion about the trusts and said she probably didn't see the whole picture but would Arty help her understand it? Confidentially?

Arty gave a long dissertation on trading practices. Emily wasn't put off by the smoke he was blowing; it made him even more appealing than he had been through the vodka-induced fog at the party.

During the second coffee, Emily learned that the Copper Skin had cashed out about nineteen million. Which meant the reports Ross gave her were dummied up for her benefit—he was willing to lie to her outright. He'd been evasive and occasionally nasty in the past but had never before lied outright. Seventeen million had gone into the trust accounts, a sliver to Brian Garrity, Managing Director (on paper) of RedSock. The rest, nearly two million, went to Ross. Ross called it "walking around money," according to Arty. It never appeared in the joint account at home.

By the third meeting, this time in a trendy wine bar, Emily came to understand that Arty desired her, a feeling which pleased her.

The fourth meeting started with vodka and progressed to Arty's loft, where Emily learned she was indeed desirable and capable of some wet, delicious activities she had nearly forgotten and several she had not experienced before. In the aftermath, Arty traced a finger over her nose to her lips, smiled and said, "I'm your back door man." She looked at him quizzically. "The guy who goes out the back door when the husband's coming in the front," he said. "Howlin' Wolf sang about it. Great bluesman."

The fifth meeting produced a clear understanding that Arty could move funds from the Sint Maarten bank where the trusts were held and introduced Emily to cocaine.

Last night was the sixth meeting. Ross was "out of town," most likely carrying on his own extramarital activities. Arty didn't have to be a back door man. They had dinner in a SoHo bistro. At his place, after cocaine and delicious sex, they hatched the plan. Only speculative at first, feeling each other out. Would she be willing to leave Ross for a life in Europe? Would he be happy to live a quiet life in, say, Iowa?

# TWENTY-THREE

Joe and Weezy had arrived in Vienna separately and checked into the Hotel im Palais Schwarzenberg. The hotel was a *Schloss*, a citified castle without the walls. It had become a hotel, run into hard times, been bought by a French conglomerate and restored to its former glory. Their room was huge, larger than Joe's apartment in New York. It had an expansive sitting area on the ground floor and stairs that led to a balcony with a bed. The bed was elegant and uncomfortable, but the view from the floor-to-ceiling windows over the eighteen-acre private park was spectacular. Even the cosseted investment bankers found this sort of old-world elegance impressive.

Joe watched Weezy balancing on an ornate chair, inspecting a wall-mounted light fixture. "This beautiful place gives me heightened awareness about the value of old things," he said, using the code phrase they had agreed on three weeks earlier. He grimaced at how stilted it sounded.

Weezy blew into the fixture, producing a cloud of dust, and stepped down from the chair. "Let's take a walk."

Ever since Weezy had left Joe to recuperate in New York, they had abided by their decision to not talk openly. It had been hard for Joe. He wished Weezy was more disturbed by having to forego the daily conversations that had been so important after the mugging.

They strolled in silence down a perfectly kept gravel path amidst ornamental shrubs. Muted traffic sounds reminded Joe of the city, but espaliered evergreens made the park a world of its own.

"The concierge says the ravens are part of the hotel's history," Joe said, nodding at the birds tut-tutting to each other on the lawn. "Been here since the eighteenth century. Sounds like they're gossiping about us." He took Weezy's hand. She gave it, but it felt cold, dry. At the far end of the path, they sat on a filigreed cast iron bench, more comfortable than it looked.

"I doubt anybody can eavesdrop on us in the hotel," Joe said.

"Let's be conservative."

"Okay, but I want to hear what Barber has. You've been pretty close-mouthed. What's he told you?"

"Not much." Weezy said. "He didn't want any of my data. He's following the legal process carefully to make sure, as he said, 'some fancy lawyer can't get my conclusions thrown out over a technicality.' "

"I thought HoHum got some good stuff before they, uhh —"

"Before the rat bastards killed him." Weezy stopped, swallowed and continued, her voice thick. "He found about twenty hedge funds trading in and out of Skins all the time. Mostly the medium risk levels. They must end up losing a percent or so in transaction costs. They're probably protecting their commodity and currency portfolios. The thing is, they never hold for long."

She cocked her head. "Then there's RedSock. They buy the highest risk tranches of Skins and hold 'em. A prescription for financial disaster, except with three Skins ZCG has put together over the last several years something totally unexpected happened."

She paused. A young couple strolled on a path a few yards away. They walked slowly, speaking German, laughing. Weezy waited until they were out of earshot, looking maybe a little defiant. Joe nodded to encourage her.

"Several years ago, a well-armed rebel group appeared out of nowhere in Mali," she said. "It disrupted the African Currency Unit just as it was getting off the ground. Earlier this year, the chaos with copper in Zambia. And now, that riot and explosion in South Africa. I mean, RedSock seems like a brilliant planner of outliers."

Joe listened to Weezy, but recent events kept intruding, shaping the story. The meeting with Ackerman and the bonus pool. The "mistake" with the implant, closely followed by Braithwaite's "test" of it. The concern about data security. The mugging and Tony's warning. The sudden inclusion of Weezy in the Vienna trip.

"One hit is good luck," Weezy said with a grimace. "But three in a row? You don't have to have Martin Docherty's fancy econometric models to see that somebody knew bad things were about to happen."

Joe said slowly, "If you can foresee the worst case scenario, you can protect against it. That's what we always tell clients."

The silence was broken only by the ravens' tut-tutting.

He finished the thought, "But if you can make the worst case happen …" He shivered. "Oh, crap. Kazakh Skin."

***

The next morning, Joe woke early after sleeping fitfully, only partly a result of the uncomfortable bed. "Must have been original equipment with this place," Weezy grumped as they both tried to get comfortable. They had stayed in the garden until dusk, trying to figure next steps. The Kazakh Skin itself was perfectly legal, designed to meet a business need. With no support from the FBI, there was no point in accusing anyone. Anyway, who would they accuse? All they had was suspicion.

The first scheduled event of the morning was a meeting to introduce ZCG's US staff and European affiliates. Joe found the reception hall down a long corridor. The room must have remembered the days of the Empire: liveried servants and string quartets playing Strauss waltzes. It must have been insulted by the severely modern conference table and straight back chairs invading the rococo gilding and elegant fabrics.

Joe found his place card midway down the table. He was seated between a senior New York colleague he'd met a couple of times and a German woman whose business card introduced her as Magister LaDonna Ginzberg. She provided a severe smile, then turned away to have an animated conversation with a European confederate.

At the head of the table, Ross Ackerman stood and cleared his throat. Conversation ceased.

"We all know why we're here. I want you to mingle, use your connections. Remind every potential client of what happened with copper and chromium."

Sure. Scare 'em, Joe thought, trying to keep the disgust he felt bottled up. The more they buy, the more you stand to profit.

Ross looked around the room, giving Joe a little smirk. Of recognition?

Apparently reassured that everyone took his meaning, Ross continued, "You all have examples of what it cost Morgan RioTinto to cover its exposure in Zambia and how that played out. Martin Docherty is available, but choose who you introduce carefully. He's a limited resource, and he'll bore the crap out of most CEO's."

Beside Joe, Ginzberg whispered "bore the crap out of" and checked the e-pad in her lap. He caught the words "Bohrung? gebar? die Scheiße aus."

Ross yielded to Eric O'Malley, who stood and beamed at the group. "First off, thank you all for being here," he said, offering the welcome Ackerman should have started with. "You will make this conference a success for ZCG." Joe felt the room warm and relax. Eric continued, "All the companies here are dealing with political risk at some level. You have lists of the people that should be … strike that … will be interested in the new Kazakh Skin. The Kazakh government has made it clear that they're open for business, and there are about a dozen valuable resources there. But it's a troubled area. We've developed this new Skin, the next generation of the single-commodity Skins we built our reputation on. We see tremendous potential for this broader-based product." He paused, picked up a sheet of paper.

"We have several activities planned. Invite potential clients to any of them you like … let Stacey know who they are." He looked toward Stacey Cheung, seated next to him.

Stacey stood and said, "There are visits to the museums, the Spanish Riding School and a special performance of the Lippizan stallions. There's a walking tour of the inner city and a tour of the cathedral." She smiled. "Mention to the Americans you invite that the Europeans mean serious walking, so be prepared. Finally, most of us will gather here on Thursday evening for a shuttle to the Donau König, which will take us overnight to Budapest. The trip will give you the opportunity to talk with potential clients over dinner. You'll find all of this and the schedule for the activities in Budapest on your e-pads."

As the meeting broke, Joe got a stiff handshake from LaDonna Ginzberg. Nick Braithwaite had slipped into the room while Stacey was speaking and was now listening to Ross. He nodded, his eyes on Joe. Joe returned his stare. Why was the security guy at a financial conference? What were they planning for Weezy and him?

# TWENTY-FOUR

ON THE THIRD day of the conference, Ross Ackerman spent a boring morning listening to several depressing reports on the state of world mineral reserves. All in all, encouraging. The more nervous people were, the more Skins they would buy. As the meeting broke, he was drawn into a conversation with a low-level representative of a Latin American conglomerate. She was pretty, so Ross was polite. He heard a tap come in from Povreshenko, which he ignored. It took a couple of minutes to determine there was no sale to be had and no chance the woman was interested extracurricular activities. Ross pointed her toward the other side of the auditorium, where a coterie of European bankers and ZCG customers surrounded O'Malley. Eric smiled at Ross and gave a thumbs up. What was that about?

Ross walked into the foyer and glanced at his e-pad. No message. He looked around the open area. A few people clustered around the coffee stand, but it was quiet where he stood. He took out his e-pad, tapped, and said, "Arty Pov."

The phone line clicked a couple of times, reminding Ross he was not in New York. Then Arty appeared.

"Good news, boss. A big slice of the midrange of the Kazakh Skin went to Morgan Rio Tinto. Order came through regular channels." That's why Eric was upbeat. "Want me to speed up the RedSock buys?"

"How much are we in already?"

"Eight hundred k, starting small early May. Tracking the Kazakh currency, so it looks like a simple trader's bet and cover."

"Okay," Ross said. "Braithwaite got the think tank article on Kazakh instability released, so I think we need to amp it up. We may have only a few more safe days. I'd like to be completely out of the market for at least twenty days before the underlying derivatives begin to mature."

Arty nodded. "Gotcha." He cocked his head, like there was more to say. Ross was about to press him, but he was in a hurry. Never know about a cokehead.

They disconnected, and Ross glanced around the foyer again and said, "Braithwaite."

Another couple of clicks, then Braithwaite's brusque, "Leave a message."

Ross put in a high priority tap. "Park across from the conference, fifteen minutes." A couple of minutes later he got a tap, "Half an hour." No explanation. Braithwaite was less deferential since the mugging fuck up. That problem could wait until later.

***

Ross strolled the Stadtpark across from the conference. Bankers and politicians filtered in and out. As usual, Braithwaite appeared without Ross having seen him approach. Always the spook.

"Where have you been?"

"Setting up systems on the ship." Conversation with Nick was annoying because he treated all information as secret, even trivial details.

"And this guy Le Pic, where's he?" Ross asked, letting his aggravation show.

Nick stared him down.

"He'll be on board when we leave." Then, "You should get ready to pull the trigger on Mayfield, too. Give your PR firm the story now. Make it vague—suspected insider trading, the firm's security staff looking into it, that kind of stuff. Get them working on a draft." Braithwaite said. "Be sure to tell them to contact the FBI. They'll want you to hold off until just before the release. Agree to hold, but you will have put down a marker."

"Releasing that chaff we talked about, huh?" Ross said. "You see a missile coming?"

Braithwaite gave him a flat stare. "Planning ahead."

A couple people walked past, discussing the conference. Ross watched them stroll out of earshot, then turned to Nick. "When is the Kazakh project going down?"

"A month, three months outside."

"Jesus, Nick. Could you be a little more vague?"

His barb didn't seem to upset the big man as much as it should. Which goaded Ross to ping again.

"Seems like you need to get your ducks in a row."

"My ducks are in the best row they can get in Kazakhstan." The steel-eyed stare was contempt, Ross realized.

"I need a better timeline to be able to—"

"—Make your Skins purchases without raising suspicions at the SEC." Nick finished the thought, further irritating Ross. "You should purchase at least sixty percent of what you intend next week."

Goddamn, this muscle-bound security guy was giving trading instructions?

Ross tried to control his anger. "I'll do the trading; you do the security." Then, knowing he was talking down, "You see, the SEC algorithm looks at consistency. Best way to beat it is to buy the same amount over an extended period."

"No."

Ross's blood rose. Don't lose control in front of this troglodyte.

"No," Nick repeated. "That's the way it works for stock options and stock sales, but the SEC algorithms for this kind of trading are event-related. Haven't you studied them?"

"I didn't major in statistics, dickhead." But "dickhead" pushed it too far. Ross tried a disarming smile and saw Nick will himself back into control.

"So, what should we do, Einstein?"

"Buy heavily right now. Prices of the commodities where Kazakhstan is strong in have been coming down for a couple of weeks. There'll be a dead cat bounce in a week or so. Lighten up the protection then and wait for the inevitable correction. Then buy heavily again. The algorithms will assume you're a stupid trader."

Ross was unsure how to respond. Braithwaite always seemed to have deeper knowledge than he expected.

"Gotta get back to the conference," Ross said.

The next morning, Ross's message was waiting on Arty's monitor. Looking at the detailed plan, he thought, "Damn, Ross knows his stuff."

***

The spouses sat gratefully in a hotel coffee shop on Stephansplatz, having spent the afternoon walking considerably farther than most expected to. Emily Ackerman excused herself. "I have to check on my Uncle Silas back in Iowa. He's recovering from pneumonia."

The hotel's coffee shop opened onto a pedestrian mall lined with small, exclusive shops. Emily called Arty's private phone, hanging up after two rings, their code for "call me back." She occupied herself examining shop window displays and listening to a brass trio costumed in the colors of some little town in the Alps. The group reminded her of happy Iowa summers and polka bands. Five minutes later, her phone buzzed and she saw

Arty, the angularity of his features magnified by the e-pad's wide-angle lens. He sat in what looked like a brown box, no desk in front of him, no monitors.

"Where are you?"

"My office."

"That doesn't look like the trading floor."

"Men's room. Private. Like I said, my office." He chuckled.

"I miss you," Emily said, the memory of past pleasures and the promise of future ones in three words.

Arty looked a little embarrassed.

"Anyway, glad you called," he said. "The project is about to heat up. I'll be buying a lot of the Skin into the trusts over the next two weeks. When are you getting back?"

"We're scheduled to fly home after the weekend."

"Okay. I know you're getting on a boat to go to Budapest. We shouldn't talk on the boat at all … too easy to monitor when you're all cooped up. Call me after you land. I should know about timing by then." He paused for a moment. "You may have to pull the trigger on distribution from over there. Do you think you can do that?"

"I'm sure I can," she said, hoping it was true.

"Hang in there," Arty said. Did he see her hesitation? Could he see her biggest question: Do I want to?

# TWENTY-FIVE

EARLIER IN THE day, Weezy broke away from the social activities to go off on her own. She left a note in the hotel room for Joe and walked to the Kartnerstrasse, far enough from the hotel to be private amid city bustle. She found a secluded bench where she could make a video call.

"Maddie, anything new on the ZCG business?"

Maddie took a sip of coffee. Weezy realized it was before nine in the morning in Bethesda.

"Yes. I got a lot more data on Mali, the copper problem and chromium. You want the short story or the long one?"

A young woman with a baby in a stroller sat down on the next bench. Weezy signaled to Maddie to hold. The woman began a singsong, one-sided conversation with the baby, speaking one of the Slavic languages. The baby gurgled and laughed, and the woman picked her up, glancing at Weezy with a smile.

"Better give me the short one," Weezy said.

"The Mali disturbance could be a lucky guess on the part of RedSock, but it's likely they had advance knowledge of the copper issue in Zambia and the chromium catastrophe in South Africa."

"How do you know?"

"Henry's analysis says—"

"Henry Barber got back to you?"

"Oh, yes." Maddie gave a little smile. "Henry came back through official channels, which meant through Keith. The upshot was something like what my Georgia grandpa would describe as the unholy combination of kerosene, a corncob and a cat's patootie. Let's just say you're lucky to be five time zones away."

Weezy rubbed her temples. "Sorry. Should I laugh or cry?"

"Neither, actually. It's been fun to watch Keith stand up and do his job without first considering the bureaucratic risk/reward continuum."

"What did Henry find out?"

"He got into the trading data in detail. He pretty much confirmed what you suspected. ZCG started putting together Skins maybe ten years ago, making small margins. Until five or six years ago, they were trying to sell the high-risk stuff off cheaply and taking a loss there.

"Then something changed, right?" Weezy said with a smirk.

"It did. RedSock started buying the high-risk tranches. They're paying upwards of twenty percent of the value they're insuring." She stopped, disgust twisting her mouth. "Well, gambling their clients' money on … but they keep cashing in big time. So it's a win-win. ZCG gets big fees from RedSock. RedSock clients make out big time, too … at the expense of other investors, of course." Weezy thought of all those Scholze accounts in RedSock and the 600% returns. Then HoHum, then Joe.

Maddie leaned toward the camera in her monitor. "Weezy, are you okay?"

"Yeah. Fine, really. Thanks, Maddie, for following up. Sounds like we're on to something." She wished she was in Bethesda pounding this case into the ground. "I should go back now," she said starting to stand. "Keep me up to speed."

Maddie's look said there was something more. Her mouth was set, her eyes sad.

"Maddie, what is it?"

"Henry found another Skins trader out there."

Weezy sat down again.

"Of course." She remembered her own research to set up HoHum. "What, twenty or thirty hedge funds buying the mid-range tranches …"

"No. Joe."

"What do you mean, Joe?"

"Henry has access to account ownership data that we can't see. About a month ago, Joe bought thirty-k worth of the high-risk Chromium Skin. Shortly thereafter, chromium went nuts. The Skin will pay out $402,000 over the next several weeks."

"Can't be. Someone's setting Joe up."

"Henry says Joe Mayfield set the account up and bought the Skin. I was skeptical, but Henry found the bonus document that Joe used. Clearly his signature. I … " Maddie's voice wound down to silence.

How could he?

"Could it be a mistake?"

"Doesn't look like it, but I asked Henry to look more carefully." Maddie forced a smile, but her voice gave away her doubt that the trace would do anything but put more nails in the coffin.

After they signed off, Weezy sat quietly on the bench. She rubbed her eyes and pushed her hair back, suddenly angry at the new stylish hairdo and the beautiful place. The woman on the next bench was nursing her baby and smiled at Weezy. She tried a return smile, but felt foreign … to the place, to the sorority of women her age who understood the beauty of motherhood, to the good fellowship of the smart, friendly people she met on the trip. Most of all to Joe. A breeze stirred the plane trees lining the boulevard. So elegant. Maybe this was what Joe hoped, to get away together and enjoy a beautiful place. A way to cover up the big lie. She remembered Maddie saying of Joe, "If it ain't love, girl, it ain't bad."

She shivered in the warmth of the Viennese afternoon.

***

Joe came back from the conference to find Weezy's note, "Out walking - back soon." He had been introduced to yet another European colleague as a "new member of the team" and an "up and comer." Don Petrescu asked detailed questions about the Kazakh Skin and said Morgan RioTinto had bought in. Ross Ackerman grilled him about RioTinto's plans in Kazakhstan, showing a down-to-business, respectful side that was a pleasant surprise. In short, it had been a good day, and Joe glowed from the compliments, the anticipation of a bonus, and the brisk walk through the center of the city.

He found a beer in the refrigerator and twisted the cap, but the Bohemian brewery in the little town of Budvar that gave the world Budweiser still used the traditional crimped top. He considered trying his grandfather's magical trick with the back of a kitchen knife to pop the top. But there was an opener on top of the refrigerator with tall crystal beer glasses. Joe used it, poured the beer and pulled a chair around so he looked out over the hotel's private park while he sipped a lager infinitely more delicious than its bland US namesake.

He drifted into a half-dream state, relishing the thought of the Morgan Rio Tinto sale and the money it would put in his pocket. New air conditioner for Panacea. Maybe a new canoe. Pocket change if Ackerman was as good as his word. It wasn't only the money. It was getting his ticket punched, being an admired member of the team.

A discordant note grew more insistent, as if arriving from a distance. He saw Weezy talking, saying something he didn't want to hear, her eyes serious and tearing up. He wanted to continue the reverie to find out what was upsetting her.

He heard a door open.

"Joe? You asleep?"

He came back to the surface. "Not really. Closing my eyes to relax a bit."

"You saw my note?" Weezy looked serious, but that was not unusual.

"I did." He looked at his watch. "We'd better start getting ready. We're supposed to be out front for the shuttle at four-thirty."

"Yeah, I know. I'm pretty much packed." Joe shifted in the chair to look at her and saw strain on her face.

"How about one more stroll around the park?" Weezy said, waving her hand at the window.

"What's wrong?"

She shook her head ever so slightly. "Just *heightened awareness* of the beauty of this place." Her face said she was not thinking of beauty. "I need one last walk."

***

Weezy and Joe walked to the end of the gardens. The ravens, a fixture on the manicured lawn, looked for all the world like courtroom lawyers discussing abstract legalities. Weezy was silent, wondering how to broach the painful subject. Joe filled the void, telling her about the conference, mentioning names of several people who wanted to talk with her about "IAC issues," probably jobs. He told a funny story about an Austrian investment banker being introduced as 'Doctor Doctor' because she had two advanced degrees. He looked at her, laughed maybe a little too long, trying to encourage her to lighten up. She raised a hand to stop him and paused, searching for words.

"I checked in with Maddie."

"Any big developments?"

"Matter of fact, yes."

She dropped her eyes and pushed some pebbles with her toe. Not like her to hold back. But then, she was usually not risking a relationship much too important to destroy with a few misplaced words.

"Maddie got Henry Barber's report. Henry thinks there really is a problem."

She stopped and turned to face Joe.

"Remember you said Emily Ackerman specially asked for me to come on this trip?"

"Sure."

"Have you seen any indication of that interest?"

"Uhh … no, now that I think of it."

"I haven't either. I told a story about my relaxed sartorial habits at lunch. I got that polite chuckle you get when people think you've said something rather odd from everyone except Emily Ackerman. She wasn't listening very carefully, but when I mentioned I wore one red sock to work, she damn near choked on her aperitif."

The ravens chuckled.

"Why were they so anxious to get us both here?"

"Maybe they're trying to keep track of us while they figure out how much we have discovered."

"I guess we need to be careful, stay together and look for anything that might help Maddie and Henry Barber." Joe checked his watch. "We'd better get packed." He turned to go to the room.

It would be so easy to put off confrontation.

"There's another thing."

Joe turned back. His face said he was preoccupied, a little perplexed with Weezy's hesitation.

"Your account at Quantitec."

Joe looked puzzled. "What about it?"

"What about it? Is that all you can say? What about it?" Weezy felt her color rising. "Feel a little richer?"

Joe moved from surprised to guarded. "I haven't checked. Is the market up?" Then angry. "Wait a minute. You've been checking my finances behind my back? Why?"

Dumbass mode took over. "You should be able to figure it out, smart guy. Did you think the FBI wasn't going to notice you while they were investigating ZCG?"

"Notice me? Why? Weezy, goddammit. Are you going to raise moral compass issues every week?" His voice rose. "What happens when I make my first sale? Will I be selling out to corporate America? What are we going to do then?"

"Just a hint here, in case you're terminally oblivious, the 'me' part is going to solve this issue or there won't be any 'we.' "

There. It was in the open. There was a moment of silence, then harsh croaking as the ravens weighed in. Joe's mouth was hanging open, his eyes wide.

"I'm leaving." Weezy turned on her heel and walked back toward the room. There was no crunch of gravel to say Joe followed.

Weezy jerked open the French door, stomped up the stairs to their elegant bedroom and threw the last few things in her bag. Her newly purchased makeup kit made her stifle a sob. Stupid to cry over something she shouldn't care about anyway. This life was not for her.

Joe's voice rose from the lower level.

"Weezy? What's wrong?"

"Everything."

Footsteps came up the stairs.

"Weezy, talk to me. I don't understand what you're upset about."

She realized she was crying.

"You don't understand? Chromium Skin? Ring a bell? Three hundred seventy thousand dollars profit from the fine fucking folks that killed HoHum. Forget about moral compass. We're talking lights-out-on-the-top-floor stupid, here."

Joe sat down on the bed.

"Weezy, this doesn't make sense." He rested his forearms on his thighs and looked at the floor.

"I love you."

First time he out and said it, but it sounded like a plea. Weezy yanked at the zipper on her bag, and it stuck.

"I can't lose you."

She pulled harder; a sob caught in her throat. Finally, Joe stood, came over to her, covered her hand with his and freed up the zipper.

"I've had the account at Quantitec for five or six years. Ever since Florida Consolidated pushed us all into 401k's. I can't invest in Skins. It's a conflict of interest. You must know that."

"But you did."

"No. I didn't." Tight-lipped, he walked down the stairs. He found his e-pad and came back up. He sat on the bed, opened the pad and said "Quantitec" then put a thumb on the screen.

"Here."

He shoved the screen into Weezy's face. It showed an account statement for Joseph E. Mayfield of Panacea, Florida. Sixty thousand dollars invested in index funds and bonds. All plain vanilla.

The only sound in the room was her harsh breathing.

"I don't understand," she said, trying to suppress the quaver in her voice.

Joe gestured toward the stairs, angry. "Heightened awareness of a problem."

Weezy stood rooted. *Get this wrong, dumbass, and there will be no Joe.*

Joe grabbed Weezy's sleeve and pulled.

"What?"

His eyes flashed warning.

He dragged her down the stairs, through the French doors, to the gravel path.

"Heightened friggin' awareness. Shouldn't have talked in there."

They walked to the end of the park in silence.

"Joe, I don't understand."

"I bet you don't." The ravens did not approve of their re-intrusion and let them know it.

"Explain what's going on … and explain why you believed whatever so-called evidence somebody fed you instead of asking me about it."

"I … I …"

"Right. You, Maddie and the FBI have been suckered into thinking good old lights-out-on-the-top-floor stupid Joe … Yes, that's what you said … is dumb enough to trade illegally using the same online broker where he keeps his paltry 401k?" His lips trembled and he drew a long breath.

"Here, maybe you can find transactions I'm not aware of."

He handed the pad to Weezy. His anger seemed to subside, but the hurt in his eyes did not. His gesture of trust broke a dam in Weezy, and her fear and tension rushed out. She checked the report and searched the Quantitec website for another account.

"Joe, the FBI found an account at Quantitec recently set up in your name. A month ago, that account purchased $30,000 of the highest-risk Chromium Skin. Henry thought whoever set up the account went out of his way to keep it secret."

Joe turned to Weezy, his look guarded. "Better have him recheck his information. You guys are missing something."

Weezy looked at her watch, trying to ignore the fact that she was suddenly one of "you guys."

"I've got to get away from here and call Maddie," she said. "I need your e-pad."

"We need to be out front at 4:30."

"If I have to, I'll get a taxi. I know where they queue up."

"I don't like you walking around the city alone."

"I'll be careful."

***

Nick Braithwaite glanced at the daily security report while he packed his bag. He was preoccupied, thinking through his monitoring plan for the Donau König. His eye caught Quantitec. He dropped his Dopp kit into the bag and tapped the reference. He'd had nothing of interest from Mayfield and Napolitani other than the confirmation that they did, indeed, share bodily fluids. Now, there it was … the slip he'd been waiting for.

Mayfield had an account at Quantitec already? That moron Garrity didn't check before setting up the Skins account? Shit!

The bitch knows. They both know.

He tapped Ackerman and left a message, "Need help on the trading security project. Meet second deck, rear, thirty minutes."

He was almost packed up, late now, when his e-pad buzzed.

"What's so all-fired important? I do have legitimate work to do, you know."

"We need to accelerate our project."

***

Weezy walked the quarter mile back to the Kartnerstrasse bench where she'd called Maddie earlier. Quiet now. She tapped her e-pad.

"Call Madeline Hollingsworth."

There was a slight delay, a click, then Maddie peering out at Weezy.

"You told him, didn't you?"

"Maddie, something's wrong. Yes, I told him. Yes, he has a Quantitec account. He showed it to me. He's had it for several years, and it has no Skin in it. It's worth about sixty k."

"Do you have data on that account?"

Weezy opened Joe's e-pad and forwarded the Quantitec account information. "It's on its way. How the hell could Barber have ignored this?"

"Maybe he was just looking at accounts connected to ZCG, but I helped him set up the scan and, if I do say so, it was pretty sophisticated."

"Yeah, but he dropped the ball," Weezy said, temper rising, "he needs some training in problem solving."

"Weezy, before you do your famous tap dance on his forehead, remember that he's the best resource we have."

Weezy exhaled loudly. "Right. Got it."

"Keep your spirits up, girl," Maddie said. "I have a feeling things are going to turn out all right." She grinned.

Weezy glanced at her watch. "Got a boat to catch. Maddie, we shouldn't be talking openly when I'm on the boat, but texts are okay. Use Cal Occult and your imagination."

Maddie's grin vanished. "Don't get on that boat."

"I can't very well pull out now, particularly—"

"Weezy, damn it. If Barber missed Joe's real account, that means someone very sophisticated set it up. If that's true, you're in danger. If they've killed before, they'll kill again. Let the authorities run this down. Don't get on that boat."

Weezy had a rush of affection for Maddie.

"Don't worry, I'll be careful."

"But—"

Weezy signed off. The last time she sat on this bench, the Kartnerstrasse seemed foreign and unfriendly. Now, the light shafting down through the plane trees and the conversation of passersby gave the boulevard an air of elegance. A pudgy man with kinky, flyaway hair came around the corner. For a moment, Weezy saw HoHum, but the guy was wearing a suit, not a T-shirt. She shook off the vision.

At a cab stand down the block, several taxis waited. She got into the one at the head of the line. The cab driver eyed her in his rearview mirror, asked her something in German. She thought of Maddie's warning, of HoHum and of Joe and said, "DDSG Ship Station Reichsbrucke."

# TWENTY-SIX

AT THE QUAY, Weezy pointed the driver to the Donau König. The ship rested gracefully, a well-preserved dowager lovingly cared for and elegantly dressed in brilliant white and teak. The ZCG party had been driven over from the hotel, and the last bags were being moved aboard when Weezy arrived. She had sent Joe a message from the taxi. He was waiting on deck when she stepped onto the quay. He came down the gangway, greeted her with a nod rather than a hug, and gave her an access badge. Weezy's looked like a charm, engraved 'ZCG' and came with a delicate silver bracelet. Joe's, also engraved, was mounted on a thin leather band. Joe picked up her bag and walked up the gangway.

"We're on the second deck, port side," Joe said. "We'll be seeing Slovakia and Hungary on the way." At the stateroom, Joe waved his wrist in front of the small access pad. The door opened. A note on the bedside table encouraged them in five languages to use the badge to call the service staff at any time. Weezy pulled out her scanner and checked to be sure the badges were not broadcasting. She resisted the temptation to do an in-depth scan of the stateroom. Her uncertainty was justification for being close-mouthed with Joe.

"Let's pretend this is a great vacation," Joe said. "How about a stroll on deck?"

"Sure."

"Let's stick together, try to enjoy." Joe's face said he knew it was a lame hope.

It was warm on deck, with a cool breeze from the hills that rise toward the Alps bringing a hint of pine. They leaned on the rail, taking in the panorama of the city. Smartly dressed sailors loosed the spring lines, making ready to cast off. Joe turned to Weezy.

"I doubt anyone would try anything here. Too many people."

*He's trying to reassure me. Maybe himself, too.*

"This trip, the hotel, Vienna, now this ship. It's like a fairy tale," Weezy said. "Trouble is, I keep expecting the wicked witch to show up. Kinda wrecks the effect."

She looked both directions to confirm they were alone, then told Joe about the FBI report. Finished, she said, "Joe, someone's willing to kill to protect what they're doing. I'm scared."

Before Weezy could say more, Braithwaite appeared, coming up the stairs from the lower deck. He was talking to a man with a ponytail, black hair shot with gray. The man was a few inches shorter than Braithwaite and slender, an Arabian stallion next to Braithwaite's Clydesdale. He had a sharp face with a prominent nose and wore an earring. Rat, Weezy thought, except he's good-looking.

Braithwaite saw Joe, took in Weezy. She saw him paint on a friendly smile. "Joe, good to see you. And this is Ms. Napolitani, isn't it?"

He reached to shake Joe's hand, then Weezy's. His hand was big, dry and strong, not quite crushing hers.

Weezy forced a smile. Did he notice her hesitation?

Braithwaite nodded toward his companion. "This is Armand Santucci. He's visiting from Ajaccio."

"Corsica, right?" Weezy asked.

"Yes, mademoiselle." Heavy accent, Italian or French. "I am from the birthplace of culture." His grin asked Weezy to forgive the hyperbole.

Braithwaite gave Joe and Weezy a curt nod, clearly wanting to move on. "Well, I hope you enjoy the rest of the trip." Santucci looked like he wanted to continue the conversation, especially with Weezy.

After the two moved away, Weezy continued, "I don't know how fast Maddie and Henry will figure out your phantom account. She's going to send us a coded message when she knows anything."

Weezy felt Joe relax a little. Maybe relief at being part of 'us' again. On the way back to the cabin, his hand brushed against hers.

She waved her bracelet at the cabin door. It opened with a soft click. Weezy's e-pad showed a new message from Maddie "re: Cal Occult. There are two points of entry, both appearing to be from the same source, but actually separate."

Weezy showed Joe the message. To his raised eyebrows, she tapped out "You've been set up" on her e-pad. Relief flooded through her, almost forcing tears. Relief contended with rage on Joe's face. She tapped out "Okay" to Maddie and put an arm around Joe's shoulder, brushing her hand over his hair, feeling a little thaw. "Be careful tonight," she said, serious. Then a grin. "I don't want those investment banker ladies closing a deal with you."

***

Swarovski lead crystal chandeliers and empire wall hangings dressed the ship's salon. The tables were set with silver and fine linen. A string quartet played Strauss waltzes. Laughter punctuated conversation as the ZCG group gathered, about a hundred in all.

Stacey Cheung greeted Joe and Weezy and directed them to a round table in the center of the room. The time-honored boy-girl-boy-girl protocol had been co-opted by the relationship template: Don Petrescu was seated next to his counterpart at Indentia Mining. Nita Solchow, ZCG's senior banker on the Indentia account, and Joe were on either end of the client continuum. Pam Petrescu and Weezy were across the table, with Santucci between them. Santucci turned out to be charming, seemingly ecstatic to be seated between, as he said, two "donne molto sveglie … that means very cute women." With the excellent wine being constantly refreshed by attentive stewards, everyone was a little tipsy by the first course. It was Knoblachsuppe, accompanied by a white Grüner Veltliner "as good as the best chardonnay," according to Santucci.

The garlic soup was followed by chunks of Csabai sausage delicately fried. Don described them as "artery blockers" to polite and guilty chuckles. Then a small salad, then *Hähnchenschnitzel* ("best goddam fried chicken I ever ate," Don concluded around a large bite) with white asparagus and julienne beets. For dessert, Linzer and Sacher tortes. The charming steward offered the tortes 'mit Schlag' from what looked like a mountain of whipped cream. "The way he said it was so … sensual," Pam said, stopping conversation and then blushing.

Eric O'Malley rose from a table near the bar to salute the audience with a short, warm recognition of fellowship. He continued, "Tomorrow, we will arrive in Budapest. In honor of a fine old Hungarian tradition, let's drink a toast with törkölypálinka … hope I said it right … a special Hungarian brandy I'm told is always drunk straight off with a toast to St. Nicholas."

The table steward appeared with a tray of small glasses of a clear, amber liquid. Santucci leapt up, a little unsteady. With a sweeping gesture, he picked two glasses off the tray and with a slight bow, presented one to Pam, then one to Weezy. Taking a glass for himself, he remained standing while the steward moved around the table. "Pace i salute," he said. "Peace and good health, in my country." Weezy, on the far edge of tipsy, took a sip. She told herself this was the last drink of the evening. Nice at first, but a bitter aftertaste. She hesitated.

Santucci shook his head. "No, no Madame. You must drink it all or Saint Nicholas will be offended."

She glanced across the table at Joe, shrugged and finished the glass.

Santucci beamed. "Now Saint Nicholas is happy."

***

Joe drank his törkölypálinka. Very smooth. Across the table, Armand Santucci said something to Weezy, and she tipped her glass up and drank. Weezy looked as if she'd had a little too much. But she seemed happier than she had been since HoHum.

Joe stood to stretch and perhaps go and inject himself into Santucci's too-intense continental campaign. A hand clapped him on the shoulder, and he turned to see Ross Ackerman's smile.

"Joe, come over to my table. Woman over there is excited … actually, titillated …" The smile became a leer. "And you'll see what I mean by titillated … by the story of RazorBlue."

***

Weezy watched Ackerman take Joe across the room. *Should have asked me, too.* Armand Santucci was charming, but a little much. His smile turned to a look of friendly concern. "Madame Louise, you look…how shall I say it…a little uncomfortable. A glass of water, perhaps? Or maybe some cool air on deck?"

Yes. I need some air, she thought.

She stood, wobbled a little. Damn, she'd had too much to drink. "Excuse me," she said, hoping she hadn't slurred her words. She went past Santucci toward the door to the deck and the ladies' room.

The breeze had stiffened, and the heavy door resisted her, but the wind felt good on her face. The deck thrummed with the effort of the big engines pushing Donau König toward Budapest. But something was off. Weezy was descending into a tunnel of altered sounds, losing her balance.

Then there was a hand on her back. "Madame Louise, are you all right?" The accent. Not Joe. Suddenly she was afraid. The hand was insistent, moving her toward the railing.

*What's wrong?*

She grabbed the railing with her right hand, tried to turn. A strong hand took her left arm.

Twisting. Pain.

She let go of the railing, reached back, grabbing hair, flesh, hooking her finger on something.

Fight, fight, fight.

Then she was spinning, coruscating light off of … water? Flat black before shock. No breath. Cold. Pulled under. Engine drumming.

Tired. Drifting. On her chest, Sappho stared at her, eyes huge. So cold. *Why is she trying to wake me? Not time to get up.* She reached to touch her. She was rough, not silky. Why was she rough? Sappho told Weezy to hold on, she would carry her.

***

Nick disengaged from his table and the wife of a stuffy, oblivious IAEC official. Her friendly, offhand touches on his arm had begun to move lower, a complication he didn't need. He leaned on the small bar next to the dance floor and ordered a beer. He had watched Santucci and Napolitani leave the salon. He caught the eye of Ackerman and gave a small nod.

Mayfield was occupied at Ackerman's table, as planned. Some couples were beginning to stand, ready to call it an evening. Nobody seemed to have noticed Santucci follow Napolitani.

Minutes later, Santucci entered, skirting the room. He approached the bar and Nick, scratching his head as if preoccupied.

"Done?"

"Yes, done." Santucci said.

"Are you sure?"

Santucci kept his hand aside his head, seeming to tell Nick a funny story. The bartender was oblivious, making multilayered after-dinner drinks. Santucci's hand covered scratches, not deep, but obvious. He said softly, "She fought, but she went over. How bad is my face?"

"You have some scratches, and she must have hitched your earring. There's a little blood. Probably best to go to your cabin. Take your badge back." He passed over the badge Santucci had left with him so he could make an invisible exit to follow Weezy.

Santucci palmed it, glanced around the salon ferret-like and slipped away.

***

Joe disengaged from the group at Ackerman's table. No one seemed particularly interested in RazorBlue, despite Ackerman's advertisement. He scanned the salon. No one at his table. Pam and Don Petrescu were dancing. Nita Solchow was standing, talking to the Indentia group. Santucci was at the bar with Braithwaite. Joe went out on deck. No Weezy, but the breeze felt good. Maybe she wanted to get away for a bit. He saw the *damen* sign a dozen feet down the deck. Maybe that was it, the ladies' room? He waited a couple of minutes. A woman he didn't know came out.

"Anyone else in there?" he asked, trying to sound matter-of-fact.

She said no.

Joe walked around to the port side, toward their stateroom, getting worried, then angry. Did she leave without telling him? After their agreement to stick together, be careful? If this was just a classic Weezy ignoring social convention …

He waved the bracelet, opened the door.

"Weezy?"

The stateroom swallowed his voice. There was only the gentle thrumming of the engines.

"Weezy?" He opened the door to the tiny bathroom, then the closet.

"Weezy?" Panic rising.

Joe sprinted back to the salon. More than half the people had left.

No Weezy. Think. Where could she have gone? Probably something perfectly understandable. He went back on deck, looked up. The sky was clear, the stars brilliant. Maybe on the top deck. He took the companionway stairs two at a time. Several romantics, but no Weezy. He walked the shadows of the third deck slowly, his pulse beginning to race.

Where else could she be? The ship was three hundred feet long. Guests weren't allowed below decks. She was not on the third or second. There was a lounge on the first deck. Maybe a group went there for a nightcap? That would be unlike Weezy, but still.

Joe pounded down the stairs, slipping on the metal wet with evening dew. The lounge was empty but for Nick Braithwaite holding a snifter of brandy, talking with the bar steward.

"Have you seen Louise Napolitani?"

"I think she went back to her cabin, perhaps half an hour ago or a little more. She was maybe a little, uh, seasick." He gave Joe a friendly smile, but his eyes were cold.

"She's not in the cabin, not any place I've looked."

"What about Nita Solchow? She is traveling alone. They may have gone to her cabin to have a female conversation."

Joe locked eyes with Nick. *He knows.*

Joe turned on his heel, hearing Nick say after him, "I'm sure she will turn up okay."

On the deck, Joe thought through the last hour, trying to remember any shred of information, any forgotten glance, that would tell him Weezy was going to turn up okay.

***

The Donau König's bridge was above the top deck. A discreet sign said, "Kein Zugang/Access Not Permitted." When Joe was halfway up the short companionway, an alarm went off. An officer blocked his way, hand resting on a holstered Taser.

"Help. I need help." Joe tried to remain calm. "My friend …" The officer raised his eyebrows, looking as if he was not understanding. "Mein Frau …" Joe said, going for his limited German vocabulary. "Ihr … she … ist …"

"Your wife is …" The officer said.

"Missing."

"She is missing? She did not get on the ship?"

"No, she's missing. I can't find her. She left the salon about twenty past eleven. She's not in our cabin. Not in the ladies' room on deck two. I've been around all the decks, and I can't find her."

Joe recited the places he'd searched.

"And her name?"

"Louise Napolitani."

"Stateroom number?"

"Uhh … nineteen."

"Was she wearing her bracelet?"

"Her bracelet?"

"The badge she was given when she boarded."

"Oh, yes. The bracelet. When we came into dinner, she was wearing it."

Now the officer looked relieved.

"We can look at where she has been."

Joe was taken aback. "You mean you track people around the ship?"

"We throw away all the data at the end of each trip, but in this case, perhaps we can see …" he stepped aside and motioned Joe onto the bridge "… where she has been." He turned to an e-pad on the bulkhead in back of the helm, tapped on it.

"Her name is Louise Napolitani?"

"Yes."

"And you are Joseph E. Mayfield, with the ZCG company, yes?"

"Yes."

"Your badges were activated this afternoon at 18:11. Štefan put your bag in the room at 18:14, and you yourself keyed the room's pad at 18:29. Ms. Napolitani was with you. You both left the stateroom at 18:52, passed the port bow indicator at 18:56, then several others … a bit of a walk around Deck Two, perhaps … and returned at 19:18." He looked at Joe, raising his eyebrows. Joe nodded confirmation. "Ja, then you left at 19:57 and went to the salon." He peered at the screen. "…And Frau Napolitani left at 23:26, as you said." The screen showed a map of the boat, a yellow line tracing Weezy's path. The line stopped at the exit from the salon. The officer looked puzzled, switched to a list. He scrolled through another two pages of text, paged up and went over the list again. "I see no more entries for Frau Napolitani. You left the salon at 23:37 and left many tracks."

The officer paused for a long moment, then tapped a button on an intercom next to the e-pad. He spoke a string of German to a person who sounded as if he had been awakened from a deep sleep.

"We will search the ship," he said to Joe.

The officer spoke briefly to the other sailor on the bridge, who saluted and hustled down the companionway. Soon, other crew members began appearing in various stages of dress and wakefulness.

Forty-five minutes later the entire ship was awake. Eric O'Malley, Pam Petrescu, and Nita Solchow kept Joe company in the salon. He grew more terrified by the minute. *They think this was an accident.* How stupid had he and Weezy been? When they saw Braithwaite on the ship, they should have gotten off, grabbed a plane to Atlanta, holed up in Panacea, and let the FBI do their job.

The captain entered the salon, his expression grim. He wore his uniform jacket over striped pajamas, bare feet in *fussgesundheit* slippers. Without his captain's cap and starched shirt, he looked considerably smaller than Joe remembered.

"We have not found Frau Napolitani. We cannot know what happened, but …" He opened his hand. "We discovered her badge near the railing outside the door." He gestured toward the salon door.

"I understand she was quite a bit affected by alcohol. It is possible she did not see … perhaps fell against the rail."

Joe was shaking his head while the captain spoke. "No, not possible. She did not like to drink too much, and nobody her size would fall over a railing that high …"

He heard himself grasping at straws. He remembered Weezy talking about the wicked witch and felt sick.

The captain shrugged in resignation. "I agree. It doesn't seem possible. We are notifying the officials on our route. It is only ten meters to the water, and the Donau water is from the mountains. Cold, maybe sixteen … umm … sixty degrees Fahrenheit, even now as summer approaches. That would perhaps wake her quickly, no?"

Joe took in the hopeful words but saw the truth in the captain's eyes.

# TWENTY-SEVEN

CONSTABLE HANS PROHOFFER was a big man. An uncharitable observer would call him bullet-headed. No one would guess he recited Goethe silently to himself in quiet moments.

That morning, he stood at the bank of the Danube near the bottom of Hainburg's main street. It was nearly light enough to start the search for a person, a woman, missing from a ship that passed Hainburg near midnight. He got the emergency message in the wee hours and sent a tap out to volunteers to meet at daybreak. They would launch a small boat to search the shoreline and walk the path along the river. Thankfully, one of the volunteers was the local baker, who was up well before daybreak anyway. He had delivered coffee and breakfast kuchen to the assembly point.

Hans leaned on his bicycle, sipped coffee and took a bite of the kuchen. Almost as good as the ones in Vienna and half the price. Hans had been in the Bundespolizei there. Because of his size, he'd gotten the hard duty. When his wife's MS flared, they decided to move to the little town where she grew up. They had been happy with the quieter life. Hans dealt mainly with drunks and vandals now. He dusted the locked assault rifle once a month and rarely had to hang the Glock on his belt.

But a bit of excitement was not unwelcome.

***

Magda Naumann was an early riser. She liked to walk the margins of the Danube and watch the sky turn from gray to rose. She and her husband escaped from Vienna to Hainburg an der Donau two or three times a year, as finances permitted.

Magda left her husband safely tucked in the lounge at the Gasthaus, digesting the *Wiener Zeitung* along with his coffee and health bread. He would be commenting under his breath on the idiocy of the politicians in Vienna, Bratislava, Prague, and America—another reason for Magda's choice of morning for her solitary walk.

She strolled the gravel path while planning the next term's lessons for her Mittelschule mathematics class. She was a neat person; well organized, not to say compulsive. Flotsam at the water's edge offended her. Trash, most likely.

She sighed. This place should be kept clean. She shook her head, reaching to adjust her glasses, then realizing she had left them in the room.

She came closer, peering at a pale, white object.

*Eine Hand?*

A form, partly covered with river debris. A body, half out of the water.

*Eine Frau?*

Chestnut hair plastered to a pasty white temple. Black dress, one shoulder strap missing. Lying face down, head to one side, one arm under her, the other stretched, hand holding an exposed root. Not moving.

*Tot?*

Hands shaking, Magda tapped the emergency responder on her phone's screen. A computer voice asked the nature of the problem. Magda stammered that she'd found a body. The emergency responder noted the location of the call and forwarded to EU 144, the emergency/rescue number.

***

Prohoffer saw bicycle lights winking as volunteers came down the gentle slope to the assembly point. His implant tapped him. An emergency call to 144. GPS put it about a mile downriver.

He told the first of the volunteers to hold off the search, took a last bite of the kuchen and mounted his bicycle. The path was gravel, a little challenging, and he was out of breath when he saw the blue light pulsing through the trees. Then the ambulance down near the riverbank. The passenger door was open, and a woman in the passenger seat looked stunned. The town emergency medical technician squatted in the shallow water, his kit open, helmet light on and a field stretcher on the gravel of the bank. Hans tapped his uniform camera, scanning the area. The tech looked relieved as Hans approached, then turned back to the motionless form half in the water—a woman, very pale. He felt in her mouth, clearing the airway.

"Help me turn her over."

"Is she alive?"

"Barely. May not make it to the hospital. Deep shock."

A slender, white hand locked on a protruding root. "But she's a fighter," the tech said.

He gently pried her fingers away, then felt carefully down her back.

"Okay. We can turn her."

She was slim. Hans could have lifted her with one hand. They turned her on her back. Her dress had slipped off her shoulder, exposing a breast, making her look vulnerable and sad. Her left arm was swollen below the elbow, a red bruise stark against bluish-white skin. Prohoffer recognized the spiral fracture. Someone twisted her arm until it broke.

Hans watched the tech putting monitors on the woman's chest, but he was back in Vienna in his mind. It was a sultry August evening, a domestic disturbance call, a woman crumpled in a corner of a dingy apartment holding her crying baby in one arm and whimpering in pain. Her other arm looked like the one on this woman. A man, drunk, sat in a ragged chair, calling her a bitch and worse. Hans was part way through the appropriate script for a domestic call when a wall of red descended. He was five again and terrified. His father, drunk, lurching toward him, pushing his mother aside, grabbing his shirt …

The newspaper story hinted at police brutality, but next time, Hans knew it would be much worse. Another reason to move to Hainburg.

The tech covered the woman and said, "Hans?" Prohoffer shook off the memory, and they lifted the woman on to the stretcher. The tech's radio crackled, and the voice of Doctor Astrid Kühn began a litany of instructions.

Hans walked Magda Naumann back to the hotel. She was silent at first, but began chattering as the shock wore off. In the foyer of the hotel, she began, finally, to cry.

Hans called off the search party, telling the men the person had been found and politely declining to provide details. He bicycled back toward the station and the well-ordered life of a small-town constable, but what he saw was the arm, the bruise. The rage ached to rise again.

# TWENTY-EIGHT

NICK BRAITHWAITE WAS the first to know. As designated security officer for the ZCG group, he had been on the bridge when the captain put out the emergency call using the ship's communication system. Not protected. Easy to tap in. So when Prohoffer called the captain shortly after the Donau König docked at Budapest, Braithwaite got a tap on his implant. His childhood Afrikaans allowed him to get the gist of what was said.

He tapped Santucci on a secure line, who went from dead asleep to wide awake in a blink.

"They found Napolitani. She's not dead, but in bad shape. She's in the town of Hainburg an der Donau, a little west of Bratislava on the Austrian side of the river."

"*Incredibile.*" Braithwaite noted a hint of admiration in Santucci's voice.

"You have to finish the job. She can't survive."

"That may be difficult. Where is she?"

"If she's barely alive, she's got to be in a hospital. Look it up."

There was a pause. Nick remembered Santucci, skilled in so many ways, was a virtual cripple when it came to technology. He could answer a tap, but not much beyond.

"Hold on," Nick said. Then, to his e-pad, "Show Hainburg hospital." A map popped open on the screen, showing a hospital near the town center. He touched the highlighted point and said, "Detail." A diagram of the hospital appeared with a live feed of the emergency room. An inset showed urgent care opened in two hours.

"I'm sending the layout of the hospital … and a map. Middle of the town. She'll probably be somewhere near the emergency room on the first floor."

Braithwaite said to his e-pad, "Autocab service to Austria." Several services appeared on the screen. "I'll order an autocab to come here." He tapped and swiped. "It will be programmed to go to the hospital. You will have to tell it where to park when you get there. I've reserved it to wait an hour after that. Got that?"

"Yes, autocab to Hainburg. But how—"

"You will have to find her when you get there. The autocab will be here in ten minutes. Better move now, before there are people on deck. Stop at my stateroom. I'll give you something that will make her death look natural." They signed off.

Nick went to his briefcase, opened it, and peeled back the liner to reveal a concealed panel. He took out a plastic cylinder and plunger and assembled them into a syringe. He extracted a needle and small vial of clear liquid from another compartment. He removed the protective shell from the needle and sucked the liquid into the syringe, then replaced the shell.

Santucci knocked lightly on his door.

Nick handed him the syringe.

"If there's an IV, there will be a port in the line. Inject all the fluid into the port and leave. If there's no IV, give her the shot anywhere, maybe the thigh. Somewhere it won't be obvious. She will expire in about three minutes. There will probably be a monitor on her. It will give an alarm. You need to be out of the area when it goes off." He handed Santucci a disposable phone. "Give me a call …" Nick hesitated. A direct call, even on a secure line, might be traced to the ship. "No, send me a chess move at Father Time, like before. Say 'RxQ' and I'll know the job's done."

Santucci gave Nick a half salute and left, all business.

Nick took two minutes to think through all the possible outcomes of the situation. Satisfied, he tapped Ackerman, who answered sounding irritated as usual.

"Yeah? Jesus, it's before six o'clock."

"They found the Napolitani woman. She's alive, but I think only barely."

"Barely? You think?" Ross said softly. Nick realized he was trying not to wake Emily.

"I listened to a conversation in German," Nick said. "What I know is she's alive in the little town of Hainburg an der Donau, a couple of hours back up the river. That much I followed. I sent Santucci to finish the job."

"Uhh ... Okay."

"The captain will no doubt tell Mayfield, and my guess is Mayfield's first inclination will be to jump in an autocab and go to Hainburg. You need to hold him back to give Santucci some time."

"So, you stop him." Whispered.

Nick was used to non-professionals not thinking through situations like this one. He stifled his irritation, tried to remain dispassionate.

"Look, I can stop him physically and risk breaking this whole thing wide open, or you can talk at him long enough to give Santucci an opportunity to help her expire quietly."

Nick added, "Do you understand?" Then wished he hadn't said it. If Ackerman adopted his normal entitled asshole persona, the plan would collapse.

"Do I understand?" Loud. "Do I fucking understand?" Louder. "Oh, sorry, baby, go back to sleep."

Then in a furious whisper, "Of course I understand. How come I have to clean up your mess ... again?"

***

Joe sat on the bed in their stateroom, catatonic. He didn't know for how long. Earlier, friends were around him, worried about the wild look in his eyes. Sleep, they said. Get some sleep.

A loop ran in his mind, starting with their entry into the salon last night and ending with his turn away from Ackerman's table and finding Weezy gone. The loop ran faster and faster against a backdrop of mental noise: their agreement to stay close, her brush of his hand, Braithwaite's cold stare.

A discreet knock. Joe sighed. He worked up a polite defense against friendly concern and advice, then cracked open the door.

The captain, looking exhausted but relieved.

"We have found Fräulein Napolitani."

He must have seen the pain in Joe's face.

"She is alive. She is in a town up the river, Hainburg an der Donau. She is not well at all, but she is in the *Krankenhaus* … pardon … a hospital."

He smiled. "We are all very much relieved. You will want to go there, yes?"

Joe heard himself say, "Yes, of course."

The captain took out a phone and made a call, speaking what must have been Hungarian.

He turned back to Joe. "The first officer's cousin. Very reliable. You don't want an autocab to go to Austria. He said he will be here in ten minutes. Do you speak Magyar?" The captain's eyebrows rose.

"Magyar?"

"Hungarian." Seeing Joe's incomprehension, the captain shrugged. "I thought not. Well, Mátyás has German and a little English, and I will direct him."

***

Eric sat in the salon, watching the light creep over the old city of Pest. He had cajoled a sleepy steward into making a cup of coffee after having tossed and turned, sleepless, most of the night.

The gangway was down. Bottled water, oranges, fresh croissants were brought on board and laundry was taken off. The man with the ponytail...Santucci, wasn't it?...went down the gangway and got into an autocab. Early flight, probably.

Mayfield hurried by the salon window.

Eric went to the door.

"Joe...Joe?"

Mayfield turned and smiled weakly. Still looked shell-shocked.

"They found Weezy."

Eric tried not to let his face fall.

"She's alive. She's at a hospital." Joe's eyes were tired, but there was a shade of hope in his voice. "Back up the river, in Austria. I'm going there."

Joe turned to go down the companionway.

"Wait up," Eric said. "I'll go with you."

"No, I'll be okay."

Eric saw Joe's look. Guarded, maybe suspicious.

"You might need someone who can speak a little German."

Joe hesitated. Finally, he said, "Okay. The captain's called a cab. It's about a two-hour trip."

The captain stood at the head of the gangway.

"Mátyás is arriving in a couple of minutes," he said as Joe and Eric approached.

Ross Ackerman came down the aft companionway.

"Hi, guys. Joe, we're all so sorry for your loss." Eric read Ackerman's phony concern. Was it just Ackerman's normal tone deafness or was there something more?

"They found Louise early this morning," Joe said. "She's alive. She's in a hospital back in Austria."

"Really? That's wonderful."

Ackerman was not surprised. Eric was certain, now. How could he know about this already? The captain, maybe? Braithwaite? Then why would he pretend to be surprised?

Eric turned away from Ackerman, rearranging his features to hide the giveaway.

An ancient Skoda pulled into the parking area next to the dock, brakes complaining as it stopped. Rust spots dotted the faded green finish, and several dents spoke to past incaution. Mud clung to the rocker panels.

The captain's broad smile tried to cover his embarrassment. "Mátyás," he said, as if the name trumped the car's appearance.

A slightly overweight young man wearing a baseball cap got out of the car. The stink of diesel rose to greet the group. He looked up at the ship, and with a broad flourish, opened the rear door of the car.

Ross broke the astonished silence.

"I'll order a car. You can't be thinking of going in that piece of junk."

Joe looked at the car, then at Ross, seeming about to agree.

"The only other cabs available at this time of the morning are autocabs," the captain said. "Mátyás knows the roads better than the autocabs. Also —"

Ackerman interrupted. "Look, Joe. You said they found her, that she's in a hospital. She probably can't have visitors yet. Let's get some breakfast, let our friends and potential clients," he looked at Joe and Eric meaningfully, "know that everything's going to be all right. Then we'll get a decent cab and send you off a couple of hours from now."

"I have to go *now*."

Ross shook his head, "No, Joe. It makes no sense to go now." He looked at Eric, then the captain. "C'mon, guys. Support me on this. You know I'm right. Mayfield may not be able to think straight, but you can."

There was something off-kilter, a strain in Ross's voice.

"Let's go ahead with Mátyás," Eric said, watching Ross.

Ross's fair complexion flushed. Anger. But in his eyes … fear?

"Goddamn it, are you guys nuts? You want to drive two hours in a car that's falling apart with some … Hungarian Gypsy driving. What the fuck's wrong with you?"

The captain drew himself up, his own color rising.

"Mátyás is a good boy. Not a Gypsy. That is a very large insult in Hungary."

Ross made a throwaway gesture. "Aw, shit. For crissake, maybe the guy's a friggin' philosopher, but his car's a death trap. Wait a while … we'll get a limo. They've probably got the woman drugged up and tied down. She probably won't even know you."

"The woman?" Joe's voice rose as he stepped toward Ross, fists balled. "It's Louise … my … fiancée."

Eric put a restraining hand on Joe's shoulder. "Ross, this isn't about clients and sensible behavior," he said. "You don't stand around weighing the options when someone you love is in trouble. We're going with Mátyás." Ross's insistence and anger were confusing. Why was he so upset?

Eric took the lead, stepping toward the gangway.

Ross blocked his way at first, but stepped aside, perhaps seeing Eric's purposefulness, perhaps reckoning that mass times velocity equals right of way. Eric knew from his look that there would be consequences when Ross had a chance to have a back channel tête à tête with Zhou Qiáng. Eric realized he didn't care. Joe followed, with the captain and the first mate trailing behind, leaving Ross alone on the deck.

On the dock, Mátyás doffed his Boston Red Sox cap, creating an explosion of dark curls.

"Beszél Magyar?"

Joe and Eric both shook their heads, not understanding the question.

"Haben sie Deutsch?" Mátyás looked from Joe to Eric.

Eric said, "Kleine … uhh … wenig."

Mátyás pursed his lips, weighing Eric's broken German, then smiled, "Alzo, I speak in English with great proficient skill."

The captain and first officer arrived to translate. There ensued an extended conversation that lapsed into German and Hungarian with frequent mention of Slovakia.

Finally, the captain turned to Joe and Eric. "The normal route to Hainburg goes through Hungary, then into Slovakia, through Bratislava, finally to Austria. There is a little difficulty near Bratislava about smuggling. Mátyás said yesterday the Slovak police were inspecting every truck and car. He thinks they will do it again today, and that will make a big delay. He is going to take you from Hungary into Austria on the Budapester Strasse. A few kilometers longer, but shorter in time."

Mátyás nodded sagely. "Yes, faster this way. Very fast."

He motioned for Joe and Eric to get in. Eric reached for the door handle and pulled with no result. Mátyás mimed a hard jerk and said, "More, More." Eric shrugged, yanked the handle, and the door came free with a groan. He folded himself into the back seat, and the car issued a suspicious creak. Joe took the seat behind Mátyás.

Mátyás strapped himself in and gunned the engine. A cloud of diesel exhaust plumed in back of them, and they were off. The autopilot asked something in Hungarian. Mátyás swore and pounded the override button.

Dodging an incoming truck and receiving the international signal of irritation from its driver, Mátyás shot across the lot toward Jane Haining rkp. The old car's speed indicator began bleating. He swore again, pulled a stocking cap out of the glove box and put it over the indicator.

As they turned on to the boulevard, Eric shifted in his seat and saw Braithwaite had joined Ackerman on deck and was apparently enduring a tirade. Braithwaite's eyes found the cab and locked Eric in a cold stare. Mátyás swerved around a double parked van, and the ship and Braithwaite disappeared from view.

***

As the Skoda cleared the outskirts of Budapest, Mátyás engaged the autodrive and turned to Joe and Eric.

"You have been taking pleasure in your voyage from Wien, yes?"

Eric shook his head at Mátyás.

Mátyás restarted. "Your lady will be okay, no? She will have enthusiastic care in the hospital. Doctors in Österreich is very excellent." He pulled a serious face entirely out of keeping with the Red Sox cap and curls.

"I hope so," Joe said, his tone flat. But Mátyás apparently felt an obligation to buck up and inform his clients. Their trip across Hungary was accompanied by Mátyás' commentary on the geography, an idiosyncratic history of the Magyar invasion, and his opinion of the quality of the "babies" in each little town. Eric whispered, "I think he means 'babes'," managing to pull a grin out of Joe.

After an hour, Mátyás pointed to a turn off the autobahn. "That way is Slovakia. Stupid computer shows a traffic clutter ahead, but still wants us to go that way. Smart computer …" He tapped his head. "Tells us to go to Austria."

Twenty minutes later, riding through neatly manicured farm fields on a quiet country road, the speed indicator's over speed warning turned from a muffled bleep to a klaxon. The car shimmied, and Mátyás indulged in a torrent of abuse. The Skoda limped to the shoulder and stopped in a cloud of dust.

"The tire is broken, but don't shake your brain about it. I fix it very quick."

They got out of the car. Joe stood very still, his breathing short, shallow. Finally, he began marching up the road. Eric called after him, "Joe, you can't walk to Hainburg." Joe kept walking.

Mátyás watched as Joe crested the hill in front of them, turned to Eric and said again, "Very quick."

And he was right. Eric could tell from Mátyás' practiced movements that he needed to fix flats often.

Two hills later, they picked Joe up.

Back on the road, Joe went silent as they approached Hainberg, a spring coiling, his face frozen. Even Mátyás kept quiet, and they rode the last several miles in silence.

***

Armand Santucci lived by a simple rule: Safety and success depended on having options. Santucci contemplated a corollary as the autocab made its way toward Hainburg: As in chess, options shrank as the end game approached.

Santucci watched the farm fields slide by and constructed his plan. The task he had been assigned would ordinarily present an array of possible solutions. To do it without raising suspicion removed many of them. Having to do it in a hospital squeezed them down to a precious few. The how-to-do-it part was difficult. It had to be done, because Napolitani was the only person who could identify him. The authorities might suspect him, but that didn't bother him much. When he got to Corsica, he could disappear into hills no sane police force would dare enter. Failure, on the other hand, had serious risks. Alive, he was the thread that connected the operation to Braithwaite. Braithwaite did not tolerate threads or loose ends.

Finishing Napolitani required charm, confidence, and speed, not muscle. The getting back to Corsica undetected was much easier.

He took out his e-pad. He ruminated on the risks presented by the several routes out of Hainburg. Presuming Braithwaite would be monitoring the cab's audio, he whistled a recent pop song while keying instructions to view where Braithwaite told the autocab to go after Hainburg. It was to wait one hour, then go through Bratislava to Tatabanya, not Budapest. Presumably, when the job was completed, Braithwaite would direct Santucci to go from Tatabanya to Vienna and home. Or maybe he would leave him swinging in the wind.

Santucci cracked a grin. He had led Braithwaite to believe he was hopeless with electronic communication. Another corollary to his operating rule: secrecy breeds and preserves options. He continued to whistle as he entered an order for a second autocab to wait on a side street in Hainburg. He set the Vienna airport as his destination. He knew he could change the route later and go to Wiener Neustadt, the town Richard Lionheart's ransom built south of Vienna. From there, he would take the high-speed rail to Graz, then to Italy and across to Livorno, to the hydrofoil to carry him to Corsica, where he could disappear.

Pleased, he closed his eyes and thought through his plan for the hospital and Napolitani one more time. He reached into his pocket and tapped one of the *pics* he had ready for action in the seams of his pants. The *pic* buoyed his confidence, and he forced himself to relax.

A few minutes later, he startled awake and found himself staring at the rear end of a large truck. The autocab threw a map up with a notation of a traffic stop for "investigation." A portly Slovak police officer appeared around the truck, tapped his data device into the exterior port on the autocab, looked Santucci up and down, grunted and said something Slavic, then "Out" in English.

Santucci got out of the autocab, calculating the damage to his carefully constructed plan, waved his hand at the stopped truck and said, "What is this?"

The Slovak officer must have seen the spike of anger in Santucci's eyes. His jaw set. "Investigation," he said, pointing to the side of the road. "Stand there." His hand moved closer to the Taser on his belt.

Santucci moved a couple of steps away, scanning the row of cars and trucks. He slipped his hand into his pocket, watching the officer engrossed in his inspection. *Maybe … But no. Get this over as quickly as possible.* The officer leaned into the autocab, checking under seats and in the small luggage compartment, taking his time. Finally, he said, "Okay," with a smirk and moved toward the next car in line.

Santucci got back in the autocab and waited, cursing the cops under his breath. After a very long fifteen minutes, the truck in front moved. The autocab continued into Slovakia, slowed for morning traffic in Bratislava, then crossed the Danube and turned west toward Hainburg an der Donau. Santucci tried to convince himself that half an hour more or less wouldn't change things.

# TWENTY-NINE

HAINBURG WAS A pretty town of red roofs, white buildings and a church spire. Not much traffic. Santucci watched the buildings and streets as he passed through the outskirts, constructing escape routes in his mind. As the cab approached the hospital, he saw the second autocab he'd ordered, waiting on a side street.

"Halt." His autocab pulled over to the curb. Santucci scanned the area around the second cab. He took the small packet of emergency supplies he always carried out of his bag. It held money, a miniature phone, a rolled-up e-pad, a debit card and a new identity, as well as a small explosive charge. He got out and slipped the packet under the leading edge of the rear tire, far enough in so people going by wouldn't see it. Back in the first autocab, he consulted his map and reviewed the layout of the hospital, memorizing exits and paths. "Right turn. Park here." The autocab obeyed.

He took the syringe out of its case and slipped it into his shirt pocket. Then he was out of the cab, walking toward the hospital.

As he approached the entrance, he held his breath and strained to give himself a flushed appearance. Then, through the door. The emergency room doubled as urgent care in this small town, and the waiting area held a couple of people. He ramped up his breathing and rushed to the information kiosk.

"Louise Napolitani, a patient in the emergency room. She just came in." He used English.

The person behind the desk, Frau Schmidt, struggled for a moment, translating. "Familie?"

"Freundin. Fiancee."

"Ahh. Fiancee. It is not possible to see."

"I am from the boat. The Donau König. She has no family here."

"Ahh." Frau Schmidt's features softened. She glanced at the hall to the emergency receiving rooms, confirming Napolitani was down there somewhere.

She pointed toward the waiting room. "Bitte setzen Sie sich."

Santucci crossed toward the corner nearest the receiving rooms, hearing Frau Schmidt call for a Doctor Kühn. On the way, he looked down the hall. Empty. Back at the desk, a woman with a whimpering child had claimed Frau Schmidt's attention. *Go. Now.*

Santucci willed himself to relax as he stepped into the corridor. *I belong here. No reason to question me.*

Each room had a window. Convenient for staff to monitor patients and a godsend for Santucci. The first two rooms were empty. In the third, a patient, covered in blankets, only the head showing. Chestnut hair splayed on the pillow. Yes, Napolitani for sure.

He watched her. Eyes closed. Out of it. Monitor showing normal heart rate. A bag of clear liquid hanging, its IV tube snaking under the sheet, no doubt into her arm. Like Braithwaite said, a plastic port at the bottom of the bag.

One more glance each direction, then Santucci opened the door silently and slipped into the room.

***

Hans Prohoffer found it hard to stay away from the hospital for the hours since they found the woman, Louise Napolitani. He kept seeing her lying on the bank, vulnerable, the hand clinging to the root and the thread of life. He told Kühn to call him as soon as she woke up.

He busied himself with preparation for a hearing later in the week, but kept an eye on his e-pad, which he had set to monitor the emergency room feed. Astrid Kühn had passed through the waiting area several times, probably checking on Napolitani.

Finally, at 8:30, his deputy, Helmut Österer, arrived, which freed Hans to go to the hospital.

The automatic doors hissed open, and Frau Schmidt looked up from her magazine to smile at him. He asked about Napolitani.

"Oh, her fiancé arrived a few minutes ago. I called Astrid … pardon, Dr. Kühn … because I can't let the poor man in to see her without …" Frau Schmidt turned toward the waiting room, surprise registering on her face. "He was sitting there, in the corner. Perhaps he's gone to the toilet?"

Hans followed her look toward the examination rooms. Astrid Kühn came toward them. She nodded at Prohoffer while she listened to Frau Schmidt's explanation about the fiancé.

Kühn turned, irritated, and motioned Prohoffer to come along. Her pace was closer to a jog than a walk. Always in a hurry, always more to do than one doctor should have to manage. Prohoffer hustled to keep up, listening to her report on Napolitani's condition. Miracle she's alive, being so thin. Exposure. Core temp dangerously low, but vital functions approaching normal half an hour ago. Some chemical in her bloodstream, lab in Vienna to report in two or three days. Prohoffer was right, it was a twisting fracture of the left radius just above the wrist. Dehydrated. Something to make her sleep.

They passed two observation rooms, then she stopped short, staring into the third room.

"Scheisse!"

She hit the door, Hans following.

Napolitani was in the bed, semi-conscious. A man was hunched over her. Kühn screamed at him. He turned, dropping the saline drip line and reaching into his pocket. There was a moment of silence. Then the alarm went off. Hans pushed Kühn aside and faced the man. Light flickered off a blade. The man crouched, a feral sneer on his face, but graceful, shifting the knife from hand to hand, reading Hans.

"Drop the knife."

The monitor was tracing an electrostatic dance. Hans was vaguely aware of Kühn reaching for the crash kit and the defib paddles.

"The IV … he was doing something with the IV," Prohoffer yelled. Kühn reached across the bed and grabbed at the IV line. She ripped the needle out of Napolitani's arm.

The man lunged, point directed toward Hans's eyes, then dropped the blade toward his heart—perfect fencing form. Hans parried, his right forearm neatly catching knife. Completing the movement, he stepped into a classic riposte, muscle memory responding to the hours of practice and the tournaments. His left hand came up to grasp the jaw of the smaller man above his Adam's apple. His follow-through lifted his attacker off the ground and carried him in an arc toward the wall. The man bared his teeth in a fruitless attempt to breathe. Then he hit the wall.

*"Hans! Hans!"*

He woke, the killer rage fading, and he loosened his grip on the smaller man's throat. The man's pallor slanted toward normal. After a moment, he gave out a gurgling cough, and his eyes fluttered open.

Hans tapped his communicator, felt a pain shoot up to his shoulder, and noticed the stiletto sticking through his arm. He shrugged and continued to tap away, ordering his deputy to come to the hospital.

***

At the reception desk, the woman leaning toward Frau Schmidt demanded to see the doctor for the third time in ten minutes. She spoke a mile a minute in school German, repeating herself, which offended Frau Schmidt. She reminded Frau Schmidt of her husband's stature as president of the Landesbank. The boy tugged at his mother's pant leg, whining in a thin, tired, drone.

Frau Schmidt almost wished for the normal boredom of the job, the book of puzzles and the endless murmur of the Healthy Lifestyle messages looping in the waiting room. Kühn, normally collegial, had been barking orders. Poor Hans Prohoffer was stabbed by the fiancé … she'd had her doubts about him all along … and the girl from the river had been attacked. Hans' deputy Helmut had arrived sweating and red-faced and took over with the false fiancé. Hans was down at Imaging, where they were deciding what to do with the knife in his arm. Frau Schmidt was about to tell the woman that, yes, the doctor was busy right now but would surely be out soon and ask if the young man wanted another hard candy.

There was a loud bang at the emergency entrance, followed by a cloud of smoke. A dirty cab spilled two men who rushed in, speaking English too fast, then ignorant German, also looking for the poor girl from the river. They, also, were not family. A second fiancé, apparently. So confusing that when Frau Schmidt paged Kühn, she mentioned this was important, not about the woman with the kid. As a result, she had four people crowding her desk, one large and hopeful, one frantic, one irate, and a small one keening.

***

Where was Weezy? Joe stood rooted to the floor, almost panting as the words swirled around him. Eric O'Malley was asking questions in pidgin German. The woman at the information desk, Frau Schmidt according to her name tag, had a little English. The severe woman with the kid was talking over both of them in German, repeating "Landesbanke" several times. Weezy was "besser now," whatever that meant. But he couldn't see her. Maybe because he was not family. There was mention of "Polizei," which seemed to promise delay. Joe's head was about to explode.

"Shut up!"

Everyone, even the kid, looked at Joe, stunned.

"The doctor? Where is he?" Joe said.

The indignant woman turned to him, angry, and said in slightly accented English, "It is 'she' not 'he.' The doctor is taking care of the idiot Bundespolizei, who can surely take care of himself, instead of mein Kaspar."

Frau Schmidt pursed her lips. "I vill—" Not finding the right English, she picked up the handset of her desk phone and paged Astrid Kühn. The phone chimed immediately, and Frau Schmidt conferred briefly. She hung up and said to Joe, "Kommen Sie," tilting her head toward the hall to her left. She stood and turned to the woman with the whining kid, nodded toward the waiting area and, wearing a tight smile, said the German equivalent of "Someone will be with you shortly." Or maybe something about where she could put the Landesbanke. Hard to tell which from the woman's reaction.

***

Joe followed Frau Schmidt a couple of doors down the corridor. She knocked lightly, then held the door for Joe and Eric to enter. A large man sat on the exam table in his undershirt. A bloody white dress shirt hung on a chair beside him, together with a blue uniform jacket with an arm patch announcing "Polizei." A woman in a white lab coat was wrapping gauze around the man's forearm, her long blond hair showing a little gray. A bloody stiletto lay in a stainless steel pan on the table beside her. Frau Schmidt began a rapid explanation in German to the woman, whose badge identified her as A. Kühn. She concentrated on the policeman's bandage, nodding at each bit of information Schmidt gave her. She applied tape, smiled at the big cop and turned to Joe and Eric.

"You are the second people claiming to know our patient. The first one did this," she inclined her head to the bandage, "to our Herr Prohoffer. You have, perhaps, a firearm? A cannon? A bomb?" She enunciated the trailing 'b.'

Someone else? Joe thought.

"Is she … Ms. Napolitani … all right?"

The woman nodded, "She will be okay, I think."

"Where is she?" Joe realized he'd almost shouted the question.

The big cop stood up. No gun, just a Taser, but it was clear he didn't need it very often. He was even bigger than Eric and looked unhappy. Not the kind of person one wants to see unhappy. He studied Joe and Eric, then spoke to the doctor in German.

"Herr Prohoffer wants to know your connection to Frau Napolitani."

"She is my … friend," Joe stumbled over the imprecision of English in explaining relationships.

Eric took over. "Ms. Napolitani is Mr. Mayfield's lady friend. Freundin, I think."

Prohoffer chuckled, not a friendly sound. He spoke to Dr. Kühn, keeping his eyes on Joe.

The doctor turned to Eric. "He said the first fiancé tried to kill her and is in custody. He wants to know what we shall do with this second fiancé?" A smile hid behind her serious expression.

Eric reached into his pocket. Prohoffer straightened and seemed to expand. Eric held up a hand. "E-pad," he said. "The ship's captain can identify us." He took out and unrolled a small e-pad, tapped it, and handed it to Prohoffer.

An extended conversation in German followed, during which Prohoffer turned the e-pad to Eric and to Joe revealing a concerned-looking captain. Their identities established, Prohoffer switched off the e-pad and handed it back to Eric.

Prohoffer looked at his shirt, shrugged, and put it on, then the blue jacket. He jerked his head toward the waiting room, opened the door, and walked in that direction. The doctor, Joe and Eric followed. Frau Schmidt began to say something as they approached the reception desk when the landesbanke woman ejected herself from her chair, mouth a thin line, ugly in her anger.

"Kühn!" she shouted. "Kühn!"

Ahead of Joe, Dr. Kühn began to weaken. Prohoffer continued toward the corridor beyond the waiting room. The woman stepped back, suddenly not so sure of herself. Prohoffer wagged a finger at her, shook his head. She stepped aside, looking furious.

They continued to the corridor and the third observation room.

Joe saw Weezy through the window.

A jolt of relief drove him toward the door.

Prohoffer blocked Joe, shaking his head. Astrid Kühn slipped by. Eric took Joe by the shoulders and moved him to the observation window, where Joe huffed great dry sobs as he watched Dr. Kühn check Weezy's vital signs. After a couple of minutes, Kühn gave a small nod, and Prohoffer stepped away from the door. Joe entered and Kühn whispered, "Gentle, very gentle."

Weezy's eyes were closed. She was doing the little lady snore Joe sometimes woke to. Her hands rested lightly on the bed. Joe stroked her fingers. Her eyelids fluttered open. She smiled, soft and sweet, and mouthed something. Joe looked to Prohoffer for approval. Getting it, he leaned close.

" 'Bout time, dumbass."

# THIRTY

HANS PROHOFFER HAD the sense these people were what they said they were. Kühn had the situation under control. He turned toward the room where he left the stiletto guy bound to a chair with Österer in charge. It was time to deal with him. This was no ordinary thug. The drug that nearly killed the woman wasn't a narcotic. Worked too fast. And the stiletto. A professional, for sure.

"Österer?"

Hans rounded the corner into the room.

Helmut Österer sat in a chair, not standing as he should be. Napping. Hans's anger started up.

"Österer!"

Hans came fully into the room, preparing to rip into Österer. The chair where they had bound Stiletto was empty. The plastic restraints lay on the floor, neatly cut.

Österer wore his navy blue uniform jacket, probably too warm today, because sweat beaded on his brow. A dark stain spread from the center of his jacket.

"Helmut?" He put his hand gently on Österer's forearm, shook it. "Helmut? What gives?" Hans knew the answer before he finished the question.

***

Santucci left by the hospital's back entrance, taking care to look purposeful, not furtive. His right hand burned, scraped raw from the effort of pulling it out of the restraint. When the constable strapped his arm to the chair, he had moaned in fake pain and arched his wrist. The constable bought it. Stupid.

He walked to the second autocab, the one waiting on the side street, pulled away the pouch he'd placed next to the rear wheel and got in.

"Wiener Neustadt. Go," he said. The cab started up, electric engine whirring to life, a display showing directions. Santucci opened the pouch and carefully fished out the small explosive charge that would have destroyed the bag in case he hadn't used the autocab. Outside the town proper, Santucci tossed the charge into a field of mounds covering next year's white asparagus crop.

He thought about disappearing but didn't like the idea of running out on a client. He didn't care about Braithwaite, and he had a significant upfront payment. But he didn't want Braithwaite bad-mouthing him. Assassination was a business, and references mattered. The woman could identify him, but only if he was caught, and he would be safe in Corsica by tomorrow morning. The cop had taken the phone Braithwaite gave him, so he used the one from the pouch to send a message to Father Time. It was supposed to be RxQ if successful. He sent pxR (resigns),clicked the phone off, rolled down the window and threw it down to the road hard. He watched it bounce several times.

The phone came to rest on the edge of the road next to a puddle, case broken, its face glinting in the morning sun. A starling, seeing the shiny object, landed next to it and pecked at it, turning it on. In its dying moments, the battery powered the auto finder to announce its location.

***

Hans Prohoffer used the cover of his rudimentary English to delay talking with the Americans. Nothing so far this morning had been what it seemed, and he was not taking chances. He called in an off-duty officer to watch over Mayfield and

O'Malley. In Kühn's office, he uploaded a couple of stills of Österer's killer from his uniform camera and sent them off to Interpol. A few minutes later, Interpol called back. So quick, he thought. But the call was patched through Interpol from the American FBI liaison in Vienna. The instructions, in keeping with the rest of the morning, made no sense.

Prohoffer found O'Malley and Mayfield where he had left them in the lobby. The irritating woman and her kid were gone, and Astrid Kühn joined them. An enthusiastic Healthy Lifestyle message played in background, encouraging meals of leafy vegetables.

Prohoffer spoke to Kühn, watching Mayfield as she translated.

"Herr Mayfield, Constable Prohoffer has been asked by your FBI to hold you for questioning in the attempted murder of Frau Napolitani. An agent is being sent from Vienna. He will arrive tomorrow."

O'Malley's face registered shock and surprise. Mayfield looked confused.

Kühn continued, "Herr Prohoffer wishes you to surrender your passport and e-pad."

Prohoffer watched Mayfield. His gut told him this was all wrong. Mayfield's sobs when he saw Napolitani and his tenderness with her. But he shrugged and took the handcuffs from his belt.

***

Prohoffer walked Joe the two blocks to the police station, part of what Joe took to be the municipal building. Inside, they passed windows offering *Lizenzen* to the end of the hall and a door marked "Polizei." The door opened on what looked like a small, neat sitting room except for the computer equipment and gun rack. Prohoffer led Joe through the gate at the desk and directed him to empty his pockets and give up his belt and shoes.

Behind the desk were two barred doors, one on each wall. Prohoffer checked the right-hand cell, held his nose and said, "Gestank," then directed Joe to the left. The cell was a room with a barred door, a bed that folded out from the wall, a stainless steel toilet and a shelf that was meant to function as table and desk. A window looked out over an incongruously peaceful garden. Still stunned, Joe sat on the bed, staring at the concrete floor.

He heard Prohoffer leave. Maybe he would find Eric and clear up the misunderstanding. Must be a misunderstanding.

Half an hour later, Joe heard Eric's voice in the hall. He couldn't see much of main room, but heard Eric try some German on the deputy.

There was a silence, then a scrape of metal. The deputy appeared at the cell door holding a metal straight chair, which he placed carefully more than arm's-length from the bars. After inspecting his work, he wagged a finger at Joe and said, "Only talk." Then he gestured back into the office.

Eric came into the picture and sat in the chair, his expression serious.

"I talked with Ackerman."

Joe nodded, sensing he should not interrupt with the questions that had stacked up while he waited.

"Quantitec?" Eric waited, eyebrows knit into one long, untamed question mark. Then anger rising. "Proud, are you?"

Joe exhaled. "Eric—"

"Napolitani found out what you were doing," Eric said. "You tried to kill her to protect the scheme, right?"

Joe ran his fingers through his hair, laced them behind his neck and gave a short, bitter laugh.

"Jesus. I should have seen it. We never should have gotten on the boat."

"Why did you do it, Joe?" There was hurt under Eric's anger. "You were paid plenty, you had a beautiful woman. You had to —"

Joe's anger propelled him to the cell bars. "The account was set up to frame me," he shouted. Eric recoiled. "I learned about it just before we got on the boat. I thought it was a way of getting rid of me," he said, blinking back angry tears. "I didn't think they'd go after Weezy." Joe pounded on the bars. "Shit, they killed HoHum, then they tried to kill me. How could I be so stupid?"

"Who's HoHum?"

Joe took long breaths.

"Ackerman, probably with Braithwaite's help, sets up catastrophes to make Skins pay out hundreds of millions. Then he buys the high-risk tranches. I suspected something was wrong. Weezy used some, ahhh, informal contacts—"

"Hackers?"

"Yeah, Eric, hackers. One of them is dead now, courtesy of Ackerman or Braithwaite, most likely. The mugging in Greenwich Village was not random. I figured this bogus account was the next try to get me. But the obvious target was Weezy."

Joe slumped down on the bed.

"I should have seen it."

His face contorted. "They'll try again, Eric. Talk to Prohoffer. Do something, please."

Eric looked for a long moment at Joe, jaw working. "Joe, I'm sorry. The evidence—"

Joe stood. "You should know better than to buy into Ackerman's bullshit," he said as calmly as he could. "If you don't believe me, call Madeline Hollingsworth, Weezy's colleague at IAC. Ask her about an FBI agent named Henry Barber."

He rubbed his temples. "But before you do that, please convince Prohoffer to make sure Weezy's safe."

***

Ross Ackerman paced the rear deck of the boat. The stateroom was too stuffy. The salon had too many helpful crew members. After he read Braithwaite's clear text message, he had knocked on Braithwaite's cabin door, intimidated the woman changing bed linens in the adjoining cabin to open it up, and confirmed his suspicion. No Braithwaite. No surprise, really. Braithwaite was always a step or two ahead of the game. The vague promise to investigate Santucci was pointless. Braithwaite knew his message to unwind the Kazakh skin would never see the light of day.

Ross was tempted to call on the secure phone Braithwaite handed him when they talked about eliminating the communication chain back in New York. But he had no leverage, and he didn't want to beg.

His phone tapped him. O'Malley.

"Yeah?"

"Ross, there have been some developments."

"Yeah? What?"

"Mayfield has been arrested."

"Why?" Ross tried to sound surprised.

"Something about him trading in Skins and insider knowledge."

So the FBI bit on the Quantitec account. Good.

Getting no response, Eric continued, "I have to stay here until we get this sorted out. I think it'll only be for a couple of days. I hate to lose the contact with Morgan RioTinto, but maybe tell everyone that Louise Napolitani is recovering, and say Joe and I have to assist with the investigation."

"Do what you have to do. I'll hold it together here."

Ross signed off, relieved.

Eric was a smart guy behind all that hail-fellow-well-met BS, not someone he wanted nosing around. Mayfield had to know something was queer about the Quantitec account. Good to have both of them out of the way. With Braithwaite out of the picture, the Kazakh plan was dead. Ross could get out from under at least some of the risky positions they'd taken. He could pitch this as an unfortunate disaster to Zhou Qiáng—move quickly to resolve it and probably come out smelling like a rose.

"Call Arty Pov. Home number."

Clicks, then the ring, then video showing Arty, more disheveled than usual, squinting into the e-pad's camera from his bed. Gray light surrounded him, and Ross realized it was before dawn in New York.

"Hey, Arty. Gotta unwind the Kazakh Skin."

Arty blinked and rubbed an eye.

"Wake up. Listen up. I'm getting some vibes at the conference. Looks like the Nazarbayeva broad is going to take the national elections and continue as premier. No matter what she says publicly, back channel said she'll be pro economic development and anti-plutocrat. And, yes, I know it'll cost us."

Arty blinked again. Probably hung over.

"Arty, you with me?"

"Yeah, but that seems pretty sudden. I should maybe slow down. Give you a chance to check it out further?"

Arty looked like he was finally waking up.

"No. We gotta unwind it now," said Ross, watching Arty's expression. He was skeptical. Maybe worried. Why?

"Don't worry, man," Ross said, thinking, Arty's a great trader but he's not so good at wrapping fresh, crusty panini around dog shit to make an appealing sandwich. Maybe he's worried it'll look like a retreat. I can spin it as a clever strategic move.

"Line up your guys," Ross said. "But hold off on pulling the trigger until I get back."

***

Ross's tap said, "I just talked to O'Malley, and something's wrong in Hainburg. Get your ass down there." Braithwaite, walking into the Delta entry hall at the Budapest airport, was not available to go to Hainburg and did not plan to be available. Ever. Too bad to lose ZCG, but this whole project was unraveling. Take the financial lumps. Develop new customers. Maybe some hints to Interpol to build deniability. For now, get back to South Africa, use his contacts to fight extradition or disappear if he had to.

He unfolded his e-pad for the young woman at the boarding kiosk. He was flying Business Class and fit the part: well-dressed, and a passport that told a story of frequent travel. He had arrived well later than the one hour normally required for identity checking, but that wasn't uncommon for frequent international business travelers.

"Returning home, Mr. de Jaager?"

"Ja." He said it flatly and did not smile at her, discouraging further conversation.

He had seen the chess move as he walked back toward his stateroom from the discussion with Ackerman on the rear deck. "Pawn takes Rook (resigns)" was bad news. The "resigns" must mean Santucci resigned, either because he had to, or …

It took him ten minutes to trace the call to its origin. It was from a different disposable than the one he'd given Santucci.

The phone was stationary about ten miles on the other side of Hainburg. That meant several possibilities, all bad.

He'd packed a small amount of gear and some cash into his briefcase. He slipped out of his cabin and passed down several internal companionways to the service deck. Using a combination of sign language, a few shared words and substantial cash, he had convinced a delivery driver to take him to a cabstand in the Old City.

On the way to the airport, he slipped a data cube into his e-pad and became Rik de Jaager, a businessman from South Africa working for an electronics supplier headquartered in Utrecht. As much as he hated Lady Fortune, she had smiled upon him in his hour of need. There was a morning flight to Schiphol with a seat available. A trip from Hungary to the Netherlands to South Africa fit the logic of his identity. Interpol algorithms would ignore it.

Sitting in the departure lounge, he analyzed the situation. Ross could distance himself from catastrophe, but only by pointing to him. Nick weighed the pros and cons of several strategies, finally sending Ross a clear text message saying he was investigating the Santucci situation. He told Ross to place the blame for the Napolitani problem on Ramos Security for not vetting Santucci effectively. Some hacker must have wanted her out of the way. He would be in touch when he knew more.

He signed off, then from another pad sent a coded message through the secure Ramos server, "Unwind Kazakh Skin." The message compromised him, but it would sink Ross, so he was confident it would never be exposed. Ross would unwind the Kazakh Skin and lose some money. Braithwaite would, of course, keep the plan intact. His bets on Uranium, chromium and the Kazakh currency would pay off.

A chime in the entry hall called his flight. The gate attendant smiled at him, perhaps a little wistfully, as she validated his boarding credentials.

# THIRTY-ONE

ARTY TRIED UNSUCCESSFULLY to go back to sleep after Ross's call. Finally, he threw off the covers, padded to the bathroom for a piss, then the kitchenette for a morning vodka. He reached for the bottle, hesitated, and made a pot of coffee instead. He stood at the counter, watching it brew, his mind a mess of questions.

Why would Ross suddenly deep-six the Kazakh Skin? He had just sent detailed instructions for the RedSock accounts that made it clear he thought something was going to happen in a month or two. He always seemed to have knowledge of when bad things were going to happen. All the recent surprises were from Africa. Must be Braithwaite had some inside line on the politics. Maybe not so much in Kazakhstan? Maybe they stumbled?

Early sunlight filtered between the buildings. Arty poured a cup of coffee, resisting the temptation to top it off with brandy.

He and Emily might have to execute their plan. The more he thought about it, the more questions he had. Dealing with cold reality was different from speculating in the happy aftermath of lovemaking, buoyed by a bump or two of coke.

He dressed for work slowly. Finally, he called Emily, hanging up after the second ring, hoping she would call back soon.

As he left his apartment, he had a vision of standing on a second floor fire escape when he was nine, his friend Igor calling him pussy for being afraid to jump. That time, he only got a broken leg.

***

Emily felt her e-pad vibrate and checked it. Arty. The tour guide was leading the group of mostly women away from the National Gallery toward the Western Railway Station for an arranged lunch. Emily was grateful for the guide, a young woman who spoke flawless English. All morning, she had kept up an in-depth, often funny commentary on Budapest's history, buildings and scandals. After the initial embarrassment of explaining Ross would not be joining them, Emily realized that the people on the tour understood overworked spouses. Now, she said to the group, "A call from Ross's office. Go on ahead, and I'll join you shortly." Nods and knowing smiles allowed her to escape to a bench overlooking the Danube.

"Call Artyom Povreshenko, private number."

After clicks and three rings, Arty answered, sitting outside the New Jersey office building.

"Arty, I'm in Budapest."

"Are you calling from the ship?"

"No, a park bench. No one will hear us. Hold on."

She glanced around her, saw that she was alone but for several people on the concourse in back of her, walking away. When she was sure they were out of earshot, she continued, "I'm not sure what's going on. Last night, Louise Napolitani ... you probably don't remember her ... fell overboard."

"Overboard?"

"Then this morning, Ross got a call really early, I think from Nick Braithwaite. Something set him off. Then he was up and out in a hurry. He didn't tell me what was going on, except he didn't go to breakfast, and he didn't come on this tour, which he was supposed to host. I've heard that they found Louise and she's alive."

"Maybe Ross was upset about Napolitani?"

"I don't think so. It was something else, maybe to do with work."

Arty nodded. "You're probably right. Ross just called me. Looks like there's something wrong with the Kazakh Skin." He paused, then said, "I think it's time for the plan."

"Are you sure?"

"Look, if you have any concerns about—"

"No concerns, Arty." Emily put on a brave face, braver than she felt.

"Me neither." But Emily saw he was scared, too.

"This is a big step. I wish I were in New York with you …" her voice drifted off. "But I should probably go. If you hear anything in the next four hours, it'll be safe to call on this phone."

"I'll see if I can find out anything more," Arty said. "But I think you should distribute the trusts today if you don't hear from me." He smiled, and his homely face transformed, letting her know she was beautiful to him. "It's all out ahead of us, Em," he said.

After they signed off, Emily sat watching a boat moving slowly against the river current, concentrating on its progress to hold her fears at bay. What was out ahead of them?

***

"Are you going to join us for lunch?"

Emily tried to keep the tension out of her voice. Not fair, making her hold the tour together while Ross ignored them.

"Be there in fifteen," he said.

The ZCG guests and bankers had split into smaller groups to enjoy the city and presumably engage in bonding that might lead to revenue for ZCG. Emily sat with Don and Pam Petrescu arrayed around a sun dappled table in an outdoor cafe, finishing their meal. When Ross arrived, he waved away the menu and ordered a pilsner and coffee. Everyone was curious about Louise Napolitani.

Ross gave the short story: Napolitani's going to be okay. Lucky she fell overboard right near a little town and someone found her early this morning. She'll be fine. Broken arm. Could have been much worse.

"Such a relief," Emily said to murmurs of agreement. Then, "Ross, honey, I'd like to stay in Budapest for a couple of extra days, if you don't mind."

Don chuckled. "How big is your wallet, Ross?"

Ross dove into the flow of banter, but Emily knew part of his brain was working on something that had nothing to do with the conversation, maybe that morning phone call.

Ross excused himself after lunch. "Conference call" was what he said. "Standard excuse" was what Emily heard.

The afternoon featured a continuation of the morning's walking tour. The guide's animated chatter left Emily free from the obligation of small talk.

This could be a catastrophe, she thought. I think I love Arty, but he uses drugs and drinks too much. Besides, love, at my age? Give up the rich life? What about the kids at the school in Harlem?

Partway through the tour, she got a two-ring call from Arty. She texted back. "On tour. I'll call later."

When the tour was over and the rest of the group had gone back to the ship, Emily found a secluded park bench and called Arty.

After a short delay, he appeared in his "office" in the men's room. "Definitely something not right with this latest Skin," he said. "I think it's time for the plan." He cocked his head. "You sure you're ready?"

"I don't know, Arty. I've been thinking about it ever since we talked. It's not the sensible thing to do, and I've always been sensible." She laughed, deep in her throat. "Maybe it's time for a change."

After they disconnected, Emily read through the detailed instructions from her cousin Bill, the attorney in Cedar Rapids. Her mouth was dry, and her fingers shook as she entered the Central Bank Netherlands Antilles website and pressed Private Banking. She put her thumb on the identifier box that popped up on her e-pad and began reading off bank names and routing numbers of sixteen target accounts.

# THIRTY-TWO

ROSS WALKED DOWN the quay to a coffee shop with an appealing terrace. Quiet in mid-afternoon and more private than the Donau König. He sipped a pilsner, searching for a little relaxation. It was late in Hong Kong, the middle of the trading day for the ZCG office there. He tapped a secure line and Zhou Qiáng answered immediately.

Ross reeled off the Dinara Nazarbayeva excuse, working to show embarrassment and contrition over the loss ZCG would take to unwind the Kazakh Skin. He kept it simple and direct. There was silence at the other end.

"How much do we lose?" Zhou Qiáng's voice was flat.

"I think I can hold it under ten million."

Ross waited for Zhou to digest, then, trying to sound reticent, "There may be another problem."

"Yes?"

The secure line hissed softly.

"One of our bankers may have been trading these Skins to enrich himself."

"Who is it?"

"An analyst, Joe Mayfield, below the level of close surveillance and not a trader."

"Who knows about this?"

"Our security chief and me."

Silence as the elder Zhou computed.

"I will be in the New York on Sunday," Zhou said. "We will meet then." Not a suggestion, Ross realized, but an order.

***

"Brian, give me a call."

Ross used the ship's communication system, expecting the call to be buried in the ordinary ones sent back to ZCG. Even if it was observed, he hoped it would look like a client talking to his broker. Ross kept a small portfolio with Brian Garrity to make conversations with him credible.

Brian's tap came a few minutes later.

Ross was on the rear deck of the ship. Most guests were leaving or had left, and except for effusive thanks for the trip and promises to get in touch on business matters, he was left alone.

Hoping to hide in plain sight, he answered, "How's trading?"

"Uhh. Yeah. Good." Brian caught on. "Dow's flat, NASDAQ's up a bit. None of your shares are moving significantly."

"Okay. I want you to buy the Kazakh Skin into that higher-risk account."

"You mean the May—"

"Yeah. That account." There was a reason this bonehead was in a third-rate firm.

"Okay. Gotcha. Lotta cash available, after the chrom—"

"Right. Put all of it into Kazakh Skin."

"Probably a good idea, you know, in general, right?"

*Jesus! The dumb fuck wants to tag along. I should let him screw himself, but I may need him in the future.*

"Wouldn't recommend it at this time for the, uhh, more conservative accounts."

Ross signed off from Brian and allowed himself a little self-congratulatory glee. This was going to work out. Too bad to lose Braithwaite, but that effectively severed the tie to the hacker and the Napolitani broad. The big accounts had been sold the Kazakh Skin, but the trades supporting them hadn't executed yet. He could go back at them with humble apologies, mention how much ZCG was losing. They'd admire his honesty. Arty must have hedged the downside, so ZCG would take a loss, but trading losses were a cost of doing business. Both Zhous would see that. RedSock would take a hit, but there would be a lot left after the chromium and copper gravy trains. Mayfield would be out of his hair. Poor bastard never knew he was rich. When the Kazakh Skin cratered, it would wipe the account, and the press release would tip the feds. Mayfield would end up in some medium security institution in east bumfuck Arkansas. Who knew? Maybe they'd bite on the story Napolitani figured out what he was doing and he tried to kill her. All in all, not bad.

A little breeze danced across the Danube, and the late afternoon sun softened the outlines of Buda. Things were going to work out well. Very well.

***

Shortly after the call from Ross, Brian Garrity was in his cubicle pitching a reverse mortgage to an elderly widow. Two guys appeared at the front desk presenting some sort of identification to the receptionist. As Brian repeated the blurb about potential yields and regular monthly payments for life, he watched the guys search across the sea of workstations. Somehow, he knew they were after him. He cut off the call and shrank down in his chair.

They had not arrested him. They asked him to come to One Police Plaza to talk about a stock trading matter. Now, he was seated at a table in a room featureless but for the mirror that made up most of one wall and the camera mounted near the ceiling. He'd been given a cup of surprisingly good coffee and left alone for about twenty minutes to marinate in his anxieties. He stared at the scarred plastic tabletop, willing himself to look as if he wondered what was going on. The room was cool, but

Brian was sweating. He shifted, tried to push the chair back, but it was screwed to the floor.

A stock matter, they said. Could be anything. Someone pushing penny stock on one of his clients. They wanted to talk. But the conversation with Ackerman kept picking at him.

A friendly-looking guy in a gray suit entered and sat down across from Brian. He looked tired and pulled the knot of his tie down. He offered a handshake and slid a card across the table. *Henry Barber, FBI.* Brian glanced at it, then froze. *Special Investigations. Washington, DC.* Barber was talking, the words seeming to arrive from a distance. "I'm working on a securities matter," he said. "Derivative products you've been purchasing for some of your clients."

The easy fifty-k for so little work suddenly seemed much too small, and Brian's hopes and speculation melted into a puddle of fear.

***

Ross's good fortune continued through dinner. He and Emily and the Petrescus had walked to a restaurant in the Inner City. Their table had a fine view of the Danube, their waiter was attentive and the food delicious. Ross's discussion with Don Petrescu about Kazakhstan, the likely Nazarbayeva victory and subsequent unwinding of the Kazakh Skin went even better than he hoped. At the end of the discussion, Don reached over to clap Ross on the back and said, eyes moist, "You're a good man, Ross Ackerman."

There was plenty of wine, plenty of friendly conversation. Afterwards, Emily slipped her arm through Ross's as they strolled toward the ship.

"Thank you for giving me a couple of days in Budapest," she said. "I really do love the city, and the way things turned out, I've had no time to appreciate it."

Her warmth surprised Ross. A continuation of his good fortune.

"I'll get the captain to book you at the Intercont," he said.

"I can do that, Ross. I was thinking of something smaller, cozier. I know you have a lot on your mind."

On the ship, Ross waved his access badge at their door. Inside, Emily disappeared into the bathroom. Ross cracked a little bottle of scotch and took a sip, savoring both the smoky flavor and his success at dodging the cannonball that the Napolitani situation could have become.

Emily finished in the bathroom and came toward the bed wearing a nightgown that accentuated her curves. Ross rolled onto his side.

"Nice. Have I seen that before?"

"I bought it in Vienna."

She slipped into bed and skipped her usual ritual of hand cream and earplugs while Ross undressed and got in beside her.

Emily smiled at him in a way he'd not seen in a while and put a hand on his chest. "I was thinking."

Ross put a hand on her hip, feeling the warmth of her skin under the silk.

"Me, too."

He kissed her for the first time in weeks. She pressed close to him, and he felt blood and breath rising.

Afterwards, Ross rolled on his back. "I'll miss you back home." He was surprised at his admission; he meant it, for once.

"And I will miss you too, Ross."

# THIRTY-THREE

JOE SPENT THE day in the holding cell, sometimes agitated, sometimes too damn tired to do anything but stare at the wall. The fact that Eric hadn't returned wasn't promising. The deputy Prohoffer left in charge spoke almost no English and shook his head when Joe tried several ways of asking to make a phone call. The deputy tapped on his e-pad, and country music Joe vaguely recognized filtered out of the station's comm system. "Tammy Wynette, ja?" he said and went back to reading a German motorcycle magazine.

Hans Prohoffer appeared in the late afternoon, relieved the deputy and changed the music to classic jazz.

"What's going on? Can I make a call?"

Prohoffer shrugged sheepishly and shook his head.

"Is Ms. Napolitani okay?" brought a smile to Prohoffer's face.

"Ja, is gut."

Night was harder. The bed was uncomfortable, and the relief that Weezy must be okay spun into worry about the FBI. Had someone called Hollingsworth? Had she gotten in touch with Henry Barber?

He must have fallen asleep, because the metallic rasp of the cell door being unlocked woke him. The deputy from yesterday slid a tray with coffee and some bread, salami and cheese on to the shelf next to the door and retreated, locking the door. Soon, classic hits from Dolly Parton and Johnny Cash suffused the small space.

At 9:00, Prohoffer ushered in the FBI agent from Vienna, who looked government-issue and very American in a gray suit, short hair, sharp features. Prohoffer opened the cell door and directed Joe to the front of the office. The agent from Vienna had taken over the desk, apparently having ousted the deputy, who leaned against the wall, irritated. Prohoffer directed Joe to a chair in front of the desk. The agent opened a file folder and began asking questions, rapid-fire.

"Seems you have two Quantitec accounts, 17-98685 and 18-00268, is that right?"

"One that I know of," Joe said. "It's for my retirement account."

"Which one is that?"

"I don't know my account number. If you give me my e-pad —"

"Did you buy the financial derivative products from ZCG?"

"No, of course not."

The questions went on for fifteen minutes. The agent seemed to exercise all the tools in his interrogation kit to try to trip Joe up. Finally, he grimaced, collected papers, and closed the file folder.

"I've spoken with some high-level people in Washington." He squared his shoulders when he said "high level."

"We have to let the brass take over on this one," he said with a sour look that let Joe, Hans and the deputy know the trip was a waste of his time.

The agent had left and the deputy had reclaimed his seat. Prohoffer rummaged through a file cabinet and came up with what looked like a very large, bright orange bracelet. He was gesturing to Joe when Eric O'Malley arrived.

"Joe, they're going to put a monitor on you. Best compromise we could get. I've talked to Maddie Hollingsworth and Henry Barber, but the Vienna office apparently wants Herr Prohoffer to be extra-cautious."

Prohoffer pulled out a tourist map of the city and carefully outlined a rectangle that included the police station, the hospital and an area to the west of the hospital.

"You will be staying with me, here," Eric said, pointing to a spot near the hospital. "It's a Gasthaus. An old monastery. And Herr Prohoffer says you will have to stay in the box he marked. You'll be able to go to the hospital, but not into the town."

Prohoffer handed Joe a bag with his wallet, e-pad, change and the bracelet from the Donau König. As Joe picked up the e-pad, Prohoffer pointed to it. "You must not call on it. Voice function *nichts, ja?*"

Joe tapped the pad and saw the slash across the phone button. "*Nichts*. I understand."

The Gasthaus, keeping in the monastic tradition, provided a meager dinner. The room looked comfortable, certainly more than suitable for a monk, with a single bed, small desk and a tiny modern bathroom. Joe was tired, more from relief than lack of sleep. But he returned to the hospital, exchanging the Gasthaus bed for a chair in the waiting room, the Healthy Living messages and nearness to Weezy.

***

Weezy woke with a start on the morning of the second day in the hospital. Or was it the third? A nurse was injecting something into her IV line. Weezy flinched and cried out, remembering Santucci's snarl. The nurse said something comforting in German, patted Weezy's arm, tapped a communicator and spoke.

A couple of minutes later a woman wearing a white coat came into the room.

"Ah, Frau Napolitani. I am Dr. Kühn. You are feeling well this morning?"

Weezy tried to sit up.

"No. Not yet. Rest a little while. I will call your fiancé."

*Fiancé?*

She must have seen the question in Weezy's eyes. "Your Mr. Mayfield. He has gone to breakfast. Otherwise, he has been under our feet all the time."

Fiancé, Weezy thought. Not bad. I like fiancé.

Her head fell back on the pillow, and she drifted. Hospital sounds mixed with the ripe smell of the forest in Panacea. Mockingbird calls, a pager blaring in German.

The door opened with a soft whoosh, bringing Weezy awake. A big policeman. And Joe. *He said I love you.* Now, she saw it in his eyes.

She tried to raise herself. Joe rushed to her, helped her sit up. She was a little shaky. Joe looked concerned, but Weezy cut off the expected take-it-easy with a shake of her head.

"Where's that rat-faced sonofabitch Santucci?"

Joe grinned. "Normal, she's back to normal now," he said to the cop. Then, "This is Inspector Prohoffer. He saved you when Santucci tried to put drugs in your IV."

The guy was a homely giant, but he took her hand gently and she saw the bulge of the bandage on his forearm. That's what the nurses were talking about … he got stabbed saving her.

"Thank you," Weezy said, and lightly touched his bandage. Then she raised her cast, nodded at his arm, and smiled.

"Ja … brothers, yes?" Prohoffer said. Then he turned serious and held up a picture for Weezy.

"Is this who attacked you?" Joe asked.

"Yes, both times."

"On the ship, as well?"

Joe looked to Prohoffer, who seemed to follow the conversation.

"Yes. After that brandy. When we were toasting. Ratface very carefully picked a glass off the tray for me. Must've had something in it. I felt woozy, and he said maybe I should get some air. Then someone was behind me, pushing. From the voice, I know it was Santucci."

Her eyes began to tear.

"Sappho saved me."

Prohoffer looked puzzled.

Weezy grabbed Joe's hand. "I saw Sappho. I reached to touch her, but she was rough, not silky smooth. She said, 'Hang on.' "

"Maybe you have nine lives, too." Joe's smile was genuine for the first time since Vienna.

***

It was nearly noon. Dr. Kühn had sent Weezy off to get an MRI nearly an hour ago. Joe, restless and tired of the Healthy Living loop in the waiting room, went to the cafeteria to get a cup of coffee. His hands shook as he stirred in sugar, and he realized he'd slept all of two hours since arriving in Hainburg.

Eric had taken over a table in the corner and was bulldozing his way through a long to-do list. The tabletop was covered with papers, an empty coffee cup, a nearly full glass of beer, and a plate of pommes frites.

Joe joined him. As he sat down, Eric signed off, slapped the phone down and sighed.

"I brought John Zhou Min up to speed and reassured Ackerman that Weezy was improving but that you are still under arrest. The doc says Weezy will be able to travel in a couple of days. I made arrangements for us to return to the States through Vienna."

"That's great and thank you for all—"

Eric's phone buzzed. He answered and listened for several minutes, occasionally asking a question. During the call, Weezy appeared at the cafeteria door, hospital gown tied demurely and the wheeled tripod holding her saline drip in tow.

Joe got up and hugged her gingerly while he whispered, "You okay to be here?"

In answer, she pulled out a chair, docked the tripod, fished a fried potato from Eric's plate, and said, "Where's the ketchup?"

"Thanks for your help," Eric said, and put the phone down.

"Anything new?" Joe said.

"Henry Barber has apparently made some progress understanding what's going on. He won't give details, but it's clear Ackerman's at the center of this. Braithwaite may be, too."

"Is," Weezy said, took another fry and looked longingly at the beer.

"Prohoffer says Interpol knows where Santucci is but is 'unable' to arrest him," Eric said. "Nick Braithwaite is 'probably' in South Africa, also beyond the long arm of the law. Prohoffer didn't get one goddam 'can do' from those bastards. Just a whole raft of 'too difficult.' " Eric looked ready to breathe fire.

"At least they have beer in the cafeteria," he said, cooling down a bit, popping a fried potato into his mouth. Chewing, he said, "Prohoffer has the right attitude, though. He wanted to march right down to Budapest and put Ackerman in irons. He talked with Henry Barber. Barber asked him to back off. He must think he has a good case if we get Ackerman back on U.S. soil."

"What about Joe?" Weezy said.

"Looks good on that front," Eric said. "Barber won't give details, but it sounds like they have someone—Ackerman or Braithwaite—giving instructions to a broker at Quantitec Financial to buy the Kazakh Skin into that account registered to

Joe. That clears you, Joe, but …" he paused, as if searching for the right words. "Apparently the Skin purchase is a relatively minor violation of securities law."

Joe tasted something sour.

Weezy twitched. "So, let me summarize here. They can't get the assassin and his boss, but they think they might have a pretty good case against the puppeteer," she said. "Have I got that right?"

Eric gave an angry grunt but nodded and stared at the plate of fries.

"And, let me see here, I bet the FBI's fancy tracking systems can't tell who made the Skins trades. That'll let ZCG off the hook. Have I got that part right, too?"

"No, they have your IAC group tracking back the trading violations—"

"And ZCG will pay a fine, right? And not miss a step." She gave a dismissive wave of her hand. "And Ackerman? What about Ackerman? A slap on the wrist maybe? A fine that will cost a second mortgage on the vacation home?"

Frail though Weezy still was, the force of her inquisition made Joe cringe and Eric shake his head, frustrated.

"Okay." Weezy's mouth was tight.

Joe's head jerked back and his mouth dropped open.

Weezy's eyes narrowed. "I said, okay. Joe, don't give me that shocked look. What you're saying is everybody skates. As usual, right? These guys make up their own rules. It is what it is. Let's move on."

"This doesn't sound like you, Weezy," Joe said.

Weezy's jaw clenched, her fury palpable.

"Well, all these fine folks are doing their best." She shrugged. "Not much more to do, is there?"

Eric stabbed the last potato on the plate.

Joe saw a hint of a smile on Weezy's lips.

# THIRTY-FOUR

IT WAS AFTERNOON, warm with a little breeze coming up the hill from the Danube. Weezy and Joe sat on the terrace outside the hospital. Joe watched Weezy eat her third meal of the day. The gaunt look of the past few days was fast disappearing. The bag of saline had been retired, but she still wore the hospital gown.

Each time Joe saw her, the pain of having almost lost her was a little less.

"Mahlzeit," she said, chewing a piece of sausage. "Must mean 'mealtime' or something like that. Whenever I say it, they cluck, bustle off and bring me food that a four-star restaurant in Bethesda would be proud to serve."

She had just finished being looked at by Dr. Kühn and an orthopod. ("The correct term is 'sadist.' ") Kühn pronounced her amazingly healthy considering what she had been through.

Joe was waiting for her to explain the 'Okay' that ended the conversation with Eric. Finally, he ran out of patience.

"So, that's it?" he said. "FBI can't run a trader down, Santucci's lost in Corsica, Ackerman cashes out and starts a new hedge fund, Braithwaite is quietly thumbing his nose at us from some South African villa behind a bought and paid for political fence. We just get on with our lives?"

"That's what they think."

Weezy looked smug. "Think about it, Joe. You painted the scenario that Ackerman & Company are congratulating themselves on. They think they're going to slide like they planned. They've probably got some clever plan to separate Ackerman from the bad stuff. Braithwaite's a pro. I bet he's covered his ass fourteen ways from Sunday. That dummy account? They were going to throw you to the wolves, Joe, but they'll be fine. Just like you, they, and most everybody else expected. But they didn't count on Barber, or you, or me."

She speared a piece of vegetable, looked at it suspiciously, then chomped down on it. She pointed at Joe with her fork while she chewed, swallowed, then spoke.

"The dumbasses are cruising, fat and happy. Exactly where we want 'em. They haven't figured out they stepped on the wrong cat's tail."

When she finished the meal, she stood and turned to put the tray on the table beside her. The bottom tie of her gown had come undone, revealing the curve of her derrière. Joe felt the memory of her skin beneath his fingers, and his breath caught.

She turned to him. "I need your e-pad."

Joe hesitated, enjoying the view, then took the folded pad out of his pocket.

"You can't call out on it. It's still under Prohoffer's control.

Weezy put her hand out. "Surely you jest."

She took the pad and began tapping.

"You're not going to do anything foolish, are you?" Joe asked.

He said it with a half-smile, trying to make his question nonchalant.

"In case you hadn't noticed, Prohoffer took the lock off this morning." Then a cloud of irritation passed over her face. "Have you ever seen me do anything foolish with data?"

"Of course not," he said, still smiling.

"Well, then quit leering and give me some privacy."

***

In the sunny breakfast nook of a modest home in at the edge of a pine forest in Wisconsin, Jake read Weezy's message. Her neighbors would be surprised to discover she was a member of

Olegarten, the Internet meeting place of twenty or so of the world's most capable hackers. She sipped coffee from the Gramma Rocks mug her eldest grandson gave her and considered her list.

Of course, all the Olegarten regulars would want to be part of the group Jake was putting together. They all loved HoHum, and this project would make reputations, no doubt. DingDing for certain: she was already familiar with the chess moves at Father Time. Motormouth, who was anything but talkative. The man from Estonia they were calling HoHumJr. Surely PeepShow for decrypting.

In the end, she selected seven members for the Posse. She would deal with the hurt and anger of those she excluded later.

***

"Adam, that's brilliant."

Maddie leaned over Adam Ambrosio's shoulder and watched as he traced through the labyrinth of servers RedSock used to get to the IAC financial trading section via Brian Garrity's trading desk.

Adam warmed to the praise and perhaps to her hand resting lightly on his shoulder.

"They thought that running the instructions through lots of servers would protect them," he said. "But they had to end up in Garrity's system. So I tracked 'em back by recursion. That got it down to a few hundred and good ol' KL Revelator put it the hell to bed."

Adam raised a hand for the skin slap, which Maddie gave.

"I think your KL is the best algorithm to come out of this section in quite a while," she said loud enough for the rest of the bullpen to take notice. Now he *was* blushing.

"But now," he said, with the panache of a magician, "the topper. I found the e-pad that made the trades."

"Whose is it?" Maddie leaned closer.

"I don't know, but …" Adam keyed his console. "I can make it think it's lost and tell me where it is."

A dot appeared, moving out of Manhattan. Adam requested location information for the last month. Green lines built around lower Manhattan. At first a careless scribble, then moving to the other side of the Hudson, filling the Exchange Place plaza to a solid blot.

"Got 'em."

"What's he doing now?"

Adam threw the image on the large overhead screen.

"Looks like our e-pad's on the Expressway—no, the train." He scrolled the map. "Going toward, my guess, Newark Airport."

***

It had been a long but exhilarating two days for Henry Barber. But now, he was waiting to catch the Acela back to Washington. The new job was prestigious and had perks–the VIP club where he was sitting, business class travel, nicer hotels. But it required bureaucratic bowing and scraping that Henry disliked. Much more interesting to be in the field again, talking to people, weighing responses. Tiring, though. He pushed back, preparing to doze.

Garrity folded pretty quickly. Essentially a small fish lured by easy money. Someone, probably Ackerman or Braithwaite, set him up. While others played by the rules, the Ackermans of the world bent them. While others followed procedure, they hired top-level lawyers and skated. He opened his eyes. He knew he was not going to doze. Too wound up. It wasn't so much the looking stupid, it was … they were the good guys, goddammit, representing the American people, and—

His phone buzzed. He dug it out of his pocket, clicked video. Madeline Hollingsworth at IAC.

"Henry, I think we've located the person making the RedSock trades."

Henry brought his seat upright and bent forward.

"Yeah?"

"One problem, though."

There was always a problem.

"The person's on the move right now, most likely toward Newark Airport."

A problem with a solution.

"Hold on, Maddie." Without waiting for an answer, Henry punched "hold," called the New York FBI office and connected to the young officer he'd worked with the day before. He rattled off the names of the ZCG employees they had reviewed.

"Can you ship those names and faces to me and the security folks out to Newark? We don't know exactly who we're after, but it's going to be somebody on that list."

He came forward and stood, going back to Maddie as he made for the exit.

"Maddie. You there?"

"Yes, Henry."

"We're going to nail this bastard and make him sing."

***

Arty needed the white lady, needed her bad. He was in a holding cell with soft green walls designed by some psychologist to keep people calm. They weren't helping. He fantasized chalking a line, the anticipation, the sweet release. Vodka would help, too. His hands were beginning to shake, a prelude to what was going to happen if he didn't get a drink soon.

It had been four hours since a young woman in street clothes stopped him at Newark. At first he thought she was going to ask for directions, but she knew his name. Then she flashed a badge.

They brought him to the Lower Manhattan station, and the agent started asking questions about Skins. Arty called ZCG's law firm, and they told him to shut up, they'd have someone over to talk to him. That was over an hour ago. The guy in the next cell had greeted him with a long tirade about the stupid cops. If they'd only look at the evidence, they'd know he bought all that stuff in good faith, he was an innocent victim of somebody called Roger, they should look. The tirade became a monotone, softer and softer, as the man ran down like a wind-up toy.

A chunky woman, expensively dressed and carrying an e-pad, marched into the squad room and buttonholed the cop in charge. They both looked at Arty, then more conversation. Finally, the cop gestured toward an interview room. The woman walked toward it as the cop turned toward Arty's cell.

In the room, Felicia Oliva introduced herself and sized Arty up.

"You need a drink, don't you?"

Arty must have looked startled.

"Fifteen years sober," she said. "So I know how you feel. If it gets too bad, I'll get 'em to put you in detox. But first, you have to tell me what's going on."

Arty started to spin a tale of his innocence, first describing his work.

"I know what a trader does," Oliva said. "Spare me the education. I need to know how you went about using Brian Garrity's account at Quantitec to purchase tranches of Skins into RedSock."

Arty feigned surprise. "That was Garrity buying for RedSock. Has to be arm's length because Ross Ackerman set up

RedSock. Ross may have…" he paused to search for the correct word, "… *suggested* that Garrity buy Skins, but I was only on the sell side of the transactions."

Oliva gave him a flat-eyed stare. "Both the FBI and the SEC think different. The FBI agent said he will forward what he calls 'definitive proof' that you managed both the buy and sell sides through a back channel to Garrity's trading account. He said whoever set it up was very good, but the trackers at IAC are better."

Arty started to sweat, and his stomach churned.

Oliva looked almost sympathetic. "They've got you in a vice, Mr. Povreshenko. We'll go for a plea," she said, not looking very hopeful. "In the meantime, you might consider some AA meetings."

# THIRTY-FIVE

ON THE FOURTH morning, Astrid Kühn declared Weezy fit to leave the hospital. Joe had gone clothes shopping the day before. Weezy was dressed in blue jeans ("universal" she said approvingly), running shoes ("very comfortable"), and a green-striped soccer shirt with *Wien Energie* splashed across the chest ("really?"). Hans Prohoffer visited, ostensibly to be sure he had contact information for Weezy, Joe and Eric. Weezy surprised herself and broke into tears when she saw his bandaged arm again, then gave him a big hug and a more than continental kiss on the cheek.

The three were free to go. At Prohoffer's suggestion, they adjourned to a table in front of a café near the hospital and a lunch of white asparagus with a subtle garlic sauce.

"I have to see where we are on the investigation," Weezy said.

"We?" Eric looked at Weezy, then Joe. Weezy unfolded Joe's e-pad and was tapping and swiping.

"I think 'we' includes Weezy's team at IAC and some others —" Weezy shot Joe a warning look Eric couldn't miss "—who probably are on the right side of the law but who really don't want to be identified."

Weezy pushed aside glasses and plates to put the e-pad flat on the table. A window opened to reveal a white-haired woman side-lit by morning sun.

"Nihow, Jake."

The woman answered, "Nihow, Hotcakes." Then, nodding to Joe and Eric, "Who are they?"

"Friends. No problem with confidentiality," Weezy said. "How goes the battle?"

"I believe we're winning. And we're certainly on the right side."

"So, how's PeepShow doing? Did you get anything?"

Jake smiled. "Oh, yes. Enough to send several of your bad guys far, far up the river. I'm transmitting now."

Another widow opened and text began scrolling rapidly. Weezy leaned closer to the e-pad, a picture of concentration, nodding occasionally, half-smiles chasing grimaces across her face. Jake's smile grew broader as Weezy continued to assimilate the flow of data. Finally, Weezy's eyes shifted back to Jake's panel. "HoHum would have loved this, wouldn't he?"

Her eyes filled.

"HoHum?" Eric said.

"One of Weezy's online associates. Killed, probably Braithwaite's doing," Joe said.

"Not probably." Weezy's eyes blazed. She held Joe in a stare for a long second, then turned back to Jake.

"Jake, IAC doesn't have this yet, right?"

"Right."

Weezy, elbows on the table, pushed back her hair.

"Okay. I'm not a lawyer, but I know IAC can track pretty much anything it wants if there's a reason. The financial manipulation is a reason. You don't want to expose Peep or any of the Posse, so let's do this: Send me the full decrypt files stripped of any identifying information. I'll pass the package to IAC."

Jake frowned. "If IAC tries hard, they can probably trace the source back to the Olegarten site."

"You're right. But I'm IAC, too. I'll make sure we don't try," Weezy said.

She read through the data for several seconds.

"I don't see much on Braithwaite."

"His firewall in South Africa is holding," Jake said. "We think he's still at his place there, but we haven't verified that. It would be nice to see what other kinds of nasties he's doing. If we can't break the wall, we'll go on a fishing expedition through the chess site he seems to use to pass instructions."

"We need to get him, Jake."

"Wish HoHum were here to help," Jake said.

When Weezy signed off, Eric said, "You can look at any transaction?"

She took a sip of beer, licked her lips. "Sure. Can, but don't."

"What about now?"

Weezy turned on Eric, cutting off a tart response. "The IAC charter is to protect the database. But here's the problem: electronic intrusion happens much faster than humans can process a search warrant."

Weezy pulled a wry face, "The SEC and FBI are the enforcement people. We can do anything they legally ask us to do, but basically we play defense. That's how I met Joe in the first place … data abuse in the IAC that both of us were trying to fix. I'm a tracker and he was a bull-in-the-china-shop hacker." She grinned at Joe. "The trades and the manipulation, we're on that like sweet on honey, courtesy of the FBI."

"But the worst crimes—" Joe said.

"Right." Weezy said. "Not much the IAC can do about my friend's murder or the bad stuff in Africa and maybe now in Kazakhstan, but …" A little grin. "The bad guys knew they couldn't go through normal financial channels to discuss assassinations. They had to use the Internet and encryption. When they did that, they put their crosstalk in the public domain."

"Yeah, but with Braithwaite involved, I'm sure they had the best encryption," Eric said.

Weezy chuckled. "And they had such a fetching belief in it. Of course, they didn't know about PeepShow and the Posse. So, if some clever person decrypts those public documents, and if that person shares that information with the authorities, well…"

She put the e-pad back in the middle of the table, "Call Maddie."

Joe looked at his watch. "It's before seven, you know."

"She won't mind waking up for this."

To Eric's unspoken question, Joe said, "Weezy's colleague in Bethesda."

A window opened, and a woman's face appeared in close-up, obviously awakened by the call.

"Oh, damn, Weezy. Slept through the alarm. Up really late."

"Don't apologize. Look at what I'm sending. You and Keith need to decide whether it gets to Barber and the SEC through you or through me."

"Hmmm." Maddie propped the pad vertical, brushed hair out of her eyes and sat up, concentrating on the scrolling filenames. She was naked. "Probably better through IAC, don't you think?" she said, concentrating on the files.

"Uhh. Maddie, feels a little breezy, does it?" Weezy broke into a broad smile.

"Oh." Maddie pulled the sheet up, but not too quickly, not blushing.

Maddie glanced at Joe, then at Eric and said in a Georgia drawl that hadn't been there before, "Glad to see you boys are impressed."

She nodded to Weezy, winked at Eric. "Now we're going to find out whether our boss has any starch," she said, and the e-pad went blank.

***

Maddie met with Keith Sanders later in the morning. He finished reading the list of thirty-six neat categories of data Weezy had forwarded and looked up at Maddie, aghast.

"Where did you get this?"

"It was submitted to us by a group that calls itself 'the Posse.' They're friends of Weezy."

"You're not seriously considering passing this on, are you?" His eyebrows showed his disbelief.

"Keith, I was as skeptical as you at first. But look at some entries to satisfy yourself. My team has traced back every important piece of information to its source and validated it. We can't spend the time to decrypt on the level they did, but we did good-size sample, and they're perfect. All of us are ready to certify that this data is valid."

There would be a firestorm when he reported to the director, and he would be in the hottest part. His fear must have shown.

"Keith, over a thousand people died in Mali, Zambia and South Africa because one guy needed more than his million-dollar salary to satisfy himself."

Keith exhaled, then met Maddie's eyes. "Send it."

# THIRTY-SIX

JOHN ZHOU MIN sat in the Manhattan conference room finishing his report to his father. The elder Zhou sat at the head of the table, still as stone. The office was nearly empty, it being late Sunday afternoon. John looked up from his e-pad, his artist's eye taking in the light shafting through the buildings of the financial district. The tranquil, golden frieze was entirely at odds with his words.

John finished, "Father, I trust Eric. His story disturbs me."

"This hedge fund you think Ackerman runs … RedSock, is it not? … Why did you not suspect something was wrong?"

John ran his hand over the table, staring at the grain of the wood, unable to meet his father's eyes.

"Ross said RedSock was a small hedge fund that needed some high-risk in its portfolio. I … trusted what he told me. "

"You trusted?"

"Yes, father."

"That is your weakness, John. I did not put you here to trust. I put you here to know why every trade is made."

Zhou Qiáng leaned toward John. "How much did this fund pay us for the Skins it bought?"

"Eighty-nine million over the last two years for the Mali, Zambia and South Africa Skins. Also, about three million to date for the Kazakh Skin."

"And how much was this office's profit during that time?"

"Sixty-seven million."

Zhou Qiáng's face did not change, but John saw the anger in his eyes.

"In other words," the older man said, "this RedSock is your only winner. ZCG USA lost twenty-two million on all the rest of its business."

"Yes." John cut off the apology he knew Zhou Qiáng expected.

"And yet," his father waved his hand at the artwork on the wall, "you purchase these trifles."

There was no answer. Of course John bought the artwork. Zhou Qiáng was, as usual, using what to him was unassailable logic to crush any other ideas. The tactic worked so well on his business associates he had made a habit of using it on his only son.

"Yes, I bought the Morisot," John said. He met his father's eyes. "The expensive offices, the bloated entertainment budgets, the ridiculous salaries, they are Ross Ackerman's."

The color rose in his father's face, but John continued, "You have often told me how much you admire American aggressiveness in business." John waved his hand, mimicking his father. "Here you see it." Through the glass wall of the conference room, the broad expanse of the reception hall was empty but for the slender bronze statue, beautifully top-lit. Zhou Qiáng would surely have put a dozen workstations there. The Hong Kong home office was drab but profitable.

As if on cue, Ross Ackerman appeared through the outer doors. He spoke briefly to the receptionist, then turned toward the Zhous. By the time he got to the conference room, he looked confident.

***

When Ross came through the door of the New York office, he didn't get the usual hit of pleasure at being home, of ownership. The jet lag had set in, not to mention the several cocktails in first class, the seemingly interminable wait to pass immigration.

The asshole INS agent extended it by slowly thumbing through every page in his passport. He was a few minutes late to the meeting with Zhou Qiáng, and he needed to talk to Arty Pov, who had been unresponsive to taps and messages. He was not looking forward to the polite, formal meeting he was about to have. He had been rehearsing his explanation most of the way across the Atlantic.

He looked across the reception area toward his office. His assistant, Kim, was not at her desk, although he'd texted her from the plane to get her butt into the office. He sent her a tap, "Find Arty Pov. Have him ready to talk in half an hour. No excuses."

In the conference room across from the entry, John rose in anticipation of Ross's approach. Zhou Qiáng stayed seated.

Ross steeled himself and strode toward the Zhous.

Pleasantries and small talk were still part of Asian protocol, but Zhou Qiáng cut off the discussion of the trip and the customers after less than five minutes.

"Where is your man Braithwaite?"

"I believe he's in South Africa. He's a contractor and has other customers to attend to."

"I expected he would be here to explain to us how a member of your group could fall overboard, be rescued and then be attacked by Braithwaite's own employee."

"He sent me a message after we realized Santucci had attacked the Napolitani woman. She is a highly placed tracker at the IAC. Braithwaite thinks some hacker must have wanted her out of the way."

Ross took out his e-pad, found the clear text message Braithwaite sent from the airport.

"Here, I'm forwarding it."

John leaned toward his father. Both read the message on Zhou Qiáng's e-pad. Ross thought he saw a microscopic change in Zhou Qiáng's frown. Maybe he was buying it.

"So, you think there's no direct connection with ZCG?"

John almost never asked questions in his father's presence. Zhou Qiáng did not silence his son.

"None as far as I can see." Ackerman gave a one-shoulder shrug.

"How, then, is it that Braithwaite brought a person on our cruise who tried to carry out an assassination connected with another Braithwaite client?" John became more and more animated as he spoke, also unusual in front of his father. "And how is it that we associate ourselves with such a man?"

"He's a contractor, John. I feel as bad about it as you," Ross said. "He's history, as far as I'm concerned." Then, hoping a change in subject would close out the meeting, "As I mentioned to you, we have a junior analyst, Joe Mayfield, who seems to have been trading Skins. He is the man who brought the Napolitani woman on the cruise at the advice of Eric. I have always been skeptical of him."—he directed a meaningful glance at John—"and it seems he set up a way to sell himself the highest-risk Chromium Skin right before the event that made it valuable."

Ross tapped his e-pad. "Here's a press release. I expect to issue it after market close Monday. We'll cut him loose after I talk with our legal folks, the SEC and the FBI."

John studied the tabletop, not meeting Ross's eyes. Then planted his hands as if readying himself to spring. "That story about Mr. Mayfield probably is not true. Eric said —"

Zhou Qiáng chopped the air. "John, be quiet."

"But —"

"I said, be quiet."

He refocused on Ross. "You arranged this?"

Ross froze. Zhou Qiáng would have had no qualms eliminating Napolitani and Mayfield and anybody else he thought was a risk. But, discuss it in front of John? John would take his deferential ass straight to the SEC and spill the whole story.

Is Zhou Qiáng setting me up?

John's head snapped up, his eyes wide. "What—"

"There is much you do not know, John." A flicker of something, maybe regret, passed across the elder Zhou's face.

Zhou Qiáng blinked once and focused his stare on Ross. "Why have you shut off the Kazakhstan project?"

Ross pulled a serious face, "Well, as I said in my earlier communication, it looks as if Dinara Nazarbayeva is going to take over the presidency from her father, and—"

"Give me the real reason, not the one you constructed for your customers."

Ross sighed. "The real reason? Too many problems." John's face had drained of color; Zhou Qiáng's expression had not changed. "Braithwaite was unable to take this tracker woman out of the picture. There are too many connections to him for the cause of the so-called accident not to be suspicious."

"That is Braithwaite's problem, not ours. You have insulated yourself from him, have you not?" Zhou Qiáng cocked his head fractionally.

"Yes. A couple of communications he sent might be a problem, but I don't think there's any way to get past him to me. As far as trading is concerned, there's a front man at a small retail brokerage who will be the obvious target of the SEC. Even if they penetrate him, they'll get to Arty Pov and no farther."

"And if Povreshenko talks?"

"Arty is loyal. He will get a few months, maybe a year in a low-security country club and enough money to retire on when he gets out. And, of course, there's Mayfield. The SEC will jump on him like a dog on a bone. Which will take the scent off us."

Ross glanced at John. He was going to have to change his underwear after this meeting. He turned back to Zhou Qiáng, thinking, be confident, appear honest, be brief. "But I had to call off the Kazakh Skin. Braithwaite can't or won't execute it, and the botched assassination, with O'Malley and Mayfield there right on top of it, raises too many questions."

"You are afraid," Zhou Qiáng said. His expression did not change, but his color deepened. "You are afraid for yourself, so you decided to throw away ten million dollars of ZCG's money … my money … to cover your mistakes."

"No, I realized that the Skin is at risk. We need to live to fight another day."

"Zhou, Cadwallon will live, and we will fight." Zhou Qiáng turned to his son. "John, fire this man."

***

Ross covered the fifty feet from the conference room to his office trying not to look stunned, pumping himself up.

John actually had the balls to fire him. Well, fine. The whole place would fall apart. These dumb bastards hadn't figured out that there was no way to make serious money on Skins without managing the outcome. With his reputation and the one hundred ten million from RedSock, he'd be running a new hedge fund in a few weeks, and ZCG's book of business would evaporate.

"Kim, did you get hold of Arty?"

Kim looked up from her console, eyes huge.

"No, I couldn't get in touch—"

"Why the hell not? I told you to have him on the goddam phone when I came out of—"

"A criminal lawyer named Felicia Oliva called about five minutes ago." Her eyes got even bigger. "He's been arrested."

The pump that had been inflating Ross's confidence coughed.

***

Ross was in his office, feeling like the time he got a mild concussion playing touch football in college. He had told Kim to call a car for him and then go home. She gave him an awkward hug and wiped away a tear, which surprised him. He had spoken with Felicia Oliva, who had asked for background, and Ross had reeled off the story he had constructed.

Yes, Arty was a derivatives trader, he had said. Yes, there was a small fund called RedSock, probably a hundred million. Yes, his wife was the trustee … and what did that have to do with Povreshenko? No, he hadn't managed day-to-day investments, that was Brian Garrity over at Quantitec Financial Management. Yeah, Garrity might be buying Skins. Yes, he put the initial funds into RedSock. It was mainly for his wife's family. Salt-of-the-earth people, but not wealthy. Farmers have a hard time when they retire, so the thought they'd … Uh, yes, the bank's in Sint Maarten. Tax management, you know. Terrible shock. She should give him a call when she had more.

Shit. They'll be after the money tomorrow.

He glanced at his watch. Nearly six. The Sint Maarten bank was closed at this hour, but his contact would be attentive 24/7, given the size of the accounts.

Ross said into his console, "Call Klaas Molenaar, private number."

Molenaar answered on video, wearing a golf shirt that announced he was not at work.

"Klaas, I'm going to need to make some transfers out of the RedSock account."

"Sure, if you send me the routing information, I can do them first thing Monday."

"I need you to move more quickly."

"Oh. Well, we will have to alert my colleague in Philipsburg. I am at a conference in San Juan right now. I will do that and get right back to you."

Lovely people, the Dutch. So businesslike.

"Call me on my private number. And thanks."

Ross disconnected. John Zhou Min stood in his doorway.

"Ross, it would be best if you leave now. I'll handle this any way you want to. Why don't you come in tomorrow for your personal things?"

John seemed embarrassed. He ought to have been.

"You'll find that your access to ZCG system has been … uhh … cut off. Standard security, you know."

"Really, John? Cut off my access?" Ross sniffed. "Hope you've been practicing that T'ai Chi you like so much, because you're going to have to be pretty flexible to kiss your ass goodbye when this hits the street."

John shifted his weight from foot to foot. "Sorry, Ross. Let's keep this professional."

Ross smirked. "I'm leaving now. Don't worry." He stood, took the e-pad off his desk and strode toward the door and John. John stepped aside for him to pass. Halfway across the reception area, Ross turned and flipped John the bird. "Oh, and fuck you very much."

***

Ross rode the elevator to the ground floor of the Mercantile Tower. The dirty hybrid waiting for him was a reminder of his fall from grace. No more limos. The cab stank of sweat and the greasy, wax paper-wrapped sandwich on the front seat. Ross's stomach did a flop, and he realized he was hungry. Nothing but beer, scotch, and hors d'oeuvres since breakfast in Hungary.

The cab driver dropped him in front of the Bank Street brownstone. Ross gave him the company card, which was rejected. He dug for cash. The guy had no change.

"Really? No change?"

The guy gave him a broad *screw you* smile. Reluctantly, Ross gave a huge tip.

As a result, he was morose, angry, and dyspeptic as he mounted the steps, thumbed the security system and entered his home.

"Oh, Mister Ross."

He was tackled in a huge wraparound hug. Dark hair, uniform, perfume and sweat. Constanza. She was supposed to be off duty at six.

"You are such a good man. You and lady Emily."

She was snuffling. Tears and snot of joy, apparently. On his coat.

"What?"

He held her at arm's length. She smiled through her tears, mascara running, homely in her happiness.

"So much good you have done. And you pretend not to know."

Ross saw another hug coming. "Uh, yes, thank you. Can you make me a sandwich?" He needed a scotch.

He mumbled something about going upstairs, and Constanza's smile became radiant, "Oh, yes, Mr. Ross. Upstairs. You are tired from your trip. I will bring you some dinner."

Ross took the stairs to the atelier. *Flowers?* The scent rode on top of the familiar smell of wax and wood.

He was halfway to the bar and that scotch when he saw the source of the fragrance. In the center of the atelier, a small table bore a huge flower arrangement, the kind on a stand like they had at Sunday services when he was growing up … or at a funeral. Ross shivered. He crossed to the table. The arrangement was surrounded by pieces of folded construction paper.

"Thank you MR and MRS. Ackerman (the last few letters scrunched up as the edge approached) … "for the e-pads!!!! — Hamid"

"Thank you Ross Ackermun and Mrs. Ackermun for sponsering the Science Fair. I am going to show how rising tenperaturs change the ice caps. — Rosa"

There were twenty-five other messages, inscribed in shaky crayon letters, surely with tongue-between-the-teeth concentration and no doubt heartfelt.

He remembered Emily lobbying for a much larger contribution to the school than he wanted to make. He'd compromised by adding the school as a beneficiary of the RedSock trust.

Ross was beginning to hyperventilate when his e-pad tapped him, the digital voice announcing a call from Central Bank Netherlands Antilles.

"Yeah?"

"Mr. Ackerman, this is Henk Vander Houten, acting for Klaas Molenaar. I understand you called asking for a transfer of funds."

"Yes, I need to have each of the trusts in RedSock, LLC closed out to the Commerzbank account you have on file. Here's my thumbprint."

Vander Houten cleared his throat. Sure, Ross thought, now we'll start the waltzing around. Of course, they didn't want to lose accounts this size. They wanted some love, some promise of future business.

"It has been done."

God, he loved these Dutch bankers. The Swiss would have taken days, protesting all the time at the complexity of the large transactions.

"Already? Wonder—"

"Yesterday." Vander Houten said.

The word hung in the air.

He continued, "Yes, your trustee directed distribution yesterday morning."

"Yesterday?" Ross's voice rose a half-octave.

"I must say, it was a surprise, but clearly within her rights."

"Where did it go?"

"In accordance with the modified trust documents—"

"Modified?"

"—Half went to an account at Bank of America to a 501(c)(3) charity called Children Upward Bound in New York and the other half to fifteen savings accounts, mostly in regional banks in the Midwest."

"Nothing left?" Ross whispered, staring at the flowers and construction paper notes.

He forced himself to get back on track, his mind running overdrive, his mouth dry. Gotta get that money back.

"You have been scammed by some very sophisticated hackers," he said, teeth clenched. "My wife doesn't know how to make … she couldn't possibly have made that transfer."

There was a short pause while Vander Houten presumably digested the implied threat. When he responded, his voice had shifted from friendly to firm.

"Central Bank has the most sophisticated security available. Existing as we do on deposits from all corners of the world, we need to be very careful. We had a match to Emily Ackerman's print, and we spoke with her and her advisor, William Scholze, at some length via secure video."

"Her advisor?"

"Yes. The lawyer is a partner at Scholze, Scholze and Carrera in Cedar Rapids, Illinois … no, Iowa. The location made me expect a, uh, less than sophisticated knowledge of banking and trust law. But I must say, their work was more than competent. You should speak to your wife. Madame Ackerman's directions satisfied our fourteen point security checklist in order to authorize the transfers."

Ross's temper rose. He was not about to take crap from some fifth-level bank clerk.

"You better start the process to get that money back right the fuck now, or you're gonna have a freight train full of New York lawyers land on your sorry-ass tropical paradise, rip your balls off and stuff 'em down your throat."

"Mr. Ackerman, I am recording this conversation, as required by our international DTC and TIEA treaties." His voice was now anodyne. "I believe the distributions were entirely correct. Your request for an in-depth review is noted, and that review will begin tomorrow. We will let you know the results. Thank you for your business, and I will disconnect now."

There was a click, then silence.

Ross stared at the flowers, wanting to lash out, smash the whole display, but steps on the stairs let him know Constanza was bringing food. He stood still, halfway between the flowers and bar, his fists clenched at his side. Constanza crossed to the bar, set out silverware, a linen napkin and a seared tuna-on-crostini sandwich with wilted arugula and the mayonnaise she made herself.

She turned to him, eyes tearing again, threatening a hug. She must have interpreted the look on his face as high emotion, perhaps remembering the several times his hands had rested too long on her backside, decided against the embrace, and retreated quietly.

She was right about the high emotion.

Ross circled the atelier, needing to move. He stopped at the bar, took a big bite of the sandwich and chewed as he walked.

Why did she do this?

Must be a way to pull that money out. Emily was in Budapest, so she wouldn't have told her family. A few of 'em may have figured it out, but he should be able to get most of it back.

Why did she do this him?

He picked up his e-pad and kept circling.

"Emily Ackerman." He checked his watch. Middle of the night there. Shit.

The phone went to voicemail.

Goddam it.

He had asked her to get implanted, and she had put him off. "Why would I need that?"

"So I can get in touch with you when I want to," he had said. The look on her face made him add, "For safety. Living here in the big city, going up to Harlem the way you do."

"They put chips in pets," she had said. "I'm not a pet."

Finally, angry, he said, "Have it your way."

So now she had only her e-pad as a phone. The one she forgot, then said she didn't have pockets. Decade old technology. Probably sitting on her bedside table. Off.

The voicemail recorder beeped.

"Emily, goddammit, call me."

He disconnected, sat at the bar and took another bite of the sandwich. A too-big gulp of scotch burned on the way down.

Constanza asked if he wanted anything more he. After solemn thanks and happy tears, she left for the evening. Ross allowed himself a second scotch and was sipping it, his mind in a random walk, when his implant tapped him.

Emily?

But it was ZCG's lead attorney.

"Ross, sorry to hear about the situation at ZCG." (The situation. Really?)

"I certainly don't know the whole story, and I can't help but think the Zhou dynasty moved a little hastily. I assume it's over these trading issues. But, to the point, we have to get you another lawyer. You know, conflict of interest."

Of course. He certainly wouldn't want to put his business with ZCG at risk, would he?

Hearing nothing from Ross, the man continued, "I recommend Elliott Stiles over at Winthrop and Breckenridge. He'll be expensive" (and you don't care, since ZCG won't be paying), "but he's the best in these … uhh … criminal prosecutions."

"Criminal prosecutions?"

"Oh, yes. The FBI arrested Artyom Povreshenko this afternoon."

"Dave, Arty is not my problem. The Zhou dynasty can defend him."

There was a moment of silence.

"The FBI has indicted you, too, possibly as a result of their interview with Arty."

"Me?"

"Yes, for a variety of charges related to trading in these Skins, but also conspiracy to commit murder and several other criminal charges. You're going to need a good lawyer."

Ross hung up and poured himself a third scotch.

# THIRTY-SEVEN

SOMEWHERE OVER THE Atlantic, Emily got the call from Ross. It was after midnight in Budapest. She should have been in Hungary, but after Ross left for New York, she packed quickly and caught the train to Vienna. She was on American Airlines squashed between a beefy German and an equally beefy Texan, wishing she hadn't flown coach. She paid cash for the ticket to Chicago so the trip would be invisible to Ross and that scary South African that did security at ZCG. She was certainly not about to talk to Ross and glad she hadn't gotten that implant so he could keep track of her like some poodle.

At O'Hare, she considered and rejected hiring an autocab to take her to Dubuque. She'd arrive before sunup and sit in that station until Cousin Bill came to fetch her. Finally, she stuck to her original plan and paid cash to ride the train from O'Hare to Union Station downtown. On the train, she dug out a disposable phone Arty had given her and texted, In Chgo. All's well. Call me.

It was almost midnight when she arrived at the station, and the Black Hawk to Dubuque didn't leave until 6:20 the next morning. She looked around the grand hall, thinking she would spend the time reading. Most people were sleeping on benches, but several were awake and observing her with an avidity that made her nervous. She realized her clothes and bag reeked of wealth and privilege, neither of which she wanted to project in this environment.

Brushing crumbs off the dirty bench, she weighed her plan to remain invisible against the comfort and safety of the first class lounge. But that would require her membership card.

One of the watchers stood and walked toward her with a crooked grin, clearly prefatory to a request or suggestion she didn't want to hear. She retreated through the glass doors to the lounge.

The tired-looking but polite woman in reception, Rosella, a 15-year employee from Santo Domingo according to her tag, greeted her. Emily sorted through her wallet for the card identifying her as the spouse of a platinum-plus member. She surprised herself by beginning to cry silently. The attendant stopped in the middle of her rote greeting. "What's wrong, Ma'am?"

"Sorry, I didn't expect this."

She handed over the card. "It's scary out in the hall, and I wanted to…"

"Yeah, it gets pretty creepy this time of night."

"I need to get to Iowa without my husband knowing where I'm going."

The woman's face softened.

"Sorry, but the card records your name in the system."

"He'll be so angry when he finds out I've left. He's a good man, but when he drinks …" *Where did that come from?* But Emily warmed to the challenge of her sudden improvisation. "When he drinks, he turns vicious. I'm afraid of what he'll do when he finds me. Maybe you'd better give me the card and I'll go back outside."

The woman handed the card back. She looked first over one shoulder, then the other. "Hold on." She tapped on her console for a full minute, then crossed her fingers, waiting. Finally, she smiled.

"You go on in. The system has registered a customer whose card really needs to be replaced and whose information is incomplete."

Emily hugged the attendant on the way into the lounge, where the men who bothered her were of a higher quality.

***

Emily found Bill Scholze waiting for her in Dubuque. He hugged her and dismissed her protestations.

"I really don't mind picking you up. Good to see you after, what, six or seven years? And Monticello is on the way back to Cedar Rapids, so we'll have a chance to talk, and I'll get to see Dad when I drop you off. Like winning the daily double."

He put her bag in the car and gave directions to the autopilot. As they pulled out of the station, he turned to her.

"It looks as if the transfers have been completed per your instructions. It's clear that the documents gave you the right to make them. Based on the asset list, it's obvious that someone pretty sophisticated has been directing the investments. Is that Ross?"

Emily nodded.

"Have you discussed this with him? I mean, you're the trustee, but doesn't he want to have something to say about timing? I thought you'd want Ross's advice before selling. As your lawyer, I act on your instructions, but I also want to understand the whole story. With the thicket of laws and regulations that are involved in offshore trusts, I want to be sure you are safe and your intentions are fully realized."

The warmth in his words brought back memories of the summer he had been infatuated with her.

"Gracious, Bill, it's a long way from slopping the pigs to 'intentions fully realized' isn't it? But you're right. I owe you the story."

Emily drew a breath and began. When she finished, they were on the road out of the small town of Monticello, driving toward Silas's farm.

***

Emily sat on the bed in the guest room of Uncle Silas's rambling farmhouse. Bill had left after a long lunch full of questions and answers. Silas had gone down the road in his old pickup to check the quarter section he rented, shaking his head in amazement. A breeze fussed with the curtains, bringing with it the smell of cut grass, cow manure and sweet summer memories.

Emily cradled the phone in her hands, fending off excuses to keep her from calling Ross.

*I have to do it. He must look at the RedSock account often. He probably knows already.*

She dialed, preparing herself for the blast she'd heard Ross unleash at people he worked with.

On the third ring, she began hoping that he wouldn't answer. Then he'd have to call her.

On the fourth ring, he answered.

First, breathing.

"Ross, I wanted to call to tell you —"

"To tell me that you've ruined us." He said this flatly, then, voice rising, "Emily. What. The. Fuck. Isgoingon?"

"Ross, I —"

"Let me rephrase that. I know what's going on. Now, Ms. Trustee, you have to put that money back. Period."

"Ross, I —"

"Maybe you don't understand that money is my money. The downstroke I need to form a new fund." Screaming. "Not money to be given to some snot-nose loser kids in Harlem. Not money to be given to some perfectly well-off farmers in Iowa who don't need it."

He paused to draw breath.

"Ross, I can explain."

"Don't explain. Get it back. I don't care how you do it, just do it. Leave the Harlem school with a half a mil. They'll be overjoyed. Tell your relatives that there's been a mistake. The money is theirs, but not yet. Then get your ass back here. I need you to be here."

"I'm not coming home."

"What?! You're staying in Hungary?"

"I'm not in Hungary, Ross. I'm in Iowa."

"Oh, my fucking Christ. You lying bitch. Iowa? Really? Iowa?"

"Yes, Iowa. If you can calm down enough to listen, I need to talk to you."

She could almost hear the wheels spinning in Ross's trader's mind as he calculated angles, evaluated his leverage, and found little.

"Yeah. So talk."

"Ross, that money, that fortune you've created, has begun to consume you. Something's wrong with how you're making it. I don't know what you're doing, talking with that man Braithwaite, making Arty Pov do illegal things. It's changed you from the man I fell in love with to a man I can't stand. We never needed a fortune, and I know you will always find a way to make money, so I exercised my right as Trustee and distributed it."

"What do you mean, 'make Arty Pov do illegal things?' Have you been talking with Arty?"

"Arty and I, we —"

"Aw, shit. Have you been screwing Arty?"

"We are close." She hadn't planned for it to come out that way. "I'm hoping to spend my life with him, Ross."

"He's a criminal, you know, and he ratted me out for stuff I didn't do. Now I've got the feds on me, and the fucking Zhou dynasty fired my ass yesterday."

After a pause, Ross said in a tone that made Emily almost feel sorry for him, "That's why I need the RedSock money. With it, I restart and punch back, send ZCG back to Hong Kong with its tail between its legs. Without it, I'm toast, just a sore loser."

Outside the window, across the yard where the field started, corn was almost knee-high, a sea of green kissed by the sun. Calming. So unlike the New York life Emily had come to hate.

"Ross, I'm terribly sorry about ZCG and your job. Perhaps this will give you the opportunity to, I don't know, peel off that shell you've built up—"

"Advice? You're giving me advice? You're sitting out there in some godforsaken corn field doing Zen koans and giving me advice? Pull the money back. Now."

It was easier that he was angry again, treating her like she was not too bright.

"Ross, I won't do that. I wish you well."

She disconnected, hoping she had done the right thing, wondering why Arty hadn't called.

# THIRTY-EIGHT

JOE RODE THE train to Vienna with Weezy and Eric. Under the combined weight of Joe's and Maddie's insistence, Weezy booked the same flights as Joe. They would spend a few days in Panacea, ostensibly to rest. The way Weezy said, "Right" too quickly told Joe they wouldn't be relaxing.

Eric insisted on taking Joe and Weezy to a quiet dinner near Stephansplatz. All three of them had been silent on the subject of the future, instead reliving the happy parts of the trip. Joe saw the light in Weezy's eyes when she caught him watching her smile. To be with friends, to be together, seemed more important to him any job or personal striving.

Halfway through appetizers and most of the way through a bottle of wine, Eric said, "I talked with John Zhou Min earlier." He paused to take a sip of wine. "Ackerman has been fired. I don't know what was in that dossier, but your friend Maddie must have sent it off. ZCG's lawyers think he's been indicted."

"For what?" Weezy was back to hard-edged.

"If it's securities fraud," Eric said, "the penalties are financial. Kind of an updated version of an eye for an eye, but with dollars. The feds love to threaten criminal action, which induces the firm involved to pony up even more of its shareholders' cash, then there's a sealed settlement, and it all goes away. Cost of doing business."

Joe stabbed at an escargot, his gorge rising. "This is the guy who probably set up mass murder, and he's going to pay a fine?"

"My guess is they'll go after the criminal charges, particularly with the FBI involved. Ross must think so too. He's retained a top-notch criminal lawyer. I'm thinking conspiracy, maybe murder."

The main course came, and they were silent for a few minutes.

O'Malley stopped, a bite of venison halfway to his mouth, and pointed his fork at Joe. "This is going to hit ZCG hard, no way around it. Maybe hard enough that we both have to consider other options."

The job I always wanted, Joe thought. Excitement. Challenge. Recognition. Now he'd been on the inside. He lifted his wine glass to Eric.

"Might not be all bad."

***

The next morning, Joe, Weezy and Eric shared a cab to the Vienna airport. The flight from Europe was as uneventful as any long trip with Weezy, who always had a hard time containing her energy. The itching in the cast didn't help. They talked about Vienna, the good hospital food, and Eric O'Malley. Not about the last few days or those to follow. When they arrived in Atlanta, there was a long line for customs. It was evening, and they were both ready for a hotel, a nap and the flight to Tallahassee leaving early the next morning. They came out of Customs, Joe carrying Weezy's bag, his own Mobibag tagging along behind. Weezy was like a kid let out of school, bouncing down the corridor.

Joe was about halfway across the Arrivals hall, moving purposefully, hoping for a short wait for a cab. Weezy was a little behind.

"Joe! Hey, Joe. You missed the guy with the 'Mayfield/ Napolitani' sign."

Sure enough, there was a tall man wearing a chauffeur's cap holding up the sign.

Weezy stopped in front of the man. "Napolitani, and here comes Mayfield."

Joe reversed course, confusing the MobiBag.

"I have your car waiting. This all your baggage?" the driver said.

"Uhh, we hadn't arranged for a limo."

"Well, I got the order to pick up two parties."

Joe hesitated. He saw Weezy was skeptical, maybe scared.

"Who ordered the car?"

The driver pulled out an e-pad and swiped through several screens.

"O-something. Like in Irish."

"O'Malley?"

"Yeah, that's it."

"Where are you taking us?"

"Fulton County airport. Lemme see here … Yeah, I'm to contact StratisAir. They must have you on a private plane."

"Hold on." Joe pulled out his e-pad. Several messages popped up. The announcement of Ackerman's "resignation" from ZCG and a *Wall Street Journal* article on the subject. Then a message from Eric: "Hope you enjoy your time off in Panacea. I've arranged transportation for the last leg. Look for a driver. Don't rest too long. Need you back in the saddle in a week."

He passed the e-pad to Weezy. "Great. Let's go."

Their driver turned out to be talkative and friendly, obviously impressed by his clientele. The limo pulled into the airport, through a gate at which their IDs were checked, and on to the tarmac. A small jet with the StratisAir logo waited for them.

The driver loaded their bags, and the plane buttoned up.

"Eric has a special talent for knowing how to do the right thing at the right time," Joe said as he took in the elegant interior. The perfect touch, knowing we'd have to spend the evening in a hotel, knowing we really wanted to get home, knowing…"

He glanced at Weezy, who had gone from bouncing on the sumptuous leather seats to out like a light.

# THIRTY-NINE

ROSS HAD LESS than a day to recuperate, steady himself. Monday, he talked with his new attorney, Elliott Stiles, who told him not to even think of going anywhere. On the phone, Stiles proved serious, leaning toward humorless, no nonsense. No doubt capable, certainly expensive.

Later that day, Ross met Stiles in his office, an older building a couple of blocks from ZCG. Stiles' office was dark, with oriental rugs covering most of the wood floor, an elegant grandfather clock metering out the fifteen-dollar minutes, and leather-bound law books. Very much in keeping with the man himself.

Stiles came around the ornate mahogany desk to greet Ross with a dry handshake and a demeanor that little gave away. He directed Ross to a conference table with a yellow legal pad and a thin folder.

As Stiles sat down across from Ross, he glanced at the clock, and said, "Tell me the story, all the details, start to finish." The lack of pleasantries offended Ross, but then he thought of the hourly rate and understood. No one wanted pleasantries at $900 an hour.

Stiles took the occasional note as Ross talked, but Ross suspected that was mainly for show. It was all being recorded in Stile's brain.

Ross was forthcoming about RedSock and the trades in Skins. In his telling, Braithwaite became a skilled security operative whom Ross discovered had a preternatural ability to sniff out political unrest, particularly in the part of the world surrounding his home base in South Africa. And, yes, he profited enormously from that knowledge. All perfectly legal.

He gave Stiles his best man-to-man look. "At first, we couldn't sell the toxic high-risk tranches of the Skins. I paid higher prices than we would have gotten from any other buyer." He closed his eyes for a moment, summoning his look of contrition, "Yes, I violated ZCG policy."

Stiles nodded and made an especially long note.

Ross continued, "Braithwaite convinced me to set up the account with Mayfield's signing bonus. Of course, that was a mistake, and I'm embarrassed to have compromised one of my own company's employees. Surely it's a trading violation, but really no big deal."

Stiles' look let Ross know that nothing relating to securities law was no big deal.

Ross went on, "The assassination attempt on the river boat has nothing to do with RedSock. The woman works for the IAC, but she's a hacker, too. Probably something to do with that."

He continued, explaining that he elected to stay conservative, which meant unwinding the Kazakh Skin. The move was in line with any reputable bank's practice, but it was expensive. Zhou Qiáng became infuriated and fired him.

He finished, pleased with his performance. He had the whole day before, two sleepless nights and several scotches to get the story straight.

Stiles made a couple more notations, looked up and said, "You look like shit."

Ross leaned his elbows on the table and massaged his temples.

Stiles moved on. "What about the distribution of the RedSock trusts?"

"I think she did a red sports car."

Stiles' scratching on the yellow pad stopped.

"Red sports car?" he said, irritated.

"You know … guy hits forty, buys a red sports car, dumps his wife for a glamorous babe. This is my wife's red sports car."

"Ahh." Stiles didn't crack a smile.

"I think she got bored with me and saw all that money … but we're going to undo those transactions. I've spoken with her, and we'll work it out, even if she does decide to stay in some godforsaken burg in Iowa."

Stiles made another note, flipped back to an earlier page.

"So, what now?"

Stiles brightened. He stood and paced to the window overlooking Trinity church, hands clasped behind him like a thoughtful Oxford don. Looking out over the Gothic spires, he said, "We need to talk to the feds. Really, the story boils down to some trading the SEC doesn't like. ZCG's done all it can to cover its ass by firing you. They won't have the stomach for the publicity if the feds come after you for having made trades they should have known about."

He returned to the table and took his seat.

"The FBI wants to nail you on conspiracy because they can't get at Braithwaite. Unless they have substantial evidence that it was you that gave orders for these alleged incidents …"

"I don't think they have much," Ross said, "but Braithwaite is a bright guy. If he made some of the bad stuff happen, he may have planted evidence that points to me."

Stiles straightened, then leaned back, lacing his fingers behind his head, staring at the clock. After a moment, he sat straight again, planted his hands on the table and stood.

"Well, let's go see what they have."

***

It was only half a mile to the US Attorney's Chambers Street office. For Ross, the trek was made worse by a scotch-headache and the fact that Elliott Stiles' good humor leaked out no matter how serious he tried to be.

*This uptight prick is looking forward to the meeting. Of course, complicated cases mean billable hours and street cred. No wonder he's happy.*

"They probably don't have much on you," Stiles said. "But play the game. They're expecting a combative Wall Street tycoon. Be repentant. Act like a beaten man." Not hard with this headache, Ross thought.

"You're going to take the fall for minor trading infractions, maybe get off with a censure." Mercifully, the light at Warren Street was red and Ross was able to catch his breath.

Stiles turned to Ross and said, "You'll probably be prohibited from using your license for a couple of years, but that doesn't mean you can't start a new fund."

The rest of the trek took them through densely packed state and federal buildings. At the US Attorney's office, they were shown into a featureless room and joined by a serious-looking young woman and a large man wearing a suit that looked like it had been slept in. Stiles introduced Tonya Williams, the Assistant DA. "Stiles" she said and shook his hand as if he had a communicable disease.

A raising of Stile's left eyebrow, quickly suppressed, was the only hint of concern when Williams introduced the man with her as Henry Barber, FBI. Ackerman's headache came back with a vengeance.

Stiles opened the discussion. "I asked for this meeting to get an idea of what the issues are. We know that a trader employed by ZCG has been arrested for trading irregularities, but we're not sure why my client is involved."

Williams gave Stiles an arch look.

"He seems to be the puppet master, according to Mr. Povreshenko and Mr. Garrity."

Stiles did not react to the mention of Garrity, whom Ross had carefully neglected in their initial meeting. Ross's stomach churned, and he hoped the pain in his chest was heartburn.

"We'll need to know what you have."

Williams smiled and produced a thin file folder.

A half smile crossed Stiles' face. "Looks like not much."

Just like he said. Ross's estimation of his lawyer swelled.

Williams opened the folder and smoothed the single sheet. "I suppose it's that I've been a clerk for an older judge, but I can't get away from using paper."

Barber chuckled, drawing a severe look from Williams.

She slid the sheet across the table to Stiles, who took it with a frown. Ackerman leaned to look over his shoulder.

It was a numbered list of thirty-six items with titles like, "Interpol background on Armand Santucci and decrypted conversations with R. Braithwaite", "Payments to Brian Garrity", "Decrypted text messages between R. Ackerman and R. Braithwaite re: Chitimukulu assassination."

Williams opened her brief case and produced a small magenta plastic tray with eight storage cubes.

"You'll get all this in discovery anyway. Read 'em and weep."

She stacked another tray, then three more on the table between them. One numbered cube for each line item on the printed list. Each cube could hold three terabytes.

Maybe it was the light filtering through the dirty window, but it looked to Ross as if Stiles turned greenish. But he squared his shoulders and took up the list again.

"About half of these items are decrypted." His focus snapped to Williams. "They were probably obtained illegally and will be inadmissible."

"Good try, Elliott. Of course, you know that conversations, encrypted or not, that involve financial malfeasance or felonies are admissible."

Elliott Stiles had no answer, so he was about to duck back to reading the list when Barber leaned forward.

"Mr. Ackerman, you're key to the actions against Mr. Garrity and Mr. Povreshenko. There are some criminal charges against you, as well."

He pushed a document across the table. Stiles fielded it. He read it over once, then a second time. Finished, he put a hand on Ross's forearm. "They're going to put electronic handcuffs on you."

Ross heard a tone he didn't recognize from his implant.

"I think they already did." Ross tried a hard stare at Barber, who smiled, not quite apologetically. "Stay on Manhattan, and don't go above Bank Street. That'll allow you to go to your office and your home."

Ross remembered Emily, across the table at La Grenouille, telling him why she didn't want an implant. "They put those chips in pets," she'd said. "I'm not a pet." He'd been angry at the time. "What the hell's the downside?" he'd asked. Now, he knew.

"Oh, and you'll need to keep this on at all times," Barber said, holding up an ankle bracelet.

"Crissake, you've already got my implant wired."

Barber smiled, "Belt and suspenders. You could probably figure out a way to interrupt the implant, but the old school ankle bracelet is much harder to get rid of."

***

The next morning, Elliott Stiles took the steps up to Ackerman's Bank Street townhouse slowly. The immaculately maintained brickwork was surely a selling point. After discharging the mortgages on the townhouse and the place in the Hamptons, there would be enough left to pay his fee. Stiles knew this. You need only one experience of having to stand in front of a judge trying to extract fees from the pretty, weeping wife of a Wall Street bandit to know you need to check the assets and the real estate before getting too deeply involved in the truth and beauty thing.

Of course, his client was a murderer. Technically a conspirator, but in the eyes of the law, there was not much difference between the guy who pulled the trigger and the guy who made the plan. And motive? Ackerman had one hundred ten million motives.

Ackerman presented himself as a conceptual guy, a maker of trades and deals. Details were for subordinates, except when he was "managing" Skins outcomes. There, he kept close tabs on the process, an unfortunate deviation which had yielded a mountain of evidence. Neither Tonya Williams nor Henry Barber were eager to negotiate. Braithwaite had disappeared in South Africa, and nobody there seemed willing or able to run him down. The only other major player was Ackerman. Williams could smell the kill and the career-making publicity.

A uniformed maid met him at the door and led him to the back of the house, where French doors opened on a secluded patio. Ross Ackerman was in chinos and a houndstooth shirt, handsome as always, sipping a beer.

"You want a beer? Got a nice lager from Bavaria here." Ackerman said, holding his glass to the sun and nodding toward the maid.

"Water is fine."

"Oh, yeah, that's right. You've got nothing to get drunk over."

This was not Ackerman's first beer.

Ackerman waved a hand at a chair, and Elliott sat, feeling a little out of place in his suit. He suppressed the urge to loosen his tie.

"This matter of conspiracy is serious. There is a lot of evi —"

"Braithwaite. It's Braithwaite, Elliott. I wanted the best intelligence on the places we worked in, but I never expected —"

"They have you talking to Braithwaite numerous times, discussing the details of events. They have you chewing out Braithwaite for not being able to accurately predict timing in the South Africa chromite incident that killed over a hundred people."

"Fabricated. It's crap off the internet put together by a bunch of hackers."

They were both silent while the maid put a sparkling water on the table and retreated to the house.

"I tried that idea out on Williams and Barber," Elliott said. "In this day and age, everything has tracking codes. I don't know which army of analysts cracked your codes, but they did a hell of a good job."

"So, negotiate."

Ackerman's voice held little hope. He was, after all, a trader. He could read the deal in Elliott's eyes.

"I have done so. They're eager to go to trial," Elliott said. "Braithwaite's out of the picture, at least for the couple of years it would take them to extradite him. You're their main focus … their only focus, really." He paused to sip his water, then continued, "They'll keep it simple. Bargain out the little guys and bear down on you. South Africa wants to extradite you in the case of the dictator. There, I can push back on any number of technicalities. But the conspiracies to murder Herman Suttermeier, Joseph Mayfield and Louise Napolitani are a lot tougher."

Elliott rested his elbows on the table and laced his fingers. He leaned forward.

"You need to prepare yourself for a plea, if they'll agree to one."

Ackerman sighed. "So we'll pay a fine, I'll lose both houses, and I won't be able to do any trading for, what, five years?"

"All that and more, Ross. They're going to put you in prison." Elliott attempted to look compassionate. "We need to try for a minimum sentence and to preserve some of your assets."

Ackerman looked down into his glass, now half empty. "Not with a bang but a whimper, eh, Elliott?"

# FORTY

BEFORE ELLIOT STILES appeared that morning, Ross had been rehearsing the speech he imagined making in the courtroom. It had started as a simple statement that as a good trader, he was trying to do the best for his company. Over a couple of days, it had morphed into a full-fledged tragic exposition. The judge would surely understand how Ross's desire to do good had been taken advantage of by dishonest, ungrateful people. The packed courtroom would be hushed as he spoke and Emily (who would, of course, be in the first row) listened with tears in her eyes. He would get probation, and Emily would return to him, bringing substantial cash with her. Federal officials, fearing adverse publicity, would not claw back the proceeds of his trades.

The whole superstructure came crashing down when Stiles mentioned prison time.

*What the fuck am I going to do?*

He spun four or five scenarios, each of which had him relaxing in a tropical paradise or a secluded cabin in the western forest at the end. None of which, he realized, would happen.

Braithwaite could figure a way out. But he wouldn't put himself out for Ross unless there was an angle, a way to profit from Ross's bad luck.

The phone! Of course.

Energized, Ross pushed himself out of the patio chair, passed through the kitchen and took the stairs to the third floor two at a time. ZCG had sent over two big boxes of his stuff, which he'd left on the floor of his bedroom. He pawed through Lucite cubes memorializing deals he'd once been proud of, pictures of family and famous people he knew wouldn't return a call if he made one. He didn't need the help of famous people. He needed Braithwaite.

He found the throwaway phone Braithwaite had switched out before Vienna at the bottom of the second box. He tapped it … still at half power, enough for a text.

```
Nick,
```

He paused, working to find words to hook Braithwaite, then slammed the phone shut.

*Can't haggle from a weak position.*

He went down the stairs, his mind engaged in the calculus of the risk-reward continuum. Braithwaite was sitting somewhere in the middle, with a little place in the Bahamas on one end and a big, tattooed guy named Bubba on the other. Braithwaite would be better off with Ross out of the way, no question. The only issue was what out of the way meant.

Got to push him to the Bahamas end of the spectrum.

In the atelier, Ross poured himself a scotch. Back up the stairs to the office next to his bedroom, he found and unfolded his e-pad. He scanned the encrypted files he had kept on RedSock. Plenty to make it clear Braithwaite was the guy who did the dirty deeds. And Braithwaite didn't know what the feds had seen. He had to believe Ross could implicate him. Then he'd help him.

Fearing the feds were recording his communication, Ross left the house and walked to the park where Bleecker meets Bank Street.

He found a Wi-Fi node at a bakery next to the park and tapped out a text.

```
Nick,
Feds have indicted me for murder.
You're implicated. Need help to
disappear.
```

He'd give it half an hour. He walked around the park, trying not to worry about what to do if Braithwaite didn't call and reassuring himself that Braithwaite would see that relocating Ross was his best and only course of action. Braithwaite must be made to believe killing Ross would trigger the release of incriminating documents.

After twelve minutes crawled by, the phone vibrated.

***

Nick Braithwaite tapped out: Go to a safe place. I will call in 15 minutes.

When Ackerman's message popped up, Braithwaite had been enjoying a morning coffee on the patio of his home in Johannesburg. He had arrived a few days ago. A conversation with a high-ranking functionary in Bloemfontein verified that Interpol wanted to speak with him—most likely not just for a chat. The next day, standard sedans trying to look innocuous appeared at the end of the street. Not that he was particularly nervous. Spend a few weeks here, protected by expensive friends. Interpol would eventually lose interest.

Nick stared at his e-pad, remembering the last phone swap, suddenly cold in the warmth of the morning. Chink in the armor.

His fantasy about evading prosecution was fine if the Americans were talking some complex financial conspiracy bullshit the lawyers could drag out. But if Ackerman spilled his guts, the charge would be murder. Eventually, they'd find a way in. If Ackerman went down, he'd drag Nick with him.

He rubbed his chin, thinking. Without Ackerman, they'd have only Povreshenko and the third-rate stockbroker who supposedly made the trades. Neither knew the whole story and, most important, no link to Nick. On the other hand, "You're implicated" must mean Ross had his back to the wall. He'd as much as threatened to release their communications in case he disappeared, a sort of dead man's switch. Ross's threat might be a trader's bluff, but maybe not. Got to be careful.

It took ten minutes to come up with a plan. Not too solid, plenty could go wrong, but a plan nevertheless. He liked it more and more as he fleshed it out. Finally, he went to his console and tapped into what would look like a shopping network to anyone tracking him. From there, he passed through to a secure site and sent coded messages to Croatia, Rumania and Nigeria. Keza could handle the office for a couple of weeks, then maybe a little R&R. He keyed the intercom.

"Keza, come here, please."

She appeared silently in the doorway. "I am going to need to leave, possibly for several months. Where is the Range Rover?"

"Is in Midrand, over near the M1, *Sthandwa*" she answered. "Where are you going?"

"I can't tell you … in case you're questioned. I will see text on the secure channel, but don't use it unless you have to."

"Sure." He saw her disappointment. They had both hoped for a little more time together. He added, "After a couple of weeks, I will call for you. Maybe then we can relax a little."

She rewarded him with a small, sad smile.

"Can you get me over there without alerting any of the three or four stakeout cars out there?"

"They follow me every time I move, but sure. I can get you out."

"Okay. Late afternoon would be best."

Keza left the patio, and Nick opened a secure channel on his e-pad and considered how to explain the plan to Ackerman.

***

Ross Ackerman walked a couple of blocks down Bleecker and found a quiet side street. The disposable buzzed. Seventeen minutes. He answered.

"Don't talk much." Braithwaite's voice. "Sound like you're calling off planned remodeling on your house. I'm covered on this end, but cops can probably pick up your end. Got it?"

"Yes, the renovation."

"Okay, good. For the next three days, you are going to take a morning coffee at the place near you where we sometimes met."

"Yes, I agree, but I may have to delay starting." Ross had always made fun of Braithwaite's cloak and dagger ways, but felt a spike of elation that Braithwaite was back on the job.

"You will receive instructions on how to meet my people. Also how to wire $500,000."

*Half a million?*

"That's a reasonable plan, but I'm tapped out right now. I can't really afford—"

Braithwaite's voice was grainy through the secure connection, but Ross heard the harsh tone clearly. "You think I don't know you've squirreled away six million and change?"

*Asshole!* Ross's elation turned to hatred. Braithwaite was always a step ahead of him. He hated being a sap, yet again, more than losing the money. Anyone who was listening in on Ross's end of the conversation heard only heavy breathing, a little odd for a conversation about redecorating.

Then, always the trader, Ross said, "I agree it's important to get this job done. I can give you half now and then half when you finish."

"Four hundred k now, two hundred k afterwards. This will be very expensive up front."

Ross started counter the increase but realized he couldn't risk an open conversation. Braithwaite won again.

Braithwaite continued, "Go to the coffee shop at nine-thirty in the morning. Now, say one o'clock for the listener to hear, and don't mention coffee."

"Yes, well, we can discuss it," Ross said. "Why don't we meet at one o'clock tomorrow?"

"We'll move you after the money moves. You'll like Dubrovnik."

***

After arranging for Ackerman's extraction, Nick Braithwaite changed credentials and became Rik de Jaager. Toward afternoon that day, he positioned himself in the boot of the Mercedes. Keza drove to the edge of the city, followed by several undercover police cars, left the car for an oil change and walked across the street to the shops. By the time she returned, trailed by two undercover agents, Nick had slipped into the bed of a small delivery truck and been driven to a run-down scrapyard. As dusk fell, he pulled the cover off the Range Rover and took off toward Lesotho. Six hours later, he was in Ficksburg. The Range Rover went into a local garage, and Nick was picked up by Joseph, to whom he paid a retainer to keep an eye on his place high above Khetisas. When he arrived well after midnight, moonlight bathed the courtyard and the dun-colored house, tinting it blue. It was cold above six thousand feet, and the breeze brought the smell of dust and flowers. Nick opened windows to air the place out, checked the security system. Finally, satisfied, he slept.

The house was comfortable but small. It looked like most other native houses in Lesotho, a little rundown on the outside, no landscaping. It advertised no wealth or position, unlike the villas built by successful South Africans, Chinese, and Europeans as vacation homes. He paid four times the cost of the house to get high-speed Internet and a quiet, efficient generator. A separate locked and monitored room had enough gear to manage his business and reach into almost any database, protected or not.

In a couple of weeks, the cops would conclude he had left Johannesburg. They would question Keza. Because she was black and beautiful, they would assume she was much less than she really was. After that, they would lose interest, and she could come to him.

***

The first two days at the coffee shop simply raised Ross's anxiety level. On the third day, he was at the shop a little early, sitting at a table on the sidewalk with a cappuccino. The barista, a young woman wearing a black leotard and T-shirt advertising an obscure band, cleared the table next to Ross. The clatter and clash plates and cups she dumped into a plastic tub startled him. She was most of the way back to the front door, in a hurry, when Ross realized a plate with a croissant had appeared on his table.

"Hey, I didn't—"

Writing on the doily peeked out from under the croissant.

*Stay calm.* He wanted to move the pastry and read the message but knew he should be careful. Was that old man reading the Times watching him? It took several nonchalant bites to read the whole text. *Eleven o'clock Sunday night, take a walk down Greenwich to Eleventh, turn right, walk slowly. No bag. Wire must clear Friday.* Then a series of numbers, transfer instructions, no doubt.

Ross finished the croissant, crumpled the doily as if to throw it away, and slipped it into his pocket.

***

Ross enjoyed the walk home from the coffee shop. Caesar, crossing the Rubicon. Why was he thinking of that? Oh, yeah. *The die is cast,* and all that. Fear and hope swirling, but nice to be moving forward. Dubrovnik. He remembered a walled city, romantic cafés and a sun-drenched harbor. He fantasized for a block or two about the shock on that supercilious DA's face when she found out he had disappeared.

Constanza had put the mail on the table in the foyer. Some legal stuff he didn't want to open and one hand-addressed letter. Curious, he tore the flap and found a single sheet folded around a picture. The picture showed an old guy—he knew him, didn't he—with his arm around a younger guy in a suit. A huge, red J.I. Case tractor loomed above them. The note said:

*Ross,*

*Never thought I'd buy a tractor new, but I'm going to buy this one. Maybe it will convince my son Bill to give up the law practice. Thanks to you, Emily and RedSock.*

*Silas Scholze*

*Monticello, Iowa*

Constanza appeared from the kitchen, having heard the torrent of profanity. She was wiping her hands on a towel, her face screwed into pity, maybe concern. "Oh, Mister Ross, what's the matter? Why are you crying?"

# FORTY-ONE

TWO AND A half days. Ross went from fearing the call to appear with his lawyer, wanting to slow time down, to movemovemove. After the Friday morning instruction-by-doily, he spent an hour figuring out how to wire the money to Braithwaite using an old e-pad not registered to his implant. Then he walked over to the park again and sent the instruction.

On his way back home, his implant tapped him. Elliott Stiles.

"Ross, we need to meet on Tuesday, and you need to be prepared to go into custody then."

"So soon?" He tried to sound terrified.

"Would have been Monday, except it's the holiday. I've filed a brief explaining that you need to wind up your affairs," Elliott said. "That may buy us a few days, but the DA is going to push back hard. She can smell the publicity juju."

Ross relished the vision of Stiles standing in the court room, trying to explain why his client wasn't present. The bastard might even break a sweat.

Friday night, Constanza made dinner, then left, fussing about whether he could fend for himself over the long Fourth of July weekend.

After a couple of scotches, he called Emily. She hadn't answered the last five times. This time was no exception. He left a message.

"Em, I miss you. I'm sorry about getting mad last time we talked. I had plans for that money, and now I'm ruined without it." As he talked, the weight of bad fortune became heavier. "They say I'm going to prison while you enjoy the fruits of my effort. I may not see you for some time." As in, ever. "We never really had a chance to say goodbye. Even if you don't love me anymore, I hope your sense of fairness will lead you to retain some of the wealth you took … for me, if not for you *and* me."

He poured himself a scotch. The good stuff; no sense in saving it for Stiles to drink when he got his paws on the house.

***

Ross spent most of Saturday and Sunday assembling a pile of things he just had to have with him, discovering they filled a suitcase, and starting over again. In the end, he took nothing but a jacket, his phone and an e-pad.

At a few minutes to eleven, as he closed the door to the townhouse, thoughts of thumbing his nose at the SEC and the Zhou dynasty were overwritten by sadness. He put a hand on the lovely red brick facade, feeling its lingering warmth. With it, a pang of longing for the trappings of success now gone, for Emily, for the RedSock millions.

He shook off the thought, walked to Greenwich and turned right on Eleventh. In the dark of the silent street, the thought that Braithwaite would be better off with him permanently out of the way returned. Just nerves, probably. The thought had been there ever since the phone call. He bucked himself up, thinking *Braithwaite's a smart guy*. He heard the subtext. He knew Ross had documents, but he didn't know the feds had decoded them. Anyway, Braithwaite had always been about the money, and he wanted the final 200k payoff.

As Ross rolled this over in his mind, a black Lincoln Town car slowed, passed him and stopped. A nicely dressed man stepped out, gave a little bow to Ross and a sweeping gesture toward the back seat.

Ross quashed the ping of fear, nodded to the man, and got into the car. The man closed the door and stepped around to the street side. He got in and extended his hand.

"Good to meet you, Mr. Ackerman. I am Marko, this—" he indicated the driver, "is Mr. Braithwaite's associate Gabor." Gabor gave a two-fingered salute, checked the mirror and began to drive slowly down eleventh. "And this is my friend Ezekiel," Marko said, nodding to the shiny-bald black man who occupied all the space on the passenger side and then some. Ezekiel gave a slight nod, about the only movement the confining space of the front seat allowed him.

Marko handed a folio to Ross.

"Here is a passport, about $5,000 in Croatian money, some other things you will need. There's a map and information about where you will be staying. Your name is now Randall Burgess. You were born Radovan Becovic in Croatia and raised in New York City. You are returning to your home country after moderate success in America. Your history is in there, too."

Ross took in the stream of information. He watched Hudson Park pass by, surprised by a pang of longing, of sadness. He would never see these places again.

"We need to get rid of your tracking devices. To do so, we are going to enter your lawyer's building, where you might be expected to go to talk about your upcoming meeting with the federal officials. Sunday night is inconvenient, but considering what you are paying him—" Marko raised an eyebrow, "it won't be surprising for you to meet at his office this evening."

"Why go to Stiles' office?"

Marko smiled. "We go in the front door, cut off your ankle transmitter, put your phone in the trash. Gabor goes around back and picks us up."

"But the ankle band will send an alarm, won't it?"

"Sure, but the bands aren't foolproof, it is the Sunday before the Fourth and you're at your lawyer's office. Police know no lawyer would allow a client to interrupt a tracking device. Cops won't suspect anything until tomorrow morning, and then with it being the holiday.... Anyway, you'll be well away by then."

"So where do we really go?"

"To Pier 11. As far as anyone knows, we're a bunch of Wall Street types taking a tour of the harbor to celebrate closing a deal. The boat will get us to a freighter, where you'll board for a trip to Croatia. It'll take about a week."

"So, I'm going to be a sitting duck for a week?"

"No worries, Mr. Ackerman. The police will interview the doorman, who will lead them to a private plane that will have flown to Miami. How do you say it? They will bust their picks searching for you in Miami."

Marko smiled and continued, "The ship has only four cabins. We've paid for all four. You'll be in one, and ..." Marko nodded toward the front seat, "Ezekiel will be in another to be sure you are not interrupted by any unpleasantness while you study your new identity."

"Unpleasantness?" Ross stumbled on the word.

"We want to be sure that nothing—" Marko seemed to search for a word "—unusual disturbs your, ahh, journey."

Marko finished with a smile that seemed genuine. Friendly.

Gabor had jockeyed through the one-ways around Trinity Church to drop them off in front of Elliott Stiles' office.

Inside, Marko had a friendly conversation with the man at the guard station, whose eyes darted from Marko to Ross then stayed on Ezekiel. A couple of twenties changed ownership, no doubt focusing the guard's undivided attention on his monitor. As they turned toward the men's room, Marko clapped Ross on the shoulder and whispered loud enough to carry, "Next stop Teterboro, the charter, then you're home free in Miami."

In the men's room, Marko clipped the ankle transmitter. With the guard studiously watching the front door, Marko, Ezekiel and Ross slipped out the back door to the limo.

***

As Gabor drove the Town Car through the streets of the financial district, Ross opened the folio Marko had given him and flipped through the contents. Leave it to Braithwaite to do exquisite planning. Expensive, but worth it. He began to relax. No one would go to this much work if he were planning to …

He turned to Marko.

"So, won't someone see us go to the freighter?"

Marko considered, then shrugged, "Unlikely. We'll be in international waters. The Coast Guard cares about incoming, not so much outgoing. The boat we're taking you to now and the freighter will never be closer than a few hundred meters. A small service boat will carry you between the two."

More good planning.

As Gabor turned right onto South Street, a yacht nudged up to the dock. No ferries active, so the pier was quiet. Perfect.

Gabor parked and Marko, Ezekiel, and Ross walked across the pier to the yacht. A shadowy figure put out the gangway and disappeared. When they were on board, Marko led them to the main cabin. It was beautifully furnished in birch panels, a bar in the center, and couches and chairs arranged to look out floor-to-ceiling windows. "It'll take about forty minutes to rendezvous," Marko said, leaning on the bar. "Let's have a drink, and we can discuss your life change. Dubrovnik is a beautiful city. You will be a little outside, in the hills."

Ross had a flashback to the Donau König, remembering the brandy toast and Le Pic. But Marko looked relaxed and Z-man had taken an overstuffed chair, earbuds in, a faraway look, head keeping time to an inaudible beat.

Ross said, "A water, for now."

"Fine," Marko said as he inspected the bottles, pulled out cognac and poured one glass. Then to the refrigerator, where he found a bottle of mineral water. He looked at Ezekiel, eyebrows raised. Ezekiel shook his head No.

Marko crossed to Ross, handed him the water, then raised his glass. "Na slobodu." Ross twisted the cap off the bottle. "Means 'to freedom' in Croatian," Marko said.

Ackerman took a sip of the water. The boat began a slow turn back toward Manhattan.

"Why are we turning back?" And why was Marko giving a quick, furious flick of his head toward Ross?

Ross stood, confused, and caught motion in his peripheral vision. Then he was wrapped up in the Ezekiel's massive arms, struggling for breath. Ezekiel exhaled, bearing down. Pizza breath. Ross's vision blurred. Something snapped deep inside, then pain.

He was vaguely aware of Marko doing something to his arm. Then being carried to the rail. Emily. Em was right about the shell. Nothing as important as—

He was released, floating in air, a hard slap when he hit. "Worst case scenario" passed through his mind. "Crazy trading day" as he sank into cold. Finally, he retreated into a tiny place in his brain where a nursery rhyme played over the bass line of the boat's propellers.

*Now I lay me down to sleep…*

*I pray …*

***

If they'd gone six hours earlier or later, Ross's body would have disappeared on the outgoing tide. As it was, the inward flow drew Ross's body toward the Battery, where it rested under water for a day, provender for fish and crabs. Buoyed by the gases of decomposition, it rose to the surface and was borne slowly up the Hudson on the incoming tide. It came to rest at Battery Park, where an early morning jogger, sweating out the excesses of a Fourth of July party, saw an arm, then a head with empty eye sockets and most of the nose missing. After he vomited, he called 911.

***

Emily Ackerman sat at the kitchen table preparing to solve the crossword on a back page of the *Des Moines Register* and to enjoy a second cup of coffee. Silas had risen at daybreak and gone to the next farm over to help with the birthing of a calf. Heavy clouds marched across the horizon, carrying the weight of an impending thunderstorm.

The knock at Silas's door surprised her. Alone, she went to the door and peeked through the small side window. A young Iowa sheriff's deputy stood holding his smoky-the-bear hat at his waist, sweating through his blond crew cut and shifting from one foot to the other. She opened the door.

"Uh, is Miz Ackerman staying at this residence?"

"Yes, I am Emily Ackerman."

"Is Silas around?"

"No, he's gone over to Haberman's to help with a birthing."

The deputy twisted his hat and shifted his feet.

"Uh, Ma'am, I need to tell you, uh, yourhusbandisdead."

Emily stared at him, part of her brain processing the words, part locked in repeating them.

"What?"

The deputy, blushing now, swallowed several times and spoke as if suddenly remembering a script. "I mean to say, the New York City police contacted us. Mr. Ackerman passed away under suspicious circumstances."

"Suspicious circumstances?" Emily tried to fit the words into some rational pattern. A crossword puzzle clue with no apparent answer.

"Yes, Ma'am. I believe he drowned."

"H-how?" She stammered, "How could he have drowned?"

The deputy looked as if this was a question he had not anticipated.

"He … uhh," retreating behind police officer formality, "I am not in possession of those details. The New York officer asked you to call this number."

As Emily's tears started, he handed over a card with "Sheriff's Department" and an embossed Fayette County logo. A number was written neatly on the back.

The deputy's shoulders relaxed a fraction.

"I'm sorry for your loss, Miz Ackerman. You want me to get Silas? I'm pretty sure Haberman's calf is gonna be born whether he's there or not."

Emily shook her head. "Th-thank you for telling me. I'll be all right. Don't get Silas." She wiped her cheek with the back of her hand.

In the kitchen after the deputy left, she poured the second cup of coffee, hands shaking as she sugared and creamed it. Finished, she collapsed into her chair and stared at the paper, seeing nothing. A gust of wind drove a flurry of raindrops to the window, then a clap of thunder, and the rain began in earnest. Emily folded the paper to frame the crossword. She picked up a pencil, paused, and only then tears came again for Ross, for herself, and for the life they could have shared.

# FORTY-TWO

WEEZY SAT AT her N-Ops console, tapping her foot, trying not to look impatient. She and Jake were in their regular conference to assess the status of the RedSock project. The FBI had closed the case; Interpol had let it languish. But to the Olegarten Posse it was anything but finished. The people who killed HoHum and nearly killed Weezy had not been brought to justice.

In the days following Ackerman's disappearance and reappearance as fish food, the Posse lost track of Braithwaite. Everyone was getting frustrated. Adeeb allowed as how tracking Braithwaite might be in the too hard column. Asked for "another pass" at decrypting one of the documents, PeepShow snapped, "I've got a day job, you know."

The guy from Estonia, HoHumJr, picked up Braithwaite's electronic trail briefly, bragged to the others about his skills, but then lost the trail.

"We've seen traffic in and out of his servers," Jake said, "but his security is very, very good. There was a series of messages between Johannesburg and Croatia, Rumania and Nigeria back a couple of weeks ago, but then all secure traffic stopped. We have pickets out around the three corporate servers, and—"

"Pickets?" Weezy frowned.

Jake chuckled. "Civil war. Guards out a ways from the camp to warn—"

"Oh, yeah. Pickets. So we have to wait him out?"

" 'Fraid so. If we can't get in directly, we'll have to try some cheese."

"Cheese?"

"Get the mouse out of the hole. One thing we know is that he used a chess site to pass commands. DingDing has an idea about what the chess moves mean, so she may be able to lure him out."

***

Shortly after midnight, Jake opened her e-pad and waited for the bait to be cast. She saw the message originate near Shanghai and latched onto a scrap of code that was part of the bait. The message was directed to a chess website called Father Time, which forwarded to a server in Columbus, Ohio, where it was encrypted.

It then passed through servers in Sevastopol, then Vilnius/ Chad/Sicily/Trinidad. As Jake tagged along, she had a vision of her late husband Kermit watching her work a bass out on Long Lake. "Play him slow. Niiiice and slow."

Finally, the message disappeared behind a firewall at Ramos Server 2 in New Haven, Connecticut.

"Two. It's Two," she said into her e-pad.

Seven sets of electronic eyes from the Posse pasted themselves onto Ramos #2.

Keza saw the bait some minutes later in Johannesburg. It was a chess move that Nick had not told her to expect. She rolled back from the console and tapped her teeth with her stylus. He told her not to contact him, but…

It had been over two weeks since he left. As far as she could tell, the stakeouts had finally disappeared. Decisive now, she ran the system security check, dragged the message to the secure channel and sent it.

***

The Lesotho morning was still, brilliant sunshine washing over the plateau. Nick's small veranda overlooked a stunning escarpment. He flopped into his chair, tired from a vigorous hike down to the edge of Khetisas and back. It had been a couple of weeks, comfortable but boring. He was beginning to relax. Not much to do but hike the rugged terrain until his lungs burned in the oxygen-depleted highlands and plan how to move his business forward. The Kazakhstan project would replace the ZCG revenue, but his business required diligent networking. His cadre of specialists needed to be replenished: working for Ramos Security was risky. He could take some more time off, but not much.

As he was beginning to doze, his implant tapped him. There was incoming on the secure system. Strange. Keza must have thought it was important. He stretched, drained the last of his water bottle, and went inside to the communications room.

He was surprised at the message, a chess move.

They pulled forward two weeks?

*Friggin' Kazakhs.*

He threw the water bottle against the wall.

*Stupid.* In control. In control. Get in control.

Hard to know what was going on. He brought up Father Time and typed the go-ahead chess move, but hesitated before hitting enter. Chess moves were fine for simple instructions, but why were the Kazakhs pulling forward?

He stopped, keyed the secure system and encrypted a message to Keza:

```
K: forward following message to Bolat:
Confirm timing of Nazarbiyeva.
```

***

The sun was not yet risen in Panacea, but Jake's note said she was onto something. Weezy shot out of bed and into the living area of the trailer, turned on the hard-wired e-pad. Now she sat, leaning forward, coiled energy. Joe emerged from the bedroom, yawning.

"You want coffee?"

Weezy waved off the offer, concentrating.

"Cream?"

"Sure." Eyes still on the screen. "Thanks."

Joe brought his cup and hers and stood behind her, watching.

The Posse sorted through the burst of messages Ramos 2 sent out to cover the relay of the original to wherever Nick Braithwaite was hiding. The guy from Estonia, HoHumJr, found the trail using an algorithm he designed for the purpose, justifying the group's decision to name him in HoHum's memory. The rest of them watched the tracer bounce through several African countries and come to rest in Lesotho.

A look of savage glee came over Jake's face.

"Got you, motherfucker." She glanced at the ceiling, embarrassed. Kermit might be listening. "He's in Lesotho. Near the town of Khetisas."

"Weezy?"

"What?"

"The message? What's in the message?"

"It's encrypted."

Joe rubbed his forehead. "Any way to see what he's saying?"

It took Weezy and Jake ten minutes to decrypt. Joe had taken a seat in back of Weezy. He repeated the letters as they came out one at a time, finally, "…O…F…N…A…Z…A…R…B…I…Y…"

"Weezy, they're doing something in Kazakhstan."

She glanced over her shoulder at him. "I thought Braithwaite cancelled it. Remember? The message to Ackerman."

"…E…V…A"

"Confirm timing of Nazarbayeva? We've got to contact Barber and Interpol."

Weezy's shoulders dropped.

"Interpol? Really? Are we talking about the same folks that diddled around for a couple of weeks, then said, 'So sorry, we really can't do anything about Braithwaite.' Those guys?"

"But we have to—"

"Braithwaite's asking for timing. He probably doesn't mean 'do it at your leisure.' "

"We ought to go through channels." Joe said. "This is internation—"

Weezy said something under her breath, then, "Jake, you still with me?"

The screen popped the picture of Jake, at her kitchen table, as usual.

"We have a situation."

Weezy explained the Kazakhstan and Dinara Nazarbayeva. Jake listened, pursing her lips as the size of the problem became obvious. Weezy finished, "Can anyone in Olegarten take this on?"

"No. I'm not sure there are any white hats in Kazakhstan."

Joe whispered, "White hats?"

"Good hackers," Weezy said. "Like Olegarten."

"...But I might know a black hat who would be toast if Dinara Nazarbayeva weren't around," Jake said. "Let me rattle his cage."

# FORTY-THREE

SIMON TSHENASE STOOD in front of the captain's desk, waiting for him to speak. The captain concentrated on a computer monitor, brow furrowed.

"Sit." The captain waved at a chair, not taking his eyes off the monitor. The invitation was an honor not often granted a sergeant. Simon sat, carefully lifting his pant legs so as not to disturb the perfect crease.

"It seems we have a delicate situation," the captain said, still looking at the monitor.

Both men knew "delicate situation" meant the kind of problem the captain sometimes called upon Simon to solve. Simon was a perfect intermediary, a quiet man who projected authority without being aggressive. Anyone could see he was a man of principle, good conduct and control. A deacon in the Anglican church in Maseru. A man who knew how to confront self-important white people only two generations removed from apartheid. A man larger than most and handsome, wearing the uniform of the International Police Association of Lesotho proudly.

The captain pushed back from the monitor, his own uniform shirt wrinkled and bearing a coffee stain and the crumbs from breakfast, buttons straining at the waist. Simon admired him. He had graduated from University, and he ran his department efficiently and honestly. But he was not the master of a happy home as Simon was, and he did not have a wife who pressed his uniform each morning and starched his shirts correctly. He was short and pudgy, with a face that the Great Maker seemed to have put together from spare parts.

"A delicate situation," the captain repeated, turning his attention to Simon. "There is a man named Rik de Jaager who lives above Khetisas." The captain consulted the monitor again. "He is South African, well-connected in Bloemfontein and apparently wealthy." He sipped from a large insulated cup. "His home is simple, but he spent a fortune to connect to the Internet. Investments, perhaps, or something else." The captain turned from the monitor to Simon. "Several days ago, I received some back channel information on a man named Rennie Braithwaite, also a South African. Very damaging information. There is no such man registered in Lesotho, but I have reason to believe he may be this Rik de Jaager."

The captain continued, "I want you to look over this information. Rik de Jaager may or may not be this Braithwaite. I do not wish to offend him, but I do want to talk with him."

***

Nick Braithwaite hadn't had an answer to his question to the Kazakh operative. Perhaps, then, he was oversensitive when the knock came at his door. Hard, authoritative, where that of his employee Jacob would have been tentative, not wanting to disturb the big white man who paid so well.

He reached into the drawer of the small table next to the door for his Walther PPK/S and peered out the side window. Never knew out here in the country surrounded by kaffirs. He couldn't see much of the outside through the narrow window beside the door, but there was fine dust in the still air. A vehicle?

"Who's there?"

"Mr. de Jaager, I am Simon Tshenase of the Lesotho International Police. Show yourself, please."

If he was alone, maybe …

Nick caressed the Walther's barrel while he assessed the situation. With Interpol looking for him in South Africa, his bought-and-paid-for friends would desert him. The Lesotho police might be easier to work with.

He put the Walther on the table, safely within reach. He slid the drawer a touch further open under it to expose the gold Kruggerands residing there for just such a situation as this. Stick and carrot. Subtle. Leniency was probably negotiable in Lesotho.

Confident now, he pulled the door open. A tall, handsome black police officer stood at ease, his hand resting on his holstered gun. His uniform was spotless, and he wore a smile that was both friendly and firm. A name tag shone in the midday sun. Tshenase.

"Please come with me," the officer said. "My captain wishes to speak with you."

"What subject?"

"My captain has not told me. Only that he wishes to speak with you." The smile changed fractionally.

"Tell your captain that I will talk to him if he wants to come up here."

"He was very specific."

"Tell him very specifically that he can come up the hill and tell me what this is all about," Nick said. Be firm. Best way to handle these situations. He pushed the door, dismissing Tshenase. "Go back down the hill, bo—"

The officer stiff-armed the door.

"Come with me now."

He unsheathed a Taser.

"I am not a boy. I am a sergeant."

Braithwaite delivered a precise, lightning-fast blow to the Taser, which skittered across the verandah.

"A fuckin' Taser? You gonna tase me, you kaffir piece of shit?" Nick grabbed a handful of Tshenase's shirt and shook him.

"Down the hill. Go down the hill."

A button popped off the shirt.

Nick released Tshenase and curled his lip into a sneer as Tshenase pulled at his shirt to straighten it.

"You must come with me now," Tshenase said. His voice quavered, and he eyed the Walther on the table, so close to Braithwaite's free hand.

Nick laughed, took a step back, and reached into the drawer. *These black folks like the feel of—*

He saw the pistol come up and stopped laughing, surprised. He wouldn't—

Three shots rang out.

The gold Kruggerand glinted as it dropped from his hand and rang when it hit the floor.

# FORTY-FOUR

THE CHIEF OF security for the new President of Khazakstan, Dinara Nazarbayeva, took her job seriously. She was aware of the nest of hackers in the capital, but they were causing trouble in the rest of the world more than at home. They were well down her priority list.

That all changed when her personal e-pad was hacked.

The information was vague but disturbing. A plot to create national chaos. The hacker identified himself. That built credibility since by doing so, he invited a visit from the National Security Committee. Such visits often proved fatal. She had met the man, who was working with other hackers, including one in the States he called Jake. He had information about a man who had set up a disaster in the South African chromite mines, and hacked evidence of him ordering the assassination of Nazarbayeva. That followed the South Africa plan. After the assassination, accidents in chromite or uranium mines would cause riots. Prices of the commodities would soar. Since most of the country's income was from natural resources, the disruptions would cause great suffering.

The information was validated the day after the security chief met with the hacker. Nazarbayeva's body double was shot at close range by a kitchen worker as she passed through a supposedly secure tunnel on the way to her motorcade.

National Security officers fanned out across the country. Their efforts produced confessions from a number of mine supervisors and bureaucrats, several of which proved accurate. Munitions were discovered and disarmed.

The hacker purchased a new Audi.

***

Armand Santucci sat at a table outside a small cafe in Majorca. He drank a coffee and basked in the wash of conversation around him. English, Dutch, some Asian language. Tourists in shorts and loud shirts. He had been alone too long. His hair was slicked back, the ponytail gone. On his right, two largish young women were speaking German, wearing sunburns that would hurt the next day and sipping Orangina. The taller one, blond and athletic-looking, tapped an e-pad and nodded to the brunette, then looked toward him. Maybe …

"Do you speak English?" he asked.

"Ja. Of course."

"You must try the ensaïmada. This place makes it very well. Like a kuchen, or a doughnut, but better."

The dark-haired one looked skeptical, but the blonde cocked her head.

"Where are you from," she asked, a hint of something more than idle interest in her voice. Maybe she was warming to his attention. It had been a long time since he had the pleasure of a woman.

"I am from many places, but home is Corsica, the birthplace of culture." He smiled to let her know he was joking, but only a little.

For luck and comfort, he tapped the stiletto in the slender pocket in his trousers.

The woman smiled at his obvious invitation, tilted her e-pad toward the other woman, who glanced at Santucci then nodded.

A chill ran through him. Why were they staring at him, then the e-pad? His smile disappeared, and he pushed himself out of his chair.

The pretty woman was still smiling.

Maybe it was nothing.

Several people were moving toward him, looking less like tourists than they had before.

Her smile changed from coy to smug, and she said, "Take him."

***

Emily Ackerman made the trip to see Arty every couple of weeks. It was five hours from her new home in Iowa to Yankton, South Dakota and the federal minimum security prison camp. She didn't go every week, not in winter. Arty had done six months of his sentence, hoping for electronic tracking. They gave him two years because he should have known better than to make the RedSock trades. During his plea bargain hearing, he convinced a sympathetic judge that he didn't understand that Braithwaite and Ackerman were engineering the disasters that cashed out so well for the Skins.

He looked different now. He had dried out and was no longer strung out. Healthier. Emily wasn't sure anymore whether what got them together in the first place was love, lust, or her desire to activate the real Emily. But it was worth the five hour drive to keep the possibility of a future relationship alive. If Arty was willing to live in Iowa.

# FORTY-FIVE

SEVEN MONTHS HAD passed since Austria.

Joe was back at ZCG, though the job wouldn't last. Ackerman was gone, of course. John Zhou Min had left the business after what was rumored to be a falling out with his father. Those losses, the SEC sanctions and bad publicity convinced Zhou Qiáng to fold the business back to Hong Kong. Eric O'Malley was in charge of shutting the operation down. He worked tirelessly to get bankers and support staff transplanted to other firms. The Manhattan office had been closed, the artwork auctioned. The Exchange Place office on the Jersey side was half the size it once was.

Joe and Weezy had taken a long weekend in Panacea. Weezy was sleeping in after a frantic week having something to do with Russian hackers. Joe had risen early and made coffee. He sat on the trailer steps, drinking in the Florida morning when his implant informed him that Eric O'Malley was calling. Inside, he opened his e-pad and accepted the call. Eric appeared at his desk in the Jersey office.

"So, Joe, what's your answer?" Eric's typical banter had been worn away by the fifteen-hour days and the pain of firing so many people he had mentored, so many friends. Morgan Rio Tinto had seen the sense in doing its own hedging, and Don Petrescu asked Joe to move to Kalispell, Montana, to head up that effort. Joe spent a couple of sleepless nights stewing … it was a wonderful job with great people, just in the wrong place.

"Eric, I'm going to turn it down," Joe said. "I love the idea and the challenge, but I can't move to Kalispell."

Eric brightened. "Remember that story everyone loved when you newbies made the western trip? The one about Don Petrescu as excited as a kid about fishing down in Panacea?"

Joe nodded, remembering the train and the camaraderie.

"This is computer work, right?" Eric grinned. "So you offer —"

"To do it in Panacea!" Joe said. "Eric, you're a genius. You think they'll buy it?"

Eric chuckled. "Tallahassee can handle jet traffic, and I bet a guy like Don would be plenty comfortable in a single-wide trailer if fishing was involved."

When she heard the story, Weezy said, "Clever, Joe. Eric is brilliant at human problem solving. I hope he comes up with a great solution for himself, too."

After a lazy breakfast, they drove north a few miles to Crawfordville, rented a canoe and paddled for an hour against the slow current of the Wakulla River. The sun cast shadows over the water when they turned downstream. Popcorn clouds hung across the horizon, promising afternoon rain.

In the slow pull of the current, Weezy shipped her paddle and turned to face Joe.

"You know, you could do the job from Bethesda. It doesn't really matter where you do your work. We can always take breaks in Panacea."

Joe leaned back, happy. They were well and truly "we." The sun off the water set Weezy's features in silhouette. All angles and shadows, that Caravaggio look that he saw on this river on their first canoe trip. "You could trot up to New York," she said, "and hobnob with all those fancy investment bankers that are now asking if the customer would prefer rare or medium rare but we-do-not-suggest-well-done, Ma'am."

"But I'd miss the fried chicken."

"I bet there are a few things in Bethesda to balance out the agony." Her eyes sparkled.

Joe smiled and started to work up an answer.

Weezy shook her head and gave him a pixie grin full of promise, "You know I'm right, dumbass.

{ The End }

Many thanks to the fine writers who have critiqued my work and helped me grow in this exhilarating and sometimes frustrating craft. My thanks as well to my friends Werner and Tina Fleischer for their hospitality in Vienna, advice on German language, and a tour of the little town of Hainburg an der Donau. Also to my editor, Miranda Kopp, whose advice improved the story. And finally to my wife, Beverly, a fine writer in her own right, for her unfailing support of my work.

Join me, Joe Mayfield and Louise Napolitani at *johnbairdrogers.com* or on facebook at *@johnbairdrogers.* I hope you will sign on to my newsletter. I'll keep in touch with offers of free books to advance copy readers, discussions about what's coming in the next book in the series. And perhaps you will help me navigate through the interesting world of a few years from now.

Next up in the Mayfield - Napolitani series: ***Fail Deadly*** is set a few years from now, a thriller that speaks to a very real threat to the United States today. When HelioCorp's solar energy project implodes, Weezy and Joe are drawn into solving a plot to hold the electrical power grid at ransom engineered by the Kobeli, Russian oligarchs who have kidnapped a brilliant hacker Weezy knows as HoHumJr and forced him to hack into the US power grid.
As the lights go out, first in Maine, then Georgia, HoHumJr manages to send a coded message to Weezy—a fail deadly he hopes will protect both him and Weezy. But Weezy has been captured by the Kobeli, and her disappearance makes her the NSA's prime suspect. Joe is soon a prisoner, too, the better to force Weezy to keep hidden data that would destroy Kobeli. If the fail deadly clicks open, Kobeli will dispose of the evidence ... *all* the evidence.

www.ingramcontent.com/pod-product-compliance
Lightning Source LLC
Chambersburg PA
CBHW031615100726
47898CB00006B/1798

* 9 7 8 1 7 3 2 2 2 6 2 5 8 *